Jack Crumpler

Sister Cathedra

By

Jack Crumpler

Panther  **Creek Press**
Spring, Texas

Published by Panther Creek Press
SAN 253-8520
116 Tree Crest
P.O.Box 130233
Panther Creek Station
Spring, Texas 77393

Cover art by Don Crouch
Imagineer, A Communication Arts Studio
The Woodlands, Texas

Cover design by Pamela Copus
Sonic Media, Inc.
Plano, Texas

Manufactured in the United States of America
Printed and bound by Data Duplicators, Inc.
Houston, Texas

1 2 3 4 5 6 7 8 9 10

Library of Congress Cataloguing in Publication Data

Crumpler, Jack
        Sister cathedra

I. Title   II. Fiction

ISBN 0-9678343-7-6

This book is dedicated to those sincere, committed evangelists, pastors, lay people and others who devote their lives to spreading the Gospel.

Many people have made important contributions to this work with their suggestions, encouragement and patience.

First, I want to thank my wife, Jeane, for enduring many hours of "writer widowhood" during this and other projects.

Dr. Guida Jackson-Laufer, through her teaching, critiques and support, has been invaluable.

I also want to thank Joyce Harlow, David Bumgardner and others in the critique groups for their constructive input.

A special thanks goes to Don Crouch, an artist friend of many years, for doing the front cover art.

Chapter 1

The Silver Broom's First Sweep

A red cloud of bloody spray burst from the left side of Dr. Culpepper's head. A guttural "umpff" escaped from his contorted mouth into the microphone hidden under his necktie.

In his room at the Century Plaza Hotel in Los Angeles, James Bresnahan sat forward, peered intently at the television news story of Dr. Jacob Zimri Culpepper's death. Bresnahan smiled at a frantic announcer's shrill: "What the...he's been shot. Culpepper's shot."

This was the fourth replay he'd watched. He sucked on a cinnamon disc and stared as the video recorded the precise moment when the rifle bullet ripped into the evangelist.

The newscaster droned, "Dr. Culpepper was shot a few minutes past seven as he addressed a crowd of forty-five thousand in San Diego's Jack Murphy Stadium. As you've heard from our affiliate in San Diego, the noted preacher who headed up the Culpepper Evangelistic Crusade, was pronounced dead at the scene from a massive head injury."

The eruption of blood from the preacher's head reminded Bresnahan of the watermelons splattering during target practice. Using the melons helped him determine the proper slug.

As he watched the broadcast, he analyzed the shooting results with clinical calm. He didn't see a human being dying, only a successful mission. "The first of many," he muttered.

When the news coverage cut to an aerial view of the stadium, Bresnahan relived the shooting three hours earlier. Stability of the helicopter's gyroscope-stabilized rifle mount, a modified mechanism normally used for photography, exceeded his expectations. He had no trouble holding the scope's crosshairs on Culpepper's head. The stolen fifty-caliber, U.S. Army sniper rifle lived up to its reputation as being accurate for up to a mile.

When he saw Culpepper go down, he signaled the chopper's pilot who flew the machine, also stolen and painted black, at low altitude over the Pacific Ocean due west of San Diego. Bresnahan jettisoned the rifle from the helicopter into the ocean and began to loosen the special mount used as a shooting platform. It took only forty seconds to release the clamps and toss it out.

"Go home," he said into the voice-actuated microphone touching his lips. He felt a turn to the right as the pilot answered, "Roger."

Bresnahan had plucked a cinnamon candy from his pocket and untwisted the cellophane wrapper. He mouthed silently, "You're dead as a fly, Dr. Jacob Zimri. The silver broom means errancy's doom."

With the barest hint of a smile in the dark cabin of the speeding helicopter, he popped the hard candy into his mouth, acutely aware of his calm, inner confidence, a feeling that came when he knew he was doing God's will. He pressed the Indiglo button on his digital watch. 19:15:05. The mission was precisely on schedule.

Within ten minutes, they touched down at an abandoned landing strip near Escondido. He and the pilot split up, and Bresnahan drove straight to the Century Plaza.

His attention was pulled back to the TV set when the reporter speculated about who fired the fatal shot and why. Bresnahan glared at the screen. "You'll know if and when the Lord ordains you to know."

He clicked off the set and stepped into the bathroom to brush his teeth. Shirtless, he stood in front of the mirror, pleased at the sight of his athletic build, one hundred and seventy-five pounds carried compactly on his five-foot, eleven-inch frame. He looked younger than his thirty-five years. Until he began his mission, he had hated his nondescript looks, size and medium brown hair color. Now, being forgettable was an asset. He could blend into any setting.

Bresnahan peered into his own eyes in the mirror. They were brown with tiny yellow flecks. He spoke quietly, slowly. "You, like the Almighty God you serve, work in strange and mysterious ways. Your mission is clear. In your hands, the silver broom shall sweep the errant vermin into their pit of eternal damnation. Selah."

Relaxed and fulfilled, he went to bed and thought about his next mission. Unless something changed his mind, he would journey to The American Church in Kansas City, Kansas. His jaw tightened as he thought about the offensive Reverend Raymond Tisdale and the equally distasteful Harmonia Tracker, the singer who brandished her exaggerated smile.

Reverend Ray, as he billed himself, pastored The American Church and appeared on TV in twenty-two states. With his gaudy costumes and flamboyant hysterics, Reverend Ray was the worst offender on Bresnahan's list now that Culpepper was dead. Very soon, Reverend Ray would feel the sweep of Mission Silver Broom. Bresnahan smiled as he thought, I'll whisk that made-for-TV smile off Harmonia Tracker's face.

Promise Under Canvas

Leeandra stood on the stage under the Stevens Evangelical Crusade tent, every strand of her long blonde hair in place. Strings of naked, one hundred and fifty-watt light bulbs sagged from the tent's brown canvas ceiling. Joe Ted Stevens, her trim, graying father, stood to one side of the podium, his arms extended toward the crowd.

"Tonight. Now. Accept Jesus as your personal Savior," he implored. "Believe in Him and have everlasting life."

Leeandra watched him turn to the left, then back to the right as he looked at the people who filled all of the wooden folding chairs and those who stood around the edge of the tent.

Her brother, Casper, stood at the opposite end of the stage, leading the invitational hymn with slow, gliding waves of his right arm, his tenor voice lost in the crowd's singing of "Only Trust Him."

When she read the note slipped to her by a local pastor, Leeandra gasped and immediately looked up at her fifty-three-year-old father. Apprehension gnawed at her as she sang the invitational hymn, glad the service was almost over. The death of a fellow evangelist made her think about how easy it would be for someone to shoot her father. She wondered why anyone would shoot a servant of God.

She couldn't bear the thought of another loss in the family. Her mother died five years ago. Her husband and two children were killed in the boating accident three years after her mother's death.

"Give your life to Jesus." Her father's authoritarian voice rose above the crowd's song, the band's subdued accompaniment and the breeze's quiet rush. The unseasonably warm October south wind blew across bare, defoliated cotton stalks in the field next to the tent pitched adjacent to the Interstate Highway 20 service road in Sweetwater, Texas.

Three people made their way to the reception area in front of the stage during the first two verses of the invitational hymn. As the fourth verse came to a close without additional response, Leeandra watched her father nod to Casper. She knew the signal well. There'd be no fifth verse.

When the song ended, she sat, bowed her head and uttered a silent prayer of thanks for tonight's three decisions for Jesus. She prayed for Dr. Culpepper's family and friends. She asked God to protect her family.

Preachers and Potato Chips

"Shoot!" Jerome K. Hoffstedtler—everyone called him Hoff— straightened up as he watched the six ball carom off the billiard table's rail, short of the intended pocket. "I don't know why I fool with this stupid game."

Larry Best, almost a half foot shorter, walked around the table to line up his shot, talking as he chalked the cue tip. "Merchandising a preacher is no different than selling soap or peddling potato chips. In fact, it's easier to sell religion because you're selling hope. TV evangelism is religion's answer to state lotteries and ten million dollar giveaways.

People need hope or they go nuts."

"Right now, I'm hoping you'll sink that shot so we can go eat," Hoff said and glanced at the television set in the walnut-paneled game room of his high-rise condo building in Houston.

"You can't rush an artist when he's...."

Hoff interrupted. "Listen!"

The stiff command caused Larry to glance at his friend before looking at the screen. A knot of paramedics worked feverishly on a sprawled figure. "To update on this breaking story," a newscaster said, "a prominent West Coast religious figure, Dr. Jacob Culpepper, is dead. He was shot tonight as he preached to a crowd of forty-five thousand in San Diego."

"Holy shit," Larry said. "We were talking about him not ten minutes ago."

Hoff listened to the announcer for another thirty seconds. "I'm done. Let's go eat." He laid his cue stick on the table.

"Didn't I tell you there's room in big-time television evangelism for a new superstar?" Larry said. "Even more room now."

"Jeez, that's cold."

"Also realistic, but lighten up. I'm the guy who was singing Culpepper's praises, remember?"

"Yeah, but this is kinda spooky."

Initially, Hoff had been ambivalent about Larry's idea for a business venture to elevate an unknown evangelist to stardom on television. Given the success of Culpepper and others, Hoff had convinced himself he could raise a million dollars from his stable of investors to fund the enterprise.

Hoff slipped on his sweater and said, "I'm warming up to your TV preacher idea. I'm ready to do another deal and it's different enough to be interesting—we've got to find the right candidate."

"We'll get a look-see at one day after tomorrow in jolly old Sweetwater when we go see that Stevens family bunch. Did you line up the King Air or do we fly commercial?"

"Commercial," Hoff said. "The King Air has an engine down. I haven't been able to find anything else yet, but I'm still trying."

"Yep. You the marketing biggie and me the ad biggie are gonna do some purely righteous preacher promotin'."

Perhaps Is the Best I Can Do

On Saturday, Hoff checked into the Big Country Motel in the West Texas town of Sweetwater, alone because Larry Best had been called to New York for an emergency client meeting. After discovering he forgot to pack toothpaste, Hoff returned to the lobby to buy some.

From doorway of the lobby, he noticed the tall, attractive blonde woman in red slacks leaning across the registration counter. She held a bill and called out, "Hello. I need change for the Coke machine, please."

Hoff liked her pleasant, singsong call to attract the absent clerk.

The front desk attendant emerged from a back office. "Oh, Miss Stevens, I'm sorry to keep you waiting." Quickly, she exchanged the dollar bill for quarters and smiled. "I attended your service night before last. You have a beautiful voice."

Hoff walked toward the desk. As the woman in red slacks turned around, he asked, "Did I hear correctly? Are you Leeandra Stevens?"

"That's right." She fixed an appraising gaze on him after a darting glance at his eyebrows.

"I'm Jerome Hoffstedtler. Everybody calls me Hoff." He extended his right hand.

She brushed errant strands of her shoulder length blonde hair from her face with her long, slender fingers. She glanced at Hoff's extended hand before she grasped it momentarily. "I'm pleased to meet you."

She reminded Hoff of Margo, the third of his ex-wives. He had a weakness for tall, slender, buxom blondes. "I've never been to Sweetwater before," he said. "Can you recommend a place to eat?"

"My father, brother and I eat most of our meals next door at the Red Rooster." Leeandra's quick smile crinkled a single set of parenthesis marks at the edges of her mouth.

Hoff felt a flush of excitement. He guessed she was about thirty. He thought she was one of the most exquisite women he'd ever seen. The blue of her eyes reminded him of Caribbean waters.

"I saw your photo on the poster outside," he said. "The Stevens Crusade, I believe it is."

Leeandra tilted her head a fraction to the left. "Right again."

"I'm from Houston. Do you stop there?"

"No, we don't." She made no move to turn away.

"I'd like to buy you a cup of coffee if you have time."

"Sorry," she said quietly, "I must get ready for tonight's service."

"I would've never figured you for a church singer."

"Do you attend church?" she asked. He shook his head. "Maybe you should. Then you'd know what a church singer looks like." The tinge of sarcasm in her voice was reproachful.

"Touché," he said.

"I hope you will attend tonight. That's our tent just down the street."

"If I do, will you have coffee with me afterward?"

"Persistent, aren't you?"

Hoff smiled. "I figure it's a good opportunity for you to entice a wayward soul into your service."

Her laugh activated triple sets of parentheses as if reinforcements were needed to contain her humor. "Persistent and extemporaneous."

"I take that to be a compliment. So—how about it? Coffee afterward?"

"Perhaps," Leeandra said softly. "That's the best I can do." She took a backward step, turning away from Hoff.

"You drive a hard bargain," he said. "Thanks for the suggestion on a place to eat. It's nice to meet you."

With a little nod, she walked toward the wing of guest rooms. He pivoted to watch her. There was a distinctiveness in Leeandra Stevens. He felt an inaudible vibration akin to a tuning fork with a frequency too high for the human ear. In addition to being one of the most beautiful women he'd ever seen, he figured she likely was one of the most untouchable. He enjoyed the give-and-take with her over the coffee invitation. He thought, she's got smarts and a streak of independence.

He watched until she turned a corner. She didn't look back although she must have known he was watching. He stared down the empty hall, savoring her subdued demeanor, each move naturally correct. She radiated a classic quality amid the tawdry flagrance of the fraying motel. He was always drawn to quality.

Baptism by Songful Voice

Hoff arrived at the Stevens Crusade tent twenty minutes early and chose a seat on the center aisle near the back so he could observe the crowd. He glanced at the strings of bare light bulbs overhead.

A man and a woman edged their way past Hoff. As the man settled in the wooden folding chair next to Hoff, he said, "Claypool's the name." Lacing, purple veins crisscrossed the misshapen, bulbous nose on Claypool's jovial, red face, and his right eye angled a few degrees too far to the right. "You from around here?"

"I'm from Houston."

"Big city. Ever go to anything like this down your way? Quite a show." Mr. Claypool spoke more softly as he leaned toward Hoff. His breath smelled of tacos. "Better than most stuff on TV. My wife and me, we've been coming for years, most every night it's in town and the weather's decent, not counting the year my wife had her gall bladder took out. My missus is bigger on the church part than me, but it's good entertainment. The Stevens family comes right after the cotton harvest each year. Folks around here got more money once the cotton's in."

At the stroke of seven-thirty, Joe Ted Stevens, his son, daughter and three musicians walked onto the stage. Joe Ted strode directly to the pulpit and convened the service with a short prayer.

Hoff liked Joe Ted's looks. Graying, about six feet tall, he was dressed in a dark suit, white shirt and wine-colored tie. Casper, his son, also wore a dark suit. Leeandra was dressed in an ankle-length, loose-fitting navy dress with long sleeves. All three would look good on television.

After the prayer and a short welcome by Joe Ted, Casper led two congregational hymns, accompanied by musicians playing keyboards, guitar and a saxophone. Casper introduced Leeandra, telling the crowd she would "minister to them in song." Hoff noted the crowd's twitter when she stepped to the podium. As she drew a breath to begin her song, the people waited in coughless silence.

"Amazing grace, how sweet the sound." She sang a cappella with the ringing clarity of strummed crystal. Her blonde hair, meticulously groomed with each straight-hanging strand in place, shone brightly under a spotlight. A thin pall of dust swarmed in the shaft of light as she sang.

"I once was lost, but now am found, was blind but now I see." Leeandra led the three hundred people under the drab tent into an admiring absorption of her song.

Each time she paused, Hoff sensed a crisp, anticipatory silence, an energetic eagerness by the crowd for her next sound. He was also mesmerized by her soprano voice—potent, alone and vibrant. Now, he understood the crowd's reaction when she was introduced.

With graceful, flowing moves, she turned, tilting her head as she sang. A glowing smile added to her statuesque beauty and the softness of her round-featured face. Her big, provocatively blue eyes were open wide. The fervent lyricism was a baptism by songful voice, washing across eyes focused on her face, across ears attuned to her message of promise.

Mr. Claypool nudged Hoff. "She's good, ain't she?"

"Outstanding," Hoff answered quietly. He felt the buzz of anticipation that came when he sensed a deal was in the making.

Leeandra hit each note with crisp accuracy, no sliding or slurring, no slippage into flat or sharp. "When we've been here ten thousand years, bright shining as the sun, we've no less days to sing God's praise than when we first begun."

The last note dissipated, and she raised her clasped hands to her chin. As her voice seeped away, a chorus of amens, and praise the Lords erupted from the crowd, accompanied by a smattering of applause and the roar of an eighteen wheeler high-balling its way through Sweetwater on I-20. The truck's roar ebbed quickly, but not the praising shouts of a crowd evoked into joyful noise by Leeandra's song.

"Man alive," Hoff said under his breath. "She has this crowd in the palm of her hand."

On the row in front of Hoff, a hefty, graying, well-dressed matron with a black, eraser-sized mole on her cheek blotted tears with a tissue.

Leeandra turned slowly toward her chair, one of four in a row on the wooden stage. She walked with a composed deliberate undulation, her hair swinging gently in counterpoint to her steps. Quickly, Casper returned to the pulpit, addressing the crowd with bouncy enthusiasm. Hoff barely heard him. He was engrossed in Leeandra, digesting the unexpected power and allure of her song. He thought she was out of place under this dingy brown tent with hay strewn on the ground to help suppress the dust. There was magic in the voice of this enchantress named Leeandra. His fascination continued as the service unfolded in a series of what were, for him, new experiences.

After another congregational hymn, Leeandra gave what she called a testimony, talking about the accidental deaths of her husband and two children. As she emphasized the importance of God's love in dealing with life's tragedies, her voice had a melodious lilt.

With fluid turns and tilts of her head, she looked at people as she spoke about God's love. She made eye contact, it seemed, with every matron with mole, every old man in blue twill overalls and every freckle-faced little boy with cowlick. There was no hint of recognition when Leeandra looked at—or was it almost at—Hoff. At the end of her talk, Hoff again saw people wiping away tears.

Joe Ted strode to the pulpit, his eagerness to preach apparent. His impassioned sermon was a tongue-gunned, urgent plea for people to surrender their lives to Jesus Christ. "Now! Tonight! For Jesus will come again in the twinkling of an eye. Repent! Be saved!"

Joe Ted was well into his sermon when halfway across the tent, a balding, chubby man in his fifties jumped to his feet and scooted with quick, hopping steps into the aisle. Hoff's face slackened with disbelief as the man began to shout in screeching, yawping incoherency. The man held his hands above his head, wrinkling four rings of fat on the back of his neck as he looked up.

Hoff couldn't understand a single word of the gibberish. Nor could he understand the crowd's favorable reaction to what he considered an abysmally bad-mannered interruption. After one long string of gibberish followed by a whistling intake of breath, the man began to bay—long, howling owww-oooo's at the tent top. He danced and skipped in place as he howled, a stridently discordant antithesis to Leeandra's beautiful solo.

Hoff squinted when the man flopped down on his stomach, began to writhe and twist frantically, kicking up a cloud of dust from the hay-covered ground. In an instant, he was back on his feet, dancing and yelling, ooowww. He flopped down again and writhed on the ground.

All around Hoff, people began to shout amen, praise the Lord as they craned and stretched to see. The cloud of dust grew above the flailing, howling man. He was up again, bits of hay clinging to his khaki pants and shirt. He hopped more slowly and his baying ow-oooooo was shorter, quieter, his utterances less frenetic.

"Bless you, brother," Joe Ted shouted to the man. "The Lord is amongst us this evening, speaking to us through this brother in Christ. Praise Jesus!"

A frail woman with graying hair tucked into an unraveling bun stepped out into the aisle and with a weak tug at his shirt, guided the now-mumbling, spent man back to his seat.

Hoff was astonished at the spectacle, but he resisted the urge to ask Mr. Claypool what it meant.

To regain control of the crowd, Joe Ted uttered a quiet prayer before continuing his sermon, building up his rapid-fire pace. Even in the fall warmth, he retained his neat-as-a-pin look despite an exertive style.

Hoff's attention kept straying from Joe Ted to Leeandra, who sat motionless on stage, looking at her father. Hoff didn't see her move a single time, not so much as shift a foot or move a hand until Joe Ted announced the collection.

Hoff was surprised when an aluminum dishpan got to him. It was more than half full of money, fives, tens and twenties mixed among the ones and coins. From the way people dressed and the cars he'd seen in the parking lot, he guessed most people were low in the economic pecking order. He passed the pan to Mr. Claypool, who dropped in a five, nudged Hoff and said, "What'd I tell you about folks having more money."

After the collection, Joe Ted issued a summons-like instruction for unbelievers to accept Christ as their Savior. "You've given of your worldly goods unto the Lord. Now I call on you to give your life to Jesus before it's too late. Tonight! Now!" Joe Ted paused for a quick scan of the crowd with his intense blue-gray eyes before he shouted, "Praise Jesus!"

Hoff wondered if the sudden death of Dr. Culpepper contributed to Joe Ted's sense of urgency. A raspy twinge edged through Hoff. It's contagious, he thought.

As the crowd sang the invitational hymn, five people walked to the reception area in front of the stage. Joe Ted stood on the hay-covered ground and welcomed each respondent with a handshake, a hug and earnest conversation. Slender and erectly dignified, he reminded Hoff of a beneficent patriarch welcoming long-unseen family members.

Leeandra stood onstage, singing happily, her voice unheard as Casper conducted with his rhythmically-waving arm.

When the hymn ended, Joe Ted returned to the pulpit to pronounce the benediction. He invited those who felt guided by God to come to the prayer tent directly behind the stage.

Hoff felt no guidance from God, but he wanted to find Leeandra and renew his invitation for coffee. He was also curious about what a prayer tent was and what might happen there.

Under the smaller tent—the size used for graveside funeral rites— two dozen people knelt in prayer. Most spoke in a babble of hushed, beseeching voices, their palms together. Joe Ted stood in the middle. He was silent, his eyes closed, looking up, clasped hands touching the chin on his slender, squarish face. His graying hair was short and neatly combed. Hoff thought he was good looking enough to be an actor.

Casper, taller than his father, not as blonde as his sister, stood to one side of the prayer tent, talking with a small group of people. Casper was a fresh-scrubbed, few pounds heavier copy of his father. Hoff guessed Casper was in his late twenties, two or three years younger than Leeandra.

In his search for Leeandra, Hoff walked slowly around the tent's perimeter, but she wasn't there.

He hurried back to the main tent. A half dozen people lingered to talk. A stubble-faced, elderly maintenance man looked up at a string of lights that had gone out near the end of the service. Except for those few people, the tent was empty. It was also dusty and smelled of hay from shuffling feet. Hoff sneezed.

"God bless you," the maintenance man said.

"Thank you." Hoff returned to the prayer tent for another look. No Leeandra. He stood at the edge of the smaller tent for several seconds. Maybe she went back to the motel. He walked slowly through the big tent and across the unpaved parking lot, empty except for a dozen cars and two pickup trucks parked nose to nose, connected by a jumper cable. Two men peered under the hood of the white truck, the one not running.

Hoff glanced at his watch. 9:38. Time passes fast, he thought, when you're getting a slam dunk dose of the gospel.

Search for an Elusive Elixir

When Hoff got to the motel, he picked up the lobby house phone and asked to speak to Leeandra Stevens. He was told by an operator with a twangy voice, "Sorry, hon, she doesn't take calls this late."

He wasn't surprised she elected not to meet him. He was sure guys hit on her all the time. Hoff headed for the motel's little bar.

The room was dimly lit, empty and quiet, devoid of so much as a bartender or Muzak. "Hello?" Hoff called out and sat on the middle of three backless rattan stools at the bar. The three stools reminded him of the four chairs on the Stevens Crusade stage. He wondered why there were four since there were only three people in the Stevens team. Was Joe Ted married? Divorced? Hoff would ask Larry Best.

Hoff helped himself to a beer nut from a plastic bowl. The nut was stale. "Hello?" he repeated.

"Be right there." A thin, gangly young man ambled through the doorway into the space behind the bar. "Sorry to keep you waiting. I'm the night auditor. Also bartender. I hope you don't want something fancy like a Singapore Sling." The man wore a wrinkled suit and loosened tie.

"A Coors Light will do nicely. Is this place always so quiet?"

"Well...." The young man put the long-neck beer bottle on the bar. "Yes, it's always this quiet." A telephone rang in the adjoining room. "Excuse me," he said and left to answer it. Hoff sipped his beer as he overheard snatches of conversation about unpaid bills.

He picked up the *Sweetwater Reporter* off the bar and moved closer to the lamp next to the cash register. It was today's edition, Saturday, October 8th. The Stevens Crusade ad on page six stopped his idle puttering through the paper. The ad was an adaptation of the poster he saw on the Red Rooster's front door. He studied the photograph of Leeandra.

He felt embarrassed about saying she didn't look like a church singer. He still didn't think she was a churchy-looking woman. Her walk and commanding carriage were better suited for a grand entry into an elegant ballroom. What a regal figure she would be in a glittering, sequined gown, its decolletage the polestar for admiring eyes. She simply was not a fit with that brown tent pitched next to a defoliated cotton field. She was a definite fit for television.

In the ad, Leeandra displayed the same reserved, guarded smile he saw in the lobby this afternoon. She had not carried a handbag then or at the service. Women who didn't carry a handbag impressed him as refreshingly carefree.

He looked up from the Stevens ad and assessed his surroundings. The stucco walls were littered with beer signs and posters, including a Dallas Cowboys season schedule. No one was filling in the scores.

What a contrast this place is, he thought, to Chasen's Restaurant in LA. A week ago tonight, he dined there as the guest of Akron Burghler, a movie producer. Hoff's investor group was helping finance the producer's new film, *The Fourth Reich*. Two weeks before that, he had been in Peru, looking after the gold mining venture his investor group owned. A month ago, he met with Dutch pension fund representatives in Amsterdam to secure financing for a shopping center purchase.

He smiled. Tonight I actually went to hear a tent preacher. He tried to remember the last time he'd gone to church. In high school, he found church boring and quit attending, except when it meant getting a date.

Until tonight, Larry's idea to transform an unknown evangelist into a television star had been abstract. He inserted the faces of Joe Ted, Leeandra and Casper Stevens into the plan. If we can't sell Leeandra, we'd better get out of the business, he thought. Hoff realized how engrossed he had become in the evening's service. That was unexpected.

He finished his beer, put three dollars on the bar, tucked the newspaper under his arm and went up to bed.

Leeandra's face, brightened by spotlight, sprang to mind. What a magnetic, powerful presence. When she sang, a plaintive quality beckoned each person to become part of her. The service was an interesting combination of glitz and gospel. Clearly, the crowd thought the Stevenses were genuine. They seemed genuine to Hoff. Good people, he thought.

Amid the beauty of Leeandra's song, Casper's enthusiasm and the sincerity of Joe Ted's urgent plea for people to be saved, Hoff sensed an irrational, collective clutching by the crowd for some elusive elixir of deliverance. They were, as Larry put it, looking for hope. How many people were looking for an antidote for life's mundane realism? Clamoring alarm clocks at five a.m. Boring jobs. Unpaid bills. Ill and aging parents. Children with mediocre grades. Dead batteries. Fading hopes and eroding dreams. Were all such travails subject to being swept away by Joe Ted's offer of eternal life or by the musical breeze of Leeandra's voice?

Behind closed eyes, Hoff visualized Leeandra on stage. Slender but not gaunt, she was blessed with natural, elegant beauty. Her complexion, flawless. Each blonde strand in place, silky bright under the spotlight. She held her interlocked hands to her chest as she sang. The song pulled him toward her through a tunnel formed by the intensity of his focus.

Leeandra's song became a summons to worship her. When he reached her, she grasped his hand and led him into a grand hall, its walls paneled floor to ceiling with beveled mirrors. The song changed into a wordless harmonic. As Hoff looked from mirror to mirror, he did not see his own reflection. He did see hundreds of Leeandras in the mirrors and heard her hauntingly beautiful soprano voice.

Chapter 2

Baptism by Jism

Dr. Henry Woods, pastor of the three thousand-member Centrum Church in affluent, far-north Austin, lay naked and alone in his bed at home. He was satiated by his love-making earlier in the evening with the prostitute named Madelyn at Motel 69, located across town from his church.

Tonight, he had again invited her to church. When she scoffed, he told her, "True, I'm interested in your body, but also in your soul."

Three years ago, the first time he invited her to attend, Madelyn asked why he consorted with a whore.

"I love too many things," he explained as his eyes twitched with a spasm of wincing blinks. "I can't discriminate. I love God. Yes. But I love sin, too. I can't love one to the exclusion of the other. Just as the Bible teaches, the flesh is weak. I'm weak. But at times, the flesh is also strong. I can be strong, but not all the time. God is perfection. He made man in His own image but He made man capable of sin. There's conflict, the severest form of conflict for he who is a man and also a man of God."

Now, as he drifted toward sleep, the paunchy and balding forty-six-year-old preacher found himself thinking about the women he would surely find in heaven. More precisely, he thought about body parts, skin textures, smells and tastes. In heaven, Dr. Woods felt with growing confidence, he would find buttocks even rounder, firmer and smoother to the touch than the young, red-haired girl in Tampa. Or was it Orlando? No matter. Nameless and placeless in his memory, her Playboy-perfect butt was a peak of recall in the forget-eroded, receding landscape of a time in Florida that was now twenty years ago. The nameless red-head loved for him to rub his freshly-shaven face against her body. She moved her body in slow, sensuous undulations when he licked her skin in long, lazy, carnal strokes. He thought it was odd he could remember little else about her except her red hair and that fantastic butt.

Madelyn, his current favorite, took the prize for the softest inner thighs, territory he came to know intimately during their numerous romps at Motel 69. He ranked Madelyn's body as heavenly, even if she did use it in the earthiest of professions.

Yes, Dr. Woods thought, heaven must surely offer many such feminine delicacies. If not, why call the place heaven? If, as the Bible promised, heaven offered more sublime pleasures than those on earth, he could not imagine what sensual delights awaited him. The prospect of streets paved with gold interested him far less than the prospect of wanton young women. He tried to envision the eternal bliss of never-ending sexual gratification. Almost asleep, he smiled at the thought of "baptism by jism". When he got to heaven, he would be delighted to continue his ministry of baptism by ejaculated jism.

Margo the Magnificent Revisited

Hoff poured coffee into Larry's cup. They sat at the conference table in Hoff's office in Houston on Monday afternoon after he saw the Stevenses.

"Yep, I thought you'd like them," Larry said.

"I think they're great, except for Leeandra. She's fantastic. Let's skip the other prospects on your list and get this show on the road. I'm ready to make something happen."

"Nope, bad idea. You owe it to yourself to see the others so you'll have a basis for comparison."

"I'm curious. How did you hear about the Stevenses?"

"At a family reunion," Larry answered. "One of my cousins is a marketing professor at Texas Tech. She's also a dyed-in-the-wool Pentecostal. I mentioned the idea of taking an unknown evangelist and making a TV star out of him. A couple of weeks later, she sent me a clipping about the Stevenses from the Lubbock newspaper. My cousin attended one of their services and liked them. Coming from her, that's like winning an Emmy. I got a copy of their schedule from the Stevens office in Amarillo."

"You've never seen the Stevenses in action?"

"Nope. Going strictly on my cousin's recommendation. I look forward to seeing them."

"Can you go with me to see those other preachers next weekend?"

"Yep. We gotta hurry. Whoever popped Culpepper might pick off one of our candidates."

"Damn, you're cynical."

"You're getting too serious-minded in your old age. If we get involved in this deal, you'll need a sense of humor."

"How so?"

"We'll be dealing with charismatic religious types, and they're like magnets. They draw all sorts of people to—oddballs of every description, people who are kooky to the tenth power, devout believers, you name it. They'll have all kinds of devotees and enemies, some of whom we'll never know about because they'll be lost out yonder in TV land."

Hoff frowned. "Why're you telling me all this?"

"You need to know what you're getting into. It's not like the pizza restaurants, the land deals and that other stuff you've done. We'll constantly be at the outskirts of crackpot city. I'm not saying everybody we'll deal with will be nuts, but we'll see our fair share."

Hoff refilled Larry's cup. "No problem. You can handle the dingbats."

"Thanks a lot. Have you talked to your big daddy investor in Midland about ponying up some serious cash money?"

"No." Hoff had intended to visit with Andy Boxx as part of the trip to Sweetwater, but the multimillionaire oilman was out of town. The father of Hoff's college roommate, Andy had invested in each of Hoff's ventures, and he felt closer to him than to his own father. He thought of Andy, a gruff rough-and-tumble independent oilman, as his mentor, one of the most honorable people he knew. Andy relied on handshakes to seal business deals worth millions. "Andy will pony up. He always does."

"Think you can really raise a million dollars for this deal?"

"Sure, if the numbers look good enough, so get your fanny in gear with those advertising and TV production costs so we can get a pro forma put together."

Larry stood. "No time like the present. When we hit the road this weekend, I'd like to go to Abilene and see the Stevenses for myself."

"Great idea. I'll have Gracie set it up."

"I'm outta here." Larry gave a thumbs up and left.

Hoff's secretary, Gracie Perry, brought a single telephone message slip into his office and dropped it on his desk. When he didn't look at it immediately, she said, "That message is from Margo. She's in town."

Hoff was surprised. He wondered why, after being gone for two years, she popped up now. Margo the Magnificent. Hearing her name reminded him of how much he missed her. He'd heard nothing from her in those two years. In the weeks following her departure, not even his private investigator could find her. He whuffed a short laugh and picked up the message slip. "THE Margo?"

"Yes. One of your legion of ex-wives."

"Thank you, Miss Gracie, for the reminder. What's she want?"

"To talk to you. She's called twice."

"Okay." Hoff laid the message slip on his desk and reached for the phone. He called Banner Tatum, his private investigator for many years. Banner answered immediately.

"Waiting for the phone to ring, are we?" Hoff did not bother to introduce himself. "Ready to pounce on some poor unsuspecting soul in exchange for filthy lucre?"

"Actually, I'm busier than a bumblebee on a blossom." Banner got his name because his father was having an outstanding year selling evaporative air conditioners door-to-door in West Texas the summer Banner was born. Banner said he wondered if his name would have been

Bummer had his father been experiencing a bad year. "How much of your filthy lucre can I do you out of?"

Hoff laughed. "Heard any more from your man in Mexico City?"

The investigator's contact supposedly could help expedite the purchase of equipment Hoff wanted to buy from the Mexican government for use in the Peru gold mine. A former Alcohol, Tobacco and Firearms federal agent who had specialized in Central and South American organized crime, Banner was well connected throughout Latin America. Small in stature and feisty, Banner always delivered on what he said he would do. He used his mixed ethnicity of Latin, Black and Caucasian to his advantage.

"My man is supposed to call Monday," Banner answered. "Why?"

"We're way the hell behind schedule down there. Press your guy for a quick answer."

"Quick-o ain't exactly big-o among la brethren Mexicana," Banner said, "but if he doesn't call me Monday, I'll call him."

"Money is big-o, so offer him more cash if you think it'll help."

"It damned sure won't hurt."

"Call me Monday?" Hoff asked. After he hung up he looked at the telephone for a moment before he called Margo.

Her voice was quiet and throaty. "I want to see you."

"Why?"

"Do I need a reason?"

"Guess not, but I figured you had one." He'd been surprised at the minuscule divorce settlement she accepted. Maybe she wanted money.

"Don't be a jerk Hoff." Margo articulated carefully to make sure he understood. While married, she called him "jerk Hoff" when annoyed.

Hoff offered to take her out to dinner, but she insisted he come to her apartment about seven. She would prepare dinner.

After they said goodbye, Hoff poured more coffee and stared out the window of his fifteenth-floor office, thoughts focused on his ex-wife. He still loved her. When she lived with him at the condo, she put out fresh flowers daily. During the spring and summer, she picked them from the building's grounds. She was the only tenant allowed to pick flowers by the crotchety old groundskeeper. In other seasons, she bought flowers. Remembering, he smiled. But the smile waned as he thought about how empty his life became when she left. Knowing she was in town made him feel better. At the same time, he wondered why he felt so forgiving. To hell with all that, he thought. She's back. That's what counts.

He arrived at her apartment ten minutes early.

Before and after dinner, they made love with the same ardent abandon as before. Sex with her always had been a wild free fall. Hoff couldn't remember her being prettier or the sex more enjoyable. Margo the Magnificent was as magnificent as ever—tan, voluptuous, still blonde. Her fellatio fantastico was no less fantastic.

She told him she'd found a job as a cocktail waitress as soon as she returned from the Virgin Islands. A high school dropout with a GED, she owned no marketable skills except her striking good looks and outgoing personality. She'd rented the apartment completely furnished, functional but sterile except for a small vase of daisies.

"I needed to get away from Gordon and St. Thomas for awhile," Margo said as they ate lasagna and drank Lambrusco on the living room floor. Naked. She always had been good with Italian food. "I need some time to decide what I want to do with the rest of my life."

"I want to know why you left," Hoff said after they ate.

She took a long, deep breath, dipped her finger in wine and ran it across Hoff's lips. "Not today," she said. She licked the wine off him. "No unhappy talk today. Please?"

He pulled her mouth to his, and they made love. Afterward, he thought about Leeandra Stevens as Margo lay on his arm and twisted strands of his chest hair into teepee shapes. Margo's blonde hair was almost as long as Leeandra's.

A Strangely Powerful New Way

Joe Ted Stevens watched the breeze toy with his daughter's hair as she stood before an overflow crowd packed inside and around the Stevens Crusade tent in Abilene, Texas, the next stop after Sweetwater.

A lazy south wind dispersed most of the dusty hay smell and caused the strings of naked, one hundred-fifty-watt light bulbs to sway as Leeandra sang "How Beautiful Heaven Must Be." Her blue eyes dazzled. Fingers interlocked, she held her hands to her chest while she sang.

As Leeandra finished the hymn's second verse, her father watched in bewilderment as people filed quietly to the open area in front of the stage. Following the lead of a teen-age girl wearing designer jeans, nine people knelt on the hay-covered ground as Leeandra continued her a cappella solo.

At the end of Leeandra's song, four of the nine people told Joe Ted they wanted to accept Jesus Christ as their personal Savior.

Looking back on his lifetime in the ministry, he could not recall witnessing such a spontaneous reaction to singing in a religious service. He was more convinced than ever that God was using his daughter's voice in a strangely powerful new way. Thank you, Lord, he thought. Thy will be done.

Chapter 3

Death of a Friend

In bed at home in the tiny Texas Panhandle town of Channing, sandy-haired Danny Don Rhodes clutched the covers tightly against his burn-scarred lips as he watched the rerun of a Dr. Culpepper service. Seeing it reminded him of the vivid images of the assassinated preacher. Battering confusion invaded his head, bombarding his mind with shrapnel-like fragments of thoughts. "Not...not good," he stammered aloud.

The plague of confusion was another debilitating legacy of the pipeline explosion three years ago that left him scarred and crippled. He remembered the spinning storm of white and fiery red-orange, recalled vividly the strange, incongruous quiet at the center of the blast as the burning maelstrom enveloped him. The explosion changed his life from good to bad in an instant.

Only in the sanctuary of his crowded little room here in the home of his cantankerous, sixty-seven-year-old Great Aunt Gertrude could he find solace from a world he believed treated him as an outcast. Watching evangelists gave him hope. He had watched Dr. Culpepper regularly and thought of him as a friend. He believed the preacher was one of the rare ones who would not turn away from the sight of the stringy, waxy burn scars on his face, making him look much older than twenty-nine. Now, that friend was gone. "Not good," he repeated in hushed anguish.

With covers pulled up to his chin because Aunt Gertrude was on her high horse about utility bills and insisted on keeping the house cold, he waited for the next religious program to begin. He watched Reverend Raymond Tisdale's usual grand entry, the church's soloist, Harmonia Tracker, at his side. Danny Don watched Reverend Ray and Harmonia every week, except when he worked late at the service station. He didn't work late often, because the little town of Channing usually fell silent at dusk. Only when there was an emergency repair job did he stay after hours to fix a flat tire or help the mechanic. He considered himself lucky to have the job. Hooper's Fina Station was among the less than one hundred businesses in Hartley County, so he never refused overtime work. Mr. Hooper was quick to say, "If you ain't willing to work, I can find somebody who is."

Propped up on his pillows against the white iron headboard, Danny Don reached for the remote control and clicked off the set. He was not in the mood to watch the rest of the telecast. He placed the remote on the bedside table, opened the drawer and pulled out the stack of pornographic magazines. He picked the one with the best pictures of people having group sex. He glanced up to make sure the bolt lock on the inside of his door was securely in place.

He opened the magazine, then reached down to fondle his penis as he studied the photos. After returning the magazine to the drawer, he clicked off the light. With his eyes closed, he imagined the up-and-down pressure on his hard penis came from the expert mouth of a naked, green-eyed, buxom woman who was tonight's choice from the magazine. Danny Don disappeared into the enjoyment of his private nightly ritual as Aunt Gertrude watched reruns of Archie Bunker in the living room. The little white frame house creaked as it was buffeted by gusting, dust-laden winds that whipped through Channing on this late October night.

See You Later, Organ-ator

"Off your ass and out of the pew, put Jesus Christ to work for you." Larry Best smiled at Hoff. "That's a good line, my friend."

Because the coffee shop was closed on Sunday night, Hoff and Larry sat in the bar of the Abilene House Motel. They waited for a pizza delivery and talked about what they had seen earlier that evening during the Stevens Crusade tent service.

"If we'd been videotaping tonight," Hoff said, "could we've captured the excitement of the crowd reaction?"

"Oh, sure. We'd need a minimum of three cameras for good coverage. It's the same principle as televising a football game."

"I don't suppose we'd use instant replay, though, would we?"

"Why not?" Larry grinned, baring crooked, irregular teeth. "We could show that fat broad in the Hawaiian print, dancing and sweating in all the commotion after Leeandra's solo. God, what a sight! Big mama in her mu-mu with megaboobs in ultra slow-mo." Larry picked up his long neck bottle and spoke into the opening with hushed urgency. "Yes, ladies and gentlemen, big mama has her mountainous mammaries counter rotating with inversely differentiated propellation. You saw it first here on Hoff and Larry's Wacky World of Weeeee-ligion! Sponsored in part by Apostolic Sacramental Wine." He spoke in falsetto, "More fulfilling!" In a lower pitch, he added, "Tastes great!"

"No wonder you're in advertising," Hoff said. "You've got a hyper-extended sense of the weird."

"Yep. But life is weird. Recognize it and you get along better. If we go with this religion TV thing, you'll see that some bizarre things can happen in church. The unknown tongue isn't exactly everyday five-and-dime kind of stuff."

"What is the unknown tongue?" Hoff asked.

"Supposedly, a person experiencing religious ecstasy receives messages from the Holy Spirit and is blessed with the gift of speaking in tongues. It happened a lot in my grandmother's Pentecostal church. She referred to it as the gift of tongues and believed it was authentic. I got a big kick out of hearing people speak it."

"Someone spoke that stuff in both of the Stevens services I've attended," Hoff said.

Larry laughed. "Speaking of oddball crap, have I ever told you about Miss Ruby? She was organist at the old Community Baptist Church on Harrisburg Road in Houston. My grandmother took me there sometimes."

"I thought your grandmother was Pentecostal."

"She was, but these were city-wide, nondenominational services of some sort. At any rate, Miss Ruby had been organist at Community Baptist since Heck was a pup. The church had a grand old Aeolian-Skinner pipe organ, and Miss Ruby loved to play the daylights out of it. She liked to play racketa-fracketa, ring-a-ding stuff, really whoop it up."

Larry gulped his beer. "One night when my grandmother and I were there, Miss Ruby damned near brought the house down. Literally. She was playing a Mulet composition, "Thou Art The Rock." It's one of those fast bombastic things that shows off a pipe organ's true colors. Not to mention the organist's ability. Mulet gave Miss Ruby a chance to remind the brethren and sistren that she was no jackleg, get-by church organist. She showered down on that Aeolian-Skinner during "Thou Art The Rock" and plaster fell off a good two-thirds of the balcony's north wall."

"No shit?"

"Nope. Damned near no plaster, either. And in short order, damned near no Wednesday night congregation. Miss Ruby kept on playing for a minute or two, the mad masher of Mulet racking out the ranks on that wonderful old pipe organ. By the time she realized what'd happened, those good church-going folks were hauling ass out of the Lord's house."

Larry laughed. "Church was out! We're talking your basic, high-impact benediction. See you later, organ-ator. Yep. Reading about the walls of Jericho coming down is one thing. Having your church house wall come down around your own ears is quite another."

Hoff chuckled. "What happened?"

"Grandmother and I went home."

"No, goddammit," Hoff growled. "What happened to the church?"

"They repaired it. But, two years later the steeple was struck by lightning and the whole building burned to the ground. This time, church was out for good. The congregation never rebuilt."

"We ought to have our butts kicked for laughing at stuff like this."

"Nah," Larry said. "I don't think so. We've got senses of humor and God created us in His image. I consider that to be prima facie evidence that God has a terrific sense of humor." Larry smiled. "Not to mention a marvelous sense of the ridiculous."

"Such as?"

"Things like aardvarks, artichokes and Adam's apples. Don't forget the likes of Dennis Rodman, Hulk Hogan and Newt Gingrich."

"Jeez, Larry, you're terrible."

"No, I'm not. We take God too seriously, just like we take ourselves too seriously. We need to kick back and enjoy the offbeat things in life. That's why all the offbeat stuff is here."

Larry grinned and went on. "Have you ever met the man who could keep a straight face when he talked about dingleberries?"

Hoff laughed. "No."

"There you have it. Case closed. God created both, man and dingleberries." Larry peeled off his corduroy jacket, part of what he called his uniform. He usually wore the tan jacket with elbow patches, jeans, cowboy boots and a button-down, tattersall shirt, open at the collar. Only when he attended high-level client meetings did he wear a suit and tie, kept at the ready in his office. He draped his jacket over a chairback. "I've advertised damned near everything from nipples to caskets, but never religion. I like the Stevenses. With them, I think our TV deal will fly. They're a damned sight better than those yahoos we saw in Dallas Friday and Saturday nights."

"I agree," Hoff said. "Leeandra is outstanding."

"Yep. Top shelf. She just about blew me away when she sang "The Ninety and Nine." There's a mystical, profound quality in her voice. You have to listen when that woman sings. I clown around a lot, but I take her seriously." Larry paused. "Don't you know she could do a number on "Memories" from *Cats*?"

"Jeez, yes, she could." Hoff recalled when he and Larry first met. They shared a rainy-night taxi from the Winter Garden Theater, where they saw *Cats*, to the Waldorf-Astoria Hotel where both were staying. In exchange for letting him and his client share the cab, Larry bought drinks for Hoff and his date. Larry and Hoff discovered they graduated from The University of Texas the same year, although their paths never crossed on the fifty thousand-student campus. They also discovered that they both liked Martin's twenty-year-old Scotch.

Hoff thought Lawrence Canaan Best was the least likely looking individual on the face of the Earth to be an "ad biggie", as Larry sometimes called himself. He was only five-feet-six inches tall, was scrawny, and his big ears stood out at ninety-degree angles.

"Yep, it took some time for those people in the San Francisco office to take me seriously when I went sailing in there as Taylor-Pepper-Coe's executive creative director," Larry had said. "I know I look and act country, but I can't help it. It's congenital." His parents had moved to Houston from the tiny East Texas town of Timpson a year before Larry was born. "Could be worse. Instead of being congenitally country, I could be congenitally ignorant. Actually, I like to think of myself as countrypolitan."

At thirty-nine, the same age as Hoff, Larry was considered one of the agency's best and three years ago was promoted to regional manager.

The Abilene House Motel's bar didn't stock Martin's, so they drank beer. Larry motioned to the bartender for another round.

"Leeandra stirred up that crowd like gangbusters," he said. "I forgot how turned on people can get in church. Touchdown Leeandra! That woman has the bluest eyes I've ever seen. I bet she wears tinted contacts, not that it amounts to a hoot from hell."

"What do you think of Joe Ted and Casper?" Hoff asked.

"Casper is the clean cut, all-American boy to the fifth or sixth power. Every Nazarene lady who sees him will want to adopt him." Larry paused. "Joe Ted...Joe Ted gives the impression he expects an eight on the Richter Scale earthquake before the top of the hour. He cranks folks up pretty good. He's handsome, looks and sounds credible. His voice has good tonal quality. All his nouns and verbs agree. He should play well on TV.

"They're doing something right," Larry continued. "There must've been more than a hundred people standing in addition to the three hundred seated in the tent. Joe Ted said they've had almost a hundred professions of faith this week in Abilene."

Larry laughed. "It tickled the shit out of me when Leeandra, Joe Ted and Casper came on stage and you said, 'That's her, the blonde.' Hell, she was the only female up there."

"You were stuffing your face with pretzels. I didn't want you to miss anything." Hoff sipped his beer. "What improvements would we have to make to videotape in the tent?"

"Jack up the lighting for one thing," Larry said. "And add a more colorful backdrop behind the pulpit. That plain, brown tent won't cut it on the tube. The audio worries me. Lots of outside noise gets into the tent, so we'd need good microphones, mixing equipment, stuff like that."

"All that is manageable?"

"We need opinions from production experts that'll have to be paid."

"I'd expect that." Hoff paused. He thought about how stunning Leeandra looked in her red dress during tonight's service, a bright exclamation point in the tent's pervasive brown. "If we use this bunch,

I'm guessing we'll need to stay with the tent format to maintain cash flow and avoid cultural shock for the Stevenses. In the figures you're working on, I think we should assume taping in the tent, don't you?"

"Yep."

The pizza arrived and they dug in. Hoff picked pieces of bell pepper off his slices and Larry added them to his.

"Overall, you believe they're merchandisable?" Hoff asked.

Larry nodded and swallowed a bite. "Yep. Although you never know what will or won't spark the public's interest. I'd guess she'll be a smash hit or a dud, nothing in between. She's gorgeous and her voice has a memorable quality. Memorability is important. All this gets back to the marketing fundamental of having a unique selling proposition to make your product stand out from the pack."

"And she stands out." Hoff grinned. "In more ways than one."

Larry ignored the innuendo and took another pizza slice. "She's our show pony. Everybody, male or female, likes to look at a show pony. That's why the game shows have a looker to hold up the prizes or turn letters. She's world-class feminine without flaunting it. I like the way her hair swings when she walks." He paused. "Have you heard her speak?"

Hoff told Larry about Leeandra's testimony during the service in Sweetwater, including the mention of her husband's and children's deaths. "It was very moving. She drifted into a singsong kind of delivery. The crowd was spellbound."

"That's good."

"Her singsong delivery?"

"The whole thing. The bit about her husband and children plucks at the heart strings, gets people on her side. That adds to her value." Larry noticed Hoff's frown. "That's a purely clinical viewpoint. Right now, the Stevenses have to be evaluated as a packaging concept, like coffee in brick packs versus cans. We're talking new and improved religious product. It's business. For us to succeed, the Stevenses must compete successfully for viewers' time and dollars. That competition is fierce."

Hoff tinkered with a pizza crust and nodded slowly.

"This doesn't mean we rule out the human side of things," Larry continued. "We can like these people, have feelings for them, treat them fairly and all that. But right now, we're looking at what cuts of meat the butcher shop can sell."

Hoff's mouth twisted into a wry grin. "Think this will sell as good as that cat house idea of yours?"

"Oh, hell no," Larry answered with a big smile. "I still think we ought to try that. Get us a drum of peroxide and an electrolysis machine, then open Blondie's Booger Barn, home of the happy, hairless hookers."

The Empowerment of Leeandra Stevens

In Abilene's Ramada Inn motel, two miles from where Hoff and Larry lingered over their beer after eating pizza, Leeandra Kay Stevens prepared for bed. She washed her face, slipped into a powder blue, knee-length cotton night shirt and sat in front of her makeup mirror to brush her hair. She felt drained. The services in Abilene were both exhilarating and tiring. She felt as if a piece of her sang its way out of her body into the crowd with each solo.

People's responses to her singing in the last seven services were the culmination of a growing sense of power. Without an invitation, people came forward during her solos and made decisions for Christ.

Leeandra brushed her hair in long, even strokes as she thought about how people looked at her during the services. She saw adoration in their eyes. She noticed how quickly people became silent when she stood at the pulpit in the seconds before she sang. Their waiting became almost breathless, a still, quiet honor. Many leaned forward.

She stopped brushing and peered into the clear blue eyes in the mirror. This power is not of my own making, she thought.

She had told her father of the feelings of empowerment, how they bubbled inside her like a pulsing, nourishing spring. How they pervaded her spirit like a gentle weather front with its cool, cleansing winds.

"God is making Himself known to people through you," Joe Ted had told her. "It is the miracle we pray for every day."

She wished for the miracle of being able to describe the warm fulfillment that coursed through her when she sang. At times, the feelings were like colored mists—soft, living colors—gregarious yellows, dusky roses, satiating blues, the new life vitality of a spring season's greens. Occasionally, she thought she heard the mists hum inside of her, music within the music of her own voice. The colorful mists pooled and gathered at times when she wasn't singing. They filled the begging vacuum that lived inside her following the deaths of her husband and two children.

Why is God giving me this power to influence people with my singing after He took so much away? she wondered. Is it God's way of saying He's sorry? Was it God's doing that they died?

Leeandra saw them die. Burton Pierce Lee, her husband. She and only she called him Bur. Burton, Jr., age six. B.J. was all boy, a sweet-spirited, tow-headed little rowdy who lived life at the same pell-mell pace as his father. Four-year-old Stephanie Leeann. Leeandra called her honey-blonde daughter Effy. A mirror image of Leeandra when she was four, Effy loved being loved. She was such a happy, carefree child.

Leeandra had seen them die a thousand times in the twenty-six months since that bright Sunday afternoon at Lake Vineland not far from their spacious home in Plano. The accident happened on August 24th. At three-fifteen, the investigator's report said, their ski boat crashed into the old concrete silo, partially submerged in the man-made lake. She saw it all from the water skis as she was towed behind the boat.

Here in the Ramada Inn, she looked at the mirror. She saw the catastrophe unfold in an agony of slow motion, as if the rectangular, plastic-framed makeup mirror were a haunting monitor to the past. She was jolted by the same spasming grab of alarm she felt when she realized Bur was allowing the boat to drift to the left toward the silo. But he knew the silo was there. He would change course. Except he was looking back at her. So were B.J. and Effy.

Leeandra shouted, then screamed her warning, unheard over the roaring one-fifty horsepower outboard motor. She pointed and all three waved, thinking she was waving. Too late did Leeandra think to turn loose of the tow rope so Bur would slow the boat, turn and loop back around to pick her up. Too late as the speeding fiberglass boat annihilated itself against the unyielding twelve feet of abandoned concrete silo showing above the lake's surface.

Sinking into the water, her body jangled with the horror before her. She screamed, "No! No! Effy! Oh, God, no!" Despite her life jacket's buoyancy, she battled to keep the water out of her mouth and eyes. She saw the splintering, spray-flinging violence of the crash. The smoke and debris. She saw Effy hurled up into the air and a bit to the right, her blonde hair blowing. Effy began to tumble. For an instant, she saw the four-year-old's happy laugh dissolve into shocked surprise, a cry taking form. The engine's noise was gone, replaced by the subsiding explosion of impact. And splashing, blooping water. And other boats playing across the lake on a carefree Sunday afternoon in summer. The random routes of pleasure had ended in crashing death for one of the boats.

Leeandra tore off her skis and fought the water's resistance as she flailed her way toward the wreckage. Flotsam bobbed in water that sought its own peace after an instant of deathly, frenzied torment. Then she was swimming toward a bobbing orange life jacket. Who was in it? Crying and screaming out her family's names, Leeandra beat the water with her frenetic swim strokes. She was never a strong swimmer. She didn't seem to get any closer.

Suddenly a boat was beside her. Hands pulled her out of the water. "No!" she remembered screaming. "Leave me in! I've got to save them! Save them, not me!" She was hauled into the boat and a blanket was wrapped around her. Someone squeezed the water out of her long ponytail.

"My husband! My children!" she shouted as she twisted in the grip of the person trying to push her onto a cushioned seat in the canopied deck boat. Wildly, she searched the water, looking from the half-submerged drinks cooler to a plastic water jug, past unidentifiable pieces of wreckage, for orange life jackets. Both Effy and B.J. were wearing them, but not Bur. "Find them, please!" she shouted shrilly. "Effy! B.J!"

A newly-arrived boat blocked her view of where she had seen Effy thrown. "I think Effy is over there," she shrieked.

"We'll find them," a woman's voice said. "Please sit down."

Leeandra resisted the pushing on her shoulders and the pulling on one arm as she twisted, looking and searching.

Other boats arrived. She heard shouts. "Over there! Check that one!"

A few feet away on the deck boat, an urgent voice spoke into a citizens band radio microphone, "Any base station ashore. We have a code ten thirty-three at the silo on Lake Vineland. We need rescue units. We have casualties. Hurry it up! Do I have a copy?"

After a few seconds came the crackling answer, "Copy. This is Vineland Harbor Marina. Help's on the way."

More boats arrived. More people jumped into the water. More people shouted, shouts upon shouts that popped and barked in a rabid bedlam of alarmed confusion and excitement. Leeandra remembered sitting down in the boat that rescued her. She shivered under the blanket as she was held and consoled by someone she never saw. She remembered the slow whitening of everything, the blurring as if she were seeing it all through thin gauze. The gauze deadened sounds and slurred voices. "Going into shock," she heard someone say. "We have to get her to shore."

"No! I can't leave them!" Leeandra knew she tried to scream the words. She wasn't sure if any sounds came out.

She did remember the penetrating, metallic voice over the citizens band radio. "Can you ask her how many were on board? We've found a boy and a little girl, that's all. Neither of them made it."

The milky blur dimmed quickly through gray into a murky, cloudy dark. She could hear only distorted, warped, growling sounds. Someone held her close as the murky dark got colder, blacker and emptier.

Leeandra jumped when the toilet was flushed in the room next door, her father's room here in Abilene's Ramada Inn. In the mirror, she saw her eyes, red-rimmed and dry, and the brush she held motionless, embedded mid-stroke in her hair. Slowly, she pulled the brush down.

How I loved to brush Effy's hair, she thought. And dress her. Effy loved to primp. She loved for me to hold her in my lap and read stories to her. Leeandra felt the desolate void inside as she remembered the next morning after the accident. She remembered realizing Effy would never see another sunrise. Leeandra would never see another of Effy's sunny smiles. Or see B.J. come tearing into the house with a frog or a lizard. Or hear Burton sing out from the back door, "Lee-Lee, you lucky doll, your man's home!"

Things that happened every day would never happen again. Wet, smacking kisses from Effy. B.J.'s effusive cries of, "Hey, Mom, look!" Bur's Saturday morning trips to Andersen's Bakery for fresh walnut scones. She knew she had not enjoyed those bright bursts of life enough...because she never thought they would end. Life was too good for them to end. She watched her eyes fill with tears.

She took a long breath to try to fill the emptiness. She brushed her hair. "There were ninety and nine that safely lay." The solo she sang in tonight's service played in her head. "In the shelter of the fold."

She must think of Bur, B.J. and Effy as being in the shelter of the fold. Not gone, not away on a mountain dark and bare. Not that. But with the Shepherd. In the shelter of the fold. She was the one left in the desert, dark and alone. Even after two years and two months, she still felt alone.

Leeandra took another deep breath as she thought, where are you now, bubbling spring? Where are you, colors? Mists? Soothing pool? I need you.

Leeandra put the brush down, clicked off the dressing table lamp and got into bed.

"In the shelter of the fold." And, she thought, in the shelter of the dark. She pulled the sheet and blanket over her. In the shelter of the covers, too. And the shelter of pushing that day on the lake—all of it— and everything that followed, into the most remote, farthest reaches of her mind. Put them away, she thought. Yes, that's good. Far away. In months of practice, she had become adept at extricating herself from the tormenting replays.

She made herself think about tonight's service. Leeandra remembered the calm, arming, inner strength as she walked toward the podium in front of the overflow crowd. She saw and felt the people's eager waiting. Before she sang, Leeandra felt music inside her, a surging sense of elating potency. During her solos, the power surged out in a gentle, enveloping wave of love, caring and salvation.

Along with the power that was usually so rewarding, she felt a troublesome anxiety. Why? Why the skim of greasy anxiousness? Erase these thoughts, she told herself. She imagined an eraser wiping across a blackboard.

A new question formed in her mind. Why was the man named Hoff at the service tonight? She worked at remembering details of her brief encounter with him in Sweetwater. The unusual eyebrows. His good looks and softly dark eyes. The tuft of black hair protruding from his open shirt collar. The expensive cashmere sweater. His gentlemanly, if direct, approach. She saw him in the audience in Sweetwater. She gave passing thought to meeting him after the service as he suggested. She was tempted to wait on the stage, to interrupt the sameness of her ten-months-a-year life on the road with the Stevens Crusade. But, she didn't. Why? She just didn't.

Indecision mingled with her anxiety. Why can't I feel uncluttered joy? she wondered. Why the wide, deep troughs of apprehension between the waves of welcome, buoying power? Why the vivid replay of Bur's, B.J.'s and Effy's deaths? Why tonight after another evening of victory for God's work? Again, she pushed the vile pictures back into the dark, now a darkness within a darkness as she lay in the quiet, lightless motel room. Why the creeping, intensifying loneliness?

She nestled under the covers, listened to the dark's quiet and tried to erase everything from her mind. Think of the imaginary road, she told herself. See the narrow, rough track leading uphill across a treeless rise toward the clear sky. Enjoy the orange and golden streaks of the setting sun's light. Hear the bird calls, a mourning dove to the left, singing its restful, down-dipping, repetitive amen to the day. A cardinal chirping somewhere nearby, answered by its mate. Gentle sounds of a restful day in a peaceful land, fanned by a soft, laying breeze.

She lay in her burrow, savoring the imaginary road and began to drift toward sleep. She saw the first intertwined laces of colored mists—the rose colors, redder than usual, mixed with purplish blues. She heard a muted sound. She first thought it was a bird call, but it wasn't. It was a pacifying hum. From the mists? Yes. A bit louder, now, as the mists began to gather, falling off the end of the breeze. The yellows arrived. The greens, too. They blended together like merging puffs of sweet-smelling, colored smoke. They sang a pooling song that began to gather and fill Leeandra's begging vacuum.

Eyes closed, safely in the fold of her burrow, she smiled when she saw her imaginary road through the mists. She felt a gentle bubbling. The calm, arming, inner strength had never come to her quite like this before. She was thankful for its presence and for the shelter of the fold.

Instead of Sham, Salvation

The next morning, Hoff leafed through the *Abilene Reporter-News*. An article on last night's Stevens Crusade service stopped him, and he read the opinion-analysis story by the paper's religion writer.

"A proverbial doubting Thomas when it comes to these charismatic crusades under canvas, I went to the Stevens service expecting the worst. Instead of rip-off, I sensed revival. Instead of sham, I witnessed salvation.

"Leeandra Stevens possesses a powerful, singing spirit. She bestows upon us a tantalizing preview of what Heavenly Hosts must sound like."

Hoff tore out the article. He would show the clipping to Ken Walker, the Stevens Crusade business manager, during a meeting he planned to arrange this week.

As Hoff and Larry waited in the Abilene airport to board the twin-engine commuter plane, Larry said, "Did you know Abilene is mentioned in the Bible?"

"Sure," Hoff said. "Same part where slant-hole drilling and foot-long hot dogs are talked about, isn't it?"

"I'm serious. I looked it up last night in the Gideon Bible in my room. Chapter three, verse one of Luke. A geographical reference to an area called Abilene in Lebanon, northwest of Damascus."

Hoff stared quizzically at Larry. "Come on, now."

Larry held up his right hand. "Honest injun. I took a couple of Bible courses in college."

"Why?"

"I knew I wanted to be involved in the creative aspects of advertising. I thought the Bible courses might provide a different perspective being as how God created the whole shooting match."

Hoff shook his head. "You never cease to amaze me."

"Besides, Bible courses were good for my grade point average."

On the way back to Houston they talked about the television plan over the plane's noisy engines. As the pilot announced their final approach for landing in Houston, Hoff asked, "Blood, guts and feathers, what do you think about taking the Stevenses to the big time on television?"

Larry looked at his cup of coffee for several seconds, watching the tiny concentric waves generated by the engines' vibrations. "Intuitively, I think it's a winner, especially with Leeandra. She's sensational. I still like the novelty of it, but deep down, I believe the Stevenses have more going for them than novelty. I think they're real. It's nice to know the newspaper's religion writer feels the same way. I say we go for it."

Chapter 4

On Your Way, Reverend Ray

"You've worshipped with Reverend Ray...showing God's way," the pastoral assistant intoned in his rich, bass voice. "Blessed be the name of Jeeeeee-sus!"

Raymond Tisdale, pastor of The American Church, greeted worshippers who flocked to the sanctuary's stage at the service's conclusion. The featured soloist, Harmonia Tracker, helped him greet the people.

James Bresnahan stood next to the center aisle and stared at Reverend Ray while rubbing the rifle slug held between the thumb and forefinger of his right hand, tucked into his blazer pocket. Tomorrow night would be the last time for the preacher to showboat, Bresnahan thought as he watched Reverend Ray, Harmonia and a gaggle of members slowly make their way off the stage. Stopping frequently, laughing and talking, Reverend Ray and his followers meandered up the center aisle. They took no notice of Bresnahan who walked nonchalantly toward the chruch's vestibule, out one of the front doors, down the dozen steps and across the wide, four-lane street. On the other side, he stood on the sidewalk.

He rubbed the cleft in his chin as he enjoyed the crisp October night air and watched Reverend Ray emerge from the building with his entourage. As they did last night, the group stopped during their deliberate passage down the steps. A black Mercedes sedan waited at the curb, a uniformed chauffeur at attention beside the open back door on the passenger side. Every movement was exactly the same as the night before.

Bresnahan reached into the side pocket of his jacket and took out a cinnamon disc. When a coat and tie were appropriate, he wore an off-the-rack navy blazer, charcoal slacks, white shirt and a solid maroon tie, attire that helped him blend into a crowd. He unwrapped the candy, watching Reverend Ray linger beside the car for a final wave before he got in. Then the chauffeur shut the door, trotted around to the driver's side and sped away. Harmonia Tracker and the others stood on the sidewalk for no more than a minute before they dispersed.

Bresnahan looked up and down the street. The post-service rush was over. His plan would work. He would park his rental in the lot across the street and shoot from the clump of oleanders near the end of the parking lot, no more than ten paces from his car. He would need only one shot from his .270 caliber Carl Gustaf rifle, among the finest guns in his collection. Again, he reached into his pocket and caressed the bullet.

This would be much easier than shooting from a helicopter.

After the shooting, he would walk matter-of-factly to the rented Taurus and drive away. The attention of anyone lingering after the service would be focused on the dying Reverend Ray on the church steps.

Bresnahan was pleased with how well his idea of shipping the rifle to Kansas City from Fayetteville by bus worked. He hid the gun inside a set of golf clubs in a locked aluminum shipping case, then test shot the weapon at a Kansas City shooting range to calibrate the scope. He would ship the gun home the same way.

Reverend Ray would not show God's or anybody else's way after tomorrow night. This would be the last time for him to be whisked away in the ostentatious Mercedes sedan. No longer would the sanctimonious Reverend Raymond Washington Tisdale bastardize God's messages.

Bresnahan reflected on the time when he intended to be a preacher. Nobody gave him that chance because he didn't attend college or a seminary. His poor grades in high school prompted a taunt from one of his sisters, "Jimmie Dan fool fails in school."

He thought about the ways he had served God since becoming financially independent at age twenty-one with the trust fund income from his grandfather. He preached on the streets of San Francisco. For two years, he maintained a store-front mission in New Orleans, an effort that absorbed much of his four hundred thousand dollar annual income.

Before moving to New Orleans, he spent two years in Central America, ministering to political refugees from Guatemala and Nicaragua. He recalled the suffocating stench in the refugee camps.

Now, at thirty-five, he served God in this new way because of the vision about the silver broom. God gave him the broom with its straws made of thousands of tiny strands of pure silver and instructed him to sweep up and save words of wisdom when they appeared on the ground. Bresnahan was continually disappointed because no words materialized.

Three months ago, he decided the vision had another, more urgent message. Following his new interpretation, he swept away errant teachings by eliminating these clerical charlatans. Begun with the extermination of Dr. Culpepper two weeks ago in San Diego, Mission Silver Broom would continue tomorrow night here in Kansas City.

He had often thought God works in strange and mysterious ways. If such were good enough for God, they were good enough for him.

#

The following evening, as the service ended, Bresnahan sucked on a cinnamon candy and watched from the clump of oleanders across the street from The American Church. Reverend Ray stopped on the porch and laughed raucously as he shook hands with well-wishers.

Then the reverend, Harmonia Tracker and the others, all holding hands, began their slow procession down the steps. Bresnahan lifted the rifle to his shoulder. As the preacher stopped on the fifth step from the top, Bresnahan steadied the rifle scope's cross hairs on the preacher's Adam's apple. Bresnahan was partial to a good, clean neck shot because it left the victim's face intact, fit for an open casket viewing—one last look at vermin exterminated. He took a deep breath, exhaled half of it and began the slow, squeezing motion with his trigger finger.

A second later, Reverend Ray was dying as his body rocketed backward from the force of the bullet. He pulled down a half dozen people, Harmonia among them.

Calmly, Bresnahan lowered the rifle and muttered, "You're on your way, Reverend Ray. But to exactly where, I cannot say."

A Turd in the Holy Water

The brightly-lit buildings of downtown Houston illuminated the hovering layer of low clouds with a muddy glow. Jerome Hoffstedtler could see them from his twenty-fifth-floor condo in Memorial Park Tower as he poured himself a half-inch of Martin's twenty-year-old Scotch. He took a sip, pressing his tongue against the roof of his mouth to savor the taste.

"The Stevenses get a good report from my fraternity brother Bob Gray, who publishes the *Amarillo Globe-News*," Hoff said. He and Larry Best sat at opposite ends of the six-foot-long sofa in Hoff's living room.

"Gray doesn't know the Stevenses personally," he continued, "but he plays golf with a preacher who knows them. Gray said the only hint of a problem is that Leeandra and her husband went through some marital troubles. They didn't separate and there was no indication of extramarital involvement, so I don't consider that a big deal, do you?"

"Nope," Larry said.

Hoff picked up another piece of paper from his file. "This is routine biographical stuff I got from Ken Walker, the Stevenses' business manager. Joe Ted is fifty-three, a widower. His wife died of cancer five years ago. Leeandra is thirty. She took her maiden name after her husband and children died in the boating accident. By the way, I asked if she wears contacts. She doesn't. She has uncorrected, twenty-twenty vision."

"Why did you ask that?"

"You thought she might wear tinted contact lenses, remember?"

"Oh, yeah. I'm sure glad we have the quasi-nuclear issue settled."

"Casper is twenty-six, holds a music degree from North Texas State. He's never been married. Nothing remarkable in this bio stuff."

"What did your investigator find out?" Larry asked.

"I'm getting to that." Hoff had recorded a portion of his telephone conversation with Banner Tatum, the private investigator. He picked up the tape recorder from the cocktail table and turned it on.

"Leeandra looks pretty clean," Banner said on the tape. "No arrest records. I used the old security clearance routine and talked to two couples in Plano who lived next to her and her husband. One said they smoked some dope with them a couple of times. When I pressed for details, they said Leeandra never actually smoked it up with them, but she was present. The couple said they suspected the husband did cocaine on occasion, but he wasn't hooked. That's not uncommon for folks who spend time in life's passing lane. Burton made a ton of money with the family's public accounting firm. Did you know he had a million dollar life insurance policy with his wife as the beneficiary?"

On the tape, Hoff whistled with surprise before he said, "No."

"Leeandra was left well heeled," Banner continued. "As for Joe Ted and Casper, they're both clean as a nun's pot. Probably never even jaywalked. There's no hint of impropriety on how the Stevens organization handles its money."

Hoff stopped the recorder. "That bit about Leeandra, her husband and drugs is the only turd in the holy water we've found so far."

Larry rubbed his forehead. "As the old saying goes, there's no dinger like a stinky dinger."

"Smoking a joint or two isn't that big a deal, even if she did it."

"Not in our circles, but the holy rollers are likely to spaz out."

Hoff returned the tape recorder to the cocktail table. "Somebody could make a big deal out of it, but nobody will want to unless the Stevenses become famous. I asked Banner to keep digging. If that's all the dirt we find, we can manage any flare-up. Do you agree?"

"Yep." Larry paused. "The deaths of her husband and kids punish the prodigal daughter and she devotes her life to Christ in her daddy's ministry. We can package that if we have to. If need be, get her to adopt orphaned kittens. Then we can put a big, red ribbon around the package."

"Jeez, you are so cynical."

"Reality, my friend. In my business, you have to know how to dress up hogs as well as heroes."

Hoff picked up the folder of computer-printed numbers. "The business plan looks good."

"Yep. With any kind of response at all from the audience out yonder in TV land, we make out like bandits," Larry said.

"That's what I intend to tell Andy Boxx on Monday."

"You still think he'll whip out his big, fat checkbook?"

Hoff nodded. "But if he fools me, maybe Leeandra will part with a few of her million bucks."

"Poor child."

"There's nothing poor about that child," Hoff said, "in more ways than one. I had that opinion before Banner told me about the insurance."

Heretic in the Church House

Andy Boxx steered his car under the Metro Club's porte-cochere. He used the club during his frequent trips to his Dallas office.

"Hey, Mr. Boxx." The valet parking attendant with "George" embroidered on his white jacket grinned. "Looking good today, sir."

"George always tells me I look good," Andy grumped as he and Hoff walked toward the ornately-carved double doors. "George tells everybody they look good. A mortician could deliver some poor, dead fucker in a hearse and he would tell the stiff, 'Looking good today, sir.'"

Hoff smiled. Only Andy would gripe about somebody telling him he looked good.

Inside the club, Andy held up two fingers when the hostess asked how many for lunch.

"I'm glad she didn't ask if you're on a diet," Hoff said. He was pleased Andy had decided to lose some of his two hundred and eighty pounds, far too many for his five-ten height.

"You obviously haven't heard," Andy said as they sat down. "October twenty-first is International Screw the Diet Day, proclaimed by the Federation of Fat Old Farts." Hoff laughed as Andy continued, "I've got the hungries for a mess of fried shrimp, hush puppies and about a half-dozen of this place's cinnamon rolls. Best in the West.

"And I'll tolerate your palaver about this screwball preacher idea better on a full stomach." Andy glanced at the waitress. "Give me the all-you-can-eat deal and coffee."

The waitress, fortyish and fadingly attractive, glanced at Hoff's eyebrows, then looked him in the eye and smiled. "And you, sir?"

"Same for me with hot tea."

"Hot tea," Andy said. "I hope you don't raise your pinkie finger when you drink it. Get on with your preacher story."

"I do believe you're in one of your more fractious moods today." Hoff smiled at Andy's frown. "I've decided to do the Stevens venture. Their operation is much bigger than I thought, so there's a good base to work from."

"How big is big?" Andy nodded as the waitress brought drinks.

"This will perk you up. They grossed over four million last year."

"Not bad." Andy reached for the basket of bread. "Want a roll?"

Hoff shook his head. "The Stevenses lose money on the road, but make up for it with contributions by mail. They have a mailing list of over one hundred thousand names, an invaluable starting point to promote the TV programming."

"And dun them for money."

"Money is part of the deal." Hoff took a card out of his shirt pocket and briefed Andy on each of the three Stevens family members, ending with the fact that Casper was twenty-six and had never married.

"Is he a fruit?"

"Just because a guy hasn't been married doesn't mean he's a fruit, for crying out loud."

Andy waved his hand impatiently. "What else?"

"They've got a well-organized, professionally run operation. Ken Walker is their business manager and he comes across as a good businessman, our kind of people."

"What's his reaction to your TV idea?"

"He's interested. He said the Stevenses have talked about going on television, but they didn't know how."

Andy reached for another cinnamon roll. "What do Joe Ted, the boy and Leeandra say?"

"They're interested," Hoff said. "Ken Walker says they want to meet with me and talk about it."

"Do you think they're legitimate, a bunch of religious tub thumpers, money grubbers or what?"

"They're legitimate. A friend of mine publishes the *Amarillo Globe-News*. He has a couple of preacher friends who know Joe Ted. They believe he's sincere." Hoff laughed. "Walker asked me if I'm a Born Again Christian."

Andy stopped chewing and looked at Hoff. "What'd you say?"

"I told him the truth. I'm not a religious sort. Religion would be up to them. I'm proposing a business deal. He said that was fine."

"So they're going to let a heretic in the church house." Andy smiled. "At least they're not overly persnickety. What kind of deal did you offer?"

Hoff delayed his answer while the waitress set food on the table.

"Go ahead and bring us more fried shrimp," Andy said to her, "so my flat-bellied young friend can have some. I'm going to eat all of these."

The waitress smiled at Hoff. Andy watched her shapely wiggle as she walked away. "I'm glad to see the lady's still got eyes for you. Say the word and she'll hit the sheets with you."

"At the moment, I'm more concerned with eating. Sure you can't spare one, measly fried shrimp until she gets back?"

Andy forked one onto Hoff's plate.

"You are too kind."

"Tell me about the deal." Andy raked in the remaining shrimp. "Help yourself to the chicken and fish. I'm pigging out on shrimp."

"So I see. The deal is the same as I talked about before. We provide money to produce the television shows and buy air time. They buy the time from us at a substantial mark-up, using contributions from viewers."

"What is their risk?"

"They don't have any financial risk."

"That's crazy."

"Not crazy at all when you stop to think they have a good base for us to build on. I'm strong as garlic on our concept after seeing what they've already got."

Andy discarded a shrimp tail in the growing pile beside his plate. "Why aren't they willing to assume some of the risk?"

"They may be. I'd rather approach this on my terms with the possibility of a much higher rate of return. I think we can double our money in a year."

Andy stopped chewing. "Come on. That's snake oil operation talk."

"We'll buy and sell each hour of TV fifty-two times a year in the ten or twelve markets we start with. That's a bunch of turns on our money."

"Assuming there'll be money to pay us back."

"There will be."

Andy shook his head slowly. "This has got to be the most cockamamie idea you've ever had, a world-class crap shoot."

"Any more of a crap shoot than drilling for oil you can't see? Three miles underground? And under ice or water to boot?"

"That's different."

"Only because you know the oil business."

Andy thanked the waitress when she set a plate of fried shrimp on the table. He grinned at Hoff. "You can have two shrimp."

"Benevolent soul that you are."

"Help yourself. Pisses me off, but I'm already getting full."

"From the looks of that pile of shrimp tails, I believe it." Hoff told him the pro forma and offering documents would be complete within a week. "I want to raise a million dollars. I'll issue ten units of a hundred thousand dollars each to fund eleven shares. As usual, I'll keep the eleventh share for putting the deal together."

"When do you talk to the tent preacher about riding him bareback to fame and fortune?"

"Tomorrow. We meet in Austin, where they are with their tent."

"Will Leeandrum be there?"

Hoff frowned. "Will you read my lips? It's Leee-annn-druh!"

"Have you seen her since your sojourn to Sweetwater?"

"She was part of the service Larry Best and I saw when we went to Abilene last Thursday. Don't worry. You know I don't wash bed linens and money in the same load. It's one of my rules."

"When it comes to pussy, I didn't know there were any rules."

"You might be surprised. Are you interested in the Stevens venture?"

Andy nodded as he chewed a bite of hush puppy.

"Good," Hoff said. "I hate to be cold-blooded, but with that Reverend Ray character getting shot in Kansas, I think our deal is that much better."

"You are getting cold-blooded, aren't...." Andy stopped before he finished and grinned. "Goddam if I just didn't have a terrible thought. You're not the one whacking these preachers, are you?"

Hoff laughed. "Sure, two down and two hundred to go. I told you we could make this deal work."

"Well, I had to ask. Have you done a background check on these Stevens people?"

Hoff told Andy about Banner Tatum's report, including the information about Leeandra's husband's occasional use of drugs.

"Whoa!" Andy barked. "Just a goddam minute. You're touting these folks as the salvation of all mankind while she and that nipplehead she was married to were into dope?"

"Hold your water. As best we can tell, she didn't use drugs and besides, that was a long time ago. She was married to a high roller, they lived in a nest of yuppies and he smoked a toke or two. No big deal."

"Could be." Andy took the last cinnamon roll and asked for the check. "Could turn out to be one hell of a big deal if some joker pops up out of the weeds and starts shooting his mouth off."

"Larry and I agree we can handle the situation if it surfaces."

"And you damned well better make sure the Stevens folks aren't up to any shenanigans with their money."

"They're clean on that score. We'll have plenty of controls to protect our interests if we get in business with them."

Andy looked at his Rolex. "We better get a move on if we're going to get you to Love Field on time."

As they left the restaurant, Hoff asked, "Are you going back to Midland tonight?"

"About six or so, " Andy said, "providing my pansy-assed pilot doesn't think it's too windy."

#

Hoff got to Love Field early enough to call his office. "Woo-woo," he train-whistled to Gracie. Only when he called from out of town did he use the "woo-woo" greeting. Gracie loved it. "What's up?"

Gracie said, "Margo called. She wants to see you."

"What for?"

"You know full well what for. Are you coming to the office this afternoon?"

"Any need for me to?"

"No."

"Then I'll see you bright and early tomorrow morning."

After he hung up the pay phone's handset, Hoff said softly, "Margo, what am I going to do with you?"

Litany of Ex-Wives

As Hoff settled into his seat on the Southwest Airlines flight, he chuckled at Andy's comment about Prince being a pansy-assed pilot. Juan Prince flew the Westwind jet owned by Andy's company, Boxx Oil and Minerals. Hoff had traveled often with Andy on the jet, always piloted by Prince, a Cuban expatriate. He enjoyed any opportunity to hear Andy kibitz.

"Every pilot has got IFR and VFR," Prince told Hoff two years ago at the company's hangar in Midland. "Me, I got to contend with ABFR, Andy Boxx's Flight Rule. If there's any air left up there, fly in it."

The two argued each time Prince balked at flying, usually because of weather conditions.

"Damned fraidy cat Cuban," Andy fumed during one dispute. "One lousy revolution and you're ruined for-goddam-ever."

Prince won the arguments by refusing to fly.

"If you get so ticked off at him, why don't you get another pilot?" Hoff asked after one memorable argument about a fast-moving weather front and its violent thunderstorms.

"Because he's good and he jaws back at me." Andy laughed. "The one time he went along with what I wanted to do, we damned near bought the farm. If you ever fly with Prince and he starts praying in Spanish, you better get busy making peace with your maker. And do it fast because you might not have time to wrap it up."

During the forty-five minute flight from Dallas to Houston, Hoff's thoughts turned to Margo and then evolved into reflections on his three failed marriages, all to women whose first names began with "M". He smiled as he remembered Andy's comment. "All three of those M-named muthahs turned out to be bad medicine for you."

His first marriage was fifteen years ago to the dark-haired, feisty Margaret Gail Foote from Dallas. The only daughter of Aylin Gill Foote, overseer of fourth generation land, oil and timber wealth, Margaret was a cheerleader at The University of Texas at Austin.

A year after graduation, Hoff and Margaret married. The union was applauded by his parents, but barely tolerated by hers. Hoff's and Margaret's relationship didn't progress past physical attraction. They separated after six months of marriage and were divorced exactly three hundred and sixty five days after they had avowed "til death do us part."

Hoff stayed single for three years until Mary Jane Bates became the second Mrs. Jerome King Hoffstedtler. First runner-up in the Houston Miss U. S. A. pageant two years earlier, she was a public relations representative for a mortgage company when she and Hoff met. After a month-long, love-at-first-sight romance, they married.

A red head with a smattering of freckles, Mary Jane wanted to have children immediately, an inclination unmentioned before marriage. Hoff was amenable, but she did not become pregnant. He changed from briefs to boxer shorts, avoided hot showers and consented to sex by the thermometer. She didn't conceive, but she did become increasingly unhappy with Hoff's business travel. Their relationship cooled quickly, and they divorced after two years of marriage.

Six months later, Hoff met the bleached blonde Margo Ann Wallace, a divorced Houston-based flight attendant for Continental Airlines. They married after an eight-month courtship. Not as tall as Leeandra, but bustier, Margo was a sexual tigress. Their sex life was abundant and adventuresome. She was devoted to Hoff.

Margo continued to fly for two years after they were married, but quit when she became pregnant. She miscarried in her fifth month.

The miscarriage was a bitter disappointment to Margo and proved an emotional watershed that set them adrift down opposite slopes. Hoff was surprised at how much she wanted the child. Despite his best efforts, including counseling, the marriage eroded.

Two years ago—following five years of being married to Hoff—Margo ran off to St. Thomas with Gordon Butler, a lawyer who owned a forty-foot sailboat. Now, she was back.

He smiled as he recalled Margo's saying, "Don't be a jerk Hoff."

He looked out the window at downtown Houston's skyline as the Seven-Thirty-Seven streaked toward Hobby Airport and muttered, "Same feisty Margo." He still felt wounded by her leaving. Seeing her the one time since her return had fanned the surviving vestiges of his love for her. He genuinely enjoyed her company, and he was glad she was back.

He called her from a pay phone at the airport. An hour later, they were making love on the too-soft double bed in her furnished apartment. Once again, Margo propelled Hoff into mindless ecstasy with her fellatio fantastico. They left her apartment shortly before eight o'clock for dinner.

Chapter 5

Down the Street from Motel 69

At ten minutes before eight, Leeandra Stevens took her place at the pulpit under the family's crusade tent pitched on a vacant tract next to Ben White Boulevard in south Austin. She felt the calming flow of God's power and was eager to impart the energy to the crowd packed in the tent despite cold weather and occasional spits of rain on this October 21st evening. When she sang, the rhapsodic beauty of her voice captured the crowd's attention.

In the audience, tears streaking down his pudgy face as Leeandra sang, sat the pastor of Centrum Church, Dr. Henry Woods. He strained to absorb the compelling, powerful sound of her voice. Earlier, he had seen the Stevens tent being erected after he left Motel 69, following an afternoon of sex with Madelyn. Curiosity drove him to attend.

His head full of Leeandra's song, all thoughts of Madelyn were gone. He was captivated by the singer, imprisoned by her flowing song. His focus on her face strayed only to assess the glow on her blonde hair caused by the spotlight. Dr. Woods suddenly realized he was shaking with excitement, and he was flushed with love for this singing goddess who stood at the podium. His feelings were not carnal. They were the same love he felt for God and for other people united by a common love of the Almighty. Dr. Woods tingled with the realization he was in the presence of a special messenger anointed by God. He cried tears of joy.

After the service, the paunchy, balding Dr. Woods sought out Joe Ted. Accompanied by spasms of exaggerated, wincing blinks, Dr. Woods invited Leeandra to sing during one of Centrum Church's televised Sunday morning worship services. "You deliver mighty messages in sermon and song," he said. "Yes. Wonderful messages."

"Thank you," Joe Ted answered and turned to Leeandra. "Would you like to sing at his church next Sunday?"

Leeandra looked from Dr. Woods' face to her father's and nodded. She said nothing about the apprehension that had crept into her when Henry Jackson Woods spoke.

Cure for a Military Mood

"Did you call Margo yesterday?" Gracie Perry asked as she penciled a meeting time on Hoff's desk calendar. His office on Friday, October 22nd, was a whirlwind of activity related to the Stevens Crusade proposal.

"Yes."

Gracie finished the note. "And?"

"And what?"

"What did she want?"

A smile flooded Hoff's face. "My, my, aren't we curious this morning, Miss Gracie. Did we have cat flakes for breakfast?"

Gracie flashed a mock grimace. "Very funny."

"It was no big deal."

"You've got a big deal hickey on your neck." Gracie, mouth drawn into a puckering grin, had an "I know something" cant to her posture.

"Maybe it was a semi-big deal."

"Margo's back. Whoop-de-doo." Exasperation was evident in Gracie's voice as she started for the office door.

"If you were older, I might confuse you with my virgin aunt."

"Around a tomcat like you, I'm surprised even family members escaped as virgins," Gracie said without looking back.

Score one for Gracie, Hoff thought. He enjoyed the verbal sparring with his secretary. She was a worthy opponent. He also enjoyed the bustle associated with getting the Stevens venture off the ground. This morning, he agreed to advance twenty thousand dollars for preparation of a media plan by the Taylor-Pepper-Coe advertising agency. He worked on legal documents and the financial pro forma, including cash flow projections.

Hoff asked Gracie to get Andy on the phone.

"What?" Andy grumped.

"Good morning," Hoff said, an exaggerated sweetness in his voice. "How are we feeling today?"

"Always the stickler for niceties, aren't you?"

"There's civil and then there's civil."

"Well, I'm in a goddam military mood this morning," Andy shot back, "so don't waste my time with this civil bullshit. Oil is down a dollar a barrel. Some nipplehead wants me to invest in an asshole preaching deal. I gained five pounds from that big lunch yesterday and you're talking good morning."

Hoff laughed. "I've got some news that will put you in a much better frame of mind."

He told Andy about the buyer for a piece of property they owned jointly. They would split two million dollars in profits after holding the land for only two-and-a-half years.

"You're right," Andy said. "That does put me in a better frame of mind. By all means, sell it. With that piece of money, I might buy three shares of the tent preacher play. Are you meeting today?"

"Yes indeedie. I'm decked out in my best salesman's suit."

"He'll never know what hit him." Andy hung up.

Hoff smiled, accustomed to Andy's curt mannerisms. Except for them, Andy was Hoff's entrepreneurial role model. He admired Andy's success in his own business after he got fed up with Magna World Oil's dictatorial corporate culture.

The initials of Boxx Oil and Minerals provoked a few ex-associates at Magna to chide, "Be careful you don't bomb with BOM, Andy." As his private jet—nicknamed The Bomber—attested, Andy had prospered.

Of his own success, Andy had told Hoff, "Just shows what a normally-intelligent person can do when given his head. The corporate nippleheads at Magna wanted to clone a bunch of organizational numb nuts in their own image. One boss insisted I say beverage units instead of drinks on my expense account. On my annual reviews, I got criticized because I never polished my goddam shoes. I'm a damned good geologist. I made that company hundreds of millions, but the fuckers were more concerned about beverage units and scuffed shoes than what they hired me to do."

Hoff was thankful he met Andy while rooming with Andy's son at The University of Texas. The oilman recognized Hoff's entrepreneurial skills and told him, "You've used your own wits and hard work to get through school. Don't ever go to work for anybody else. You're smart enough to make it on your own."

Starting with the Joe College Pizza chain he founded while attending the university, Hoff had made himself a multi-millionaire.

As he looked out the window of his office, Hoff said softly, "Meeting Andy was the best thing that ever happened to me."

Presentation in The Foothills

An hour after his conversation with Andy, Hoff was driving toward Austin for his one o'clock lunch meeting with the Stevenses. He drove at a leisurely pace, listened to a Scarlatti harpsichord tape and thought about Margo the Magnificent.

Last night at his condo. Margo had been as exciting, sweet and naively childlike as ever. She did not like his condominium's decor, redone after she left to erase her imprint.

"Obviously you haven't had a took-up living here with you," she said. "It doesn't look like you do much living here period."

She was right, he thought. He did most of his living elsewhere—at the homes of friends, at restaurants and on out-of-town trips. He realized his home and his entire life lacked the magic of a woman's touch. One woman he could love and who would love him.

He was tired of pursuing women he did not want to catch except for sex to prove to himself that at age thirty-nine, he was still in the hunt.

Being married to Margo had been wonderful. She was spontaneous in doing things she knew he would enjoy. Wearing a particular dress. Or no dress at all. Making sure his suits were clean. Buying his shirts and neckties. Her ingenuity in bed.

She enjoyed the things he did for her. Opening doors. Gifts like the Egyptian mummy bead necklace for no special reason. Hoff wondered about the possibility of a reconciliation with Margo. Could he ever trust her again? Could life with her be as good as before the miscarriage?

Halfway to Austin, he quit thinking about Margo and concentrated on what he would say to the Stevenses. Ken Walker had told Hoff not to expect a decision today. He felt the buzz of excitement that came when it was time to sell a deal, and he looked forward to seeing Leeandra again.

Hoff arrived at the Hyatt Hotel in downtown Austin fifteen minutes early and strolled into the lobby. He stopped when he saw the stocky, dark-haired Ken and Leeandra standing halfway across the lobby, talking. Ken lacked an inch being as tall as Leeandra.

She laughed at something Ken said. This was the first time Hoff had seen her laugh, and she brightened everything and everyone around her. She was dressed in a plain, long sleeve, gray wool dress. Every strand of her long, blonde-as-straw hair was combed into place. She was prettier than he remembered. Once again, she did not carry a handbag.

Hoff joined them and shook Ken's hand.

"Leeandra...Hoff...I believe you two have met," Ken said.

"Miss Stevens," Hoff said, not sure why he addressed her so formally.

Leeandra smiled and extended her hand. Hoff grasped it briefly. He enjoyed the cool touch of her long, slender fingers.

"Mr. Hoffstedtler." Leeandra said his name with a tilting nod of her head and a glance at his gull wing eyebrows.

"It's Hoff, remember?"

"Yes, I do. Please call me Leeandra."

He studied her, admiring her creamy, clear complexion. Faint hints of crow's feet fanned out in tiny deltas from the edges of her blue eyes.

"I attended your service in Sweetwater after we met in the motel lobby," Hoff said. "I'm sorry it didn't work out for us to have coffee."

Leeandra's smile activated the dimples at the corners of her mouth. She glanced away, then looked back at him. "Yes, I saw you."

Hoff expected her to say something else. She did not. "I enjoyed your singing. I've heard you twice. You have a lovely voice."

"Thank you," she said with the quiet aplomb of someone accustomed to receiving compliments. "You were also at one of our services in Abilene, weren't you?"

He was surprised. "Yes. I took my advertising friend with me. He and I are collaborating on the proposal to put you on TV."

"We have news that might be applicable to that," Ken said. He told Hoff about the invitation for Leeandra to sing on the following Sunday's televised service in Austin. "Central Church, isn't it?" he asked Leeandra.

"Centrum," she answered.

The conversation was interrupted when Joe Ted and Casper joined them. After introductions, they took the elevator to The Foothills Restaurant on the top floor. They sat next to a window, with a clear view of the city's skyline. Hoff sat next to Leeandra.

At Joe Ted's suggestion, they ordered immediately, and he steered the conversation to business. Hoff liked Joe Ted's direct, take-charge demeanor. Concisely, Hoff explained the plan to put them on television. He watched all three family members carefully to gauge their reactions.

Joe Ted listened closely. With his pale blue-gray eyes, the preacher maintained unwavering eye contact. Hoff figured most women considered him handsome, despite his slightly-pocked complexion. The irregularities added a rugged dimension to his slender face, a face that remained expressionless. Hoff noticed the auguring intensity in Joe Ted's gaze and felt uneasy at the lack of a nod or any other positive reaction.

Casper was eagerly receptive from the start. Leeandra spent much of the time looking out the window. Hoff wondered how much she heard.

When he finished, he answered questions and they discussed details.

"Ken tells me you're prepared to invest as much as a million dollars to put us on television," Joe Ted said. "Why would it take so much?"

"A million assures a valid test for a minimum of thirteen weeks on the air. A half-baked effort wouldn't do you or my investors justice. I believe in doing things right or not at all."

"We think alike on that score," Joe Ted said.

"When would all this start?" Leeandra asked.

Hoff ran his finger around the rim of his glass. "Part of that depends on what you decide and when." He explained his plan to produce at least three shows before the Stevenses began their two-month-long break for the Thanksgiving and Christmas holidays. "I'd like to start airing our programs in January. Television audiences are larger during the winter."

"Isn't that rushing things?" Joe Ted asked.

"Perhaps, but there's no reason to delay."

"We're not equipped to implement any of the technical aspects of what you propose," Joe Ted said.

"Don't worry about that," Hoff said. "We'll provide equipment, production staff. Our people will buy the TV time. You folks can continue with your ministry. The only differences will be learning to contend with equipment, attending production meetings, wearing special makeup."

"Special makeup?" Leeandra asked.

"TV cameras have hypercritical eyes," Hoff said. "I don't think you'd be happy with how you look on television without makeup."

She laughed. "I'm not always happy how I look with makeup."

"My advertising friend agrees with me that you'll look terrific on television." Hoff was pleased with Leeandra's slight blush.

They discussed other details. Hoff sensed Joe Ted was about to launch into something different when the entrees arrived.

"Looks good," Casper said as the rib eye steak and baked potato were set down in front of him. Hoff and Leeandra had both ordered grilled chicken with fettuccine.

As they ate, Joe Ted asked questions about Hoff's experience in various kinds of business, and he told Hoff more about the Stevens Crusade. Joe Ted's father, Preacher Bob, had started the ministry sixty-four years ago. He preached from the tailgate of his wagon, pulled by a matched pair of mules named Nutty and Putty. Preacher Bob bought his first tent in 1928 and managed to keep going during the 1930s depression by accepting chickens, hay and other commodities from people with no cash. Now, the Stevenses moved their tent from city to city by truck.

During a conversational lull, Hoff asked Leeandra, "How do you keep so still while your dad preaches? I've been to two of your services, and I didn't see you move a muscle either time."

Joe Ted laughed. "She knows I'll flail the hide off her if she fidgets."

"That's right." Leeandra grinned at her father. "He's a real meanie. I try to think of something interesting while he preaches."

Her comment set off another round of laughter. Pleased, Hoff interpreted the humor as evidence of the Stevenses' feeling at ease.

After coffee was served, the business discussion continued.

"I share Ken's quandary about why you're willing to do this without our putting up any money," Joe Ted said. "Is it, in fact, financially risk free for us?"

"Yes, sir," Hoff answered. "The potential returns for my group are sufficient to justify our taking all of the risk."

Joe Ted looked at Hoff for several seconds, a penetrating, grading look. "We've worked hard to build up our resources, to expand on my father's start of this ministry. I don't want to jeopardize what we've worked so hard to accomplish." He paused. "Nor do I want to jeopardize the faith people have in us as messengers of the gospel."

"I understand," Hoff said.

"At the risk of being redundant, I'll ask this again. All matters of religious content would be up to us?"

"Yes, sir. You'd have complete say-so."

"Good," Joe Ted said. "Delivering the gospel is the biggest thing in our lives. We don't want to do anything that might interfere with our ability to preach God's Word."

"Your being on TV won't interfere," Hoff countered. "As I've said before, television will help you reach many more people."

After more discussion, Joe Ted said, "We need to think on this and talk it over among ourselves. We want to pray about it. I like your concept. For some time, I've wanted to expand the horizons of our ministry, but my thinking was always limited to buying a bigger tent." He smiled. "It's hard to teach an old tent preacher new tricks. Who knows? Maybe we'll be more like PTL than PLT."

"I don't understand," Hoff said.

"An inside joke." Joe Ted smiled. "PTL means Praise the Lord, a successful broadcast ministry. PLT stands for poor little tent."

When the laughter subsided, Leeandra said, "I have one other question. What gave you the idea of putting us on television?"

Hoff had noted Leeandra's silence during the meeting. She had been friendly, but with a tinge of aloofness. Maybe she was shy. He found her calm beauty and quiet demeanor refreshing. "Actually, my advertising friend came up with the concept. I'm an entrepreneur and I see a business opportunity, one that's good for all of us."

Joe Ted stood. "I hope so."

After they rode the elevator to the lobby, Hoff asked Ken to call him when the Stevenses made a decision.

Following the good-byes, Hoff stopped at a pay phone to call his office. "Woo-woo."

"Oh, that's a happy woo-woo," Gracie said. "Did it go well?"

"Of course, Miss Gracie. Was there any doubt in your mind that Hoff would pull it off?" As he spoke, he wondered if he had.

"No. But you're the one who always says meat ain't meat until it's in the pot. Did they say yes?"

"They will. Call Larry and ask him to get me a tape of a television program." Hoff gave her the details of Leeandra's upcoming appearance on the Centrum Church telecast.

She laughed. "Adding church services to your video library?"

"Hardly. But, it's a good opportunity to see how she performs in front of a TV camera." When Hoff finished talking to Gracie, he called Margo and told her he would pick her up at seven for dinner.

On his way back to Houston, Hoff called Larry and told him the deal was as good as made. Larry agreed to get started on plans for the television production. Hoff also told Larry that Andy's three hundred thousand dollar commitment had completed the funding.

"That's great," Larry said. "I just talked to Gracie. I'll get a tape of Leeandra's performance at that church in Austin."

After the call, Hoff assessed the meeting. He was impressed with Joe Ted, how quickly he grasped details. He also liked the preacher's questions, his quick wit and leadership. Neither Leeandra nor her brother said much. Hoff thought Casper was a light-weight. Leeandra was not.

In addition to her stunning beauty, there was something about her that captivated him. Something he could not put his finger on. He felt drawn to her, but in a different way than when he saw her in the lobby of Sweetwater's Big Country Motel. His feelings for her seemed to be some kind of love, he thought. That jolted him.

"Jesus," he said aloud. He continued talking as he tapped the brakes to slow down at the Giddings city limit speed zone sign. "Andy will ring my neck if I get it on with Leeandra." He slipped a Jean-Michael Jarre tape into the stereo and turned up the volume.

Introduction by Different Name

After meeting with Hoff, the Stevenses and Ken Walker drove to the Ramada Inn where they were staying. They gathered in the coffee shop and each ordered iced tea.

"What do you think of the television proposal?" Ken asked.

"On the surface, it sounds acceptable," Joe Ted answered.

"Just acceptable?" Ken's disappointment was obvious.

"It's a new idea and takes some getting used to. Actually, I'm hard pressed to see anything wrong with Mr. Hoffstedtler's proposal. Based on first impressions, I like him. I sense he'll do what he says and I believe we can work with him."

Ken picked the lemon wedge out of his iced tea and deposited it on a paper napkin. "This is the growth mechanism we've been looking for. Television can increase our evangelical outreach immensely."

"I say we jump on it," Casper said. "It's made to order for us."

Leeandra remained silent as they talked for several minutes.

"You're awfully quiet," Joe Ted said to his daughter. "What do you think?"

"I'd like to know why he's willing to invest a million dollars to put us on television," she said.

"Obviously, he thinks he can make a profit," Ken answered. "Profit is an honest, clear-cut motive. If the proposition can help us, too, then so much the better."

"Will we make money out of it?" Leeandra asked.

"Yes," Ken said.

"If it's such a good deal, shouldn't we consider using my insurance money to finance a television campaign ourselves?"

There was no reaction for several seconds until Joe Ted spoke. "I don't think that's something we should consider. First of all, that's your money. Secondly, we'll have nothing at risk if we decide to go on television using Mr. Hoffstedtler's plan. Thirdly, we know nothing about television. I wouldn't know where to begin and, frankly, I'm not interested in devoting the time necessary to find out."

"We could hire someone," she said. "That's what Hoff will do."

"If your heart is set on doing it that way, we can take a look at it," Joe Ted said. "But I believe our energies should be focused on our evangelism, not on trying to find a bevy of television experts. I prefer to leave those headaches to him."

"My heart isn't set on doing it ourselves," Leeandra said. "I just thought I'd mention it."

"Your offer is generous. I appreciate it," Joe Ted said to Leeandra, then looked at Ken. "When do we owe Mr. Hoffstedtler an answer?"

Ken told them Hoff would like an indication no later than Monday.

"Why is he in such a hurry?" Leeandra asked.

"He's a charger," Ken said. "He's put this proposal together very quickly. Less than three weeks have elapsed since he attended the service in Sweetwater. Obviously, he thinks we should start in January when TV viewership is higher."

"You're convinced he'll stay out of our hair as far as the gospel is concerned?" Joe Ted asked Ken.

"Oh, yes, he has no interest in that."

Leeandra spoke up. "Could that be a problem...his obvious lack of interest in the gospel? This is just a business deal to him." She turned to Ken. "Right?"

Ken nodded.

"I see nothing wrong with that," Joe Ted said. "That's the way it works with printers, electricians and others we hire."

"We would not hire him," Leeandra said. "This would be more like a partnership."

Joe Ted nodded. "That's an excellent point. Do you think being partners with him might be a problem?"

"In Second Corinthians, the Bible says we're not to be yoked to unbelievers," Leeandra said.

"The Bible also admonishes us not to sit in judgment of others," Joe Ted said. When there was no response, he suggested they adjourn to prepare for the evening's service.

They resumed the discussion the following morning at breakfast. Ken and Joe Ted were the first to arrive at the coffee shop.

"This is a gift from Heaven," Joe Ted said. "It's what we need to move forward. We've slogged along for years in the same old way. I prayed hard last night and again this morning. I believe God brought Hoff to us. I think we should accept his proposal." He paused. "But I want us to be unanimous."

"Leeandra is the only one with reservations," Ken answered.

"She's the one I'm talking about."

Casper arrived next and was still supportive.

When Leeandra arrived, Joe Ted asked her opinion.

"I had the strangest dream last night," she said. "We were in some big place like a football stadium with a tent over it. There was a huge crowd and TV cameras all over the place. When you introduced me, you called me by a different name." She smiled at her father. "Crazy dream."

"What name did I use?" Joe Ted asked.

She frowned. "I can't remember."

"I hope it wasn't freak face or anything like that." He laughed.

"No, nothing like that. It was a serious, religious-sounding name, but for the life of me, I can't remember what it was."

"Any thoughts on whether we should go ahead with Hoff's proposal?" Joe Ted asked.

She raised her eyebrows. "Hoff? Not Mr. Hoffstedtler?"

Joe Ted smiled. "He did ask us to call him Hoff. It's easier to say."

She said, "I'm willing to go ahead with his idea."

"Reluctantly?" Joe Ted asked.

"Carefully might be a better way to put it. Two television evangelists have been killed, you know."

"The Lord will protect us from that kind of harm." Joe Ted reached across and patted her hand. "Nonetheless, being careful about this undertaking is good counsel. I think we all feel that way."

After breakfast, Ken tried to call Hoff, but got the answering machine.

Hoff spent the night at Margo's. Ken's call was the first Hoff returned when he and Margo arrived at his condo.

"Terrific!" he said when Ken gave him the news. "I'll have paperwork to you in two or three days." When Hoff hung up, he let out a whoop.

Margo asked, "What's that all about?"

"A business deal. I just made a sale." He walked across the room, put his arms around her and pulled her close. She had changed into one of his dress shirts with nothing on underneath. As they kissed, he slid his hands under the shirttail and massaged her buttocks.

Chapter 6

A Peaceful Thanksgiving

Alone on Thanksgiving, James Daniel Bresnahan ejected the videotape of the Philadelphia church service, provoked at his own indecision about whether the evangelist was a candidate for Mission Silver Broom. He felt a restless irritation as he thought, I know the errant vermin are out there. I am not diligent enough in my search.

Also contributing to his irritation was being alone on a holiday. Even though he had spent virtually all holidays alone for many years, they were bothersome reminders of the alienation from his family and their lack of understanding, even when he was a child.

When he was nine, he had the beautiful vision about Jesus' pet dog, Manger. At the foot of the cross on which Jesus was nailed, Manger licked drops of his Master's blood. From the cross, Jesus told his dog, "As long as you live, you can heal sick injured animals by licking them."

With a child's enthusiasm, he told his mother, but she scolded him for having an overactive imagination, just as she had when he told her of other visions. His parents thought the visions, along with his outlandish behavior, such as dipping his siblings' toothbrushes in urine, were part of his competition for attention. He was the middle of five children.

His two brothers and two sisters teased him unmercifully. Everyone in the family called him Jimmy Dan. During a prolonged bout of teasing, his oldest sister chanted, "Poor Jimmy Dan, the little idiot man" as she marched around beating on the bottom of a tin pail with a stick. From that day on, he insisted on being called James. He never let the use of Jimmy Dan go unchallenged. Each time one of his siblings called him that, he found a way to get even. On one occasion, he killed his sister's pet rabbit, roasted it and served the meat to her. After she ate it, he told her it was her rabbit. Thereafter, he was called James.

His contrarianism resulted in added discipline and coercion to conform. No matter how hard he tried, his parents never seemed pleased.

He did conform eagerly to his father's love of guns, hunting and marksmanship. All of the Bresnahan children learned to shoot at an early age, taught by their father. James fell in love with guns. He bought his first weapon at the age of eighteen and now owned an extensive collection of rifles. He appreciated their form, dictated so specifically by their powerful function. To him, guns were instruments of power. He saw a parallel between the power of a gun and the power of God. Both reflected precision in creation and the power to destroy.

At age ten, James was invited to hunt with his father. His first kill was a cotton tail rabbit. His first shot wounded, but did not kill the rabbit. Its hind quarters incapacitated, the helpless animal sat with its front legs rigid and stared unblinkingly at James as he shot it between the eyes. Shooting the creature excited him so much he wet his pants.

Bresnahan emerged from his thoughts with a start and sat for a moment before he went to his safe and retrieved the .270 caliber Carl Gustaf rifle used to kill Reverend Ray. Since returning from Kansas City thirty-four days ago, he had not fired the gun, one of his favorites. Target shooting would allay his anxiousness.

At the practice range on his ten acres of woodlands where he lived near Bentonville, Arkansas, he erected a cardboard target before he sat at the shooting bench. Carefully, he adjusted the scope and loaded a round into the firing chamber with the bolt action.

He was about to put his eye to the scope when a movement to the right of the target caught his attention. A moment of apprehension evaporated when he saw the bitch dog pass into full view from behind a large pine tree, her milk-filled tits hanging low. She stopped and looked back as first one puppy, then another, followed her into view. The bitch's rib cage bones were clearly visible. A stray, he thought, looking for dinner on this Thanksgiving Day.

For his own Thanksgiving meal, Bresnahan had dined on red seedless grapes, Swiss cheese, a broiled chicken breast and wheat crackers. He ate a large red apple for dessert.

Suddenly, the bitch looked in Bresnahan's direction, alert to his presence. He sensed the dog's alarm and slowly raised the rifle to look at her through the scope. She stared at him, her appraising eyes open wide. She looked back at her pups briefly, then resumed staring at Bresnahan. Standing there so passively and defenseless, the dog reminded him of the wounded rabbit he shot between the eyes as the creature stared at him, awaiting its fate.

"You tempt me," he said in a whisper. After another ten seconds of looking at the bitch through the scope, Bresnahan hooked his index finger around the trigger. He positioned the cross hairs between the dog's eyes. After the shot, he quickly found the dog again with the scope. She lay motionless on the ground. He swung the scope to the right until he found one of the two pups. It crouched on the ground in terror, then began to inch its way toward its fallen mother. Bresnahan used the bolt action to push another cartridge into the firing chamber. He shot the puppy in the head. Still looking through the scope, he was unable to find the other puppy. He lowered the rifle and worked another round into the chamber.

Most probably, he thought, the remaining puppy retreated into the woods. He would wait for a moment. The puppy knew no other haven than its mother, now dead but still warm. No more than a minute passed before he saw the second puppy creep into the clearing. In a slow, crouching crawl, the little animal inched toward its dead mother. He lifted the scope back to his right eye, targeted it and shot it in the head.

As Bresnahan lowered the gun, he felt an overpowering urge to urinate. Quickly, he laid the gun on the firing bench and stepped to the edge of the crushed limestone surrounding the bench. He unzipped his trousers and relieved himself. He heard a hawk's cry and looked up to see the big raptor bank to its right and out of sight. He wondered if the hawk might have had its eye on one of the puppies for its Thanksgiving meal. He fingered the cleft of his chin as he finished urinating and enjoyed his inner peace, so compatible with the quiet and order of the forest.

Celebrating with Prayer Chicken

Joe Ted Stevens leaned back in his wing chair. Clasped hands held to his chin, Joe Ted's index fingers formed an A-frame that he tapped lightly against his pursed lips. He stared at the blank, gray television screen. Built into a bookcase, the television set hissed quietly as if trying to shush the ticking Seth Thomas mantle clock in the den of the Stevens home in Amarillo on November 25th, the Friday after Thanksgiving. One month and three days after the Stevenses agreed to be participants in the television venture, they watched the first show to be completed.

Leeandra, Casper, Ken Walker, Larry Best and Hoff looked at Joe Ted, who sat in the middle of the semicircle. They waited for his reaction to the first one-hour Stevens Crusade television program. Dressed in navy slacks and a white golf shirt, he was expressionless.

Hoff made a mental note never to play poker with Joe Ted. Thoughts of full house, church house and shit house mouse almost made Hoff grin.

On Wednesday, Hoff and Larry had been ecstatic when they saw the initial show at Bayou Bottom Studio in Houston. Now, they tolerated the slow-crawling seconds, each articulated by the mantle clock's metallic ticking, as they awaited Joe Ted's verdict. Hoff brushed his fingers back and forth across the long hair on the back of his left hand.

A smile dissolved the grim, contemplative mask on Joe Ted's face. "I like it," he said, taking jerky glances from Leeandra to Ken to Casper.

Casper and Ken were effusive with praise. Leeandra said nothing.

Joe Ted looked at his daughter who stared down at her clasped hands. "Leeandra?"

She continued to look down for a moment before lifting her eyes to meet her father's inquiring gaze. "I like it." Her voice was quiet and flat.

"Are you sure?" Joe Ted asked. "I want all of us to feel good about this. If there's something you don't like, tell us."

"By all means," Hoff interjected. He was perplexed by her reaction. Her performance was flawless, much more moving than when she sang in the televised Centrum Church service. During the Stevens Crusade service used for this show, twelve people had made spontaneous confessions of faith at the end of her solo.

Leeandra looked up again, first to Hoff, then to her father. A smile fled across her lips. "I guess I'm not as quick to accept change as all of you." She glanced over to Larry and back to Hoff. "I like it." Her head and shoulders shuddered with a quick shrug. "I had no idea what to expect. It's really good." She smiled. "To tell you the truth, I'm surprised at how good it is."

"I'm glad you're pleased," Hoff said coolly. He was peeved at her reaction. Why would she expect anything other than a good job?

"This is a quantum leap forward for our ministry," Joe Ted said as he stood. "I'm elated. Would it be too vain to watch it again?"

"Not at all," Hoff answered.

"But, a break first." Joe Ted laughed. "This is as bad as public television. No commercials."

"Or a long-winded tent preacher," Ken chimed in.

During the second showing, Joe Ted, Casper and Ken were relaxed and chatty as they commented on details of the service. Casper complimented the taupe and teal canvas panel behind the pulpit. Leeandra said nothing, watching as intently the second time as she did the first.

When the tape ended, Joe Ted said, "Boy, time flies when you're watching yourself on TV, doesn't it?" He slapped his thighs and stood. "I feel like celebrating. I'm going to prepare my specialty, prayer chicken. You're all invited to stay for dinner."

"You're not!" Leeandra said.

"Come on, it's not that bad," Joe Ted retorted.

"It's that good," she said. "I'm delighted. We haven't had it in ages."

"She's delighted now," Joe Ted said with an impish grin. "The first time I fixed that dish, I made the mistake of telling Leeandra and Casper about it first. They came up with the name prayer chicken. They said one long, powerful prayer would be necessary to make it edible."

"What is it, for Pete's sake?" Larry asked.

"Boneless chicken breasts in pickled green tomatoes. You'll like it, or I'll refund your money. On the dinner, that is. Not the TV program."

Larry laughed. "Can't beat a deal like that."

"And I won't be offended if you make a quick trip to get a burger," Joe Ted added.

"I'll give you a hand in the kitchen," Larry said and peeled off his corduroy jacket.

Ken excused himself to attend an early evening meeting at his church, again complimenting Hoff on the program. Hoff told him enough tape was shot for five television programs. Editing on the other four would begin in Houston tomorrow, even though it was a long holiday weekend.

After Ken left, everyone gathered in the spacious kitchen. Leeandra and Hoff stood to one side, watching Joe Ted, Casper and Larry start preparation of the meal.

"I've got to hand it to you, Hoff," Joe Ted said as he removed the skin from a chicken breast. "When we met in Austin a month ago and you told us what your schedule was, I didn't think you'd make the deadline. My hat's off to you."

Hoff grinned. "Just proves what I've always said."

Larry laughed. "Uh-oh, here it comes."

"I'll ask," Joe Ted said. "What have you always said?"

"Do not write off a man named Hoff."

They were all in the mood to laugh and did.

"Drat!" Joe Ted spat the word. "I was sure we had French bread, but we don't. Somebody has to go to the store."

"I'll go," Hoff said and turned to Leeandra. She was dressed in a dark blue velour jogging suit with red accent stripes. Hoff wondered if she wore a bra. "How about navigating for me?"

Leeandra hesitated for a second before she answered, "Okay."

"Get some Falfurrias butter, will you?" Joe Ted asked. "Salted?"

"Okay." She said to Hoff, "Give me a minute to get my coat."

Hoff was pleased with the prospect of a few minutes alone with Leeandra. He had not seen her since the meeting in Austin one month ago. Suddenly, he remembered when he was in the seventh grade and had a crush on Patricia Lee Burnett. She was a cheer leader and was voted the most beautiful girl in school. He was stricken with long periods of dreaming, puppy love paralysis fantasizing about her. She rode to a school event with Hoff and his father one evening. Hoff pretended he and Pat were on a date. His father stopped at a convenience store for cigarettes. During that alone-with-Pat vacuum, he managed to locate a voice within his seething enchantment enough to say a few intelligible words. In the Stevens kitchen, he felt a similar sense of awe. He smiled.

Wind-whipped granules of snow peppered Hoff and Leeandra as they hurried toward his rented Cadillac, parked at the curb.

"Brrrrrr," she said as he opened the car door for her. "This weather is getting nasty."

In the car, Hoff let up on the gas after spinning the wheels and said, "Much of this and we won't be able to fly home tomorrow."

She smoothed her wind-blown hair. "Getting caught away from home over a holiday weekend wouldn't be too nice."

Spending the rest of a long weekend with Leeandra would be nice, he thought, especially since Margo was in Gladewater with her mother.

As Hoff and Leeandra chit-chatted during their supermarket errand, he quickly settled into feeling comfortable with her. She was a good conversationalist and laughed easily. Again, she did not carry a handbag, but paid for the groceries with a twenty from her overcoat pocket.

When they got back to the Stevens home, they found Joe Ted busy cooking. Casper and Larry helped between spurts of conversation about New Age music. Hoff went into the den to revitalize the fire in the fireplace. He added two pieces of split mesquite wood and was putting the screen back in place when he noticed Leeandra standing behind him.

A gust of wind rattled a window. When he stepped away from the fireplace, Leeandra backed up to it to warm herself. Hoff sat in one of the two wing chairs in front of the fireplace.

"Can't beat being at home in front of a fire on a day like this," she said. "I've warmed myself many times in front of this fireplace."

"How long has your dad lived here?"

"Fifteen years. When I moved from Plano two years ago, Daddy converted the guest bedrooms wing into two apartments, one for Casper and one for me. The apartments give us privacy." She turned to face the fire, held out her hands for a moment, then sat in the chair next to Hoff.

"I guess you enjoy the break from being on the road, don't you?"

"Very much."

"How long have y'all taken a break over the holidays?"

"It started before Daddy took over from Preacher Bob. I think they always came home for a few weeks around Thanksgiving and Christmas."

"And you go back out the second weekend in January?"

"I think so." She laughed. "Daddy, Casper and I are like the old fire horses. We charge out when the bell clangs."

"By the way, I haven't complimented you on your solo at Centrum Church in Austin. You were terrific."

"You were there?" A small frown furrowed her forehead.

"No. I got a tape of the program. If you were nervous about being on television, it didn't show."

"You're kind."

"As good as that was, I thought you were better in our first TV program. It's obvious you enjoy singing. Have you had voice lessons?"

"No."

"There's something else I've wanted to ask. Where are you when Joe Ted and Casper go to the prayer tent after the services?"

She smiled. "Why do you ask that?"

"I looked for you in the prayer tent in Sweetwater and in Abilene. You were not there either time."

"I sit in the van with Billy Dean Smith, our road foreman, until Casper and Daddy are ready to leave. I don't care for the prayer tent." She stared into the fire.

Hoff wondered why she didn't like the prayer tent and was soon lulled by the leaping flames and glowing coals. He liked being here with Leeandra. He felt a contented excitement, regulated by the mantle clock's rhythmic ticking. She continued to stare into the fire, lost in thought.

Hoff realized he harbored a mixture of perceptions about Leeandra. When she was in front of a crowd, he saw her as a powerful figure wrapped in delicate, finely appointed beauty. At other times he saw her as a skittish doe, alert with caution. At times she seemed poised for flight. He saw that wariness in Austin when he presented his proposal and again this afternoon when Joe Ted asked for her reaction to the program. He sensed it for a moment before she agreed to go to the supermarket with him.

He enjoyed her company, here in the wavering, frail light on this darkening, wintry afternoon in the Stevenses' comfortable den. Firelight danced on the soft rounded features of her face. In his head, he heard her voice as she sang "Amazing Grace" in the program they watched earlier.

"Ten minutes," came Joe Ted's announcement from the kitchen. "Leeandra, would you see what all these good folks want to drink?"

She stood. "What will you have?"

"I'd like to see the wine list." He looked up at her and grinned.

She smiled. "Do you prefer domestic or imported?" Hoff laughed, and she added, "Actually, we don't have wine."

"Water will be fine. But with all this religious firepower, is there any chance of getting it turned into wine?"

She had a mock frown. "I don't think we have that kind of firepower."

After dinner, they sat in front of the fire with coffee and slices of fruitcake sent to Joe Ted by a preacher friend in Corsicana. Hoff and Larry complimented Joe Ted on the chicken dish.

A few minutes before ten o'clock, Hoff and Larry prepared to leave. "We'll stay in touch," Hoff said and looked at Leeandra. "Good night."

She gave him a tiny smile, but said nothing.

A Slop Bucket Has More Charisma

At their motel, Hoff and Larry stopped in the bar for a beer. Both were tired and they were silent for several minutes.

"You were right about Leeandra being essential to the TV show,"

Larry said. "She had people eating out of her hand. That lady is stronger than a horny gorilla."

Hoff nodded.

"I think we should increase her exposure," Larry said. "She's the strongest of the three, much more charisma than Joe Ted or Casper."

"A slop bucket has more charisma than Casper. He's a nice kid, but he's duller than dog shit."

Larry laughed. "Yep. Casper is not Mister Excitement, but he does what he's supposed to do."

"You're right. I'm O-D'd on being nice. It gets tense having to be so careful about not letting any no-no's slip out." They were silent for several minutes before Hoff said, "It's waiting time, now. That's the part I hate."

"Yep. It's always scary when the public gets the chance to decide if what you've done is worth a tinker's damn."

#

In his motel room, Hoff took a long, hot shower and went to bed. He lay with his hands clasped under his head, wondering how the public would react to the Stevens television program.

He listened to icy spits of sleet peck at the motel room window and thought about sitting in front of the fireplace with Leeandra. It had been a cozy, comfortable time. The image of her face in the fire's wavering light struck him as being a visual song. He smiled.

Hoff imagined he and Leeandra were in front of a fireplace far away from anyone. Popcorn and hot chocolate added a nice touch. Coffee laced with Kahlua would be better, but she doesn't drink. What the hell, he thought. It's just make believe. Might as well make it coffee with Kahlua.

Focus on a Smile

Leeandra lay in bed, unable to sleep. She smiled as she thought of going to the supermarket with Hoff. She was glad he did not insist on paying. It takes a confident man to let the woman pay, she thought. She felt at ease with him, liked his small talk about things other than the ministry. Too many people thought that was all she wanted to talk about. She thought he was caring and sincere without being solicitous. She liked the natural way he opened the car door and positioned himself to walk between her and the parking lot traffic.

She replayed the conversation about the prayer tent. She would not go there because it reminded her of the graveside service for her husband and children.

Quickly, she banished thoughts of them and let Hoff's face come back into focus. She wondered when she would see him again.

Chapter 7

Scar Boy

"I got the date mixed up," Danny Don Rhodes said when Annabelle Morton, waitress at the Panhandle Cafe in Channing, asked why he came in after nine o'clock, over two hours later than usual. "I thought I had a doctor's appointment today, but I don't. I got mixed up."

Annabelle smiled. "The usual?"

Danny Don ran his fingers through his sand-colored hair and shook his head. "Just coffee. I had a bowl of oatmeal at home."

Annabelle was placing the white ceramic mug on the counter in front of him when one of the men from the co-op grain elevator said, "What's old Scar Boy doing in here this time of the morning?"

When Danny Don squinted and began to turn to look at the man, Annabelle said in a hurried whisper, "Don't. Don't pay him any mind. He's just trying to get your goat."

He said, "Some day he's gonna shoot off his fat mouth when I've got my three-fifty-seven. Then it'll be my turn to shoot something off."

With a threadbare white cotton hand towel, Annabelle rubbed the stained, mottled blue Formica counter top for no good reason and smiled. "With any luck, I'll be there to watch him get his come-uppance. Got any plans for New Year's?"

Danny Don slurped the hot coffee through his scarred lips. "No." He spoke barely loud enough for Annabelle to hear.

"That was bad about the preacher in Kansas City getting killed, wasn't it?" Annabelle asked. Sometimes they talked about television preachers when business was slow enough for her to talk about anything.

He nodded. "The radio news said Reverend Ray and Dr. Culpepper might've been killed by the same man."

"Or woman," she said. Her smile crinkled the fifty-six year collection of wrinkles on her long thin face. "Never rule out the weaker sex."

"You really think it might be a woman?"

"Aw, you know me. Just flapping my jaws. I got no idea whatsoever."

"Hey, Annabelle," came a voice from somewhere behind Danny Don. "Got a coffee cup over here with a dusty bottom."

"Coming up." Before moving away from the counter, she lowered her voice and said, "Coffee's on the house this morning. Help a little to make up for you losing a morning's pay, huh?"

He nodded, and whispered, "That son-of-a-bitch better not call me scar boy ever again."

Critique by Margo the Magnificent

On Sunday night, January 15th, Hoff invited Larry Best and the Bayou Bottom Studio production crew to his condo for a party to watch the first Stevens Gospel Crusade television broadcast. He also invited Margo.

He thought about flying to Amarillo to watch the first show with the Stevenses, but they didn't invite him.

Before the Stevens show began, Larry played a video of Leeandra's appearance on *Gospel Music Showcase* earlier in January. The syndicated program appeared on stations throughout the nation. Leeandra was invited to sing after someone—Larry could not find out who—sent a video tape of her Centrum Church appearance to the program's producer.

Leeandra sang "Amazing Grace" on *Gospel Music Showcase*. Her performance drew compliments from the Bayou Bottom crew members, none of whom was partial to religious music.

Despite the Stevens Crusade show's religious nature, everyone was drinking and eating when it began. Because of their familiarity with it after the editing process, they continued to eat and drink, laughing at mistakes only their expert eyes would see.

Hoff watched closely, silently. This was his first look at the program since he and Larry showed it to the Stevenses two months ago in Amarillo. He was impressed with the production quality achieved despite the tent's crude surroundings. Leeandra's solo was the highlight. In the next round of shows to be produced, she would sing two solos per program.

After everyone else left, Hoff and Margo sat on the sofa, drinking Scotch. He draped an arm around her. "What do you think of the show?"

"It's okay," she said listlessly.

"You didn't like it?"

"Not my thing."

"It wouldn't be mine, either, but I have a special interest."

Margo gazed off through the glass doors at the downtown skyline.

"Actually, I think they're quite good at what they do, especially Leeandra," he continued.

"She'd sound better with a band."

Her snide tone nettled him. He moved so that they no longer touched.

"She'd look better with a little more makeup," Margo added.

"It's not your thing, you don't know boo about TV production, but you pick things apart." Hoff's voice was crisp.

"You asked my opinion," she said, equally crisp. "I'm voicing it."

"Thank you," he said icily.

She scooted away from him. "What's with the sudden jerk Hoff?"

He glared. "What's with you is the question! It pisses me off that you nit pick what happens to be a good program put together by people who know what they're doing."

"Meaning I don't know shit about the whole thing?" she shot back.
"Precisely!"

Her eyes were a boiling blue. "Well, mister big shot, little Margo dumb ass isn't quite as dumb as you think. I saw the way you looked at Miss Prissy Bitch while she sang. You wouldn't give a goddam if I said Casper is a piece of shit or the old man looks like a fruit bat."

Hoff glared at Margo. She looked away from the hostility, got up and walked to the glass doors. After looking outside for a minute, she turned to face him. She started to speak, then took another sip from her drink. A smile broke the tightness in her face. "Got the hots for her?"

"What if I do?"

She shrugged. "What if you do?"

"It's my business," he said coldly. "I have no formal attachments at the moment, in case you've forgotten."

"I haven't." Margo sat on the far end of the sofa. She laughed sardonically. "Big bad Hoff and the preacher's daughter. Who would...."

"Would you just shut up?" He repeated, "Just shut up!"

Her eyes were instantly full of fury. She glared over the rim of her glass, the heat draining from her eyes. "Okay," she said quietly. "But next time you ask me a question, tell me the answer first and we can avoid an argument." She put the drink down and picked up the phone.

"What're you doing?"

"Calling a cab."

"Always the cut and run artist, aren't you?"

Margo slammed the phone down. "Now, shithead, you can just shut your goddam mouth!" She stood in a spurt of angered motion. "Yes, goddammit, I left. Yes, goddammit, I came back. And yesssirreeee, goddammit, I am leaving again!" She strode toward the coat closet.

"Margo." His voice was soft. She stopped halfway to the closet, but didn't turn around. "Margo," he repeated.

She turned, her eyes watery. "What?" The word was a flat bark.

He bit his lower lip and stood, but made no move toward her. "I do think Leeandra is special, but there's nothing happening between us. It's a business deal." He walked slowly to her and grasped her hands. "I'm sorry I cut you down. I've worked hard on that show. If this deal succeeds, I'll make a lot of money. I guess I'm a little up-tight about it." He smiled. "Ego thing in addition to the money. You know I don't like to fail."

She looked at the floor.

"I shouldn't have said what I did," he added quietly. "I'm sorry." He lifted her chin and kissed her tenderly on the lips.

She leaned against him. Hoff hugged her close, chastising himself for lashing out at her and wondering why he had flown off the handle. He breathed in her faintly sweet odor, a smell he loved, and felt her hot tears on his neck. As they held each other, he stroked her hair and asked himself how he could keep from loving Margo. When her tears subsided, they walked arm-in-arm to his bedroom.

The Cash Register Ringeth

"We have an avalanche of mail!" Ken Walker, the Stevens Crusade business manager spoke to Hoff over the phone from his Amarillo office in short, excited bursts. "We're up to eighty-eight thousand dollars. Our people are still counting!"

You're shitting me, Hoff thought. He said, "Eighty-eight thousand?"

"Yes! And here it is only Friday after the first weekend of programs. Unbelievable! Leeandra is getting nothing but the highest compliments."

Ken promised to fax daily updates. Pleased, Hoff hung up and told Gracie about the contributions to the coded post office box used to track donations generated by the Stevens show. "That's more than double the pro forma." Hoff reached for the phone. "I've got to call Andy."

Andy answered gruffly. "What do you want?"

"Shall I do my niceties routine or do you want the good news neat?"

"If it's really good news and not bullshit, I'll take two shots straight."

"How about eighty-eight grand worth of good news?"

"Goddamit, speak English to me! What're you talking about?"

Hoff told him about the donations. Andy said, "You're shitting me."

Hoff laughed. "Believe it or not, that's what I came within a gnat's whisker of saying to Ken, but I'm not shitting you."

"Christ almighty. Go find a wad of those preachers," Andy said. "I'll sell my shit-for-steel oil rigs and put my money into tent preachers and television."

"If this keeps up, we'll gross four-and-a-half million bucks for the Stevens TV venture the first year," Hoff said.

"Not bad," Andy said.

"The cash register ringeth." Hoff laughed. "Whoa! I'm beginning to talk like a preacher."

After the conversation with Andy, Hoff told Gracie to call a meeting for Tuesday, January 24th, following the second weekend of Stevens TV programming. By the time they met, contributions were up to two hundred thousand dollars. Hoff told Larry Best to double the number of markets in which the Stevens Crusade program was being televised.

"You called it, my friend," Hoff said to Larry. "You predicted

Leeandra would be either a smash hit or a dud, nothing in between. You nailed the smash hit part of it."

Beyond Our Wildest Dreams

Leeandra picked up another letter from the box of correspondence forwarded from Amarillo. This one was from a woman in Brownwood. "Miss Stevens, you are an angel put here on this earth to sing about the glory of God. I pray that your voice will be the last sound I hear before Jesus calls me home." Leeandra placed the letter in the growing stack of ones she had examined. She had stopped reading all of each letter and began to scan through them because there were so many.

She selected another, from an elderly couple in Anson. "Your beautiful singing gives us a lift, helps us forget our aches and pains. May God be with you. We would love to hear you sing more."

Leeandra looked away from the box of correspondence toward the vase filled with two dozen long-stemmed yellow roses. The flowers had arrived an hour ago. She picked up the note from Hoff that accompanied the roses and read it for the third time. "Congratulations on your success. The future holds many achievements for you, your dad and brother. Fondly, Hoff." He sent fruit baskets to her father and Casper.

She touched one of the roses as she thought about Hoff. Despite the infrequency of their visits, his handsome face was clear in her mind. She especially liked his dark eyes. His eyes always told her he cared about her. She smiled and thought, Hoff is the man who can make me happy.

She glanced at her watch and decided to rest before the evening's service began here in Harlingen. She stretched out on the king-sized bed, closed her eyes and tried to quiet the whirl in her head.

"Beyond our wildest dreams," her father had said about response to their first television programs.

"You're getting nothing but rave reviews," Ken had told her.

She hadn't decided how she felt. A nagging apprehension dampened her enthusiasm for the successful debut on television.

Outside, a cold, steady rain peppered down. People here in the Rio Grande Valley were thankful for the moisture, but Leeandra wondered if it would keep worshippers away from tonight's service.

Three-quarters of a mile away, at the Stevens Crusade tent, Billy Dean Smith, the road manager, double checked the time. With more than an hour to go before the service started, the tent was one-third full and people continued to stream in despite the rain. He shook his head in disbelief and walked toward the truck where he would eat his sandwich. Hopefully, the coffee in his Thermos was still hot.

Chapter 8

Passing Grade for Joe Ted

In the basement of his home near Bentonville, James Bresnahan ejected the videotape, sauntered across the room to his antique S-curve rolltop desk. He peeled the cellophane off a cinnamon candy and popped it into his mouth. On his word processor, he wrote a letter to a friend in Oklahoma City, thanking him for the videotape of the preacher named Stevens. He and several others throughout the Bible Belt exchanged videotapes and letters examining the motives, theologies and techniques of evangelists. The others were unaware of Mission Silver Broom.

The thank-you letter printed, he created a file on the Stevens TV ministry and typed his observations. "Joe Ted Stevens is an adequate pulpiteer. He possesses a controlled sense of delivery, but is also effective in generating a sense of urgency. He demonstrates no appreciable evidence of formal training or study; however, he does utilize New Testament references with some efficacy. I expect he believes in the inerrancy of the Scriptures. His appearance is credible, unlike others with exaggerated television styles. Neither he nor other family members rely on excessive makeup, hairdos or costumes. I believe I would find this man as much at home at the pulpit of a modest, mainstream church as on television.

"Casper is adept at leading congregational singing. He is cheerful, polite and deferential to his father — a functionary.

"Leeandra's singing is compelling. She possesses a beautiful, albeit untrained voice and does not embellish or adulterate the traditional hymns. She sings a cappella with great care, focusing upon spiritual content. I find her vibrant and refreshing. She contributes in a meaningful way to this new broadcast ministry.

"While at first blush this group seems imbued with a genuine sense of mission, they must be watched carefully lest they be corrupted by success and the pursuit of money."

Bresnahan re-read the entry, fingering the cleft in his chin, mindful of the slightly longer whisker hairs he missed in the indention when he shaved after his usual, five-mile morning run. He transferred the entry to a diskette, removed it from the computer and placed it in the walk-in safe, the same place he kept his gun collection.

I Shall Call You Leeandra

"An extra fifty dollars?" Madelyn asked Henry Woods. "What for?"
"Indulge me," he said, pulling the prostitute to him. "Nothing of

great consequence."

As the fully clothed Madelyn took the naked Centrum Church pastor's penis into her mouth and fingered the isthmus between his scrotum and anus, Dr. Woods said, "Today, my sweet little Madelyn— perhaps always—I shall call you Leeandra."

She took his member out of her mouth and asked, "Who is this Leeandra chick, anyway?"

"Shut up and suck my cock. I've already given you a fifty dollar answer. Just tend to business and earn your money."

Madelyn frowned as she put his penis back into her mouth. Later, as they fornicated in the missionary position, she became angry when he told her she should be taller, more buxom and blonde, like Leeandra. But she didn't respond until much later, after their ordered pizza arrived.

"You shouldn't say things like that to me," she said after she ate a second slice of pizza. "You're not fucking that Leeandra chick, whoever she is. You're fucking me."

Dark Memories of Skeeter

Danny Don Rhodes chewed a fried pork rind and watched the credits at the end of the program. The last one read, "A Stevens Evangelical Television, Inc., Production." Joe Ted Stevens said it was their first program, and he asked for everyone's prayers. Danny Don nodded as he finished chewing the pork rind. He was not the praying sort and didn't intend to start simply to help this newcomer on television, but he thought Joe Ted's request for prayers showed good intentions.

Danny Don liked the Stevenses. He thought Joe Ted was genuinely concerned for lost souls. Even though he never sent money to any of the television preachers, Danny Don liked the fact that Joe Ted seemed apologetic when he asked viewers for contributions. The request for money came only after Joe Ted asked for suggestions on how to improve the program. Danny Don had none. He especially liked the singer, the blonde-haired daughter. She was pretty. Her voice was pretty.

He thought Leeandra was the type of person who would care about people, even somebody like him who was crippled and scarred by an explosion, who limped because of an improperly-set triple compound fracture of his left leg. Somebody with a gimpy left arm because the deep lacerations damaged nerves and severed tendons. She was genuine. She would be there when people needed her.

He used the remote control to turn off the TV set. A rerun of Reverend Ray was starting. Danny Don wondered how long the reruns would last. He wondered when The American Church would get a new preacher.

Would they replace Harmonia Tracker? In Leeandra Stevens, Danny Don had found his replacement.

He pulled the covers to his chin. Outside, a blustery north wind whipped through Channing, Texas. The night's low was forecast to be eighteen. Aunt Gertrude adjusted the thermostat upwards a few degrees after last month's gas bill showed a decrease. Still, the house was cool enough that the quilt felt good. With the bedside lamp still on, Danny Don folded his hands and thought about Leeandra.

Joe Ted beamed with pride when he introduced his children. Who wouldn't be proud, Danny Don thought. Both were nice looking. Parents had it easy being proud of attractive children. He assumed Casper and Leeandra had kids. His mood darkened as he wished for a mother like Leeandra, one who cared and would be there, unlike his own mother, Clare Jean. Everyone called her Skeeter. When he was eight, she ran away with an over-the-road trucker, disappeared into the maze of highways. Her good-bye note, scribbled with a black crayon on the inside of a ripped-apart cereal box, read: "I've got to get away from here. Go ahead and hate me."

Because of the things she did, he felt no great loss that Skeeter was gone, but he was sorry that he had no mother.

Thoughts of her prompted vivid memories of when she entertained her gentlemen friends. "Entertain" was Skeeter's word. Over the years, Danny Don had tried to forget, but he couldn't. He could still see Skeeter, naked and on her knees, fellating one of her paramours as the nude man sat on the couch. After he ejaculated, she rubbed the globs of semen on her face and spread some of it on her nipples, moaning in satisfaction.

Danny Don tugged the quilt tighter under his chin as he remembered the time his mother had sex with two men at once in the little one-room garage apartment. He could still hear the men's grunts and guttural commands, his mother's moans and shuddering cries. He was afraid they were hurting her. Maybe she was dying. He watched in terrified silence for fear they would hurt him.

He was also afraid because Skeeter slapped him and jerked him around by the hair the one time he talked while she was entertaining. All he wanted to do was to make Skeeter's friend like him too.

Skeeter had threatened "to tie his weenie in a knot" if he said anything to his father, who often worked nights at the auto repair shop. She had grabbed his little penis as she made her threat, twisted and squeezed until he cried and begged her to stop.

Above all else, he remembered how Skeeter played with the gluey ejaculate that men spent on her. He couldn't picture his mother's face without the smears. He tried to suppress the thought, but failed.

Did Leeandra Stevens do such things? Did she let men shoot spunk into the same mouth that sang such beautiful hymns? No. Surely not. But would she? Not with him, he knew that. Not even the kindest and most caring of women would do such things with a man whose face was half covered with waxy, stringy burn scars.

The scars on his face and arms were why Joyce left him. She was his childhood sweetheart. They married two days after they graduated from Dalhart High. She said she left because he got so mean-tempered after the explosion while welding on the pipeline in Borger. He knew better. The scars. His limp. She was ashamed of him. That's why she left.

Long before the accident, Joyce worked at a nursing home while he attended trade school to learn welding so they could have a good life. That prospect had been blown away by the explosion.

Now he was alone, working for subsistence wages at Hooper's Fina Station. Living with his Great Aunt Gertrude. Counting his pennies. Reading second-hand newspapers to save quarters. Scrimping and gimping while beautiful people like Leeandra savored their good lives rich with popularity and attention.

Most women winced at the sight of him. He saw the revulsion even when there was no grimace or frown. Some looked away. Others stared as if he were an animal in a zoo, caged by scars instead of steel bars.

Suddenly, Danny Don felt confused. Inside his head, he began to see a mixed image of Joyce running backward, away from him. Of Skeeter, her face smeared with ejaculate. And of Leeandra, standing naked, her face bright with light as she sang a hymn. He closed his eyes tighter, angered by the blended image, angry for having such thoughts about this person named Leeandra, enraged at the invading confusion.

The confusion made him unable to remember when—was it two, three years ago?—he got the last letter from his father, who took a job overseas working as a mechanic. Danny Don lost the letter and couldn't remember the name of the country.

His eyes snapped open. From a bedside drawer he removed the small stack of porn magazines. Reading them helped push the roaring chaos out of his head. He shuffled through until he found the one with pictures of three men and two women having sex during a picnic on the shore of a lake. He knew all of the magazines by heart, each photograph, each nuance. Danny Don fondled his penis. After several minutes, he turned out the light and imagined he was part of the group beside the lake.

Unwelcome Wake Up Call

The explosive clanging tore through Hoff's deep sleep, then mercifully went away.

The ringing resumed, extracting an unsaid goddammit in Hoff's head. He groped in the dark for the telephone and was seething when he jerked it to his ear and hissed, "Yes!"

"Hoff, this is Gracie. I know I woke you, but I have bad news. Joe Ted Stevens suffered a heart attack this morning. He's dead."

Gracie's words were clearly intelligible, but the hammer blow of her message took a few seconds to beat its way through the sleep and the shock-absorbing mental mechanism that slows comprehension of calamity.

"Hoff?" Gracie asked. "Did you hear me?"

"Yes," he said thickly. "When did it happen?"

"This morning in Harlingen. Ken Walker just called. He wants you to call him. He's at his office in Amarillo."

"Holy shit," Hoff mumbled. He struggled to clear his head as he pulled himself into a sitting position on the edge of the bed and rubbed his face. He found the switch at the base of the bedside lamp and turned it on. "I didn't know Joe Ted had heart trouble."

"Me neither."

He continued to rub his face. "How's Leeandra?"

"I don't know anything other than what I just told you. Ken was very shook up, could hardly talk. Are you awake enough to take down his number? He wants you to call him right away."

"Yes, uh...I have to find a pen. Okay." He wrote down the number and glanced at the bedside table clock. 7:04.

Hoff was at the Hyatt Hotel on Union Square in San Francisco, had arrived late last night for a meeting today with Stewart Wong, representative for a wealthy Hong Kong group interested in real estate investments. "Will you call Larry?" he said.

"Wouldn't it be better to wait until you talk to Ken? We'll have more details."

"You're right." Hoff took a long, deep breath. "I'll call Ken now. I meet with Stewart Wong at nine-thirty. I'll try to get a flight around noon." He had planned to take a couple of extra days to enjoy San Francisco. Margo was scheduled to join him this evening. That would change. "I'll get back to you as soon as I get a fix on this." He hung up.

Hoff got through to Ken on the first try and sat in stunned, motionless silence as Ken gave him details. Joe Ted had stopped at a vending machine to buy a newspaper on his way to the motel coffee shop for breakfast. As he bent over to remove the paper, he pitched forward, then rolled onto the floor, clutching his chest with both hands. Casper was with him and administered CPR until the ambulance arrived. The paramedics rushed

Joe Ted to the hospital even though he failed to respond to their treatment at the scene. He was pronounced dead on arrival.

Ken said he was about to make arrangements to fly the body, Leeandra, Casper and Billy Dean Smith to Amarillo.

"Ken, I'm sorry. And it's from the personal perspective, not business."

"I appreciate that."

"Did Joe Ted have a history of heart trouble?"

"Years ago he had an irregular heartbeat, but no recent symptoms. He watched his weight, got regular checkups, never smoked." Ken paused. "He was only fifty-three."

"How is Leeandra taking it?"

"Surprisingly well, but Casper is all to pieces. It happened right in front of him. He's been sedated."

"I want to call Leeandra. Do you have her number?" Hoff copied the number and added, "How are you doing?"

"I'm okay, I guess...under the circumstances. Joe Ted was like a father to me."

"I'll fly to Amarillo, but I don't know if I can make it tonight. If not, I'll get there as early as possible in the morning." Hoff paused. "Can I help or will I be in the way?"

"I think you can help."

"Okay. And, Ken, my sincerest condolences. I didn't know Joe Ted all that well, but I thought the world of him."

After his conversation with Ken, Hoff called room service to order coffee and promised a ten dollar tip if the waiter got to his room within five minutes. He slipped on trousers and a pullover shirt, chocked open the door to his room with a balled-up sock and called Leeandra. Her room phone was busy and he was put on hold. Hoff glanced at his watch, more mindful of the February 7th date than the time. The coffee came while he was holding and thinking about the impact of Joe Ted's death on the Stevens Crusade TV programming. He sipped coffee until the motel operator put him through to Leeandra.

Her voice was quiet, but steady. "I'm holding on, trying to come to grips with what's happened."

"I'm in San Francisco but plan to leave here about noon. I hope to get to Amarillo early enough this evening to come by your house."

"That would be nice."

"Anything I can help with now by phone?"

"Thanks, but I can't think of anything. We have lots of friends here in Harlingen. Between them and Billy Dean, I have all the help I need."

"My thoughts are with you, Leeandra." Hoff felt a heavy helplessness.

"We'll see you tonight," she answered. "Be careful."

Hoff hung up, poured more coffee and sat thinking. This was his first conversation with Leeandra in over a month. Hearing her voice revitalized his mental image of her soft beauty in the wavering light from the fireplace in the Stevens home the day after Thanksgiving. She sounded quiet but strong on the phone, no hint of the skittish doe. He was glad to hear calm control in her voice. She was showing her reservoir of strength. She would need it. For that matter, Hoff thought, we could all use an extra dose of strength.

The numbing sadness of Joe Ted's death left him queasy and tight. It's unfair, he thought. Joe Ted was delighted with public response to the television programs. Not because of money, he said, but because he thought it validated a higher worth of the Stevens Crusade. Last weekend was their third week on the air.

"I've always thought we could and should reach many more people with the gospel," Joe Ted had said over the phone four days ago. "There's an urgent need for people to hear about Jesus. Each time I pronounce a benediction, I'm mindful of lost souls who may die before they hear about Jesus. God sent you to help us preach the gospel. Your motives and ours may be different, but God's will is being served. We'll all be blessed."

Is dead being blessed? Hoff asked himself. I don't understand. Maybe I'm not supposed to. Anger simmered inside him as he thought, this kind of thing makes no sense. I hate things that make no sense.

He reached for the phone and made his flight arrangements. Then he called Gracie, omitting the woo-woo, and told her about his plans to fly to Amarillo via Dallas. "There's one other thing," he added. "I need for you to call Margo. She was to fly out here tonight."

"Oh?" Gracie hadn't made Margo's flight arrangements.

"No sermon, Miss Gracie."

"I'll call her."

Hoff called Andy and told him about Joe Ted's death.

"Anything I can do on the business end?" Andy asked. "I don't mean to sound heartless, but I'm not involved with them personally."

"I'm not thinking about business ramifications just yet," Hoff said. "The funeral will probably be held Thursday or Friday. I doubt we'll talk about the crusade until after that."

"I hope not. I guess Leeandra and Casper are in shock."

"Congratulations! You actually pronounced her name right."

"Do I win a prize?" Andy asked.

Hoff laughed. He and Andy used humor to help metabolize anything that happened. Hoff was thankful for the dash of levity. "Your prize is my undying friendship."

"Shit fire if I'm not a lucky peckerwood. Listen...use me as a standby.

Anything you need, you say the word."

"There is one thing. Is The Bomber available to fly Joe Ted's body, Leeandra and the others to Amarillo?"

"You've got it," Andy said. "I'll get Carla to set it up."

"Thanks. Have her call Ken Walker in Amarillo." Hoff gave Ken's number to Andy. "The TV venture will pay for the plane."

"The hell it will. It's the least I can do."

Hoff thanked Andy and hung up.

When Hoff met with Stewart Wong, he explained the circumstances, left as soon as essentials were covered and caught an 11:50 a.m. flight to Dallas.

He settled into his first-class seat and ordered an Anchor Steam beer. After takeoff, he forced himself to work, making notes in the Hong Kong investors file. He would locate prospective land parcels in Texas for their consideration. If they purchased any, he would earn a sizable finders fee.

But Hoff's thoughts and feelings were drawn to Joe Ted's death. He put away the file, asked the flight attendant for another beer, put on the stereo headset and dialed to the classics channel. A Rheinberger concerto for organ and orchestra played. Hoff closed his eyes. The back-and-forth, antiphonal passages between the orchestra and pipe organ made him think of the most fundamental opposites for humankind—life and death.

Joe Ted was dead. Wham! His sense of urgency was warranted, Hoff thought. He was gone, as Joe Ted himself would have put it, in the twinkling of an eye—an eye now closed in death.

Hoff opened his eyes when the flight attendant asked him to rebuckle his lap belt because of possible clear air turbulence. Her eyes were almost as blue as Leeandra's, and his thoughts focused on her. He wondered what it would be like to hear her sing a featured part with a large chorale in that mirrored hall he dreamed about the night he saw her in Sweetwater.

In such a hall, she should be accompanied by a magnificent pipe organ and an orchestra. Would such a grand performance be any more moving than when she sang "Amazing Grace" a cappella under the drab canvas and sagging lights of the Stevens Crusade tent? Maybe, he thought. Maybe not. There was no maybe about the fact that he looked forward to seeing her again, even under these deathly disastrous circumstances.

He listened to the concerto and asked the question: Who can lead the Stevens Crusade?

Timequakes All Around

Hoff's watch read nine minutes after ten when he rang the bell of the

Stevens home in Amarillo. The house was ablaze with lights as if extra wattage would fend off the added darkness that comes with death. A cold, blustery wind whipped his hair until he was admitted by a woman he didn't know. A blaze crackled in the den's fireplace.

Leeandra got up from the sofa to greet him with an extended hand. He shook her hand and gave her a quick, fraternal hug.

"Thanks for coming." Leeandra's voice was huskier than when they talked this morning. She was pale, obviously tired. The beauty of her rounded facial features was even softer, as if he were seeing her in smudged focus.

"How are you doing?" he asked.

She smiled weakly and exhaled a long breath. "I'm beginning to realize what happened. I'm sad." She licked her lips. "Feeling vacant."

No one else sat on the sofa with her, so Hoff did. "Is Ken here?"

"He's at the funeral home tending to details. He should be back any minute."

Someone offered coffee and Hoff accepted. "For what it's worth, I think you're holding up well."

Leeandra looked at the fire then back to Hoff, another weak smile on her face. "When people close to you die, you start to go on living the minute they're gone, like it or not."

"I guess if anyone knows about that, you do."

She nodded and sipped a Diet Coke. "Lots of other people do, too." She looked past Hoff toward the front door, responding to the sound of someone's arrival. "There's Ken."

The three of them sat on the sofa with Ken in the middle. "The funeral will be at eleven o'clock Friday morning," Ken said.

Leeandra squeezed Ken's hand. "Thank you. I couldn't stand the thought of going to the funeral home tonight."

"Makes me feel a little less helpless," Ken answered and looked at Hoff. "We can't thank you enough for arranging for Mr. Boxx's jet to bring them home. I want his address so we can thank him."

"Yes, that was very generous," Leeandra added.

"He was glad to do it," Hoff said.

"Do you have a place to stay tonight?" Ken asked.

"No."

"You can stay here if you'd like," Leeandra offered. "The garage apartment is empty."

Hoff accepted quickly. He sipped his coffee, listening as Ken and Leeandra talked about details of the funeral arrangements. They were interrupted now and then by a person with a question or someone leaving. Leeandra declined to take two phone calls.

"I'm just about talked out," she explained.

By eleven-thirty, everyone was gone except an older woman who would spend the night, Ken, Hoff, Leeandra and Casper, who was sleeping off sedation in his bedroom. The older woman went to bed and an hour later, Ken left to go home.

Hoff and Leeandra returned to the sofa after he added two pieces of split oak to the fire, got another Diet Coke for her and refilled his cup.

"Do you have anything to help you sleep?" he asked.

She shook her head.

Hoff thought she was very much in control. He wondered if she had cried.

"I had a good cry in Harlingen." Her statement came as if she sensed his question. She talked slowly, speaking into the distance as she peered into the fire. "And on the plane coming home. I'll probably have another one after I go to bed."

They sat in silence for several minutes, looking at the fire. He listened to the ticking Seth Thomas clock on the mantel, remembering how loud it sounded when he and Larry waited for Joe Ted's reaction to the first television program. Now, the clock ticked a cadence of finality. Hoff thought the ticks sounded quieter, a respectful, resolute continuation of time's measurement. He thought about how fast time had passed since he first met Leeandra.

"A lot has happened in the four months since I ran into you in that motel lobby in Sweetwater," he said.

She nodded slowly and continued to stare into the fire.

"That day turned out to be a monumental surprise," he said.

"How so?"

"Your service that night was a real eye-opener. I'd never attended anything like it. I didn't know what to expect, but I was very favorably impressed—enough to pursue the TV venture."

She brushed strands of hair away from her face. "Lots of changes since then, but changes were already going on, even before we met you." She was quiet for several seconds. "After my husband and children died, I was devastated. Confused. My world had caved in right in front of my eyes and I couldn't understand why. I was angry and scared, full of questions and accusations. Why did God let it happen? That sort of thing. I came to Daddy's house in full retreat, even took my maiden name back as if that would help it all go away. Then I started singing in the tent services because Daddy suggested it and because I needed something to do. I sang in the services sometimes when I was a kid.

"When I first started singing again, I just went through the motions, but I began to enjoy it and take it more seriously. The audiences were responsive. Daddy made me feel like I was contributing to the evangelism." She paused, glancing toward the fire. "Then, bit by bit, I started feeling whole again, began to feel alive on the inside as if the part of me that died with my husband and children was growing back. I felt something new and strong."

Leeandra sipped her soft drink. "That new strength is still there, even now, right this instant, in spite of Daddy's death. You're aware of what's been happening since the services last October in Abilene?"

"People responding when you sing?"

She nodded and looked at Hoff, but also through and past him as she talked, the songful lilt back in her voice. "It's like some living, powerful force inside of me rides my voice into those people's souls." Leeandra blinked and again was looking at him. She smiled, triggering one set of parenthesis marks. "Goofy?"

"Not at all." He noted the difference in her face. Her voice was stronger and a liveliness played in her eyes.

"I don't know exactly what will happen to our ministry. Casper and I always depended on Daddy to lead the way. With God's help, we'll continue." Leeandra blinked rapidly. "Daddy's not gone entirely. His love for people, his belief in God, his sense of mission...all of those things that were in him are now part of me. It's as if these last two-and-a-half years with Daddy happened so I could learn to recognize the power of God's love the way he did." She smiled. "I'm afraid I haven't said all this very well."

"To the contrary. You said it eloquently."

"Daddy liked you, you know."

"I thought so. Thanks for telling me. I liked him, too. He let me be who I am."

"He was like that."

"You've got lots of good memories about your dad, don't you?"

"Both Mom and Daddy."

"When I was in high school, I knew a preacher's son who was the biggest heathen around, rebellious as all get-out. Did you ever rebel against church?"

She laughed softly. "One year during the holiday break when I was...oh...ten or eleven, I told my parents one Sunday morning I wasn't going to church. They said 'fine', got ready, took Casper and went without me. For the first time in ages, they had lunch at a restaurant afterward. Without me, of course. It hurt my feelings something terrible. When they got home, I bawled like a baby."

"What did your parents do?"

"Daddy and I had a long talk. I really don't remember what he said, except I knew he loved me. We all went to church that night and Daddy took us out for hot chocolate. We hardly ever did that. But I knew everything was okay again. That's the only time I pulled a stunt like that. Going to church with them was fun because they enjoyed it so much." She was silent for several seconds, then looked at the mantel clock. "It's after one. Would you mind if I suggest we call it a night?"

"Not at all. I hope I haven't kept you up too late."

She smiled. "I needed to talk."

#

Hoff took his bag to the garage apartment, unpacked and went to bed. He lay on his back in the dark, hands clasped under his head and listened to the quiet. This seventh day of February turned out to be a violent, jerking upheaval in time's fault line. He thought of how many timequakes must happen every day to people around the world. But only when they occurred nearby did they crash through the ticking routine of everyday events.

A siren's wail rose from the night's windy, cold darkness. There were timequakes all around.

A Song about Precious Memories

At Chapel of the Plains Funeral Home before the start of Joe Ted's service, Hoff was introduced to Dr. Henry Jackson Woods, pastor of Centrum Church in Austin.

Dr. Woods stood two inches shorter than Leeandra, and his protruding eyes were set close together. He hovered close to Leeandra, constantly touching her elbow or letting his hand rest at the base of her back. His loud, authoritarian voice dominated conversations.

Hoff bristled with an instantaneous, total dislike for the man. He stayed away from Dr. Woods to observe. The Austin pastor set off all of Hoff's alarms. He asked himself if he was jealous of the man's overt attentions to Leeandra. No, he answered. There's more to it than that. This character is a gob of living spit if ever I saw one.

Hoff sat at the back of the chapel until all the seats were taken, then got up and gave an elderly woman his place. Ken had apologized for not seating Hoff with the family. Although Joe Ted was an only child, there were many relatives plus his deceased wife's family.

Leeandra cried soundlessly as she and Casper led the family's entry though a side door to the reserved seats in front.

Hoff was surprised when halfway through the service Leeandra was called on to sing. Her tears were gone as she sang "Precious Memories." A charismatic lilt infused Leeandra's voice with hope. Strummed crystal never rang with more clarity. "In the stillness of the midnight, precious memories linger still."

Hoff's eyes moistened. He couldn't remember the last time he felt the urge to cry. He derived a strange comfort in knowing the capability still existed somewhere deep inside.

At the cemetery, a piercingly cold north wind prevailed over the sun's brightness. Gusts flayed the tent, which reminded Hoff of the Stevens Crusade prayer tent. This one was not a shelter for new converts to Christianity. It was shelter for the newly dead Joe Ted in his casket, protection for an open, freshly-dug grave and for the huddle of family members, pallbearers and the pastor. The minister tried to spread petals from a red carnation on Joe Ted's coffin, but the wind blew them away. The petals, said the pastor, represented Christ's blood shed for the salvation of mankind. The minister pronounced a benediction, its amen ominous with finality.

Leeandra, still seated, sobbed as Casper and Ken tried to comfort her. Hoff watched from the edge of the tent, absorbing her agony into his stomach's churning gruel. Absently, he rubbed the hair on the back of his left hand. He noticed Dr. Woods standing on the other side of the tent looking at Leeandra, his pudgy face a passive, staring blank.

Bad Vibes a la Beady-Eyed Bisqueen

"Damn! Another preacher investigation," Banner Tatum, the private investigator, said. "What have you got going with all these preacher persons?"

"Maybe too much," Hoff said. "I want you to bore in on this one. I smell a bad hombre."

"How bad?"

"A slime ball that stomps baby chickens. Remember Robert Bisqueen?"

"Oh, shit," Banner said. "Beady-eyed Bisqueen, we called him. Yeah, I remember that piece of non-humanoidal, dope-running trash. He's the only son of a bitch I ever got mad at for wishing me merry Christmas. You think this Henry Woods preacher person is that bad?"

"Woods set off the same bad vibes that Bisqueen did when we worked on the Belize land deal," Hoff said. "I never ignore my instincts on this sort of thing."

"And you're usually right. We'll see how your batting average holds up. I'll jump on this right away and get back to you pronto-like." Banner laughed. "Beady-eyed Bisqueen. I wouldn't have thought about him for fifty bucks. You sure know how to fuck up a perfectly normal Friday afternoon."

Chapter 9

Death Amidst a Forest of Life

James Bresnahan looked up from the Sunday paper after reading an article about Joe Ted Stevens' death. It detailed the brief history of the Stevens television program and its growth.

Bresnahan folded the newspaper and laid it on the table next to his chair on the back porch of his home. He fished a cinnamon disc candy from his shirt pocket, loosened the cellophane wrapper and slipped it into his mouth.

He scooted his chair to the left to get back into the sunshine, warm and soothing on this clear, calm winter afternoon. The weather was cloudy and chill this morning during target practice when he shot the .243 caliber Winchester M70.

The woods were quiet except for distant birdcalls. The deciduous trees were devoid of leaves, but the pines' green needles gleamed in the sunshine.

He enjoyed the woods' peaceful order and celebration of life. Their cones, acorns and seeds brought new life as pine begat pine, oak begat oak. Occasionally, one of the big trees died. Death amidst a forest of life. Just as Joe Ted's death came in the midst of a world of life. Bresnahan wondered why a man of God was struck down at a time when his ministry was growing so fast.

Later in the day, he came to a conclusion and entered his opinion in the Stevens data file. "I believe God felled Joe Ted Stevens. Evidently, he was not as pure as he would have us believe. Should it continue, the Stevens ministry bears watching. Whatever impurity existed in him could well be perpetuated by his successor."

Something Bresnahan did not type into the Stevens file was his belief that this act of God upon Joe Ted ratified Mission Silver Broom. Among the most overt practitioners of errancy was Reverend Andrew Peter Webber in Tampa, Florida. God willing, Webber would be felled a week from today. Bresnahan felt a revitalized commitment to his mission.

Antidote by Songful Voice

Danny Don Rhodes frowned at the television set in his room as he watched Joe Ted Stevens preach at the regular Sunday evening time. Danny Don thought it was wrong for the program, obviously on videotape, to be aired without an explanation of Joe Ted's death. He continued to watch, fascinated by the evangelist's plea for lost souls to accept Jesus Christ before it was too late.

His frown went away when he thought, Joe Ted's own death bore out the truth of his message. His thoughts about death brought an onslaught of confusion. "Not good," he stammered aloud.

The confusion subsided when Leeandra sang "The Balm of Gilead." He liked the peaceful beauty of her voice. She was a balm, a comforting antidote to boring days at Harper's Fina Station, Aunt Gertrude's ill temper and his own limping, scar-imprisoned, directionless days.

Thank God Leeandra did not die. Danny Don hoped she would continue to appear on television even though her father was dead.

Bullshit or Brilliance?

On Monday after Joe Ted's funeral, Hoff and Larry Best sat in Hoff's twenty-fifth floor condominium watching the afternoon fade into a drizzly, mid-February evening. Houston's downtown buildings seemed to huddle together in the fuzzy, gray cold. A newly-opened bottle of Scotch sat on the coffee table. A Scott Joplin CD played and Larry, wearing his corduroy jacket, shucked off his goat skin cowboy boots. Larry hated funerals and did not attend Joe Ted's.

Hoff told Larry about the service. "I was astounded. Leeandra was a paragon of strength. When she and I talked the night I flew into Amarillo, I got the impression she accepted her father's death as a pre-ordained event. There was not so much as a single quiver in her voice when she sang at his funeral."

Larry sat in thoughtful silence before he said, "I figured she's made from strong timber, but I never figured her to be that strong. Do you still think she and Casper will carry on with the ministry?"

"Yes. She made that clear Saturday when she, Ken, Casper and I met. There are lots of details to iron out, but there's no doubt in her mind they'll continue."

"Does Casper feel the same way?"

Hoff sipped his drink. "Casper just trots along behind. Set the pace, pick the direction and Casper follows. He's not quite a weenie, but he's damned close."

Larry laughed. "Now, let's take a look at this. Is it better to be a weenie or a semi-weenie?"

"A semi-weenie, I guess, if those are the only choices. Neither is a good alternative."

"You sure do have a hard on for Casper."

Hoff scrunched up his face. "It's not that I dislike him, but I don't see much there to like. He always tags along, content to stare at the asshole of whoever is ahead of him. I don't like that action."

Larry took a sip of his Scotch, held the glass up and watched the fingers of liquid drain down. "This whole thing has shifted to an unexpected wavelength, hasn't it?"

Hoff nodded. "I'm not sure I know what to make of it all. Leeandra, Casper and Ken are in Corpus Christi. They didn't want to delay getting back to the scheduled services. They'll recruit a local pastor to help with the preaching."

"Who do you think will handle the preaching over the long haul?"

"I'd put my money on Leeandra."

"Can she preach?"

"If she decides to. She believes there's some kind of divine power growing within her. I think she sees Joe Ted's death as a directive to become more involved in the ministry." Hoff looked at Larry and grinned. "Want to hear a crazy idea?"

"Yep. I live in a world of crazy ideas. I love 'em. That's how I make my living."

"Here we have a woman who's knock-your-dick-in-the-dirt gorgeous. She sings like the proverbial lark. I'll lay odds she turns out to be a stem-winder of a preacher, if she decides to. And if that happens, she's our product."

"She's always been a main selling proposition in our product."

"Yeah, but now she's the whole enchilada," Hoff said. "New, improved industrial-strength evangelist in a curvaceous package. Leeandra the beautiful."

"Aren't you counting your chickens before they hatch? We don't know if she can preach."

"True, we don't know. But, I'm betting she can and will, so I'm thinking ahead. She'll be different from other evangelists on the tube. She's a terrific singer and good-looking enough that people go the tent or watch her on TV just to see her, but she's not a glamour-puss type that turns other women off. Everybody adores her. Like you said back in Abilene, she's our show pony. She's a complete package." Hoff sat forward on the edge of the sofa. "I believe we should pick a new name for her."

"What kind of new name?"

"Sister Cathedra." Hoff paused. "I've run through a whole laundry list of possibilities—Sister Hope, Sister Faith, all of those. They strike me as kind of corny. Sister Evangel sounds okay. That might work. I gave some thought to Sister Grace because of the way she sings "Amazing Grace." If we use that name, the song would be a natural theme. But, I think Sister Cathedra is more distinctive. We rename her Sister Cathedra.

Not legally, of course. For lack of a better term, it will be her stage name."

"Are you saying cathedra or cathedral?"

"Cathedra. No 'L'."

"Did you make that up?"

Hoff laughed. "I can't believe I know a word that you, the consummate ad biggie, don't. A cathedra is a bishop's official throne. I ran across that word on a vocabulary test in high school. I missed the definition so it stuck with me. A cathedral is a building that contains the bishop's throne."

"But she's not a bishop, for crying out loud," Larry countered.

"The word is also used in connection with someone who is an authoritative source. Who's to say she's not an authoritative source?"

Larry shrugged. "Nobody, I guess. Certainly not me."

"What do you think?"

Larry sipped his Scotch, looked out the window, then back at Hoff. "Sister Cathedra...." Larry began, then paused. "Sister Cathedra. I'm sitting here trying to make up my mind whether it's bullshit or brilliance."

"Which way are you leaning?"

Larry sat for a long time without answering. He stared through the glass doors to the balcony into the fast-darkening gloom.

"Which is it?" Hoff asked. "Bullshit or brilliance?"

Larry looked at Hoff for a moment, then smiled and nodded. "Brilliance." Larry was quiet for a moment. "Damned if it isn't a brilliant idea. Sister Cathedra." He paused again. "Yep, it's got a good ring to it. We can test the name with focus groups to assess public reaction. I wonder what she'll think?"

"If it's presented in the right way, she'll go for it."

"I suppose you've figured out what the right way is?"

Hoff examined his Scotch for several seconds and was somber when he spoke. "Yes. Leeandra realizes she's the only family member who can perpetuate the ministries of her father and grandfather. She believes she's ordained by God to preach the gospel. It's up to me to convince her that using the Sister Cathedra name is a better way to get people to listen." He sipped his drink. "Want to hear something else crazy?"

"Yep."

"Damned if I'm not beginning to believe that's the way it is."

Sister Cathedra's Time Has Come

Unlike the other times Hoff saw Leeandra introduced under the Stevens Crusade tent, this crowd was silent. Absent were the buzzing babbles of excitement, the craning to see, the crackling undercurrent of anticipation. On a breezy, uncomfortably cool February 14th Tuesday night in Corpus Christi, Texas, the overflow crowd of four hundred was as silent and still as so many graveyard headstones.

Appropriately so, Hoff thought, on the fourth day after Joe Ted Stevens' burial under a wind-flayed tent in a brown, winter-dead Amarillo cemetery.

Standing at the edge of the Stevens Crusade tent, he watched Leeandra walk from her chair to the pulpit. She wore a beige, hip-length sweater over her navy dress. The sweater masked her slender, buxom curvaceousness, but it did not conceal the difference in her walk. This was not the subdued, undulating, casual walk that made her long blonde hair swing in counterpoint to her steps. This was a purposeful stride.

Leeandra rested her hands on the pulpit instead of clasping them in front of her as she always did before she sang. She lowered her gaze to the pulpit for a full half-minute before she raised her eyes and looked at the silent audience.

Even from outside the tent, behind two other rows of standing people, Hoff could see the teariness in her eyes. Gone was the blue of clear Caribbean waters. This blue was clouded by the turbulence of death and grief. A taut weariness hung on her face as she completed her scan of the audience. She lifted her chin.

In that fraction of a second, Hoff wished she would sing. A profound wish for the lyricism of Leeandra's hauntingly beautiful soprano voice to warm this chill, windy night with her a cappella delivery of "Amazing Grace" or "The Ninety and Nine."

Instead, she spoke in a slow-paced monotone. "The Lord giveth and the Lord taketh away. Blessed be the name of the Lord." She paused. "A week ago today my beloved father was called home by his Heavenly Father."

Soft scattershots of amens broke out among the crowd.

"Just four days ago, we lowered my father...." Her voice tailed to a pause. She swallowed twice. "We laid to rest the body of God's servant."

She paused again, leaving a ringing silence as if the headstones were holding their breaths. A night bird's call sounded from the darkness outside the tent. Hoff saw the minuscule softening on Leeandra's face as she resumed speaking. "Joe Ted Stevens was a minister of the gospel. He preached about God's love, but his words were whispers compared to the eloquence of the way he lived his life for the glory of Jesus' name."

She raised her voice to continue over a louder outbreak of amens. "God's love showed itself in my father's clear countenance, shone in his eyes because it glowed with such fervent passion in his soul and spirit."

A new round of shouts came like artillery bursts from throughout the crowd. She stood silent, looking from person to person until the hubbub subsided. Her face was now relaxed with a pleasant calm.

"What a triumph of God's everlasting love and grace that in this season of sadness, we remember those things about my earthly father that live on in the eternal majesty of our Heavenly Father." The singsong lilt was back in her voice. Her eyes were once again provocatively blue. "The mortal eyes of my Daddy are closed in death. Yet, his joyous message of God's love, the memory of his eyes aglow with the eternal light of our Lord and Savior Jesus Christ, are with us as we gather to worship our Redeemer tonight."

A wave of exclaiming voices stopped her. As she waited for the outbreak to subside, Hoff stood on his tiptoes to scan the crowd. The audience was now festively alive. All eyes were focused on Leeandra, her long blonde hair shining under the lone spotlight.

She let the crowd lapse into whispers, then into a still, unmoving quiet. Only the wind stirred, making the strings of naked, one hundred and fifty-watt light bulbs bob and sway. That same wind whirled shining dust particles through the spotlight's shaft as she stood looking at the silent crowd for another moment.

Hoff saw her take the tell-tale breath as she clasped her hands and lifted them to her chest. Leeandra sang a short passage. "In the stillness of the midnight, precious memories linger still." She held the last note, letting the musical fragment wane slowly, a soothing, short-form baptism by songful voice.

Hoff felt warmth in his own eyes as he saw people throughout the crowd daub and blot away their tears.

She let the note die away, dropped her hands to the pulpit and spoke again. Her voice was almost as musical as when she sang. "And so, my brothers and sisters in Christ, the Lord giveth and the Lord taketh away. But what He gives us in the life of a messenger like Joe Ted Stevens is of such powerful majesty that not even God can take it back. Because God gave us part of Himself when He gave us my father. And God has made a covenant with us. What God in His infinite wisdom gives us—once we accept His gift—will never be taken away."

Leeandra paused and stood at the pulpit in the blotting, total silence and smiled, her face alive with joy. "It is the wonderful message of redemption. The Lord giveth us that which is everlasting. The Lord taketh away only that which, in the scope of eternity, does not matter." She looked up at the swinging, sagging strings of light bulbs as she added with a forceful, rising voice, "Blessed be the name of the Lord!"

The crowd erupted into shouts and almost in unison, people jumped to their feet on the hay-covered ground. Many began to sing, an extemporaneous welter of different songs that came together in an improbably joyful sound.

Hoff watched Leeandra's face tilt slowly toward the pulpit as the crowd's noisy worship became a celebration. Some people danced. Others waved handkerchiefs. Others held their hands in the air. At Casper's instruction the three-piece band onstage began to play "Blessed Be The Name" and the crowd joined in to sing.

With slow steps, Hoff backed out of the standing fence row of people crowded at the edge of the tent. He shoved his hands into his jeans pockets and walked swiftly toward his Lincoln Town Car parked a block away. He faced a three-and-a-half-hour drive back to Houston. He had his answer. We've got ourselves one hell of a preacher lady, he thought. Sister Cathedra's time has come. He was perplexed with the scrap of doubt that kept him from feeling elated.

The Barnum Treatment

Hoff called Andy Boxx to tell him about the Sister Cathedra idea.

"Shit fire, the poor girl's dad hasn't been in his grave a week and you're putting the Barnum treatment on her. Sister Cathedra, of all the goddam things! Pre-fucking-posterous!" Andy's voice was brittle, which meant he was not fuming. His disagreement was serious. "Sounds to me like you're open pit mining these people. Are you sure this is the right thing to do?"

"Yes." Hoff had asked himself the same question during the drive home from Corpus Christi the night before. He continued with his answer to Andy. "Ferdinand Porsche didn't put a precision machine in a square box with wheels on it. He designed an exterior package commensurate with the quality of the machinery inside. That's all I'm doing. The change to Sister Cathedra is a marketing decision. I'm convinced we're making the right move."

"I know you're a smart young man. I realize most of your decisions work out, but this one stinks."

Hoff took a deep breath. He didn't like genuine disagreements with Andy. "I'm going with it. We're doing something right. Our contributions have jumped to more than three hundred thousand dollars a week."

"Money is one thing. People are another. But do what you think you have to," Andy said heavily. "When do you discuss this with Leeandra?"

"Larry Best and I meet with her, Casper and Ken Walker day after tomorrow in Corpus Christi. You're welcome to attend."

"It's your game," Andy said in a flat tone. "You play the hand."

Chapter 10

Planning Time at T-3

James Bresnahan stood alone at the street corner in Tampa, Florida. As he waited for the traffic signal light to change, he scrutinized the imposing edifice of The Tampa Tabernacle. Earlier in the day, he picked up his rifle, packed inside a set of golf clubs, from the Tampa bus station, drove to a shooting range and sighted in the weapon.

Absently, as he looked at the church building, he rubbed the cleft in his chin with his left index finger. Reverend Andrew Peter Webber conducted his services in the large sanctuary, part of a sprawling complex of buildings. Locally, The Tampa Tabernacle was nicknamed T-3.

In addition to a four thousand-seat sanctuary, the complex housed post-production facilities where final editing was done on Reverend Webber's weekly television programs. It included a wedding chapel, meeting rooms, fifty thousand square feet of office space and a gym.

Bresnahan thought the buildings were extravagant. He saw them as testimony to Reverend Webber's commitment to commercialism. At last night's service in the T-3 sanctuary, Bresnahan concluded beyond any doubt the unctuous Reverend Webber's only regard for the gospel was using it to expand his personal realm.

The traffic light changed to green, but he continued to study the building, concentrating on the array of small, round windows near the pulpit and choir loft area at the front of the sanctuary. It had always seemed strange to him that a person could walk through the front doors of a church building and suddenly be at the back of a sanctuary.

"Sir! You at the corner!"

Bresnahan jerked around in response to the commanding words. Instinctively, as he saw the police officer wearing silvery, reflective sunshades, Bresnahan pointed at himself with his index finger.

"Is this your car?" asked the officer, standing in front of the rented Oldsmobile Cutlass.

Bresnahan saw the officer's motorcycle parked behind the car and stepped toward him. "Yes, sir, it's mine. Is something wrong?"

The officer pointed to a sign. "You're in a no parking zone."

"I'll move it right now," Bresnahan said quickly. "I apologize for not noticing."

"I see you're driving a rent car. Where're you from?"

"Joplin, Missouri." Bresnahan spoke without hesitation and maintained eye contact with the officer. Before a mission, he practiced answers to incidental questions to avoid telltale delays. He carried a fake driver's license to confirm the information.

"Welcome to Tampa. Sorry for the interruption, but it's the law. Enjoy your stay in our city." The officer retreated toward his motorcycle.

Bresnahan was angry with himself for his foolish mistake. As he took the keys from his pocket, several cinnamon discs fell out. He picked them up, got in the car, drove to the corner and parked on the side street.

He got out and, walked back to the corner, looking for the cop. He was gone. Bresnahan crossed the street and entered the main sanctuary, empty on this Saturday morning. He strolled down the aisle and stepped onto the dais. From the pulpit, he could see second-story windows in the building across the street where he had parked illegally.

As anticipated, there was a line of sight to the pulpit from the building occupied by a civil engineering firm. The last employee went home by six-thirty on Thursday night and by six last night. Today the building's parking lot was empty. Getting into the building would not be a problem. None of the windows was protected with security wiring.

He stepped off the dais and sat in the second pew next to the right center aisle. His plan was to shoot the verminous Reverend Webber tomorrow night. Bresnahan had selected the .307 caliber Dakota 76 rifle from his collection.

Because of his encounter with the officer, he decided to revise his plan. He would check the Cutlass in at the Tampa airport as soon as possible today, fly to Orlando, rent a car and drive back to Tampa tonight. That would obscure his movements in the unlikely event he was being watched. If police checked records on the rented Cutlass seen by the officer, they would find it was checked in before Webber's death. He smiled, got up and strode through the back of the church, out one of the front doors and into the bright sunshine of this 18th day of February.

On his way home, he would stop in New Orleans to get another falsified driver's license and new credit cards from Doctor Document. Bresnahan became friends with Doctor Document—who liked to be called Doc Doc—during the two years he operated the store-front mission in the French Quarter. Bresnahan provided papers for illegal aliens who accepted Jesus Christ as their Savior.

He stopped the practice when he realized most of the aliens' interest was in being saved from immediate deportation instead of from eternal damnation. He resented their taking advantage of him. He also resented not being taken seriously by members of his own family. He had overheard his brother say, "Jimmie Dan jerk, doing God's work!" Despite what anyone said, he was doing God's work when he operated his mission in New Orleans. Tomorrow, he would do God's work when he swept away another verminous apostate in accordance with Mission Silver Broom.

#

The next evening, Bresnahan waited in the office building across the street from T-3. As the crowd gathered, he watched Andrew Peter Webber swagger onto the dais, dressed in a long, white robe. The white, Bresnahan thought, would soon be stained by the blasphemer's own blood.

When Reverend Webber stood at the pulpit to begin his sermon, the sanctuary's overhead lights dimmed. The targeted preacher was illuminated by spotlights.

Bresnahan got down on his knees next to an open window in an office identified as belonging to a senior civil engineer. He rested the rifle on the window's ledge, using the engineer's mouse pad as a cushion. He aligned the scope's cross hairs on Reverend Webber's neck, took the usual deep breath and exhaled halfway. Ever so slowly, he squeezed the trigger. The Dakota's slug struck Webber in the right side of his neck, two-and-a-half inches below his ear.

Bresnahan said quietly, "Andrew Peter, your time is done. I slay thee in the name of Yahweh's Son."

Three blocks from T-3, as he drove away from the murder scene, he met an ambulance screaming its way toward the church. "No need to be in such a hurry." He smiled and popped a cinnamon candy into his mouth.

Mister Sissy and Sister Cathedra

Hoff turned his Town Car toward the surf. He parked facing the sea on the moist, hard-packed sand at the edge of the North Padre Island on the outskirts of Corpus Christi. He and Leeandra sat for a while, looking at the Gulf, listening to the waves. A south wind warmed the sunny day.

"How about something to drink?" Hoff asked.

"Sounds good."

"No 'perhaps' this go-round?"

Leeandra wrinkled her nose and smiled. Hoff nudged off his loosely-tied sneakers and pushed them under the front seat. He got out of the car, opened the back door and fished two soft drinks out of the cooler.

Barefoot, wearing blue shorts and a white sleeveless top, Leeandra leaned against the driver's side front fender. Her long, blonde hair flew in the gusty sea breeze. She thanked Hoff when he handed her a Diet Coke and nodded toward his Diet Dr. Pepper. "I thought you might choose something stronger."

He held up the can. "This is my first choice when I go to the beach with church soloists." He smiled. "I bet you don't know this is also called a mister sissy."

She frowned.

"I used to drink beer with a bunch of guys at Lloyd's Ice House. If I gained weight, I swore off beer and drank these. Lloyd wouldn't serve you if you ordered a Diet Dr. Pepper. You had to call it a mister sissy. Then you got the big razzaroo from the regulars. You didn't realize how incomplete your life was without that gem of minutae, did you?"

"I do feel fulfilled." Leeandra laughed softly, rippling both sets of parenthesis marks at the corners of her mouth.

They set out in a slow walk along the edge of the water, chit-chatting.

Jeans rolled to his knees and wearing an orange golf shirt, Hoff lagged a few steps behind her. He watched her mosey along the beach. This was his first time to see her in anything other than a dress or slacks, and he noted the subtle ripple of her leg muscles. Her legs were firm and perfectly proportioned with light, flawless skin. He imagined how creamy soft her upper inner thighs must be. She probably had a temptingly sparse pubic tuft. Her shorts were tight enough to define the firm roundness of her buttocks. He was getting an erection. He slipped his left hand into his pants pocket and made himself think of something else.

He felt peeved with himself for lusting after Leeandra and also felt a twinge of confusion about why he should be. He walked faster to catch up with her.

Leeandra said, "This is a good time of year to walk on the beach, so peaceful and quiet; very few people. Nothing smells as clean and alive as wind off the ocean."

Hoff was enjoying the sun's warmth and glanced up at the cloudless sky. "You're right."

"Thanks for coming out here with me," she said.

"It's my pleasure."

At the end of yesterday's meeting when Hoff suggested the Sister Cathedra name, Leeandra asked if he were staying overnight. He was surprised when she suggested they drive to North Padre Island the next day. She said the beach would be a good place to talk after she took time to think and pray about the new name.

Now, she stopped walking and faced him, her blue eyes open wide, boring into his with studied intensity. He saw that same intensity several times in Joe Ted's. She said, "I want us to be completely candid."

She maintained the lock-eye, penetrating gaze for another few seconds before she resumed her slow pace along the water's edge. "I have mixed feelings about the Sister Cathedra name."

"That's understandable."

Leeandra glanced at him, then looked back down at the hard-packed sand. "Mixed feelings and a lot of questions."

"Let's work on finding answers."

She stopped again. "If this comes off as vanity, then so be it. I'm concerned about making a fool of myself if I do the preaching. Do you and Larry really think I'm good enough to handle it?"

Hoff restarted the walk. "Yes, or we wouldn't have made the suggestion. You obviously have doubts."

"It's logical for me to have doubts," she shot back. "I'm not trained, nor am I formally ordained. I have no experience." She paused. "And the world is not exactly full of female preachers."

Hoff laughed softly.

Leeandra stopped abruptly and glared at Hoff. "This may be funny to you, but it isn't to me. This ministry is important. Daddy's and Preacher Bob's work deserves to continue. This is hardly a laughing matter."

"Hold on," he said, surprised by her anger. They were standing close to each other. Hoff reached out and clasped her arms lightly. Her skin was cool. Touching her sent an eddy of excitement through him. "I recognize the importance. I wasn't laughing at you." He diverted his look past her, out to the water, then back to her. "I often laugh to cope with things, always have. Not everyone appreciates that. I apologize. The last thing I want to do is upset you." He paused. "And as sure as dogs bark, I don't want you to be angry."

Leeandra was expressionless. He knew she was taking stock of his answer, so he asked, "Can I smile?" She tilted her head a fraction, brushed the wind-scrambled hair out of her face and nodded.

"That's better." He patted her arms and released his hold. "I drove down on Tuesday and heard you speak to that crowd. You were terrific. You're a gifted communicator, when you sing and when you speak. You were every bit as much at home in front of those people as I am walking along this beach. You're that way under the tent, and you're that way on television. I have a lot of faith in your capability to handle the preaching."

"I didn't see you Tuesday night."

"I stood outside."

"Came to check me out?"

"You could put it that way. Remember, I have a stake in this, too. Where we go from here is also important to me."

They walked in silence for several minutes. She stopped to examine a shell, but didn't pick it up. She faced the water and said, "Sister Cathedra." She said the two words softly. "It's....it's so...."

"New?"

"Yes, but the name seems like show business or something you might see on one of those tacky trailer signs with a flashing arrow." She laughed. "Sorry. That struck me as being funny for some reason."

"Good," Hoff said. "Laughter helps process new ideas. I bet you don't know that laughter releases beta endorphins, chemicals in the brain that help relieve stress."

"No, as a matter of fact, I didn't know that." She was somber again and they walked for a long time before she stopped and turned to him. "Isn't Sister Cathedra too...too glitzy?"

Hoff looked up as a sea gull hovered in the breeze and said as they watched the bird watch them, "No."

"Just 'no'? No explanation?"

"I don't have an explanation. Sister Cathedra doesn't seem right to you because it's new. It's like a different hairdo or meat loaf recipe. Anything new takes some getting used to. Cathedra is a religious type of word, not at all glitzy to my way of thinking. Sister Cathedra is a refined, distinctive and appropriate name. As I told you yesterday, Larry tested Sister Cathedra to assess public reaction. People like it. Using Sister Cathedra will help gain attention for this ministry you want to perpetuate. It'll help entice people to try out your product, so to speak."

"Product?" Leeandra snapped. The penetrating look returned to her eyes. "Is that what we are to you? A bar of soap?"

"Not at all, but I'm the marketing guy, remember? Call it product, service or ministry. No matter what name you use, isn't the purpose to get your message to people who haven't heard it?"

"Yes, but product sounds so...lifeless."

"I didn't mean it that way. I care a great deal about all of you, and I respect what you do. My goal is to help you reach out to a larger audience. I hope you believe me."

She nodded almost imperceptibly and started to walk. A flock of gulls took off and whipped their way seaward against the breeze. For a long while they sauntered without talking. Often, she stopped to pick up a shell or flip one over with her toe. Her toenails were painted bright red.

"Why do women paint their toenails?"

She looked at him. "Why do you ask that?"

"Just curious. Painting them is bound to take a lot of time. Usually, nobody but you sees your toenails."

She turned into the sea breeze and shook the hair from her face. He wondered if her husband had liked for her to paint her toenails. Maybe he kissed her feet and licked them sometimes during sexual foreplay.

She smiled. "Painted toenails make me feel more feminine."

"Make yourself much more feminine," he said, "and the world's males won't be able to stand it."

"A compliment, I trust?" She glanced at a low-flying gull as it banked into the wind. The Caribbean blue was shining in her eyes.

"Most definitely. But, I'm not telling you anything new. Women know when they're beautiful. Knowing is part of what makes them beautiful."

She looked Hoff squarely in the eyes, a serious, probing look.

"You are a beautiful lady," he added.

"Thank you," she said, barely above a whisper.

Hoff's hands were in motion to take her by the arms when she turned away. As she did, he admired her breasts, more apparent as the wind pressed the lightweight blouse against her body. He wondered if her movement was happenstance, or if she purposely avoided being touched.

Leeandra pressed two fingers against the top of her right thigh. "I sunburn like crazy. Let's head back to your car." They walked in silence until she asked, "What did Ken have to say at breakfast this morning?"

"Ken is undecided on the Sister Cathedra name. He told me he'll abide by your decision. He thinks you're capable of handling the preaching, and he said Casper would rather see you take over than bring in somebody from the outside."

She stopped walking and dug into the sand with her big toe. "Sister Cathedra. I wonder what Daddy would think?"

"Is that a rhetorical question?"

The brittleness was back in her eyes.

"He would approve," Hoff said.

"I'm not so sure," she said as they moved on. "The Stevens Crusade is sixty-five years old. This would end it."

"I disagree. The name may be different, but the effort doesn't end. Joe Ted changed things. He brought you into the operation. That was a change. Going on television was a monumental change. I think your father would've been the last to resist using Sister Cathedra because the Stevens Crusade name might be downplayed."

"Maybe." She was silent for several steps. "And there is the question of whether, pure and simple, this is the right thing to do."

"Right in what way?"

"Every way. Most importantly, is it God's will?"

"If it is God's will for you to carry out this ministry, why wouldn't it be His will for you to do so in the most effective way?"

She kept silent, intent on looking for shells as they neared the car. She straggled behind Hoff and he whirled around when she shouted, "Sand dollar!" She snatched the sand dollar from the beach and held it up as she ran toward him. "Look, it's in perfect condition."

He smiled at her enthusiastic reaction.

"I love the beach," she said. "I want to go to the Caribbean some day. Everybody says the beaches are beautiful there." She looked up from the sand dollar to Hoff. "Have you been there?"

"Yes. It's as beautiful a part of the world as I've ever seen, especially sunrises and sunsets. On a calm, clear morning, the sun comes up with a grin on its face and the water answers with its own rippling laughter."

Leeandra tilted her head and smiled. "You sound like a poet."

"The Caribbean makes poets out of people." He laughed. "I heard that description from an old Black gentleman on St. Croix."

"Where all have you been?"

"I was born on Aruba, but we moved away when I was a kid. I've been to the Virgin Islands, Dominican Republic, Antigua, Nevis, Barbados and Puerto Rico, mostly for vacations."

"How come you were born in Aruba?"

"My father worked for an oil company and he was stationed at their refinery down there. We moved around a lot."

They resumed walking. She stepped into the water and immediately hopped out. "Wow, that's cold!"

"After all, this is only February. The morning paper said the surf is fifty-eight degrees." He leaned against his car and brushed the sand off his feet before depositing their empty cans under the front seat. She declined when he offered her another Diet Coke.

On the way back to Corpus Christi, they stopped for lunch at Pelican's Perch Restaurant adjacent to the Intracoastal Waterway. They sat on the screened porch and ordered fried shrimp. Both settled into a quiet mood.

"I'm concerned about the appearance of coming on too strong if I step into Daddy's shoes," Leeandra said suddenly.

"I don't see that as a problem." He smiled. "Would you have a problem if I order a beer? I don't think I can eat fried shrimp without one."

"Won't bother me."

"Back to your stepping into Joe Ted's shoes," Hoff said. "There's a law of physics that says nature abhors a vacuum. Organizations abhor a lack of leadership. You have natural leadership ability and it makes sense for you to take over."

The waitress set a Coors Light beer in front of Hoff and he sipped it. "I'm also convinced you have an immense inner strength."

"Why do you say that?"

"Among other reasons, your singing at the funeral. I'm not real big on going to funerals, but I've never seen a family member sing at one."

She moved her water glass around expanding circles of moisture on the red plastic table cloth. "'Precious Memories' was one of Daddy's favorite hymns." Leeandra looked at Hoff, a tiny smile on her face. "Daddy said even the angels stop what they're doing and listen when I sing 'Precious Memories.' That's why I sang it. I knew he would hear me."

"Good reason." Hoff felt a knot of emotion in his throat.

Leeandra continued to make circles with her glass, and their silence held as they watched a tugboat pass on the Intracoastal Waterway. A flock of diving, squawling sea gulls searched for fish in the boat's wake. When their shrimp was served, they talked little as they ate.

"What time is it?" Leeandra asked after she finished her meal.

"Almost three."

"I've lost my watch," she said absently.

Hoff began to unbuckle the band of his. "Here, take mine."

"Take your watch?" She grinned. "I can't do that."

"Why not? I've got several." He held it out to her. "No great shakes. It's a cheap-o."

She took the watch. "Somehow, I can't envision you wearing a cheap watch. A cheap anything, for that matter."

"I take that to be a compliment. But, I've got a thing about spending money on watches. I make my ego statements in other ways."

Her smile faded slowly into a somber, lingering look. She glanced at the watch, now on her left wrist, and said softly, "Time for me to get back to the hotel."

Hoff wasn't ready to stop being with Leeandra. He felt a sagging discontent and sensed the same feeling in her. They were quiet during the short drive to Corpus Christi. When they got to the hotel he asked, "When will you let me know about Sister Cathedra?"

"A few days. A week at most." The blue of her eyes was soft. She didn't speak for several seconds, then she said, "I enjoyed the day."

"Me, too. Maybe we can do it again." He paused and when she said nothing, he added, "I hope the service goes well tonight."

They exchanged good-byes and he watched her fluid, undulating motion as she walked toward the door. Before disappearing inside, she waved. Once again, she did not carry a handbag.

"I'd give five thousand bucks to know what she's thinking right now." He shifted into drive. "Damn. She's got me talking to myself."

Strain on the Brain

Hoff drove to the Marriott Hotel overlooking Corpus Christi Bay and found Larry Best in the bar. "Sorry to keep your ad biggieness cooling his heels, but I think the day was productive. Helping Leeandra get to know Sister Cathedra, as it were."

"That's good. I've been productive, too. You'll be pleased to know that I've composed lyrics for the world's next big country-western hit."

Hoff laughed. "And what might that be?"

Larry struck a theatrical pose and sang with an exaggerated twang,

"Why am I the toilet bowl of my sweetheart's life? Yah-tah-dah-dah." He looked at Hoff. "What do you think?"

"Your country music taste buds are in the wrong orifice." At Hoff's suggestion, they retrieved their bags from the bell captain's station and left the hotel.

When they were in the car, Larry asked, "What did Leeandra have to say about Sister Cathedra?"

"About what you'd expect. She's not sure, wants time to think. She'll let me know next week. She asked if we're convinced she's good enough to handle the preaching, said she doesn't want to make a fool of herself."

"Do you think that really worries her?"

"Enough that she asked the question. Ken tells me Leeandra has never been one to take charge, but she feels a strong obligation to perpetuate the family ministry. Given a little time and practice, I think she'll get over her self-doubt. Actually, I think she wants to take charge. She just may not know it, yet."

Hoff lapsed into silence, thinking about his conversation with Ken at breakfast. Ken had said, "Right now, with the emotion following Joe Ted's death, she might be motivated to take over. But I don't think she's an incisive enough thinker to foresee everything being a preacher entails. She won't realize how big the job is until she's done it for awhile."

Hoff, as he turned off Shoreline Drive toward the freeway, wondered again if he were pushing Leeandra too fast with the Sister Cathedra suggestion. If Ken was right, now was the best time to thrust her into the leadership role. Her emotions would help her get off to a stronger start. The better the start, he thought, the better the odds for a strong finish.

Larry asked, "Are you down in the dumps about something?"

Hoff scrunched his mouth to one side. "Nah. Just thinking."

"Did you and Leeandra have words?"

"As in fight? Actually, we had a very good conversation."

Hoff set the cruise control on seventy-five. Several minutes passed in silence. "I think she'll do it," he said. "She'll become Sister Cathedra. Get your people started on ad ideas. We need a strong public relations firm to get more news exposure. I want to expand awareness outside of the normal religion-oriented media channels."

"Don't you think we should wait for her answer?"

"I'm not big on waiting. Let's get on with it. Supposedly, faith can move mountains." He grinned. "Let's see if it can move a Leeandra."

They rode in silence for several minutes until Larry spoke. "I want to ask a serious question and I don't want you to get the red ass. Okay?"

Hoff laughed. "Let me guess. Am I a pathetic herpetic?"

Larry didn't laugh. "In your mind—at this red-hot instant—where is the line between Leeandra the woman and Leeandra the product?"

Hoff stared ahead as he drove, but felt Larry's examining gaze. A long time elapsed before he answered. "There's not a line. It's more like a wind shift zone that gets fuzzier as time passes. Is that vague enough?"

"Yep. So vague that I think you're ready for a career in politics. Say the word and we'll get you jump-started." Larry slumped in his seat. "All this Leeandra and Sister Cathedra stuff puts some kind of strain on the brain, don't it?"

"Yes. On some other body parts, too."

They both laughed.

After a few miles, Hoff heard Larry's deep, regular breathing. He was asleep, leaving Hoff alone with his thoughts, all about Leeandra. He concentrated on what she'd said, how she'd reacted and what he saw in her eyes at the beach. The flare of anger was a surprise. Never before had he seen her angry. He diagnosed it as uncertainty. The wary doe was apparent in her concerns about becoming Sister Cathedra. Her strength was there, too, and he sensed her resolve to carry on the ministry.

Several times during the day, particularly when he let her out at the hotel, he saw a look of caring interest in Leeandra's eyes. But the caring also vented itself like a scent, an ancient cue that bridges space between members of the opposite sex. Hoff smiled at the realization he probably telegraphed the same thing. He knew the signals and the feelings well. These, however, were being transmitted over a different frequency.

Hoff was confused about his feelings for Leeandra. He felt protective, was genuinely fond of her and realized he wanted to let himself care for her romantically.

Suddenly, he found himself thinking about the contrast between the complexity of his feelings about Leeandra and the simplicity of his relationship with Margo. Sex and the lingering half-life of love kept him and Margo together. He was satisfied that he knew and understood her. The only uncertainty, trust, was clearly identified. Except for that, she was a known quantity.

Leeandra was more unknown than known. As he drove through the darkening late afternoon, he was perplexed because he couldn't even begin to decipher the "something different" he sensed in her.

Only part of his reluctance to become romantically involved with Leeandra was wanting to avoid mixing business and pleasure. He didn't want another ill-starred relationship. The business connection and her commitment to the ministry were, he thought, barriers to romance.

He wondered what her feelings were. The signals she sent were not yet clear. Unclear, he thought, but definitely there. Signals from women were nothing new to him. The uncertainty over what they meant was.

Fear of Standing Alone

In her hotel room, Leeandra relaxed on her bed, her head propped up on three pillows stacked against the headboard.

She sipped a Diet Coke, looked out the window at the dusky sky and thought about her day at the beach with Hoff. She wondered why she felt the bothersome sadness. In a season of unhappiness brought on by her father's death, this new sadness felt different.

Hoff's Sister Cathedra idea scared her although his argument about the name as an effective marketing tool made sense. After all, Leeandra thought, his idea to start the television ministry had turned out to be very successful. She believed him when he said he cared about her and the others, but his reference to "product" was an unsettling insight.

For reasons she could not define, taking over the Stevens Crusade under her own name didn't seem as imposing. She feared having to stand more alone as Sister Cathedra. Not totally alone, she knew, because Casper, Ken, Hoff and others would be with her.

Her thoughts zeroed in on Hoff. How close did he want to stand? How close did she want him? How much of her consternation was about the Sister Cathedra idea? How much was because of her growing feelings for this dark-eyed, easy-smiling, attractive man with such expressive, unusual eyebrows? She wished she could talk to her father. Not being able to was another detail in her mounting recognition of the enormity of his absence.

The ball of heavy feelings inside grew as she confessed to herself: for the first time since her husband's death, she was interested in a man. Right now, she felt lonely because that man wasn't with her.

Margo Time

When Hoff got to Houston, he called Margo. She was home and he accepted her offer to heat up leftover lasagna. He was so quiet during dinner at her apartment that after she cleared the dishes, she asked, "Is anything wrong?"

"Yes, but you can make things right." He turned out the lights, leaving a single candle burning on the dining table. He sat on the couch. When she joined him, he put his arm around her and held her close for several minutes. He made no move to fondle or arouse her.

"Hoff," she said, barely above a whisper. "Are you sure nothing is wrong?"

"Shhhhhhhhh. I just want to sit here and hold you close."

Chapter 11

Pre-Biconjugation Meditation

Dr. Henry Woods locked the door to the parking lot from his Centrum Church study thirty minutes after the Wednesday night service ended. He enjoyed being alone in the rambling structure at night. He liked the physical reminder that under his leadership, the congregation had grown from a handful to over three thousand in twelve years. His visitors were due to arrive in an hour. He wanted this time to think about the idea that popped into his head minutes after he learned of Joe Ted's death. Dr. Woods wanted to join forces with the Stevens Crusade. He felt compelled to move quickly, before decisions were made about who would carry on the ministry.

"The Stevenses need me," he had said aloud to himself after Joe Ted's death. "I am the perfect addition to their team. Yes. Leeandra is the perfect addition to mine. Together, we would be abundantly powerful."

He wanted to preach in the Stevens Crusade because of its growing television network. Leeandra's singing would strengthen Centrum Church's radio programming. Unaddressed was how Leeandra would have time to do anything in addition to her role in the Stevens services.

His thoughts about Leeandra inevitably focused on her beauty. At Joe Ted's funeral, she was surprised to see him, but friendly. She seemed to enjoy his presence. He enjoyed being with her and relished touching her, always in a sympathetic, circumspect way.

Now, as he sat in an upholstered black leather chair on the visitors' side of his desk, he thought that more than anything, he wanted to be with Leeandra. She was sixteen years younger than he. He realized she was unlikely to find him physically attractive, but they shared a love of God and God's work. He was on the way to making himself believe Leeandra could, given the opportunity, love him physically as well as in the context of their shared evangelism. Given time, she would appreciate his contributions to her personal life as well as to the ministry. He slumped in the chair and rested his head against the soft leather back.

His musings about Leeandra continued until he jumped, startled by a loud knock on the study's door. Moving swiftly, he admitted Madelyn and Cuddles, the same prostitute friend Madelyn brought the only other time he insisted they come to the church because he was in the mood for "biblical biconjugation". Within minutes, Dr. Woods, Madelyn, who cooingly called him Woodsey, and the curvaceous, milk-white Cuddles were naked in the baptismal pool, enjoying its soothingly warm water.

Votes for Sister Cathedra

"Instead of Dine-A'Lite, it ought to be ding-a-ling," Hoff said.

On Tuesday after his walk on the beach with Leeandra, Hoff met with Andy Boxx in Dallas about a new franchise food proposition. Andy was considering a low-calorie, health appeal concept called Dine-A'Lite.

"People are always going to eat," Andy said.

"True," Hoff answered. "The question is what they'll eat, where and how much will they pay?"

"Shit fire, I know all that," Andy grumped. "This health kick has people eating sissy food, even me. I think we ought to buy the master franchise for the whole state."

Both glanced up when the secretary in Andy's office handed a note to Hoff.

"I'll take the call here." Hoff looked at Andy. "Leeandra Stevens. Shouldn't take but a minute." Hoff answered on the first ring.

"This isn't why I called," Leeandra said, "but I wanted to tell you again that I enjoyed our time together at the beach."

Hoff smiled. "I did, too. That would've been reason enough ."

"I guess so." Leeandra paused. When she continued, her voice was flat. The moments-before songful lilt was gone. "Ken, Casper and I agree that Sister Cathedra is the way to go."

"You sound as if you still have doubts."

"At this moment I do, but I am getting used to the idea. Part of me likes it. Part of me doesn't. All in all, I like it more than I don't. As you already know, I can be a little slow to accept change. I think it would be a mistake to delay or not do it because I'm a slow poke."

"Okay. We'll start implementing the change."

"I'm late for a meeting with a group of pastors, so I need to run. Maybe we can talk more about it tomorrow."

"Understand that I don't want you to go along with the Sister Cathedra name to appease me or anyone else."

"I'm not."

After good-byes, he hung up and stared at the phone for several seconds.

"What did the good-looking Miss Preacher have to say?"

Hoff told him.

"Looks like you're off to the races, taking her to the big time."

"That's where she belongs."

Andy rubbed the flaking top of his right ear. "I don't mean to sound like a wimp, but I think you're pushing the girl too fast."

"In the first place, she's not a girl. She's thirty years old. Nobody makes her do anything she doesn't want to."

"That may or may not be a lot of crap. Has it occurred to you she may not know what she wants? Her nest is severely unfeathered. Hell's bells, her daddy just died. That can knock the props out from under anybody."

"What is this, the Andrew Boxx chapter of the protect Leeandra Stevens society?" Hoff was irked and it showed.

"No, it's not." Andy spoke with a quiet, firm tone. "It's the voice of experience. You're dealing with people here, not warranty deeds or chicken sandwiches on an oat bran bun. I don't jack people around, never have."

"I don't either."

"I'm not saying you do. I am saying you have a volatile mix here— religion and people, mostly young people. You've got a good-looking woman involved." Andy smiled. "And you with a hard on better than half the time. I'm not running on you, Hoff. I am asking you to be careful."

"Just because she's good-looking is no reason to think she's some kind of hare brain. A bright mind doesn't have to be packaged in ugly, you know." Hoff reached for the carafe on the table and poured himself a cup of coffee. "Want some?"

Andy shook his head. "When we first talked about this deal, I brought up the question of doing right by these folks. That's still important. I want to make sure we're not misusing them."

"Don't you think I feel the same way?"

"I hope so."

"Rest assured I do," Hoff said. "I'm fully aware of the difference between people and chicken sandwiches. I don't want to do anything that will gore their ox. I like these people."

"Leeandra more than the others?"

Hoff smiled. "Yes, dammit, Leeandra more than the others."

"That computes." Andy laughed. "I'm beginning to think I ought to meet Leeandra. I'd like to tell people I knew her before she walked on the goddam water."

"You'd better get yourself grounded real good. You're going to get struck by lightning some day as sure as dogs bark."

"Could be. For right now, though, I'm alive and well, one hell of a lot more than you can say for these preachers that're getting their lights put out. I saw on the news that another one got whacked in Tampa. What do you make of all that?"

"There's no doubt in my mind that the killings are related," Hoff said. "Ken Walker is taking a close look at security arrangements around the Stevens' tent."

"Good move. Those preacher killings smack of some lunatic that got off the leash. Damned if I don't think the loonies are breeding faster than rabbits."

Before leaving Andy's office, Hoff called Banner Tatum. "How about using your Florida contacts to check out that latest preacher killing in Tampa. I'm wondering if we should take precautions."

Might There Be a Second Time?

Hoff ordered coffee and raspberries for dessert, and looked across the table at Margo. "Like old times, isn't it?"

"Yes," Margo answered with the hint of a smile. "You've always known how to order. My lobster was delicious."

They were in Vincent's Restaurant on Midway Road in Dallas. She was delighted when he invited her to make the trip with him. While he met with Andy, she shopped, using Hoff's credit cards.

"You're right," she added. "It does seem like old times. Old and very good times."

Hoff looked at Margo for a moment. "I haven't pressed you on this, but I've got to know. Why did you leave me?"

Margo took a quick breath, and a smile flashed across her face, but was gone by the time she answered. "I've asked myself that question a million times."

"How did you answer yourself?"

Margo lifted her eyebrows, crinkling her forehead, and took a slow, deep breath. "I'm afraid I never came up with a very good answer." She paused and added quietly, "No answer at all." Her eyes were instantly awash with tears as if an emotional dam had collapsed. Tears streaked her cheeks and she looked away.

Hoff felt knotted inside. He hated to make her cry. "I haven't brought this up to be ugly," he said softly. "I need a way to understand."

"I know." Margo's voice squeaked. The tears stopped and she smiled. "Excuse me for a minute, will you? I'll go put myself back together."

Hoff stood as she left the table. He watched her cross the dining room as did almost every other male in the restaurant. Margo the Magnificent. If anything, she was more magnificent than ever.

The waiter served the raspberries and poured more coffee. When Margo returned to the table, Hoff stood to seat her. The tears' damage to her makeup was repaired. She wore less makeup now than when she was a flight attendant, a difference he liked.

They ate dessert in silence.

"Could we wait until we get back to the hotel to finish our talk?" she asked. "For some reason, I feel conspicuous here."

On the way to the hotel, Hoff bought a six pack of beer.

"Make love to me, Hoff," Margo demanded the minute they got back to their room. Her voice was a quavering, breathy imperative as she embraced him with a clutching hug.

Hoff had intended to finish the conversation, but he couldn't resist Margo's heated invitation.

Their love making lasted for almost an hour. As they lay naked and satiated, sipping a beer, she talked. "I've thought a lot about why I left you. You and me, our trips, the fun, the sex—all such perfect times. Being pregnant with your baby was better than perfect, if that's possible." She paused. "Then, the miscarriage. I felt like I'd failed you. For some reason, I got to thinking that being married to you was too good to be true. That it wouldn't last. You were so perfect. You still are, for that matter. I couldn't figure why you would stay with me. You could have any woman you wanted. I ended up convincing myself that you wouldn't stay with me. It seems like I've always expected to fail, have always looked for a place to land when I bail out. It was a classic case of self-fulfilling prophecy."

After a moment, he said, "I really did love you, you know."

"I know," she squeaked. Her tears were back.

Hoff hugged her closer.

"God, I wish I had a better answer." Margo cried hard for a minute, then added, "I wish I had it to do over."

"Is that why you came back?"

Margo sniffed and wiped away the tears with the edge of the sheet. "Probably." She took a deep breath. "Yes."

He was quiet for a long time, then he smiled at her.

"Do you think there might be a second time around for us?"

Again, he was quiet for several seconds. "I really don't know. I guess we've got to decide that, don't we?"

She twisted the long, black hair on his chest and answered, "I guess so." Slowly, she moved her hand down his stomach. In minutes, Margo's fellatio fantastico had coaxed rigid life back into his flaccid penis.

Chapter 12

The Worshipful Henry Woods

Leeandra was glad to get to her hotel room after the evening's service, the last during this trip to Corpus Christi. Physically and mentally spent, she was drinking a glass of water when she heard the knock. As always, Billy Dean Smith, road manager for the Stevens Crusade, had escorted Leeandra to her room. She wondered if he had forgotten to tell her something. She stepped to the door. "Yes?"

"Leeandra, this is Henry Woods from Austin. May I see you?"

A tidal bore of unpleasant surprise heaved through her. She frowned through the peep hole. Dr. Woods peered directly at the hole, hands in the side pockets of his lime green sports jacket. The nose on his pudgy face jutted out bulbously in the distortion caused by the wide-angle lens.

"It's important that I talk to you." His penetrating voice made him sound as if the door didn't exist.

She hesitated before she unhooked the safety chain, twisted the dead bolt and opened the door. "I had no idea you were in Corpus."

"May I come in? I won't stay long." A lifeless grin clung to his lips.

Leeandra stepped back from the door. "Come in."

Dr. Woods closed the door behind him. She motioned him to one of the side chairs near the king-sized bed. She sat at the dresser.

He took out his handkerchief to daub beads of sweat from his forehead. His smile was forced and discomfiting. "I've talked to Ken Walker about this, but I felt led by the Lord—no, compelled—to talk to you. Tonight." His smile glowed and faded like a lamp with a short circuit. "Has Ken talked to you about my proposal to combine our ministries?"

"Yes." Leeandra was already sorry she let him in. His nervousness was contagious. She knew that Ken had tried to refuse the merger suggestion diplomatically.

"To tell you the truth, I feel unduly put off by Ken. He hasn't been responsive, not even to my invitation to have you sing again at my church." A spasm of wincing blinks interrupted him. "Your ministry in song is so powerful. Yes, so powerful. I would like for you to use Centrum as your home church. It is ideal for producing the television programs. Yes. Now that your beloved father is gone, I sense you need someone to share the preaching load. Heading up a large ministry is a mighty task." Dr. Woods sat forward on the edge of his chair. "You have a special commission from God. Yes, a special talent. I was at your service tonight. I saw God working through you."

"I didn't see you."

"I arrived late, had to stand outside. God has ordained you to be His special messenger. With our facilities at Centrum, better use can be made of your talents. I can spare you the burden of having to conduct every service yourself."

Leeandra stared at Dr. Woods, at the fatuous expression on his face. How could she feel so suspicious of and repelled by a fellow preacher of the gospel? "I'm flattered. I'm also very tired right now." She laughed softly and brushed strands of hair away from her face. "You've caught me completely off guard."

"Yes, I see that. I apologize." He spoke in a rush, accompanied by a flutter of exaggerated blinks. Exhales of breath whooshed out with the words. "I do apologize. Yes. But God has directed me to speak with you. Tonight. I need only a few minutes."

"Surely you'll be spending the night in Corpus. Casper, Billy Dean and I can meet with you at breakfast before we leave for Victoria."

"I appreciate that. Yes. But I was hoping you'd see the value of my offer. Tonight. I hope to persuade you to see the impact we could have by collaborating." Dr. Woods blotted away more perspiration with his wadded handkerchief. Beads of sweat dappled the top of his balding head.

Leeandra wondered why he was perspiring. The room was cool. He looked fatter than she remembered at her father's funeral. His flustered, beseeching behavior was at odds with the self-assured, in-control demeanor she saw when he appeared unexpectedly at Joe Ted's services. "I can't decide something like this on my own," she said. "We just don't operate that way."

"Leeandra, the Stevens Crusade is nothing without you. Absolutely nothing. You can decide anything you want, by yourself." Dr. Woods' labored blinking seemed to absorb all of his energy and he paused. "You are the one with control. You are in power."

"No, it's not like that with us. We're a family, a team."

"You are the central force of this ministry." He tried to smile as he talked. All he accomplished was to bare his small, white teeth. "God ordained you, not them. Yes. He empowered you."

She did not hesitate. "Thank you, but...."

"Don't say no! Not yet. Just...."

"I'm only telling you I would never presume to make such a decision alone," Leeandra said firmly. She stared at him. A clutching urgency seemed to fuel his bursts of breathy speech. He was the image of a man on the verge of panic. Why?

"How can I convince you that this is God's will?" His voice was stridently high pitched, his face awash in perspiration.

She took a deep breath. "Again, I'm flattered, but I will not decide anything...." Her mouth popped open with surprise as Dr. Woods dropped out of his chair onto his knees.

"Please, my dear Leeandra, I beg of you." He inched forward on his knees, labored breaths whistling in and out. "God directs me to prostrate myself before you."

Her eyes widened with alarm as Dr. Woods fell face down on the floor, extended his arms and grasped both of her feet with his hands. A clinching mix of fear and surprise paralyzed her.

His face pressed against the beige carpet, he continued in a burbling voice. "I succumb to God's will and to you, dearest Leeandra. Yes. I am but a clod of inconsequence before you." He pulled up on all fours, then straightened and knee-walked until he was close enough to grasp her knees with his fat-fingered hands. "I beseech you to hear me out."

She felt the heat from his hands through her skirt. She took a deep breath, trying to calm herself, fighting back the urge to wrench free and run for the door.

His face was contorted. "It is God's will, can't you see that?"

"Stop it!" She spat the words. Anger boiled off her fear as she hissed, "Get you hands off me!"

He jerked his hands away.

"You will leave my room! Now!"

On his knees, he sank back on his haunches and drew his clasped hands to his chin. His face twisted as he cried soundlessly. Tears spilled from his wincing eyes to mix with the trickles of sweat on his face. "No, please, no," he whined. "Don't send me away. Let me stay with you. I've come to worship you. Yes. Worship you."

He flinched as she stood. Before she could take a step, he lunged and wrapped his arms around her ankles, his face against the carpet between her feet. He cried in convulsing, raspy sobs. "Dear God, help me. Help me, dear beautiful Leeandra. Yes. I am your servant." Slowly, he released his hold.

She stepped away and stared aghast at the pitiful spectacle of Dr. Henry Jackson Woods, face down on the floor, his body heaving. The sparse hair strands combed across his balding head were plastered by perspiration. His rumpled jacket looked as if he had worn it for days.

"Dr. Woods." She waited for a moment. "Dr. Woods!" She almost shouted his name.

With inching slowness, he looked up. Sweat darkened his white shirt collar and the knot of his yellow paisley tie.

"If you do not leave my room right now, I'll call the police." She glared at him. "Leave this instant!"

"Have you no mercy?" His voice was barely audible. On his hands and knees, he continued to look up at her. "No mercy?"

"Yes, I have mercy," she answered, her anger yielding to pity. "But you must leave." When he didn't respond, she added, "Now."

He made no move other than to look down at the floor.

She strode to the door and yanked it open noisily. "You have two seconds to get out of here!" Her anger was rekindling.

Dr. Woods' face was a humiliated blank as he struggled to his feet with a wheezing effort and shuffled toward the door.

"I'm sorry," he mumbled. He stopped two feet from her. "Please. Would you not tell anyone about this?"

"You must go," she said softly. "Now."

He looked down and plodded out.

She slammed the door, twisted the dead bolt, latched the safety chain and peered through the peep hole. Dr. Woods stood for several seconds with his back to the door, then shambled out of view.

Shaking, Leeandra slumped against the door, feeling its cool surface with her hot, flushed cheek. After a few seconds, she rushed for the phone, traced her finger down the emergency call list Billy Dean always made sure was there and dialed Hoff's home number. She fidgeted as it rang. "Answer the phone," she breathed on the third ring. When Hoff's answering machine clicked on, she hung up, sat down on the bed and dialed Billy Dean's room number.

"Hi," the road manager answered cheerfully.

"I'm sorry to bother you. Everything's okay and he's gone, now, but an unsettling thing has happened." Leeandra told him about Dr. Woods' visit. "Could you come baby-sit me for a little while? Until I calm down? And would you bring me a Diet Coke?"

Nearer My Prod to Thee

"Public reaction is overwhelmingly in favor of Sister Cathedra," Hoff told Andy. On Monday, March 27th, the day after the first weekend of Sister Cathedra broadcasts, Hoff talked through a smile, his feet propped on his credenza. As he spoke into the phone, he watched the freeway traffic fifteen floors below his office. "Ken Walker says calls are running a hundred-to-one on the positive side. You really ought to watch her."

"I invested in the deal, but damned if I'm going to watch her on the tube. I'm keeping some folks waiting. Are you finished?"

"Yes."

Andy hung up. Hoff smiled as he listened to the dial tone for a moment before Gracie announced Banner Tatum was on line two. Seconds later, Hoff sat impassively listening to the private investigator's report.

"Henry Woods is not a graduate of Georgia Seminary as he claims. I'd wager he's not a graduate of anywhere. But, that's small potatoes. The district attorney in Austin has begun an investigation of Woods for misapplication of church funds."

"Bingo," Hoff said.

"You haven't heard the juicy stuff, yet." Banner began to laugh.

"What's so funny?"

"This big cheese preacher person has a thing for whores. He consorts with hookers in Austin regularly, two at a time on occasion. It's not because he's doing missionary work, either, although I'd wager he gets into the missionary position with them."

"How...."

"You have to hear this next bit," Banner said, his voice wavering as he struggled to keep from laughing. "A couple of times, Woods had two hookers meet him at his church late at night. Can you believe it? He bonked them right in the sanctuary, up on the stage. He pranced around naked singing lewd takeoffs on hymns." Banner laughed for several seconds. "'Nearer my prod to thee. Shall we gather with a rubber.' I've been around for a long time, but I've never heard anything like this."

"Are you sure of all this?" Hoff asked.

"I'm sure. I tailed Woods to a porno movie motel—Motel 69 no less—on Austin's south side, a long way from his church. He picked up a rent car near the Austin airport, then met a hooker named Madelyn at the motel. When they finished, I followed her. It cost me a hundred finely-engraved portraits of Jackson to get her to talk, but talk she did and I've got it on tape."

"You paid her in twenties?"

"Yeah. Lucky I had my walking around stash up to snuff. As you might imagine, she had no interest in taking American Express. Or anything bigger than twenties. Madelyn has street smarts. She made sure my payoff was in circulated bills, no consecutive serial numbers."

"Why did she rat on him?"

"Two thousand bucks didn't hurt. She told me she wants to move to California. She has a sister living out there. Two grand will get her there in style."

"Good work. Anything else?"

"Isn't that enough?"

"Probably," Hoff answered. "But I want the whole story."

"There's nothing else on the down side. Woods is married, but his wife doesn't play a role in the church or his life. She's a real house mouse. My gut feel is she may be afflicted in some way. I don't know what you'll do with this info, but you need to know that Woodsey—

Madelyn said she called him Woodsey sometimes—has a pot full of fans in Austin. Damned near everybody I talked to thinks he hung the moon."

"How so?"

"What you'd expect. Good preacher. Good at raising money for the church, which he's built from scratch. In fact, he does some neat stuff. He has prayer breakfasts for street people, serves them coffee and doughnuts. The church distributes food and gifts to the needy during the holidays. The guy isn't all bad."

"He's bad enough. Send me the bill. Will you take a check or do I have to send well-worn twenties?"

"Send dimes for all I care."

"You'd shit if I sent you two thousand dollars in dimes."

"No sirreeeee. I might herniate myself lugging them to the bank, but I'd be glad to get them. Do you want a copy of my conversation with Madelyn?"

"Nah. Might give me some strange, new ideas. I've got enough vices." Hoff paused. "There is one other thing. Woods dropped in on Leeandra in Corpus Christi last week, begging her to take him into the Stevens Crusade. He acted crazy as a loon, spooked the hell out of her. I want him to know that we know about the DA's investigation, the hookers and so forth. I also want him to understand that he is not to contact Ken Walker, Leeandra—not anyone in the Stevens organization except me. If he does, we'll call a news conference on the steps of his very own church and play that tape of your conversation with Madelyn. Would you do the honors?"

"Okey-doke."

"Perhaps you should give him a spiffy little cassette player. Make sure batteries and a tape of your conversation with his little playmate are included."

"Nice touch," Banner said. "I'll deliver it in person."

"And pronto-like," Hoff said.

"I'll do it tomorrow. I've got something else," Banner said. "Remember you asked me to keep my ear to the ground on this string of preacher killings? I've got a first cousin who's a detective in the Miami Police Department. He tells me the Tampa police have tied all murders to one perpetrator."

"Who?"

"A John Beckman from Joplin, Missouri," Banner answered, "but it's a bogus name. More than likely, the shooter gets his I.D. from a counterfeiter. A cop may get lucky and recognize the counterfeiter's modus operandi. Or, a snitch might come forward. The Tampa cops put out the word they'll pay for good information. It's a long shot, but that's what they've got to work on right now."

"Not much, is it? Keep me posted, will you?"

"When I know something, you'll know it."

"As always, I appreciate the good work." Hoff hung up, smiled at the thought of Banner delivering the tape to Dr. Woods, and thought, it's fun to play dirty once in a while.

He called Ken Walker and told him only about Dr. Woods' seminary misrepresentation and the district attorney's investigation. "I'm taking steps to discourage Woods from contacting you or Leeandra in the future."

"Oh?" Ken responded. "What kind of steps?"

"They're not things you're accustomed to. Would you be offended if I suggest you don't really want to know?"

Cosmic Princes and Public Relations

"The ides of agony," Hoff said to Larry Best as he hung up the telephone. "Sorry to keep you waiting. The accountants are working on my tax return and had questions."

"I truly love income tax filing time," Larry said. "About like I love standing in a fire ant bed while I'm having a root canal."

Hoff laughed. "You're dressed to the nines today. What gives?"

Larry adjusted the lapels of his dark gray suit with an exaggerated tug. "Big meeting with our airline client on a twenty million dollar ad campaign. That, my friend, is suit-and-tie time."

"Looks as if Ott fixed you up with a dandy set of rags."

Ott was the nickname Hoff and Larry used for Omar The Tailor. Omar Bubar-Shar was blond, spoke accent-free English and refused to say where he was from. When Hoff asked about his background, Omar answered, "I was a cosmic prince, transmogrified to Earth as a tailor to help would-be princes look their best. Interesting, don't you think?" Omar had not smiled.

Larry launched into his report on Leeandra's second *Gospel Music Showcase* appearance. She got rave reviews and would be invited back. The new public relations agency helped generate widespread media coverage of her appearance. Larry showed Hoff clippings from the *Miami Herald* and *USA Today*.

Hoff noticed the PR/America stamp at the top of each clipping. "George makes sure you know where these come from, doesn't he?"

"It's all part of selling his service," Larry responded. "He's doing a damned good job."

Hoff thought George Lee, general manager of Public Relations Agency of America's Houston office, was a windbag, but he was delivering media coverage for Sister Cathedra. Contributions were up by more than fifty thousand dollars per week since adoption of the new name. Hoff had decided to add another dozen cities to the television network. After this expansion, the program would be aired in forty-one markets.

"We need a talent agent for Leeandra." Hoff looked out the window at the clear, early April sky. "I want to get her booked on non-religious programs to increase her exposure, help ring the cash register. Between you and George, can we find a top-notch agency to represent her?"

"We can try. Leeandra's a big fish in our pond, but she's an entertainment unknown."

"All the more reason to hire expert help. Convert unknown into known. Will you chase that rabbit?"

"Yep." Larry glanced at his watch. "I got to go talk about getting twenty million bucks worth of airline advertising off the ground. Up in the air, junior adman," he sang, then laughed. "Yes, I know, what you said. Keep my daytime job. Do you see Leeandra today?"

Leeandra was in Houston for a video taping session to update television commercials by adding more Sister Cathedra emphasis.

"I'll see her late this afternoon," Hoff said.

Larry headed for the office door. "Tell her hello for me."

Gracie stood outside Hoff's office with her "I need your attention" pose. "Margo is holding, has been for five minutes."

"How are things between you and Margo?" Larry asked.

"Okay."

"Life can be grand when it comes to dealing with ex-wives."

"Grandly complicated." Hoff waved good-bye to Larry and returned to his desk. He picked up the phone, pushed the blinking button and said, "Are you naked?"

Margo laughed. "No."

"Too bad. I thought we could talk dirty."

"We can. Come over and we'll do it in person."

"No can do," Hoff said. "I've got a busy afternoon."

"How about tonight?"

"I've got a client in town tonight."

"I want to talk," Margo said, the levity gone from her voice.

Hoff hesitated. "About St. Thomas?"

"Yes."

"Has he given you a deadline?" Hoff knew that Margo's lawyer friend had called three days ago from Miami while on a business trip. Margo said he mentioned marriage, even though she declined his request to return to St. Thomas with him.

"No deadline. But I do owe him an answer. I owe me one, too."

Hoff recognized her dilemma. She didn't want to risk losing the option of rejoining her attorney friend in St. Thomas. His patience might be wearing thin. "What do you want to do?"

"I'd rather talk about this in person."

"Me, too, but I'll be tied up till tomorrow. Can it wait till then?"

"I guess it'll have to."

They agreed on a seven o'clock dinner date the next evening.

Magic Bowl of Chili

Hoff steered his Town Car into the parking lot next to the two-story red brick warehouse that was home for Bayou Bottom Studio. It was one of several TV and movie production companies located on the east edge of downtown. The dashboard clock read 5:53 as Hoff turned off the engine.

After a quick look at rough edits of two updated TV commercials, Hoff and Leeandra left the studio. As they walked toward the car, Hoff asked, "Do you ever carry a handbag?"

"Hardly ever. Why do you ask?"

"It's one of the first things I noticed about you."

"In school, I always carried scads of books and heaven knows what. After I had children, I lugged around diaper bags and everything else. When I got active in the crusade, I decided to quit carrying stuff. When you move around as much as we do, you learn to travel light." Leeandra smiled. "Short question, long answer."

After they got into the car, he asked, "How about a short tour around town and then we'll grab something to eat?"

"Suits me, but remember, dinner is on me tonight."

Hoff drove through downtown and the posh River Oaks neighborhood. He pointed out the sights, then headed toward the Galleria area. "Can you stand seeing one more thing before we eat? I want you to see the water wall next to Transco Tower." In minutes they were there and parked. Holding her elbow, he guided her toward the curved water wall with its three arched entries.

"Let's go up close," he said. They stopped ten feet from the face of the brightly-illuminated, three-story-tall cascade.

"I've never seen anything like this," Leeandra said.

"Step closer." He led her to a spot in the middle of the arc formed by the water wall, only five feet from the flow. "Look straight ahead."

She slipped her arm inside his. "I feel like I'm going up on an elevator." She was quiet for several seconds. "The water looks like flowing, white light. It's beautiful."

"I'm glad you like it."

"I love it, but I'm getting wet."

They stepped back out of the spray, through the middle arch and strolled down onto a long, recessed grassy area. When they got to level ground, she withdrew her arm. They walked to the end of the five-acre lawn and looked at the water.

Leeandra clasped her arms across her chest.

"Too cool?" he asked. He slipped off his suit coat and draped it over her shoulders. One hand lingered at the base of her neck.

A tiny smile lit her face. "Somebody raised you right. Your good manners come naturally. I noticed that in Amarillo when we went to the supermarket."

"I enjoy impressing a beautiful lady." Hoff savored the quiet caring nestled in her eyes. He felt her tremble and pulled her closer. "I believe the time has come to see if my manners can hold up over dinner. Hungry?"

"Yes. I haven't eaten since breakfast."

She took off the suit coat and handed it to him when they got to his car. As he started the engine, he said, "What sounds good?"

"Something simple."

"How simple? Hamburger? Salad bar? Hot dogs and chili?"

She laughed. "Hot dogs and chili? I can't remember the last time I had that."

"Then I know the place. James Coney Island. It gets five stars in the Jerome K. Hoffstedtler good eats guide."

"Let's go. My mouth's watering. By the way, what does the 'K' stand for?...Your middle initial."

"Oh. It stands for King."

"Appropriate," Leeandra said and they both laughed.

At her request, Hoff walked ahead in the cafeteria-style serving line. Each got a bowl of chili, two hot dogs and corn chips. As they neared the drink station, he turned to her. "Remember my telling you that I can't eat shrimp without a beer? Same goes for hot dogs and chili." He ordered a Coors Light. She asked for iced tea.

When they got to the cash register, Hoff said to the attendant, "My purseless lady friend is paying tonight." He nodded toward Leeandra and added, "I think."

She looked at him coyly, head tilted a fraction. "Now, Mr. Hoffstedtler, I bet you think I don't have any money with me, don't you?"

"The thought crossed my mind. But you said dinner is on you."

She reached into the side pocket of her dress. With a flourish, she produced a sheaf of folded twenty dollar bills. "Ta-dah!"

Hoff laughed. "Touché." He stepped aside to let her pay.

They sat at one of the white, plastic-topped tables. She slumped in her chair and let out a long sigh. He asked, "Tired?"

"Sort of. I've been run ragged with meetings, appointments, you name it. I'm glad to have a night off," she said.

"Ken and I've discussed cutting down on tent services."

"I hate to eliminate any services, but something has got to give." Leeandra took a bite of her hot dog. "Oh, boy, that's good!"

"Your reward for another hit performance on *Gospel Music Showcase*," he said.

"Nice reward."

"There's been lots of good media coverage on your performance."

"It seems strange to read things in the newspapers about myself. I still have a hard time believing it's me they're talking about."

"You make a good Sister Cathedra."

"At times, Sister Cathedra still sounds a little highfalutin."

"Have you had comments to that effect?"

"No. A few people have told Ken they don't like the new name, but nobody has said it to me. People tell me it is pretty, sounds important."

"Fits you well."

A smile played across her face. "Still selling the idea?"

"Just an observation." He told her about the upcoming additions to the television network.

"I can't believe how fast the crusade is growing," she said.

"Thanks to you."

"Not entirely. But I do realize I have a role as God's messenger." She smiled. "I wish I could express the difference I feel when I sing or preach in a service. I'm a different person, not at all like who's sitting here eating a hot dog with you."

"I've seen the difference."

"During a service, I feel as if God is right there on stage with me. The music and the words flow out so effortlessly, but with so much energy." She laughed. "I made that statement to Casper and he told me I was making myself out to be a ventriloquist's dummy."

Hoff thought a remark about a dummy coming from Casper was appropriate. Instead of voicing his opinion, he said, "You're having a big impact, that's for sure."

A customer asked if he could take one of the chairs away from their table. Hoff nodded assent, then turned to Leeandra. "I've meant to ask this for the longest time. Why do you always have four chairs on the stage? Even when only you and Casper are up there?"

She told him about Joe Ted's insistence on having a chair on stage in memory of his wife. "Now, we have chairs for both of them."

"I wondered about that the first time I saw you in Sweetwater."

"So much has happened since." She sounded pensive. "Some good, some not so good. Thanks for having confidence in me when I didn't have it in myself. Sometimes I think this is all a dream."

"Success feels good, doesn't it?"

"It's a confusing kind of good, hard to come to grips with. All in all, you're right. And I have the feeling more is on the way."

"Me, too." He told her his plan to hire a talent agent. "I'm thinking about a big crusade in early fall in the Astrodome."

Leeandra's eyes widened. "Are you serious?"

"Absolutely. By fall, I think we'll need a major event to maintain momentum. The worst thing we can do is not look ahead. A major crusade service will also be an opportunity to produce a TV special."

In an eye blink, the happy, inquiring expression on her face was gone, replaced by distant thoughtfulness. With a quick shake of her head, Leeandra said, "This is amazing!"

She told him about her dream after their meeting in Austin when he broached the subject of putting the Stevenses on television. "What's amazing is the similarity between my dream about a covered football stadium with TV cameras and your idea to have a service in the Astrodome. In the dream, Daddy introduced me with a different name. Now, I'm being called Sister Cathedra."

"Joe Ted didn't call you that in the dream, did he?"

"No. I couldn't remember the name he used. What kind of television special are you thinking about?"

"I don't know. The thought just popped into my head."

Leeandra laughed. "You really are a mile-a-minute sort."

"It's a mile-a-minute world."

"It's turning into that for me." She took a slow, deep breath. "At times I wish for the old days before we went on TV."

"Those days aren't all that old. Less than six months have passed since we first talked about the television proposal. I believe you're more adaptive than you think."

"Maybe." Leeandra glanced at her watch, did a double take and said, "It's ten o'clock!"

Hoff checked his own watch. "Sure as hell is." He grimaced. "Oops."

She smiled impishly. "Forgive him, Lord, for he knows not what he says." She pushed up her left sleeve and began unbuckling the watch band. "I'm glad I remembered. Here's the watch you lent me in Corpus."

"It was a gift. Keep it."

"Daddy told me never to accept gifts from strange men."

"Strange men!" Hoff exclaimed. "Strange as in odd or strange as in you don't know them?"

Leeandra blushed. "I don't know why I said that. Erase it."

"Strange men!" he said with mock disgust. He took the watch and put it in his suit coat pocket.

"Save it so you can bail me out the next time I forget mine." She smiled. "And by no means are you strange. In either sense."

Hoff smiled back. "I take that to be good news."

A wistful light shone in her eyes. "I've got to go. I have an eight o'clock flight to Dallas tomorrow. We have a big meeting with one of the congregations we work with in Grand Prairie."

"Got another minute for me to tell you something?"

Her round blue eyes bore a savoring expression. "Yes."

"It's been a long time since I've met somebody as...as distinctive as you. I see a complexity that's hard to figure out. There's a complexity in my feelings about you that's hard to figure out. You're special. My feelings for you are becoming...."

"I can say the same."

"I don't know exactly what my feelings are." He scuffed the label off the empty beer bottle with his thumb nail. "They change. I feel a genuine affection for you, sometimes in a brotherly way, sometimes in a not-so-brotherly way. Sometimes in a way friends feel." Hoff paused. "I've always tried to keep business and personal matters separate. But my feelings for you seem to be headed in the personal direction. I guess...well, I wanted you to know." He shrugged. "End of bumbling statement."

She brushed a strand of hair from her cheek. "That's sweet of you. Thanks." She hesitated. "I have sensed a change in your feelings for me. Just as I'm sure you've sensed a change in mine for you.... Haven't you?"

"Yes."

"I also admit to some uncertainty what my feelings are." She smiled. "But one thing is certain. This has been a fun, carefree evening—a nice, laughey time. I've enjoyed being Leeandra instead of Sister Cathedra."

"We were on the verge of a good time like this at the beach."

She nodded slowly.

"It took the truth serum in a pot of good chili to bring it out."

Hoff drove her to the hotel. He stopped in the driveway before reaching the entrance, took her hand and kissed her cheek. "It's been many moons since I've enjoyed being with someone the way I enjoy being with you. The next time you have a break in your schedule, I'd like to come see you and treat you to a bowl of chili."

"May I make a suggestion? Bring some from James Coney Island."

Sunrises, Sunsets

When Hoff got home, he loosened his tie, poured a Scotch and sat on the balcony of his condominium. Through that drink and another, he gazed at the city and tried to sort through his feelings for Margo and Leeandra.

When he was with Leeandra, he felt a fresh vitality. Not since his schoolboy days had he treated a female with such deference. Tonight, he'd felt timid at times, almost as timid as when he was in the car with Patricia Lee Burnett. With Pat, it was puppy love. With Leeandra it was...what? What is it about Leeandra that makes her so different?

And Margo? Learning to trust her again continued to be a problem. Loving her again as much as before would come easily when and if he let himself. From the tone of this morning's conversation, he knew the time to decide was near. He didn't like having a deadline. Margo the Magnificent. He smiled. She could be so inventively erotic. Most of the time, he thought of her only in a physical sense, but she possessed a sweetness he couldn't shrug off. She could be so completely childlike, playful and dependent. He was certain Margo still loved him. He sipped his Scotch and thought, I still love her.

When he thought of Leeandra, sunrises came to mind. For some reason, Margo elicited thoughts of sunsets.

Wishing for the Beach

At her hotel, Leeandra lay in bed, imagining a picnic lunch of chili and hot dogs on a clear, crisp day at the beach. She walked herself toward sleep, holding hands with Hoff, moseying along the edge of a gentle surf. The only time she stopped, the only time she turned loose of his hand, came when she found an intact sand dollar.

Decision Time at Shanghai Red's

"I'll fix something at my place," Margo offered.

"Dinner is on me tonight, so we're going out," Hoff answered. Left unsaid was his preference for having this encounter on neutral ground. He knew he could never think straight making love with Margo as they inevitably would if they ate dinner at her apartment.

Margo chattered as they drove to Shanghai Red's Restaurant on the Houston Ship Channel and as they ate. After dinner, Hoff ordered another beer and she ordered a Kahlua Alexander. He said, "We're here to decide about a second time around for us, are we not?"

"Yes." She looked somber. "I already know your answer....It's a good thing I like St. Thomas, isn't it?"

"What makes you so sure you know my answer?"

"Because we're here." She scrutinized him solemnly. "If you were close to saying, 'Margo, let's give it another go', we'd be at your place or mine right now, fucking our brains out. Right?"

He thought for several seconds before he said, "Yes."

Margo stared at the water, her eyes misty. She took a deep breath, blinked back tears and smiled. "But we still love each other, don't we?"

"Yes." He glanced at the water as he rubbed the hair on the back of his left hand. "When will you leave for St. Thomas?"

"In a couple of days. As soon as Gordon can arrange for my ticket."

"I'll take care of the ticket. No strings attached. I'll get the ticket to you tomorrow morning."

"Okay. You're being generous. Thanks."

When they left the restaurant, they walked to the car arm in arm. They held hands on the way to Margo's apartment, but said nothing. He was thankful she did not mention Leeandra.

"I've got a fifth of Boodles," she said at the door. "We haven't gotten tanked on gin together in a long time."

"God almighty," Hoff said. "Remember how drunk we got on gin that night in New Orleans?"

"Do I ever. You banged me standing up on Rampart Street."

Hoff chuckled. "What saved us from getting thrown in jail?"

"We were having too much fun."

"Lots of fun." He kissed Margo softly on the lips then hugged her tightly. "Good luck, magnificent one. I wish you well." Gently, he pushed her away and added, "I'll miss you."

"Come in for a little while?"

"I'd better not. Stay in touch?"

Margo nodded. As he turned to walk away, she murmured, "Good luck, preacher lady."

Hoff smiled as he walked to his car.

At his office the next day, Hoff told Gracie to arrange for Margo's ticket to St. Thomas. "Make it first class. She deserves that much."

"Did I hear correctly? One way?"

Hoff nodded.

"Ergo there go Margo," Gracie said quietly.

#

A week later, Hoff received a note from Margo. "Made it to St. Thomas. Flying first class was a treat. You've always known how to make me feel special. I love you. Margo." She printed her St. Thomas mailing address and telephone number at the bottom.

He wrote the information in his book, stared at the neatly printed entry and wondered if he would ever see her again.

Chapter 13

Sister Counterfeit

In the tiny town of Channing, Danny Don Rhodes scowled at the twenty-one inch television set occupying its place of honor atop the chest of drawers in his cramped room.

Fifteen minutes earlier, Leeandra's singing had calmed the bombarding confusion in his head. The mental storm erupted when Aunt Gertrude bawled him out for dropping the dish of sweet pickles on the floor after supper. Now, the roar was back, a storm of swooshing chaos.

Danny Don had scarcely believed his ears when Leeandra explained why she would henceforth be called Sister Cathedra.

With a snapping jerk of the remote control, he had turned the television set off and watched Leeandra shrink into a dot of white light that faded into nothing.

"Not good. Sister Ca....," he said angrily, unable to articulate the new name. Since the accident, he had trouble comprehending new words. His anger bloomed into seething agitation. He hated changes. Why couldn't things he liked stay the same?

He wondered what this would do to the beautiful, caring Leeandra. He knew in his heart that she was unlike those other beautiful women. She would never look away from him, would never stare. Not Leeandra with her pure, blue eyes and long blonde hair that must feel as soft as corn silk. Not the Leeandra whose voice was the calming Balm of Gilead.

But now she would be different. A different name. She's not Leeandra anymore. She's Sister Ca.... Goddam her filthy soul to hell! Who does she think she is? She has no right! She's Leeandra!

Danny Don shook with anger, his mind full of the furious, battering bedlam. He wanted to scream, to beat his fists on the bed. Instead, he sputtered aloud, "It's...it's not right! You're Leeandra! Leeandra, not Sister Ca...Sister Ca...." Tears filled his eyes. He hissed, "You are counterfeit, that's what you are! Sister Counterfeit!"

Fallout from Banner's Visit

"Boy, being a preacher, you sure do give a new meaning to that term 'laying on of hands.'" Cuddles, a prostitute Madelyn brought along for a "biconjugation" with Dr. Henry Woods, giggled at her own humor.

Dr. Woods thought Cuddles' tinny, high-pitched voice was unpleasant and he wished she would shut up. Cuddles habitually talked at inopportune times, like now when he preferred to think she would be stimulated by his ministrations. He massaged Cuddles' splendidly ample breasts while he nuzzled and licked the white, unblemished softness of her inner thighs. Neither he nor Cuddles paid attention to the television, showing a man and woman engaged in grinding, mechanical fornication.

This was the Austin preacher's second time with Cuddles, chosen to succeed Madelyn who left town unceremoniously without any effort to get in touch with him. Cuddles had said she thought Madelyn moved to Los Angeles, but she didn't know how to get in touch with her. He was not sure if Cuddles was telling the truth.

At the time of that conversation with Cuddles, Dr. Woods was at a loss to explain why Madelyn picked up and moved on such short notice. He had asked, "Is she in trouble?"

"Not her," Cuddles answered, "she's a straight shooter."

"Shootee is more like it," he grumbled, vexed by her departure and by his own inability to extract more information from Cuddles.

He had enjoyed a one-on-one afternoon with Madelyn eight days ago. The day was nothing special. He didn't sense anything was wrong. She was her usual, compliant self, seeming to enjoy the sex. He felt rejected by her sudden departure. She was more than a whore to him. He never felt a romantic attachment, but three years of sex, seldom less than once a week, fostered feelings of closeness. He always sensed she thought of him as more than a routine john. Now, she was gone, as if plucked from the face of the planet.

Last Friday, feeling the need for physical relief, Dr. Woods sought out Cuddles. He relieved himself, but the Madelyn-less sex was far from exciting, too coolly matter-of-fact to suit him. Cuddles required coaching on every move. She didn't let him kiss her on the mouth. Her grating, whinny-like voice was a supreme bother.

On Saturday, the man named Banner Tatum had paid his visit. After the shock of being discovered wore off, Dr. Woods felt rage.

His first torrent of anger was focused on Jerome Hoffstedtler for initiating the investigation by this slight, rude hooligan. Banner's evil, calculating smile bared his yellowing teeth during his brief visit to the Centrum Church study. The hooligan obviously enjoyed recounting the story of how Hoffstedtler scorched the left ear lobe of somebody named Bisqueen with the flame from a cigarette lighter. Banner laughed when he described Bisqueen's howls of pain as Hoffstedtler adroitly held the lighter in place despite Bisqueen's writhing efforts to escape. Such behavior was inhuman. Banner's story caused Dr. Woods to feel fear, and that fanned his ill temper. He remembered being introduced to Hoffstedtler at Joe Ted's funeral, but he recalled little about the man, only that he was tall with dark, probing eyes. At the time, Dr. Woods sensed malice in those eyes.

His second surge of wrath was aimed at Madelyn. Suddenly, he knew why she left without telling him. The mouth that sucked in countless shots of his semen spat out his secret in vivid detail into Banner Tatum's tape recorder.

Now, in room thirty at Motel 69, Dr. Woods felt totally uninspired, far from turned on by Cuddles, as delectable as her body was. The first time he saw her, he imagined she was a younger and chubbier Leeandra.

He loved to have a beautiful, naked woman on her back before him, legs open, available without qualification. The subservient posture usually made him feel in total control, stimulated him into a "blue steeler" erection. Not this afternoon. He could not focus on Cuddles' inviting nakedness. Madelyn's betrayal and Banner's visit preyed on his mind. Dr. Woods quit his nuzzling.

"Anything wrong?" Cuddles asked.

As he scooted backward off the bed, he resisted the urge to repeat her question in a mocking falsetto. He did not resist the explosion of fury. He stepped quickly to the luggage stand, snatched up his boxer shorts and put them on.

Cuddles watched. "What's wrong, honey?"

He pulled on the fire engine red golf shirt without answering and reached for his khaki pants.

"Did I do something wrong?" Her tone was quiet, eyes full of fear.

Dr. Woods jerked his belt tighter so he could buckle it, binding into the roll of fat around his middle. "You're all alike," he muttered with a flurry of exaggerated blinks.

His mind was crammed with thoughts of betrayal and rejection. Betrayal by Madelyn. Rejection of him personally by Leeandra. Betrayal of his long-protected secret. Rejection of his efforts to join forces with the Stevens Crusade. He plopped into the room's side chair and reached for his shoes in which he always tucked his socks.

"Bitches," he said, loud enough for Cuddles to hear.

"Why are you pissed off at me? I didn't do nothing."

Dr. Woods snapped to his feet and in three lunging steps, slapped the button to turn off the television set. Her eyes widened in alarm and she reached to pull the sheet over her. With catlike quickness, he snatched the sheet away. "You stay naked until I say otherwise. You're my whore!"

He returned to the chair and began putting on his left sock.

She stared at him. "I...."

"Shut up."

"Look, I don't know what...."

Before Cuddles could finish her sentence, he pounced on her and drove his left fist into her stomach. The blow made her grunt a forced exhalation as he slapped her right cheek and eye.

"Oh, God," she cried.

"Don't let God's name come out of your whoring, cock-sucking mouth," he screamed, his voice breathy and hoarse with rage and exertion. He slapped her again with the palm of his right hand, then back-handed her on the other side of her face.

"Oh, please," she wailed, "please stop."

He slapped her hard on the right breast and was about to strike her again when his hand stopped in mid-air. On his knees, straddling her tightly-clinched thighs, he glared at her. Slowly, he knee-walked backward toward the edge of the bed. He looked down at Cuddles, her arms crossed over her large breasts. What he could see of the right one was reddened by his stinging slap.

When he got off the bed, he blurted, "Slut." He spat on her, the small projectile of saliva splattering on her left collar bone. "Bitch whore," he rasped with heavy breaths. "You're all bitch whores."

In another sudden movement, he grabbed his cordovan loafers from underneath the chair and stalked out of the room.

Forty-five minutes later, after he checked in the rent car and retrieved his own Cadillac, he slid to a stop in his reserved parking spot outside the door to his private study at Centrum Church. Banging and slamming every door he passed through, he stalked through halls and anterooms until he reached the two thousand-seat sanctuary, strode onto the dais and to the pulpit. The empty, quiet hall was bathed in subdued light from unseen, recessed fixtures high on the walls. Dr. Henry Jackson Woods grasped the edges of the pulpit, his knuckles white from the force of his grip.

"My beloved brothers and sisters of Centrum Church," he said, his voice booming as it did each time he preached. "Tonight, God has led me to reveal unto you the pestilence bred in our hearts by the vile canker sores of humankind. Vile canker sores who, with every breath, every thought, every action and deed, seek to extinguish that tiny light of the Creator's omnipotence that lives within each of us.

"Tonight, though repulsed by them, we must see those diabolic blasphemers who would suck us into their hell of paganism. Repugnant though it may be, we must reach down into the muck and stench of their spiritual pigsties to lift them from the destruction of their own, profane quicksand. Verily, verily I say unto you, we who are washed with the Blood of the Lamb shall remain clean even as we plunge our hands into the squalid filth from which we seek to save these wretched souls lost in the offal of their own making."

For twenty minutes, he railed out his scourging message. Sweat dripped from his face and darkened his red shirt. He pounded the pulpit and shouted his message to the emptiness of Centrum Church until exhausted by his wild oration. His handkerchief, soaked with mopped perspiration, lay in a wad on the pulpit in front of him. Dr. Woods slowly sank to his knees and sobbed.

"Oh, dear God...." His words gave way to more sobs. "Oh, blessed Jesus," he managed to gasp as his wrenching cries subsided. "Oh, merciful Savior, I beg Your forgiveness." He snuffed out several short breaths, the aftermath of his crying. "Please, dear God. Please relieve me of this torment. Deliver me from this vexation of being a mere man created in Your image." His raspy voice tailed to a whisper. He slumped to a sitting position, propped up by his right hand. Dr. Woods looked up as a spasm of wincing blinks wracked his contorted face. "In the name of God the Father, God the Son and God the Holy Ghost, I ask for deliverance from this pestilence that rages inside of me. Dear God, Thou art my one hope, my one salvation."

Mumsy's Little Numsy

Hoff waited for Andrew Numsen Boxx at Hobby Airport in Houston and recalled a drunken conversation with Andy.

"I hate that freaky middle name of mine," Andy had said. "When I was a little fart-knocker, my mother called me Mumsy's Little Numsy. Jesus Christ, save me from Mumsy's Little Numsy. My older brother told me about it later, along with every-goddam-body else in the neighborhood. It took me several tries, but I finally whipped his ass to shut him up about that crap." Andy had fixed a bleary, bloodshot stare on Hoff. "If you ever mention Numsy or Numsen, I'll whip your ass!"

Hoff spotted Andy among the people hurrying off the airplane. As they shook hands, Hoff took the carry-on garment bag.

"I can't believe I flew halfway across Texas to attend a church service," Andy said as they headed for the parking garage. "This is one October I will never forget. Do you really think you're going to fill the Astrodome with this high-powered lady preacher of yours?"

"Everything points to a full house."

"Out of curiosity, what's the tariff on using that place?"

"Basic rent is thirty thousand dollars a day," Hoff said. "That's for the building only, no staff, no use of the scoreboard. All that stuff is extra. Blood, guts and feathers, our costs will be close to seventy thousand. Keeps the riff-raff out."

"No fooling. What are we calling the girl these days? Leeandrum? Sister Catheter?" Andy laughed. "Damn! Wish I could've kept a straight face to see how bad I got your goat."

Forty pounds lighter than a year ago, Andy was hungry for Mexican food. Fifteen minutes after leaving the airport, both had cold Carta Blanca beers in front of them. They ordered fajitas. Then Hoff asked, "Did you see Leeandra on the Johnny Cash special last weekend?"

"I damned sure did. Johnny had tears running down his cheeks when she gave that little talk about all the deaths in her family."

"That was a hellacious shot in the arm for tonight's service. We got all kinds of media coverage."

"How did she get on the Cash show?"

"The talent agency arranged it."

Andy shook his head. "I'm amazed. You found this gal in a nip-shit tent preaching show in a piss ant little town, and here she is on network TV a year later. Hell of a deal."

"Time flies when you're making money, doesn't it?"

"Damned sure does." Andy flashed a wicked grin at Hoff. "Gives us something to offset the loss on a certain movie project."

Hoff grimaced. "Looks like we're about to conduct last rites for *The Fourth Reich*. One major league tax write-off coming up."

"Thrills me to the core," Andy said sarcastically as he watched the waiter serve the platter of sizzling fajitas.

As they ate, Hoff told Andy a crowd of sixty thousand was expected. Andy shook his head. "Shit fire, the Oilers didn't draw sixty thousand people before they hauled ass to Tennessee."

"The Oilers didn't have Leeandra. She's on a roll. We got a half-page story in *Time Magazine*. An article in the *Atlanta Constitution* says she's the hottest thing in religious programming. She was on five TV programs in Houston this week."

"How's she handling all this?" Andy asked.

"Like a champ. I've seen her up tight a time or two, mostly due to the fast pace. There are lots of pressures on her time."

"And her brother?"

"Casper goes with the flow." Hoff shook his head slowly. "Ken Walker tells me Casper is showing signs of jealousy because Leeandra gets all the attention. Casper is weak as used wash water."

"Why don't you get rid of the little nipplehead?"

"He serves a purpose in addition to being Leeandra's brother. She wouldn't stand still for getting rid of him."

Andy nodded as he chewed. "What's the story between you and Leeandra?"

"There's good chemistry between us."

"Is Margo still in St. Thomas?"

Hoff nodded.

"Good place for her. I never rehire an employee who quits, and I damned sure would never let a woman back in my house after she walked out on me."

Hoff smiled. "Never?"

"Abso-goddam-lutely never!"

Hoff told Andy that a *60 Minutes* crew would be at the stadium to shoot video tape of Leeandra for possible inclusion in a segment about TV evangelists.

"Sounds like trouble. They may do one of their hatchet jobs."

"Our PR people don't think so. They say we'll get good national exposure."

Andy pushed his plate toward the middle of the table. He took another flour tortilla out of the basket. "These damned things are habit forming. I'm stuffed. I hope I've got time for a nap."

Hoff looked at his watch. "You do."

Andy had insisted on staying at the Warwick Hotel instead of spending the night at Hoff's condominium. "I need my space. Your place is too damned little. I don't want all your neighbors to feel sorry for you every time I cut a big old fart."

Hoff told Andy he would pick him up at 4:30.

"Why so early?"

"The service starts at six. I want to get there by five."

"Six? That's an oddball hour."

Hoff explained Ken Walker chose the time so people coming from outlying towns could get home early. "Tomorrow is a school and work day, you know."

Andy grinned. "I guess these churching folks don't observe cocktail hour, do they?"

Hoff drove Andy to the hotel's front door. "You're not going to chicken out at the last minute and not go tonight, are you?"

"I'll let you know if I get a better offer," Andy said as he got out of the car. "Compared to going to church, any offer will be better."

A Dome Full of Sister Cathedra

Leeandra Stevens' face filled the Astrodome scoreboard's huge television screen, a giant-sized Sister Cathedra dominating the crowd. Winking pops of flash bulbs, a buzzing roar of excited conversation and people's stirring, craning movements subsided as she stood at the pulpit on a portable stage.

Leeandra wore a plain, long-sleeved, dark blue dress. She wore no jewelry. Her long blonde hair shone like a golden waterfall down her back under the battery of high-intensity overhead lights.

Hoff leaned forward in his seat. Absent were the smells of hay and dust. No strings of naked, one-hundred-fifty watt light bulbs sagged from the domed stadium's arching, steel structure. From his vantage in a luxury suite high above the stadium floor, Leeandra was dwarfed by the immense scale of the building. He felt a swell of pride at their progress in the year and nine days since that night in Sweetwater when the Stevens Crusade tent was pitched adjacent to a defoliated cotton field. He wondered what Mr. Claypool would think.

Hoff lifted his binoculars. In the middle of the rounded field of vision, Leeandra's face shone with a commanding radiance, her eyes fiercely blue. She stood in silence for almost a full minute.

A flutter of excitement raced through him as he thought about the contrast between this authoritarian figure on stage and the quiet, distant Leeandra in her dressing room before the service when he wanted to introduce Andy to her. She seemed remote, coolly indifferent when she asked him to wait until after the service's conclusion.

Through the binoculars, he saw her take a breath and the first note of "Amazing Grace" sang its way through the cavernous stadium. She sang with a joyful smile as she dispensed another dose of elusive elixir with her flowing, delicately tuned soprano. As always, she sang a cappella. When she paused at the end of the first stanza, he heard the quiet as sixty thousand people sat mute, soothed by the balm of her voice.

As she sang the second verse, he examined the crowd. Each person he saw was gazing at Sister Cathedra, a commanding figure, the nerve center of this sports stadium packed with worshippers. Hoff felt a quick burst of apprehension when he saw the movement begin in the crowd. Thoughts of the evangelist murders raced into his head, and he was mindful of the fifty extra off-duty police officers added to the security force. His concerns about danger faded as he realized people were responding to her song.

First one, then tens and hundreds of people made their way to the large open area in front of the stage as Leeandra sang. Some rushed. Some walked prayerfully. Some limped. An elderly, white-haired man sat slumped and bent as he was pushed in a wheelchair. A majority of the respondents knelt in front of the stage. Others stood with heads bowed.

Throughout the stadium, Hoff saw people dab at their eyes with handkerchiefs. He swung the glasses back to Leeandra as she neared the end of her song. She held her clasped hands high against her chest and tilted her head back, her eyes turned upward as she sang the final words, "We've no less days to sing God's praise than when we first begun."

She held the final note with possessive clarity before letting it go to diffuse itself into the gathering. Applause, shouts of amen, hallelujah and praise the Lord erupted into a roar.

She bowed her head and stood for several seconds before she turned and walked slowly to her seat, her long hair swinging gently. The instant she stepped away from the pulpit, Casper had the band playing and the choir, composed of volunteers from area churches, singing. One of the guest ministers stepped to the pulpit to address the respondents.

Hoff focused on Leeandra. She sat in a folding chair on the stage with her head bowed, hands in her lap. He glanced around the luxury box. Winston Peacock, the producer from *60 Minutes*, bent forward in his seat, elbows on his knees, chin resting on his interlocked fists. He was absorbed in the crowd's reaction.

Larry Best, in his corduroy jacket uniform, leaned toward Hoff and whispered, "Touchdown, Sister Cathedra!"

Twenty minutes passed before all the respondents returned to their seats. Casper led the assemblage in singing another hymn. When it was over, Leeandra returned to the pulpit.

The crowd lapsed into silence as soon as her hands touched the podium. Smiling, she sang the short first stanza of "Sweet Hour of Prayer." Then she spoke.

"We are here to worship the holy name of Jesus Christ, our Lord and Savior, the only-begotten Son of God. This service is dedicated to the memory of my father, Joe Ted Stevens. Although he is not with us in body, I feel the power of my father's rich spirit as he worships with us in this sweet hour of prayer."

A flurry of amens and hallelujahs ricocheted through the stadium.

"Tonight, we gather in a venue normally used for sporting events and entertainment. I ask each of you to envision a house of God, a sanctuary of His saving grace. Envision an altar of prayer and supplication made holy by the spilled blood of Jesus Christ."

He was impressed with Leeandra's calmness as she emoted the message of salvation, eternal life, inner peace, death and resurrection. She spoke without notes, smiled much of the time as she told what sounded like a simple story. As she spoke, he again scanned the crowd with his binoculars. People sat quietly, listening to her sermon delivered in the songful voice that had become her style.

"Believe in Jesus Christ as you believe in your next breath of life on this Earth. Jesus is your breath of life everlasting. Believe in Jesus Christ as you believe in tomorrow's dawning. For in so doing, your tomorrows will be filled with eternal light from His never-ending beacon of grace and love."

Her face glowed as she bathed the attentive throng in her canting, singsong delivery. Hoff lowered the binoculars. He saw her in the context of the huge crowd and wondered how a single person could exercise such complete control over an assemblage of this size.

Suddenly, the sermon was over and hordes of people streamed toward the stage. Many skipped and danced, waving their hands.

"Look at that!" Ken Walker said. His voice wobbled with excitement.

Winston Peacock stood, watching wide-eyed.

"What the hell's going on?" Andy whispered to Hoff.

Hoff continued to look at the streams of people converging on the stage. "They're responding to Sister Cathedra." He thought, I hope that shooter lunatic isn't among them.

Casper replaced his sister at the pulpit, leading the band and choir. The stadium was alive with singing voices. She stood to one side, arms outstretched, turning one way and then the other, back and forth again and again while the small army of volunteer workers received the respondents. The area in front of the stage was a swarm of milling, kneeling, dancing, singing, praying humanity. The people reminded Hoff of a colony of ants reaping their bounty from the mother lode of sweet-tasting elixir.

"Amazing!" Ken said.

Hoff heard Winston Peacock tell his associate, "If we don't get dynamite footage out of this, I don't know where we will."

Hoff sat looking down at her. A flood of mixed emotions filled him as he thought about the difference between Leeandra Kay Stevens and Sister Cathedra.

Enraged at the Rag Knots

Downstairs, off the stadium floor, Hoff and Andy walked into the crowded reception room. Most of the people were volunteers from local churches who had helped with the service. More people were coming in. The gathering was noisy with festive laughter and success-excited conversation. People clustered around a long table holding punch, coffee, sandwiches, chips and cookies.

"This may not be a drinking crowd, but they're giving that food hell," Andy said. "I guess the Lord loves a sober, cheerful chubby."

Hoff spotted Leeandra and Billy Dean Smith on the far side of the room. They were hemmed in by one of the guest ministers and a knot of people, including Larry, who was shaking Leeandra's hand. Larry had told Hoff he would leave as soon as he congratulated her.

"Follow me," Hoff said to Andy. "I'll introduce you to her."

Hoff led the way toward Leeandra, now engrossed in conversation with two well-dressed people. Hoff stopped to make sure Andy was keeping up and saw Ken working his way through the crowd. By the time Hoff and Andy got close to Leeandra, she was looking down at the floor and listening to Ken speak into her ear. Hoff was about to say her name when she moved away, following Ken. She didn't see Hoff. "Leeandra," he called out, but she didn't hear him.

"Where's she going?" Hoff asked Billy Dean.

"To be interviewed by reporters." He grinned. "Isn't this great?"

"Sure is." Hoff turned to Andy. "Misfire. She's going to see the newsies. Want something to drink?"

"Yeah, but not here. This place is a frigging madhouse."

"Let's see if the media room is calmer." They made their way across the reception area, then down a hallway. A uniformed police officer stopped them at the media center door. Not until George Lee, the public relations man, vouched for them were they allowed in. Immediately, Lee scurried away.

"Sometimes I really don't like that flannel-mouthed son of a bitch."

"You're pissed because you couldn't get in here without his say-so," Andy said. "Big shits don't like to be controlled by the say-so of little shits."

When Andy excused himself to find the toilet, Hoff walked closer to where a radio reporter was interviewing Leeandra. A local television news crew was busy setting up nearby. Leeandra faced three-quarters away from Hoff as she was interviewed.

"You are convinced that God chose you for the ministry?" the radio reporter asked.

"He led me into this ministry, yes," Leeandra answered in a fluid, quiet voice. "Many people are anointed by God to do His work. This ministry is one small part."

"The Astrodome full of people is hardly small," the reporter countered.

"It is compared to God's universe."

When the reporter finished, a young woman Hoff saw earlier with George Lee summoned the waiting TV reporter and cameraman. The public relations staffer began talking to Leeandra, who listened intently as she sipped from a Diet Coke before handing it back to the staffer.

When the TV interview began, Leeandra exuded confidence as she handled the reporter's questions with ease. Hoff felt an impatient vexation at not being able to speak with her.

The staffer was back at Leeandra's side the instant the television lights clicked off. "Newspaper reporters are next, group interview." The staffer continued talking as she ushered Leeandra in Hoff's direction.

"Don't make a statement. Just answer questions, okay?"

Leeandra was nodding, swallowing a sip of the Diet Coke when her glancing look swept past Hoff, then back to him.

"Looks like you're busy," he said. He beat back a rushing urge to take hold of her.

"Yes." She slowed as she passed him, but didn't stop. "See you in a little while?" Then she was past him, ushered on to the opposite corner where newspaper reporters waited.

Angry conflict brewed inside Hoff. Leeandra's "See you in a little while?" sounded almost like a plea. The up-tilted inflection was augmented by two seconds of her soft, caring look. But she didn't stop. He felt vacant and peeved, unceremoniously dismissed, the same way he felt when he tried to introduce Andy before the service. He was irked with her for not stopping to talk and irked with himself for what he knew was a childish reaction to her limelight hour. He was jealous of these nameless people and their tape recorders, cameras, pads and pens, with first liens on Sister Cathedra.

"Still in a holding pattern?" Andy asked when he returned. "What's going on?"

"More interviews. Looks like this may take quite a while. Do you want to stick around and meet her or boogie?"

"Might as well stick around. I'm too damned old to boogie. Besides, I sat through two hours of churching to meet this star preacher lady. What's a little heels cooling time on top of that? Let's get a cup of coffee."

They got coffee and returned to where they could hear the questions and Leeandra's answers.

"Is the Sister Cathedra name a marketing gimmick?" a newspaper reporter asked.

"No. The name is a mechanism for reaching more people with the gospel."

"Some people regard your ministry as the fastest-growing of its kind in the nation. Is it true a promotions specialist orchestrates your efforts?"

"Many people assist our ministry. Hundreds of volunteers from eight churches in the area helped tonight. Acceptance of our work by people like those who attended tonight is the biggest factor in our growth. Our ministry delivers God's word to people in a way they both want and need. Souls are being led to accept Jesus Christ as their personal Savior. That is the true measure of our success."

"She's doing a good job," Andy whispered.

Hoff nodded, already thinking that Leeandra was at her queen bee finest. There was no hint of the skittish doe. He was restive with a scratchy mingle of feelings. She was the Sister Cathedra he wanted her to be. But not the Leeandra he longed for, to stroll on the beach with or to share a bowl of chili. And, perhaps, to love. Could she be both Sister Cathedra and Leeandra? Would she want to be? Would she enjoy the cloak of standing alone too much to ever take it off?

During the past six months, their relationship had waxed and waned. Each time they began feeling close, one took a backward step. Sometimes, he couldn't figure out who backed off. He thought both he and Leeandra were wary of getting too close, but each back and forth movement left them a fraction closer than before.

The newspaper interview lasted another ten minutes before the staffer stopped it, explaining that Leeandra was overdue to meet with invited guests and volunteers at the reception.

"Let's catch her on the way out so I can meet her and we can get the hell out of here," Andy said. "I've had my quota of churching."

"Leeandra," Hoff called out as she and the staffer bustled by.

"Hi, Hoff." She stopped and smiled warmly. She didn't take her eyes off him to look at Andy until Hoff spoke.

"I want you to meet Andy Boxx. Andy, this is Leeandra Stevens."

She took Andy's extended hand and said, "I'm glad to meet you. I've never had the chance to thank you personally for letting us use your airplane when Daddy died."

"You're welcome. I'm pleased to meet you."

The staffer interrupted. "Miss Stevens, we're keeping a lot of people waiting." The staffer looked at Andy, then Hoff. "Why don't you gentlemen join us at the reception?" She grasped Leeandra's arm and steered her toward the door.

"Glad to meet you," Leeandra said, looking back at Andy. With a brief, somber glance at Hoff, she was gone.

"Let's get the fuck out of here," Hoff hissed and raced out of the media room.

"Are you pissed off?" Andy asked from two steps behind.

They were now out into the hallway. "I damned sure am! Come on," Hoff barked.

Andy hurried to keep up. Not until they got to the car did Andy say, "Boy, I almost forgot how quick you can get your dander up. Why're you so riled?"

"Goddam bunch of sanctimonious assholes!"

Andy sat in silence until Hoff steered his car out of the parking lot. "I'll be glad to take a cab back...."

"That's not it."

When Hoff did not continue, Andy asked, "What the hell is it? You're acting like a king-sized shit."

"I feel one, passed over and pissed off. A turd at the bottom of the bowl."

"This is a big night for her."

"Hi, Hoff," Hoff said in a mocking falsetto. "How's that for not even getting the fucking time of day? She could've told that public relations pussy to buzz off or some goddam thing. Chaps my ass!"

"I can see that."

"I've wet nursed these sons of bitches, her included, from back when they were sucking a dry tit. Last October, they were a bunch of minor league rag knots on the edge of a goddam cotton field. She tastes the big time and can't even take a second to say 'how are you, Hoff?', 'glad to see you, Hoff', 'stick around' or any other jack-butt thing." Hoff paused. "Gripes my scalded, money-making ass is what it does." He gunned his car into the intersection, but the traffic light turned red before he got through. "Oops." After a few seconds of silence, Hoff glanced at Andy. "Hungry?"

"Yeah."

"Me, too. A big piss-off always piques my appetite."

Andy laughed. "One of us better have lots of bucks."

"There's a good pie place up the street. Does that suit you?"

"Yeah. Maybe I can fatten my skinny self up."

They sat at the counter to avoid waiting for a booth. Each ordered coffee and a serving of fudge pecan pie topped with vanilla ice cream.

"Is this place always crowded?" Andy twisted around to look across the packed dining room and spoke quietly. "Is it my imagination, or is this place about half full of joy boys?"

"Probably. A lot of gay people live in this part of town."

"I didn't see prick pie on the menu."

They both laughed as the pie was put in front of them.

"Suffering Jesus," Andy said. "There must be five thousand calories in this." He dug in and they ate in silence. Andy called for a coffee refill, then asked, "Are you going back over to the Astrodome?"

"No."

"I think you should. Because Leeandra will want you there."

Hoff looked at Andy. "Think so?"

"I know so. And you wouldn't have blown your stack if you didn't want to be with her. Right?"

"Maybe." Hoff sipped his coffee.

"Aw, cut me some slack," Andy grumped. "Go back over there, pick her preachership's cute little ass up, throw her over your shoulder and haul her out of there. She'd love it and so would you."

"No way."

Andy shrugged. "Okay. Sometimes, an old fart like me has eyes that don't see quite as many things as they once did. That's the bad news. The good news is, when us old farts do see something, we usually see more of it."

"Meaning?"

"She'll want you there when the festivities are over. I saw the look she gave you when that public relations gal hustled her off."

"What makes you so sure?" Hoff asked.

"These old eyes."

"Maybe you're right."

"Maybe, my diet-shrunk ass. But you're going to have to take the initiative. Because she won't."

"Why not?"

"She's too timid."

Hoff snorted. "Timid? Leeandra? She preached to sixty thousand people tonight and you're telling me she's timid?"

"You weren't looking tonight, my young friend. That was Sister Cathedra up there in front of all those people and, no, she's not timid. Leeandra is, though. And it's Leeandra you're after."

Message Well Left

Despite being asleep and groggy from the Scotch he drank with Andy at the club on the top of the Warwick Hotel, Hoff reached for the telephone on the first ring. The cloud of sleep and alcohol kept his usual anger at bay over being awakened. "Yes," he said thickly.

"Hoff?" Leeandra's tone was tentative.

He held the telephone to his ear, trying to beat back the confusion that stopped him from responding.

"Hoff, is that you? This is Leeandra."

"Leeandra," he repeated and rubbed his face. "Where are you?"

"At my hotel." She paused. "I'm sorry to wake you, but the message says call you, no matter how late."

"Message?" he asked, his voice still husky and thick.

"I'm sorry I woke you. I almost didn't call. It is awfully late."

"That's okay." Hoff looked at the bedside clock. 2:33. He thought, I didn't leave any message.

"It took us a long time to get away from the Dome," she said, "then we stopped to eat. I'm glad you called. You left and...well...I wanted to talk to you. Why didn't you stick around?"

"It looked like you were tied up, so we left."

There was another short silence. "I'm sorry I was so busy."

"I understand." Hoff smiled when it dawned on him that Andy must have left the message.

"Hoff...." Her silence lasted for several seconds. "I was disappointed because you didn't stay. I thought you would be there when the reception was over." When she spoke again, her voice was low and husky. "But you weren't."

Hoff's voice conveyed the warmth of his feelings. "There was a lot going on. Sister Cathedra was pretty busy."

"Yes. Too busy." After a long pause, she added, "Everybody said it went well."

"The service was terrific. You did a super job."

Leeandra was silent for a moment. "When I realized you were gone, I...I was angry with you."

"Why?"

"Because you weren't there. I guess that's dumb."

"Not really," he said. "I left because I had my nose out of joint."

"Not at me?"

"Andy had a good explanation. He said I was out of sorts because of Sister Cathedra."

She laughed. "I can't believe this happened." After a deep breath, she asked, "You're not still angry, are you?"

"Well, let's see. This is Leeandra calling?"

"Yes."

He laughed. "No, I'm not angry. How about you?"

"Me, neither."

"That's good. Do you think we could have breakfast tomorrow? Better make that today."

"I'd like that," she answered quickly.

"You'll want to sleep late. Why don't we make it brunch? I could pick you up at your hotel at ten-thirty."

"Even better. I look forward to it." She hesitated. "Hoff, Sister Cathedra is different, isn't she?"

"Definitely."

"I'm not so sure I like the difference."

"Sister Cathedra has her place."

"I guess so."

After the good-byes, Hoff lay back with his hands clasped behind his head, looking into the dark. I'm falling in love with her, he thought. And I think she's falling in love with me. He smiled at the idea of loving Leeandra Kay Stevens. The only vacancy now was her absence. In a few hours, he'd be with her. He hoped Sister Cathedra would stay away.

Chapter 14

Stars Rise, Stars Fall

James Bresnahan shook his head in disgust when Sister Cathedra's picture was shown at the pulpit in Houston's Astrodome with her image in the background on the scoreboard's huge screen. He was disappointed with her participation in such blatant theatrics.

Watching the videotape in the basement office at his home, a cinnamon candy tucked in his right cheek, he questioned the Stevens ministry's meteoric rise to prominence. Who was orchestrating their growth? Additional research would enable him to learn more about her and the organization's people. She was not to be taken lightly after filling such a large venue.

He decided to go see her as soon as possible, because stars can fall as quickly as they rise. Seeing an evangelist was crucial to confirming his television-induced perceptions.

His trip to Nebraska resulted in an Omaha preacher's being taken off the list of evangelists who required Mission Silver Broom's remedial sweep. The next trip would be to Tempe, Arizona, to check out the motorcycle-riding preacher named Harley Mann. Bresnahan was determined to remain vigilant. Daily, he reminded himself of his mission. Vermin beget vermin. They must be controlled. He was God's vigilante, designated to maintain that control.

What a Friend We Have in Leeandra

Danny Don Rhodes was surprised at how fast the hour passed when he watched the televised program of Sister Cathedra in the Astrodome. When it ended, he turned off the television and the bedside lamp, and lay still in his bed. He listened to the quiet in his head. Leeandra's singing again quelled the confused roar.

Gone was his anger at Leeandra for calling herself Sister Cathedra. He whispered the new name aloud, now comfortable with how to say it. He could not remain angry with her. She was too beautiful, and she preached too powerfully. Her voice was a musical balm. No wonder people by the hundreds responded when she sang.

As he lay in the quiet darkness, he decided she was destined to accomplish great things. He hoped she wouldn't change. Even though she was a commanding figure in the televised service, Danny Don could still envision her as a person. He could be friends with a person like Leeandra and talk to her like he talked to Annabelle Morton at the

Panhandle Cafe. "What a friend we have in Jesus." Words from the hymn she sang played in his head. He modified the words, "What a friend we have in Leeandra."

Stay Away from the Antichrist

"Sister Cathedra is the Antichrist. Stay away from her Astrodome crusade tonight." Before Hoff arrived at his office, Gracie had circled the classified ad in red and left it on his desk. Hoff stood as he unfolded the newspaper page to look at the dateline, Monday, October 16th.

"This is today's paper." Hoff spoke to Gracie who stood in the doorway to his office. "Why would the ad be in today's paper?"

Gracie shrugged.

"Was it in yesterday's?"

"No. I read the *Chronicle* personal ads every day."

"Sister Cathedra is the Antichrist," Hoff said aloud. "I wonder what this is about. Antichrist," he said quietly. "Do you suppose that means what it says?" Without allowing time for a response, Hoff said to Gracie, "Call George Lee and get him to find out who placed the ad."

"Can he do that?"

"He can try. And get Ken Walker on the phone for me, will you, Miss Gracie?" A clump of apprehension grew in his stomach. He wondered if this was a warning from the evangelists killer. Gracie told him over the intercom Ken was on the line.

Ken bubbled with enthusiasm. "There's a great pic in today's paper of the Astrodome crowd with Leeandra's face on the scoreboard screen."

"I'll take a look," Hoff said. "Any count on contributions?"

"Not yet. We probably won't have a final tally until early afternoon, but I'm guessing we'll go over three hundred thousand."

"Good." Hoff paused. He didn't want to sound like an alarmist when he mentioned the ad. "Do you have the *Chronicle* handy? Turn to the last page of the classified section. Look under the personals column, fifth ad down." He heard sounds of rustling paper.

"I'm getting close," Ken said, then there was a short silence. "Antichrist! What is this? This is crazy! Antichrist?"

"I figure the ad is in today's paper by mistake," Hoff said. "It wasn't in yesterday's. Our public relations people are trying to find out who placed it."

"Who would say this about Leeandra?"

"I don't have the foggiest notion. It mentions Sister Cathedra by name, not Leeandra. Probably some nut." Hoff resisted saying the nut could be the same person shooting the evangelists.

"This beats all."

"Do you think it might be Henry Woods?"

"Surely not," Ken said. "He's got nothing to gain from this."

"Did you see him at the Dome last night?"

"No."

Hoff paused. "This might be Woods' way of getting even with us for turning down his merger proposal."

"He doesn't strike me as the kind of person who'd do this."

"Hopefully, we'll find out who did. Exactly what does Antichrist mean?"

"Some people use the term for anybody who opposes Jesus Christ's teachings. Others use it referring to one great force that opposes Christ."

"We may get a media inquiry or two about the ad. If so, refer everything to George Lee." Hoff took a note from Gracie. "Ken, I've got Andy Boxx on another line. Let me know when you get a final count on the contributions."

"I will. You let me know what you find about this crazy ad."

Hoff promised he would, pushed the blinking button and heard Andy ask, "Is your ass back to normal flesh color?"

"Yeah. You didn't have anything to do with it, did you?"

"What're you talking about?"

"The message at Leeandra's hotel that I wanted to talk to her."

Andy laughed. "She called you, did she?"

"Yes. Did you leave the message?"

"Be damned if I can remember. Some nipplehead kept pouring whiskey in my face last night. Classic case of too much of a good thing. I must've crapped out."

"Would you believe she got mad at me because I wasn't around when she got through with all the goings-on at the Dome?"

"I told you."

"That you did. By the way, I forgot to tell you last night. You looked plumb spiffy all dressed up. I can't remember the last time I saw you in a suit and tie. Your shoes were even shined."

"Plumb spiffy, huh? I thought I looked plumb extinguished."

Hoff laughed. "You sure you don't want me to take you to the airport?"

"Nah. Say, I think we ought to franchise that pie joint where we ate last night."

"Any Freudian significance in your use of the word joint?"

"I hope not. That place had more joy boys than a goddam fairy forest. Think Boston cream pie has a different meaning to joy boys?"

"You're terrible."

"I know it," Andy said. "I've made a career out of it. Except you'll notice that when the game gets down to the nut cutting, I'm good. Are you going to see Miss Cawonderful today? Tell her hello for me. I'm impressed with her. She's good people."

"You barely said hello. How do you know she's good people?"

"These old eyes."

"There may be something to that old eyes crap."

Hoff was about to say good-bye when he heard Andy hang up.

Gracie walked into the office. "George Lee called. He confirms the ad didn't run in the paper yesterday. George said he will personally go over to their office today and try to find out who placed it."

She stood in front of Hoff's desk. "If I didn't know better, I'd think we're a little hung over this morning."

"I didn't get much sleep," he said.

"I didn't realize religious services kept you up so late." There was an impish tone in Gracie's voice.

"Blame Andy and a mutual friend named Scotch."

"Things must've gone well last night."

"They did. I didn't see you there."

Gracie smiled. "I had better things to do."

Hoff's private line rang.

"I'll get it," Gracie said, but Hoff was already reaching for it.

Leeandra's voice was stiff. "I might not be able to make brunch at ten-thirty. Casper is upset, threatening to pull out and go home. He wants to talk with Ken and me."

"Why?"

"He's jealous because I'm getting so much attention. At least, Ken and I think that's the problem. It's been brewing for some time."

"Let's have lunch after your meeting," Hoff said.

"I'd like to. But if I can't, would you take me to the airport?"

"Of course."

"I'm sorry to foul up our plans, but Casper really is undone."

"Why don't you just let him go on home? We can find somebody else to handle the music."

"He is my brother. I don't want him to be unhappy. We need to thrash this out."

"Would it help if I attend the meeting?"

"I think we'll get down to brass tacks quicker with just Ken, Casper and me," she said. "Will you be available if we need you?"

"Yes." Hoff paused. "If lack of attention is bothering Casper, I've got a couple of suggestions. We can give him more exposure in our promotional materials. Maybe we could publish a song book under his name, a collection of favorite hymns."

Her silence was followed by a quick laugh. "You amaze me."

"How so?"

"I spring something completely new on you, and you come up with two really good ideas just like that."

"I'm trying to be helpful."

"Oh, believe me, I appreciate the suggestions. Maybe they'll help settle Casper down."

As a contingency plan, Hoff told Leeandra he would pick her up at two o'clock if he didn't hear from her again. As he hung up the phone, he growled, "Casper, you are, in fact, a goddam weenie!"

Good Cheerer-Upper

Leeandra stood in the hotel lobby, her luggage and a bellman at the ready when Hoff arrived. Her smile was soft and warm when she saw him. He kissed her on the cheek.

"How'd it go?" he said as they followed the bellman to his car.

"Exasperating. I don't think Casper knows what's bothering him. I used your suggestions. They seemed to make him feel better. I think he wants attention as much as anything. To tell you the truth, I'm a little put out with him. He's acting like a brat."

When Hoff got into the car, Leeandra was slumped in her seat.

"Tired?" he asked.

"Drained. The last twenty-four hours have been a roller coaster. Such a big high in last night's service and then this mess with Casper."

"Why don't you stay until tomorrow?"

"There's a dinner tonight in Abilene with a group of pastors and lay leaders." She brushed strands of hair away from her face. "I'd gladly trade the pastors dinner for a bowl of that magic chili."

"That can be arranged."

"The dinner has been scheduled for a long time. I owe it to them to be there. They're among our most faithful supporters."

"Okay. Is there anything I can do to help with Casper?"

"I don't think so." She stopped for a second. "There's one thing. You can talk about anything in the whole wide world except him."

"Gladly." He accelerated onto the freeway and merged into traffic. "Let's talk about you and me." He glanced at Leeandra. "I enjoyed our conversation last night."

"Me, too. I'm glad you wanted me to call."

"Is our conversation part of the roller coaster you mentioned?"

"Yes and no." She took a deep breath. "I feel kind of...I guess I'm feeling mixed up right now. That's part of the problem."

"What problem?"

"Being part Leeandra and part Sister Cathedra."

Hoff divided a series of quick glances between Leeandra and the freeway. Her expression darkened with a sad, troubled look, her blue eyes cloudy. He reached for her hand. "Tell me about it."

So much time passed that Hoff tightened his hold on her hand. Then he saw tears on her cheeks.

"I feel a great deal of conflict." She sniffed. "I guess I'm a little frightened. Part of me is a normal woman with a lot of my life left. But I'm moving away from any chance to live a normal life. The other part of me believes I'm chosen to sing and preach the gospel, believes I'm obligated to carry on Daddy's work."

She paused. "There's such a big difference between Leeandra—the plain me—and Sister Cathedra when I'm in the pulpit. Right now, one doesn't seem to go with the other. I feel like I'm caught in some kind of tug-of-war." She sat still, her teary eyes open wide, pleading.

"I think I understand," he said. "I wish I had an easy answer."

"I'll settle for any at the moment. It doesn't have to be easy."

He drove in silence for several seconds. "Ultimately, I guess you have to decide whether to be Leeandra or Sister Cathedra. Or both. We can get professional help, but the decision is up to you."

"And God."

"Okay. But my point is, don't be unduly influenced by Ken or Casper or me. Or anyone else with a vested interest. Work out the solution that's best for you, the one you'll be happy with."

"But I feel trapped. I would let so many people down if I quit."

"Like who?"

"You."

Hoff steered his car to the freeway shoulder and braked to a quick stop. He turned to her, cupped her left hand between both of his. "You wouldn't let me down if you quit. If you're happy as Sister Cathedra, so be it. Same goes if you choose to be Leeandra. No matter, you won't let me down as long as you're happy."

"Do you really mean that?" She sighed. "You have a lot of money tied up in this."

"Truth is, we can stop the television operation now and my group will have recouped its investment and a nice profit to boot. Even if that weren't the case, there's a wonderful thing about money. There's plenty of the stuff. You can always make more money. But each minute you live is gone. You can't make more time." Hoff smiled. "I guess I gained a new appreciation for time when I turned forty. Don't worry about money. I want to see you happy."

He squeezed her hand and glanced at the dash panel clock. "We have to get rolling or you'll miss your plane." With reluctance he slipped the car into gear. "Am I guilty of preaching to the preacher?"

"Perhaps, but you've been helpful. Thank you. I do realize it's my decision, but I was worried about how you'd feel."

"It's not long until Thanksgiving. Maybe getting away from the daily grind will give you time to think everything through."

"I hope so. I'm looking forward to a break."

Hoff exited from the freeway as he asked, "Got any plans?"

"To sleep late, be lazy and wear my old comfies."

"Sounds good. I'm due for some rest and relaxation time myself."

"You're kidding. You're the mile-a-minute type. I figured you're always on the go, even when you're on vacation."

"Not when I'm on vacation. I like to set my bucket down and do what I jolly well please. I can be an expert at doing nothing."

As Hoff drove up the ramp at Hobby Airport, he said, "I'll drop you off at the front door. We'll find a skycap. You check in while I park, and I'll meet you at the American Eagle counter."

"You can just drop me off."

"Nothing doing." He stopped curbside at the terminal. "I insist."

He parked and then hurried to the terminal building to meet her. "Is the flight on time?" She nodded, and he added, "Shoot. I was hoping it'd be canceled. We still have a few minutes." He put his hand on her waist to guide her toward the departure gate.

She said, "Twice in the past twelve hours you've been a good cheerer-upper. Thanks."

"My pleasure." He stopped talking as they passed through security. After clearing the checkpoint, Hoff slipped his arm around Leeandra's waist as they continued their slow walk. Touching her and feeling the movement of her undulating walk excited him. "I'll call you tonight. Think you'll be back to your motel by ten?"

"Easily."

"Maybe I can come to see you in a week or so."

Hoff stopped and they stood at the edge of the corridor facing each other. He put both arms around her and pulled her closer. Her eyes were a deep caressing blue. He kissed her briefly on the lips.

She looked down and said nothing.

"Am I complicating things?"

She glanced up at his gull wing eyebrows. "Things are already complicated insofar as you and I are concerned."

"At the risk of sounding gallant, I'll get out of the way if it'll help. I don't want to, though." He kissed her quickly on the tip of her nose. "I like being with you."

With a quick, tiny shake of her head, she said, "I don't want you out of the way." She hesitated for a moment. "Thanks for letting me cry on your shoulder. I'm still not at ease being in charge. Sometimes, being out in front, I feel like I can see too far, too much."

"You're not out there by yourself. Ken, Larry, me—especially me—we're always ready to help. We'll get more help if we need it." He kissed her again, as lightly as before. "When Andy really likes someone, he says they're good people. You're good people."

"By his definition or yours?"

"Both. Andy likes you. He asked me to tell you hello. At the moment, however, I'm saying it for my account." The second boarding call for the flight to Abilene was announced, and Hoff ushered her toward the gate. "Next time, those pastors will have to do without you."

She nodded, handed her boarding pass to the gate attendant and said to Hoff, "Talk to you tonight." She kissed him on the cheek.

He watched her disappear through the gate. She reappeared on the ground outside as she walked toward the small, twin-engine plane, long blonde hair swung gently with each step. Before boarding, she turned and waved. He watched until the airplane took off, banked and disappeared from sight. He already missed her,missed her songful voice, even though her voice was not songful today. Today, he'd seen the trembling doe. She didn't mention the Antichrist ad. He wondered if Ken told her about it. He also wondered what was eating at Casper. With a fleeting thought, he wondered if Casper placed the Antichrist ad, but he dismissed the idea as preposterous.

Who Is R. C. Kiola?

Gracie was on the phone when Hoff got back to his office. He took a note from her outstretched hand, read it and nodded. The count on last night's receipts was nearing three hundred thousand dollars. The crowd was estimated at sixty-three thousand.

He returned a call from George Lee at the public relations agency.

"No luck on finding out who placed the Antichrist ad," George said. "The ad came from a walk-in at the *Chronicle*'s office. The individual paid cash. A receipt was issued to an R. C. Kiola."

"Same name as the soft drink?"

"K-I-O-L-A. There's nobody by that name in the telephone directory, information service or in the paper's subscriber records. A friend checked that for me."

"Nice touch."

George ignored the compliment. "I have sources who can check computer records on credit cards, criminal records and such, but I'm confident the name is made up. The ad came in near deadline. A pure screw-up caused it to run on Monday instead of Sunday. If whoever placed it tries for a refund, my contact will let me know. I don't expect that to happen, so I figure we're out of luck. The clerk who took the ad doesn't remember anything about the customer—not red, yellow, black, nothing."

"Isn't that odd, the clerk's not remembering the ad?" Hoff said. "It's not a run-of-the-mill classified."

"Doesn't strike me as odd. She takes those damned ads all day every day. She's seen and heard just about everything. She was probably sitting there thinking about her grocery list or last night's fuck or something."

Hoff laughed. "I can identify with that. Thanks for checking."

George said there'd been no media inquiries about the Antichrist ad. Hoff hung up and buzzed for Gracie to come into his office.

Among the things he gave her to do was to make sure plans were on track for the next indoor crusade, scheduled for November 16th in Lubbock.

"This venture has really taken off, hasn't it?" Gracie said. "How are Leeandra and Casper holding up?"

"Remarkably well, I'd say. A few aches and pains, but nothing an Ace bandage or two won't take care of." After Gracie left the room, Hoff muttered to himself, "Not."

Maybe-So Shopping Plan

Hoff called Leeandra from his condominium at 9:30 p.m.

"Hoff who?" she answered and laughed.

"You and your preacher buddies didn't get into the sacramental wine, did you?"

"Heavens no. We're all part of the confirmed grape juice set."

"In retrospect, I wish I'd taken a wrong turn to make you miss your plane this afternoon."

"That's nice," she said quietly. "If it's any consolation, the pastors were glad to see me."

"No consolation whatsoever. I'm taking each and every one of them off my Christmas list."

"They'll get even, you know. They'll take you off their prayer lists or put you on, whatever you don't want."

"That prospect aside, next time I'll take a wrong turn."

"Sounds fair." Leeandra paused. "Thanks again for letting me cry on your shoulder this afternoon. I'm glad you and Andy think I'm good people. Especially you."

"Actually, I think good people is an understatement."

"That makes things even better."

"I looked at your schedule," he said. "You have next Monday, Tuesday and Wednesday off. I'd like to see you then. Have you made any plans?"

"I'm thinking about going to Dallas to do some shopping."

"Good choice. I hear Goodwill has an exceptional selection."

"I'm partial to Salvation Army," Leeandra shot back.

"Hey, that was quick."

"I've worn more than a few Salvation Army clothes in my time."

"Are you kidding me?"

"No. When I was a little girl, we went through some hard times. It's no big deal, but when you mentioned Goodwill, I thought of it."

"Times have changed," he said. "Now, you can shop anywhere you please—Nieman's, Saks, lots of neat places."

"How would you know about places to shop?"

"I've gone shopping a time or two in my life. I did a lot of scouting around Dallas when I worked on that Hong Kong investors deal. I'll make a good tour guide."

"You're hired."

"I'll make reservations for us at the Anatole Hotel." The pause at her end was so long that he asked, "Leeandra?"

"I...uh...I'm not sure."

"I'm not hinting at anything untoward." He felt a prickle of peevishness at her reaction. "We'd certainly have separate rooms at the hotel, if you're concerned about that."

"I just don't know."

"Tell you what. I'll make the reservations. If you'll feel better about it, bring someone with you."

Leeandra was quiet for a time. "Don't think it's because I don't want to see you, Hoff. It's...well...I don't know."

"I promise to re-read the gentleman's handbook." He laughed. "I won't take advantage."

"I'm not worried about you."

He was surprised. "I'll make the reservations. If you change your mind, we'll meet in Amarillo. But I'll tell you one thing, Leeandra Kay Stevens. I'll see you during those three days if for no other reason than to get a McBurger."

Leeandra laughed.

"If I have to walk. Are we on?"

"We're on," she said.

"Terrific!" He hung up, perplexed by her reaction, shook his head and muttered, "This has got to be the most complicated situation I've ever gotten myself into. Her name might as well start with M."

Chapter 15

Looking for the Dark Secret

Dr. Henry Woods sat in his study at Centrum Church in Austin after he finished watching the videotape of Sister Cathedra's Astrodome special.

He had leaned forward to absorb every nuance of Leeandra's singing, her sermon, her powerful invitation at the end of the service.

Despite his on-again, off-again fits of anger about the Stevens organization's rejection of his attempts to affiliate with them, Leeandra's allure drew him toward her. She was an excellent Sister Cathedra. He thought the new name was a stroke of genius.

Dr. Woods tried to figure out the power of her pull on him. He knew she wanted nothing to do with him. She made her position imminently clear when she rejected him last spring in Corpus Christi. Still he was compelled to find a way to be near her.

He had not stirred during the hour-long program and stared at the television set until the last credit dissolved from the screen. With slow movements, as though his hands were weighted with lead, he clicked off the TV with the remote control. He sat for a moment before he turned off the desk lamp, darkening his office except for the weak light leaking in through the shuttered window.

Dr. Woods knew he must find a way to be near her. In the quiet of his office, he toyed with an idea. If a dark secret lurked in his own life, perhaps she had one. Discovering hers was his only hope of being at her side. Tomorrow, he would track down Rodrigo Como.

Thirteen years had passed since Dr. Woods lived in Miami, since he knew people like Rodrigo, a shadowy promoter with an uncanny knack for finding what people didn't want found. What Leeandra didn't want known was exactly what Dr. Woods had to know.

He jerked with fright at the loud knocking on the study's outside door. After an instant of paralyzed alarm, he clicked on the desk lamp and looked at his wristwatch. Cuddles and her friend were precisely on time. Last April, he had given Cuddles five hundred dollars to make up for slapping her around during his snit over Madelyn's betrayal, Leeandra's rejection and Banner Tatum's visit.

Dr. Woods and Cuddles had become frequent companions. She now let him kiss her on the mouth, and she was a more passionate French kisser than Madelyn. Her voice was not as whiney and offensive, perhaps because she felt more comfortable with him. Tonight, she was bringing a friend. Dr. Woods was in the mood to biconjugate in the church house.

Fifteen minutes after admitting Cuddles and her friend, all three were naked, sprawled in a daisy chain on the dais of Centrum Church. Dr. Woods buried his face between Cuddles' legs as he partook of what he laughingly referred to as a "lordly supper."

Christianity and Condoms

James Bresnahan hung up after the ninth ring. For three days, he'd tried to reach the Document Doctor. He wondered where Doc Doc was, although it wasn't uncommon for him to disappear for days at a time. In addition to forged documents, he furnished weapons and was an expert at getting counterfeit currency into circulation.

In his basement office, Bresnahan turned on his word processor and retrieved the data file on Sister Cathedra. He renamed the file after Leeandra adopted the new name. With flying fingers that made the keyboard sound like ticks of a rabid clock, he entered the dates for upcoming Sister Cathedra Crusades he'd found on the Internet.

He added a notation. "I see a mounting body of evidence that attests to inherent evil in Leeandra Stevens, a.k.a. Sister Cathedra.

"I was most disturbed to discover the involvement of the investor group led by Jerome K. Hoffstedtler, who obviously looks upon the Sister Cathedra ministry as nothing more than a mechanism for making more money. Taylor-Pepper-Coe, advertising agency for the Sister Cathedra Crusade—or, should I call it Sister Cathedra's Circus?—also works for purveyors of condoms, liquor and gambling. The gospel is being sacrificed to the gods of promotion and greed."

Bresnahan read his entry, corrected one typographical error and hit "Save." He said to the computer screen, "What must Sister Cathedra do to save herself?"

For now, though, Bresnahan knew which errant evangelist would be the next target of Mission Silver Broom. His trip to Tempe had confirmed his suspicions about Harley Mann.

Cookie and Conflict

Hoff stood at the ground-level window and watched the twin prop commuter plane taxi toward the Love Field terminal in Dallas.

After yesterday's diffident telephone conversation with Leeandra, he wondered what her mood would be. She seemed reluctant to make the trip, and he gave her every opportunity to change her mind. Throughout that conversation, he sensed a new, complicating alloy of feelings in her.

Hoff stepped outside to greet Leeandra and kissed her on the cheek. He took her garment bag, and they went into the terminal. "How did everything go in Abilene?"

"Everybody said the services were fine, but I felt they lacked something. We had big crowds. Many made decisions for Christ."

"Sounds like you're tired," he said. "A case of the blahs, maybe."

An attendant delivered her checked bag inside. Hoff picked it up and, carrying both bags, backed through the exit to the parking lot, holding the door open for her.

She reached for the carry-on. "Let me help."

"Sorry, but I can't do that. I'm considering a skycap career. I need to find out if I have the dexterity. I'm ready to practice accepting tips, too."

She laughed. "You have me confused with a big spender."

"In that case, I may have to call you Sister Skinflint."

Leeandra got into the rented Town Car while he put the bags in the trunk. When he got into the car, he saw the tenderness in her eyes. He smiled. "I wasn't altogether sure you'd come. I'm very glad to see you."

"Same here." She looked away.

After checking into the Anatole Hotel, they drove to the Galleria to shop. Leeandra tried on a midnight blue dress at Marshall Field's.

She emerged from the fitting room. "What do you think?"

"Wow. Only if it were red could it be any better. You're smashing in red."

She tilted her head."When have you seen me wear red?"

"Last year in Abilene. You also wore red when you sang on *Gospel Music Showcase* the first time. Why don't you wear it more often?"

"I feel too conspicuous in red." Leeandra laughed. "How's that for a dynamite reason?"

"It's the world's loss."

She bought two dresses, the midnight blue and a forest green.

"This is shopping heaven." A happy lilt brightened her voice.

"And, I imagine, hell for a few husbands."

"For you, too?"

"No. I like to shop. Instead of being a skycap, I might become a full-time shopper."

"I know where you can find an assistant," she said.

He grinned. "You've got the job."

They window-shopped until five. Both were hungry, chicken fajitas sounded good and they stopped at Mercado Juarez Restaurant.

"Save room for dessert," Hoff said. "The Anatole lobby snack bar serves the best chocolate chip cookies known to man."

At the hotel, each got one of the oversized cookies, a cup of coffee, and they sat at a table near a large Ficus in the towering atrium lobby.

"Oh, my," she said after her first bite. "I see what you mean. These are sinful."

"Fifty calories a bite. But not to worry. I have it on good authority calories don't count when you're having a fine time with a lovely lady."

Instantly somber, Leeandra changed. A tenseness sprang into her face, exciting a flinty edge in her eyes.

He frowned. "Did I say something wrong?"

"No." Her quiet response was barely audible above the hotel lobby's bustle and the nearby stair-step waterfall's gurgling.

"Something just happened," he said. "What is it?"

She shook her head slowly. "All of a sudden I...it's...I'm eaten up with the all-overs."

"I don't understand. You've been so completely at ease."

Leeandra toyed with her paper napkin for a few seconds. "I'm not completely at ease with anything right now. Things are so hectic. And these Antichrist ads keep showing up."

"Don't let that bother you. It's just some nut."

"It does bother me," she snapped. "I don't like it one bit. Those ads aren't good for the ministry."

Hoff didn't tell her R.C. Kiola also placed the ad in Abilene and did so by mail, enclosing cash.

"Why didn't you tell me about the Antichrist ad in Houston?" Leeandra asked, an accusing tone in her voice.

"I assumed Ken told you. You had a lot on your mind that day after Casper's flare-up. For all I knew, it was a one-time thing. I didn't think it was a big deal. I still don't."

She furrowed her forehead. "Protecting me?"

"Perhaps. Mostly, I wanted to talk about us."

Her testiness dissolved into a distant quiet. She took another bite of cookie and chewed absently.

"If my not telling you about the ad is what's bothering you, I apologize." He thought her eyes were as blue and clear as he could remember, but a taut wariness showed in her face.

"That's only part of it. A very little part, actually."

"What else? Let's talk about it."

She tinkered with her napkin. "Okay," she said quietly. "It's our relationship. I'm falling in love with you."

He started to speak, but she held up her hand.

"Let me finish. For a good while, I've cared for you, known that I could fall in love with you. Now it's happening. In Houston, I told you about the conflict between the ministry and other parts of my life. But there's more to it than that."

She sipped her coffee. "I was very much in love with my husband.

We'd been married nine years when he was killed." She stopped, looked down and resumed talking very softly. "I loved him every day, even when things weren't going so well between us. Then, that day came...that awful day. I saw them die." Leeandra's voice cracked. Her face was pale and her lips trembled. "My husband...my children...I've seen them die a thousand times. Sometimes I see them die in a grotesque, creeping slow motion. Other times it's like fast forward on videotape, all jerky and speeded up."

She folded and unfolded the paper napkin as she talked. Her voice was a heavy, halting drone that bored through the rustling din of other people's conversation, laughter and movement. At the lobby bar, the pianist played "Oh What a Beautiful Morning." In vivid detail, she told Hoff about the accident.

"Three people I loved so much." She stared up into the expanse of the Anatole's ten-story atrium, capped with twin pyramidal, glass tops. She bit her lower lip as she looked back down at Hoff, her eyes reddening, but still dry. Her voice quavered. "They were gone and I was left. All alone. I wasn't even hurt, but I felt like part of me died. Sometimes I think part of me is still dead."

He swallowed. "How about a warm-up?" He got refills for their coffee and came back to the table. She was gazing up at the one hundred-foot-tall, red-and-yellow Sri Lankan batik hanging in the atrium as he put the coffee in front of her. He squeezed her hand.

"Thanks." She forced a weak smile. "I've told you about going home and how Daddy got me involved in the ministry, made me feel useful."

She brushed strands of hair away from her face. "Things were going so well. You found us and put us on television. That started off with a bang." Leeandra stopped, her face suddenly pale again. "Then, Daddy died. I became Sister Cathedra. At least, part of the time I'm Sister Cathedra. Now, somebody is putting those ads in the paper calling me the Antichrist. I love the Lord with all my being. Nothing could be farther from the truth." She looked at Hoff, her eyes softer. "There's you and me." She glanced down at the tattered napkin, then back up through the Ficus tree into the atrium.

"When I was married," she continued, "my life was like that big tapestry up there. It wasn't perfect, because Bur and I had problems. Church was one of them. He hated church. For a short time, he experimented with drugs. He quit when he saw how much it upset me. Our life together was comfortable and well-woven with two lovely children. Bur loved me. Then it was like some monstrous vandal burst in and tore it all up— ripped my life to shreds right before my eyes. I've wished over and over that I'd also died."

Her hand shook as she sipped her coffee. She looked down into the cup. "I've gone through periods of hating God for tearing up my life. And I've felt guilty, because I know that's not how God operates. I've wondered if Bur's and the children's deaths happened to direct me back to the ministry." She raised her head; her eyes were a watery, deep blue. "But because I believe He's a God of love, I can't believe that's why Bur and the children died. Or why Daddy died."

Hoff watched her take a deep breath that seemed to go on and on as if she were trying to fill a vacuum inside her.

"I'm messed up, Hoff. I see glimpses of how good life could be with you. Like when we had hot dogs and chili. Like how much you cared for me last week when you took me to the airport. Like shopping this afternoon." She continued to fold and tear the paper napkin as she talked. "Since my husband's death, I'd never considered seeing a man until I met you. I want to love you, but...I'm afraid...afraid of another loss, afraid of something else that starts out good, then gets out of kilter. I'm also afraid the ministry will keep us apart."

He picked up his unused paper napkin and handed it to her. "I want you to know, if you don't already, that I love you, too." He grasped the tatters of her napkin and wadded them into a ball.

"Are you sure?" she asked quickly, the piercing blue eyes filled with the same assessing look that Joe Ted had used.

"Yes, I'm sure. While I haven't experienced deaths in my family like you, I have been through three divorces. I know something about emptiness and emotional hurt. I feel some risk, too, you know. I detest the thought of another failed marriage. But you're a warm, caring, loving person. Whether it's me or someone else, you'll love a man again." He paused. "I want to be that man."

She took another deep breath and glanced up at the peak of the atrium's roof, two hundred feet above. "Right now, I just seem to be a gnat in the immensity of all this...life...death....God's will...my will...Sister Cathedra...our ministry...loving you. I'm lost in it all."

Hoff reached across the table and rested his hand on hers. "You'll find your way. Remember what I told you on the way to the airport. I want you to be happy. I meant it when I said it's okay with me if you decide not to be Sister Cathedra."

"I believe you."

After several minutes of silence, Hoff glanced at his watch. "It's early, not even seven-thirty. How about a movie or a drive around town?"

She shook her head slowly. "I'm going to my room and try to have a good cry."

"Okay. If you want to talk more or go out, give me a call, will you?"

She nodded and stood.

"I'll see you to your room." He walked beside her and slipped his arm around her waist.

"Don't!" Leeandra twisted away suddenly.

Tears filled her eyes, hot with anger or fear. He couldn't tell which. He pulled his arm away and faced her. "It's the most natural thing in the world to want to touch you. Right now, I wish I could bundle you up in my arms and make all of your troubles go away."

"I'm sorry," she blurted. Tears streamed down her face as she turned and ran toward the elevators.

Stunned, he watched her disappear around a corner. A flare of rage subsided quickly. He strode to the lobby bar and ordered Scotch to help contend with his own inner vacuum. After each drink, he called his room to see if Leeandra had left a message.

Far-Away God

Leeandra sat at the window of her darkened, tenth floor hotel room staring at the lighted office towers in downtown Dallas. She wanted to cry, to purge herself, but no tears came.

She felt a tormenting, gouging loneliness. Crashing crosscurrents of what she did and did not want spun together in a welter of distressing indecision.

What I really want is to know what I want, she thought. If only I could talk to Daddy. He could help me sort through all of this.

She envied the well-defined structure of the lighted office towers.

If only she could hold Effy in her lap and cuddle her blonde little daughter to her breast. Or brush Effy's hair. That would bring purpose and meaning back into my life, she thought. But there is no Effy, just as there is no Daddy.

I'm alone and I'm a half-breed. Half Leeandra Kay Stevens, half Sister Cathedra. I don't like it up here, so high, out in front. I see too much. I see too far. I see too many questions. Oh, Daddy, why can't you be here to help me? God, why are You so far away?

Going Separate Ways

"I'm going home today," Leeandra said in a leaden voice to Hoff over breakfast the next morning.

He glared at her. "Okay." His voice was crisp. He felt no inclination to try to change her mind.

"I'm sorry I messed this up."

He struggled to keep from getting angry. "No need to apologize."

"I need some time to myself." Pleading brimmed in her eyes and swept away his incipient displeasure.

"Patient soul that I am, would fifteen minutes do?" His smile faded. "You're worth the wait."

"My flight leaves at eleven," she said. "Are you going back to Houston?"

"Yes. I'll give you a ride to the airport."

"Would you mind terribly? I'd rather take a taxi."

"My rate is better."

Leeandra tried to smile. "All the same."

"I'm going to leave things in your hands. I'll wait for you to call."

She hesitated a long time before answering, then shook her head and laughed with clattering mirthlessness. "This is so messed up. Here I am leaving you when I don't really want to. I was about to agree with what you just said, but I don't want to do that, either." A plea showed in her eyes. "What am I going to do?"

"When you're ready to abide by my answer, ask me again."

She bowed her head. "Okay," she whispered.

He reached across the table and lifted her chin. "I didn't say that to be ugly."

"I know."

"I have an answer in mind that's very clear cut to me, so ask any time you're ready."

She said nothing.

Hoff leaned back and tucked his thumbs in his belt. "There's a wonderful old Chinese saying. Fall down seven times, get up eight." He waited for a moment. "You'll get up."

"I hope so. I've got to pack." She stood. "Be patient with me," she said in a small voice.

Hoff answered, "I love you, Leeandra."

The caring flooded her eyes for the moment she looked at him before she turned and walked away.

Chapter 16

Letter from Henry

"I am fundamentally convinced I can help save Leeandra from many of the pressures associated with the burden of her ministry." Dr. Henry Woods paused to read the first paragraph of his letter.

Tears formed in his eyes earlier when a Fort Worth colleague told him about the Antichrist ads. Heartsick that someone made such an accusation, he decided to write to Jerome Hoffstedtler:

"I recognize your personal reluctance to have an association with me and my ministry. That reluctance notwithstanding, I am ordained to preach God's word, even as Leeandra is so powerfully ordained. I believe the successes we have both achieved are evidence of God's special blessing. This commonality of purpose, of ordination and of commitment to Jesus Christ are in themselves ties that bind.

"True, you discovered things about me that are unflattering. Elements of my personal behavior are, I realize, nonconforming. They are sins of the flesh because I am flesh. I want you to know that I shall abandon those interests. I do this in the spirit of clearing one obstacle to your acceptance of me in the Stevens ministry.

"I beseech you to set aside your grievances. I implore you to set them aside not only in the name of the Lord, but also with a view toward Leeandra's well being. My prayers are with her ministry.

> Yours in Christ,
> Henry Woods"

He wrote similar letters to Ken Walker and Leeandra and made a special trip to the post office to mail them. When he got back to his study, the light blinked on his private phone's answering machine. He listened to the message. "This is Rodrigo Como. I have information of immediate importance."

An Offer to Lip Sync

"We have a death threat against Leeandra." Ken Walker, the Stevens business manager, spoke in a frantic rush. "A man called the office about an hour ago."

Hoff stifled the urge to say "holy shit" and sat in stunned silence, holding the telephone to his ear.

"The Amarillo police are in our offices right now. We're trying to decide whether to hold tonight's service in Lubbock." Ken told Hoff the police questioned the Stevens Crusade office receptionist, but she could provide few details.

"Leeandra is in Lubbock?" Hoff asked. "What's her reaction?"

"Disbelief. But, she doesn't want to cancel tonight's service. What do you think we should do?"

"Cancel it, by all means."

"Do you think this threat could be from the same person who placed the Antichrist ads?"

"Could be." Hoff took a deep breath. "Could be anybody. Did the caller say he would shoot her? What exactly did he say?" Hoff looked at his watch. It read 10:49 a.m. on the Friday after Hoff's and Leeandra's ill-starred meeting in Dallas. Hoff pressed the intercom buzzer to summons Gracie.

"As best our receptionist can recall, the guy said, 'Sister Cathedra, the Antichrist, will die.' He said that twice, then added something about he couldn't allow it to go on, but he wasn't specific about what 'it' was. He said something else, but the receptionist couldn't understand him, and he hung up."

Gracie stood in front of Hoff's desk. "Hold on," Hoff said to Ken, then spoke to Gracie. "See how soon I can get to Lubbock. Okay, Ken, I'm back."

"I asked the police if the threat against Leeandra could be from the same person who shot Reverend Culpepper and the other two preachers," Ken said. "They don't know."

"I doubt it's the same person," Hoff said. "I don't remember hearing anything about warnings. Sounds like a whole different deal to me, but we can't take chances. You said Leeandra isn't taking this seriously?"

"I wouldn't say that, but she doesn't want to cancel tonight's service."

"I'll call her," Hoff said. "Is she staying in the usual place? I'll try to talk her into canceling. But if the service is held, make double-dog sure there are uniformed officers. Hire a bunch. An obvious police presence will be a deterrent." He took a note from Gracie. "I can get to Lubbock by four-fifteen. I'll talk to her before I decide on going."

When he hung up, he called out, "Gracie, is my go-bag ready?"

"Yes," she replied from her desk.

Hoff tapped out the number of the Ramada Inn in Lubbock. Leeandra's room phone was busy. "This is an emergency," Hoff told the motel operator. "Tell Miss Stevens Hoff is calling."

In twenty seconds, Leeandra was on the line.

"Ken just told me about the threat," Hoff said. "I agree with Ken. Tonight's service ought to be canceled."

Leeandra was slow to respond. "I don't want to do that. We've been full every night."

"There's no way to protect you in that tent. Someone could shoot from the street, a passing car, almost anywhere. You're a sitting duck."

"Would canceling one service do any good? If someone wants to kill me, how can we stop them? I won't crawl in a hole and hide."

"The death threat in addition to the ads worries me." Hoff was also worried because Banner Tatum was unable to discover who placed the Antichrist ads. "We've got to take this seriously."

"But not cancel the service," Leeandra said. "I won't do that."

He was irked by her insistence, but instead of conveying his vexation, he took a deep breath. "I asked Ken to arrange for uniformed officers."

"Good idea."

"I can make it up there before the afternoon is out," Hoff said. "Maybe I can help. I could stand in front of you and lip sync the service." When she laughed, he said, "Seriously, I think I should fly up there."

There was a very long pause. "On the security side of it, I don't see any reason for you to come."

"How about personal reasons?"

"My time isn't up, is it?"

"No."

"Then how about a rain check? I'm not being insensitive to your concern, but I'll be fine."

"How are you doing otherwise?"

"I miss you."

"I take that to be good news," Hoff said. "I hope you keep on missing me. I miss you, too."

Leeandra sighed. "I've got this big emotional granny knot inside of me. It sure would be nice if I had a mommy to get it undone."

"You'll get it undone."

"You keep encouraging me," Leeandra said, "but I don't seem to make much progress."

"I bet you're making more progress than you realize. And you'll make more. I'll call you tonight after the service, about ten o'clock or so. Don't let all this grind you down."

"I won't." Leeandra paused. "I love you."

"I love you, too."

He hung up the phone and looked at it until Gracie, standing in front of his desk, spoke.

"Are you going to Lubbock?"

He shook his head. "I love her. I think. She loves me. She thinks. Yet, we can't seem to get together. It makes no sense, Miss Gracie."

She smiled. "When love starts making sense, it won't be love."

After Gracie returned to her desk, Hoff propped his feet up on the credenza and looked out at the traffic fifteen floors below. Dissatisfaction gnawed at him. The Antichrist ads, Casper's behavior and now a death threat. Hoff wondered if they were connected. No, he told himself. Casper is too much of a weenie to do those things. Hoff's thoughts focused on Leeandra's distress. He wondered if she was about to fold under the responsibility of leading the fast-growing ministry. Barely aloud, he said, "Are the wheels coming off the wagon? Maybe I ought to pull the plug on this thing."

Even Preachers Use Aliases

In Tampa, Florida, Banner Tatum sat in the police department office of Detective Mike Bridges. Bridges finished reading the short newspaper article about the Sister Cathedra death threat and handed it back to Banner.

"What's with this about preachers?" Bridges said. "Do they provoke this kind of passion because they're so good? Or because they're so bad?

"Damned if I know," Banner answered. "Any advance warning when the Tampa preacher was killed?"

"No. Ditto in San Diego and Kansas City. All three came like bolts out of the blue. It all stopped just as suddenly in February."

"Sounds like you guys are at a dead end," Banner said.

"We're stumped." Bridges rubbed his nose. "This whole preacher thing amazes me. Take that death threat deal in Texas. One minute she's Leandra Stevens, the next she's Sister Cathedra. Even preachers are using aliases these days."

Banner laughed and stood. "Thanks for seeing me. If I stumble across anything, I'll let you know."

"Thanks. We need all the help we can get."

Cure for a Blue Funk

The call from Andy Boxx did not lift Hoff's spirits. He phoned about Leeandra's appearance on *60 Minutes* last night. "Damned if your preacher lady didn't come off looking like a water walker."

Hoff stared out his office window at the rain. The downpour began yesterday afternoon when a cold front sludged its way into Houston. He had intended to drive to Larry Best's townhouse to watch the program, but stayed home because of flooded streets.

Roger Concord, the *60 Minutes* interviewer, introduced Leeandra as the brightest, fastest-rising star among TV evangelists. At times, Hoff thought, Concord seemed awed by the smiling, blonde beauty who spoke with such quiet authority about Christ, the will of God and saving souls.

Despite last night's exposure on national television, Hoff felt low, his spirits as soddenly gray as the weather. He propped his feet on the credenza and watched the billowing curtains of rain blown by the gusting north wind. Crummy weather, he thought. His bad mood had more to do with Leeandra than with the weather. He hadn't talked to her in a week. She hadn't return his calls. The growing distance between them accounted for most of his funk.

Also contributing was this morning's call from Henry Woods. He insisted on meeting in Dallas on Thursday. When Hoff pressed to find out why, the Ausin preacher said, "Suffice to say, it is important enough that your interests will be served by meeting with me. I suggest you come with an open mind."

Hoff agreed to meet. Dr. Woods' patronizing tone added to his disgruntlement. Wonder what that slimey prick of a preacher has up his sleeve? Last week, when he received Woods' hand-written note, he scribbled "fuck off" at the top of the letter and mailed it back. Dr. Woods said nothing about the reply in today's conversation.

Another part of Hoff's bad mood was the fax informing him of another strike threat by workers at the gold mine in Peru. If the strike occurred, he would have to make another trip to Lima.

He glanced at his watch. 11:11. He was hungry, but had no lunch plans. He thought about calling Leeandra, but decided not to. He glanced at the calendar blocks on his credenza. Monday, November 6th.

His mind fouled with funk, he could think of nothing he wanted to do. Except, he thought, some fucking off. Or just plain fucking. I could use a touch of de-Leeandrafication therapy.

He thumbed through his book of women's names and numbers until the listing for Lucy Mazziotta stopped him. After Margo left three years ago, he met Lucy on a Friday night at a restaurant grand opening party promoted by the radio station where she worked. Their first encounter turned into a weekend of love-making. They saw each other off and on for a year. He hadn't talked to Lucy, a late evening radio talk show hostess, for more than a year. She should be awake by now. He didn't know if Lucy was still single. He would call. If a man answered, he'd hang up.

Lucy answered on the third ring, was pleasantly surprised to hear from him and liked his idea of bringing Chinese food over for lunch.

Lucious Lucy, he thought. With any luck at all, she'll be my fortune cookie for dessert. As he slipped on his raincoat, he wished Margo was still in town. Her fellatio fantastico was still the best. He also missed her for nonsexual reasons.

"Lunch?" Gracie asked as he strode by her desk. "Back when-ish?"

"When you see me, Miss Gracie."

Chapter 17

Ride, Harley, Ride

James Bresnahan was pleased with his plan to exterminate the verminous Reverend Harley Mann.

To begin each televised service, Reverend Mann rode his white motorcycle from an outside ramp through a garage door and onto a platform between the dais and the choir loft of Saved Souls Church in Tempe, Arizona. Revving the cycle's motor, he sped into the sanctuary then slid to a stop, jumping from the machine as an aide steadied it, then pushed it out of view. As the preacher rode in, eight shapely young women, dressed in tight, black leather pantsuits, sang, "Ride, Reverend Harley, ride. You've got Jesus at your side. Ride for Jesus, Harley, ride. 'Twas for us that Jesus died." The singers were billed as the High Octane Octet.

Bresnahan parked his rented minivan on the freeway service road, fifty feet from the end of the ramp the preacher used during his motorcycle-mounted entry. The preacher would ride in a straight line away from the van, an easy shot. The motorcycle's roar would mask the rifle's blast.

He had attached magnetic signs reading "EnviroTekCo" on both sides of the van, had dressed in khaki overalls and placed two stolen orange traffic cones at the back of his vehicle. He found a long, narrow cardboard box and rested the .270 Winchester rifle in it so passersby could not see the weapon.

He watched an assistant wheel the motorcycle out onto the ramp, start it and wait for Reverend Mann, who always dressed in a dark, tight-fitting, tailored suit, his platinum hair combed in duck tails.

Crouched in the front seat, Bresnahan watched the preacher stride jauntily toward the cycle, get on and rev the engine. Bresnahan nestled his right index finger against the trigger, and steadied himself as Mann began his run toward the door into the sanctuary.

Bresnahan waited until the preacher was almost to the opening before he fired. He watched Reverend Mann's back arch when he was hit. He stiffened as the motorcycle sped into the sanctuary and began to veer to the left, the direction Reverend Mann was falling. The assistant waiting to take charge of the cycle scurried out of the way as did the eight singers.

As he stowed the rifle and drove away, calmly so he would not attract attention, he sang softly, "You died, Harley, you died. Jesus wasn't at your side."

Making Somebody Pay

Danny Don Rhodes got to Hooper's Fina Station in Channing twenty minutes before time to start work. The Amarillo newspaper was in its usual place on the filing cabinet in the cramped, cluttered office, warmed by the butane heater. He flipped the pages hurriedly until he saw the headline. "Local Evangelist on National TV."

He had watched Sister Cathedra on *60 Minutes* last night. He thought she was treated so gently because she was a beautiful woman. He read about her network appearance and the upcoming crusade in Lubbock a week from Thursday. Also the New Orleans crusade on December 8th.

During his shift, Danny Don was preoccupied with Sister Cathedra, trying to organize his jumbled, confused thoughts. Sister Cathedra's face would melt away to become the departed Joyce's face that, in turn, became Skeeter's face. His mother's face was covered with globs of semen that hardened quickly into stringy, waxy burn scars. Then, a blurred blend of the women stared at him with wide, blood-shot eyes as a cackling laugh mocked him between repeated utterances of "scar boy, scar boy."

He hammered a flat tire away from the rim in the service bay with hatred-fueled anger. Confusion roared in his head. It's not fair, he thought. Not fair for people like Sister Cathedra to have it so easy. Not fair for me to be stared at like a common zoo animal, trapped in a cage of scars.

How would Leeandra feel if she was trapped like me? He felt a new rush of confusion. Is she Sister Cathedra or Leeandra? She shouldn't pretend to be somebody else. Maybe she's Sister Pretender. Maybe the death threat meant she should die. Now she's a TV star, too high-toned for me. His anger boiled as he thought about Sister Cathedra, free from troubles that made his own life a living hell.

He slowed his hammering as he thought, somebody has to pay. Sister Cathedra talks about lambs and sacrifices. What better sacrificial lamb than the beautiful pretender, Sister Cathedra, to pay for the sins of the world against him? She would do nicely, he thought as he resumed hammering the flat tire loose from its rim. He grinned as best he could through his burn-scarred lips and swung the heavy hammer. Making somebody pay would make him feel better. Believing he deserved that small bit of justice, he swung faster — again and again and again.

Confrontation at Gate 24

A foaming slurry of anger and distrust seethed inside of Jerome K. Hoffstedtler as he hurried off the jet at Love Field in Dallas. He turned right and strode along the concourse toward the gate where he had agreed to meet Dr. Henry Jackson Woods. Hoff stopped at a water fountain. Dry, pressurized airline cabins left him thirsty, even after short flights. He spotted the Austin preacher in the waiting area, empty except for him.

Dr. Woods stood. His eyes winced in a flurry of exaggerated blinks. Hoff was relieved when the man did not offer to shake hands.

"Thank you for coming," Dr. Woods said. The start of a smile evaporated when he saw Hoff's eyes, dark harbors of hostility.

"What do you want?" Hoff's voice was husky and quiet.

"Have a seat," Dr. Woods said as he backed up three steps, sat and looked up at Hoff. The preacher's jocular air was gone.

Hoff sat, leaving an empty space between them.

Dr. Woods was dressed in denim jeans, a red sports shirt and an expensive-looking, western-cut suede jacket. A roll of fat folded over the top of his pants. "I have a proposal," he said in a low, self-assured voice.

"Let's hear it."

"On several occasions, I've suggested a merger between Centrum Church and the Stevens Crusade."

"I'm aware of that."

"I've been rebuffed." He smiled mirthlessly. "Without so much as serious consideration, a look at the books or a formal meeting. I've been extended no courtesy. Last week I received your rude reply to my note."

"You took 'fuck off' as a rude reply? How perceptive."

Dr. Woods held up his hand, palm toward Hoff. "You know what you know about me and that's that. You don't like me and that's that. Being hostile won't help us accomplish anything constructive here today."

His chest crammed with the fury of his violent dislike for Dr. Woods, Hoff glared and spoke softly, "Say what you've got to say."

A spasm of blinks and the mirthless smile flicked across Woods' puffy face. "I anticipated a negative response to my merger proposal." He glanced around even though no one was within earshot. "Nevertheless, my suggestion stands. I have leverage that warrants your support."

"What kind of leverage?"

"I've learned certain things about Leeandra of public interest."

Hoff clinched his jaws as he thought, God, I detest this gob of gospel-spewing spit. "Go on."

"I know about Leeandra's husband's involvement with narcotics. His name was Burton Pierce Lee. Marijuana. Cocaine. I realize there's no clear evidence Leeandra used drugs, but the association is close enough to be damaging. Her tacit approval would not sit well with people who support her ministry. I know you had Leeandra investigated. I assume you already know about these unfortunate episodes. Unpleasantries, to be sure, and I hate to bring them up. But, even the ministry has its business considerations. These facts warrant review of your decision."

As Woods talked, Hoff controlled his anger. He made himself speak with less hostility. "Just how have you come up with these allegations?"

"Facts, not allegations. I know about them the same way you know. Your man's name is Banner Tatum. Quite a gentleman, your Mr. Tatum. I trust he passed along my thanks for the nice tape player?"

Hoff smiled. "Afraid not. He must've forgotten."

"Too bad. My man's name is Rodrigo Como, a resourceful gentleman I met in Florida before I moved to Austin. Mr. Como is as talented and thorough as your Mr. Tatum."

"I'll pass along your compliment to Banner." Hoff grinned. "It'll mean a lot to him."

Dr. Woods frowned. "We can spar or we can deal. Or we can each go our separate way and do what we have to do. Mr. Tatum was good enough to tell me about the time you burned a certain Mr. Bisqueen's ear lobe with a cigarette lighter. I am not intimidated. You should know that Rodrigo and I can be as unpleasant and vicious as you and Mr. Tatum. So—what's your pleasure?"

Hoff glanced away momentarily, then back at him. "Do your friends call you Henry?"

Dr. Woods' expression brightened. "Yes, they do."

A steely tightness snapped across Hoff's face and he hissed, "Then I'll call you asshole."

The preacher flinched. The expression in his eyes hardened. "That...."

"Shut up, asshole," Hoff barked. "Keep quiet and listen. What you and this Como character may or may not know is immaterial. Would you like for me to enlighten you as to what is material?"

Dr. Woods frowned through a flurry of blinks as he nodded.

"Health." Hoff smiled. "Perhaps life itself." His smile grew. "Certainly life as you've always known it with various pieces of your anatomy intact." He spoke with malicious slowness through his forced grin. "Pieces like your tongue...toes...testicles."

Dr. Woods' flexing jaw muscles were visible in spite of his fat face. He drew a breath to speak, but Hoff continued.

"You're probably not a student of Texas history, but I think you'll find this interesting. When Texas was being settled, the Indians did a lot of raiding, raping and pillaging. When some supposedly civilized white men caught those Indian braves, do you know what they did to them?"

Dr. Woods gaped at Hoff. The earlier flintiness in the preacher's eyes yielded to a confused cloudiness. He shook his head a single time.

"Those white guys cut off the braves' penises and testicles." Hoff smiled at him for several seconds. "And stuffed them in the braves' mouths." He snorted a short laugh. "Can you imagine such a thing? Fill a man's mouth with his own prick and balls?" Hoff let the steel-hard look snap back onto his face.

Dr. Woods glanced away in darting moments of visual retreat from Hoff's burning stare.

"End of history lesson. Except the white guys have improved their methods during the intervening hundred or so years."

"You...."

"Shut up!" Hoff commanded quietly and after a pause, added, "Asshole." He took a deep breath. "So we get back to what is material to this discussion. And it isn't what you think you may or may not know about Leeandra. That's irrelevant." He grinned as he watched the preacher's eyes dart from place to place, landing occasionally on Hoff's smiling face. "*Comprende*? Do you know what *comprende* means?"

Dr. Woods started to answer, but a gargling croak emerged and he cleared his throat. "Yes."

"No merger. And that's that. Period. Punto."

Dr. Woods took a handkerchief from his inside jacket pocket and mopped beads of sweat from his upper lip. "You are forcing me to do something I'd prefer not to."

Hoff laughed softly. "What's that? Walk around with your prick and balls stuffed in your mouth? That's not a preference I would expect your assholey-ness to choose."

Dr. Woods frowned. "That's offensive."

"Ah, now, there's something we can agree on." Hoff laughed. "Although I don't think offensive does justice to the notion of having your genitals stuffed in your mouth. Of course, it may not end there. Or may not be exactly that." Hoff's laughter was gone. He squinted at Dr. Woods. "I might jam a red-hot poker up your fat, whore mongering ass. Or baptize you in battery acid. Or beat the living shit out of you."

Dr. Woods took a long, deep breath and looked down at the floor, his eyes wincing with a rapid flutter of blinks.

"Now, you may be sitting there thinking we have a Mexican standoff, but we don't. Why don't you be a good Christian asshole and look at me when I talk to you?" Hoff paused until Dr. Woods slowly raised his head, his eyes filled with stunned defeat.

"I'll...," Dr. Woods began.

Hoff rose and held up his hand. "Quiet, please, asshole. I'm not finished. Inside of me, waiting to get out, is one of those bad white guys. All it'll take is finding the right Indian." He paused. "Right now, asshole, you've got Indian written all over your fat face. You'll do well to back off and keep your goddam mouth shut. And know this: I will never back off. You give me the slightest provocation—the slightest—and it's 'you Indian, me white man time'."

Hoff turned suddenly and strode away, headed for the main lobby area of the terminal. When he was out of the preacher's sight, he stopped at a pay phone and called Banner Tatum. On the fourth ring, when the answering machine clicked on, Hoff hung up. He called Banner's beeper and punched in the number of the pay phone he was calling from.

In less than a minute, the private investigator called back.

"That was fast," Hoff said. "Where were you?"

"I was coming out of the crapper at this service station on the Gulf Freeway. Got the goddam squirts. Why'd you beep me?"

Hoff told Banner about his conversation with Dr. Woods.

"Jesus!" Banner said. "What do you think Woods'll do?"

"Nothing. He's a coward."

"You and those damned preachers. I hope you never get involved with truly unsavory characters. What do you want me to do?"

"First, tell me what kind of idiotic story you told Woods about me burning Beady-eyed Bisqueen's ear lobe."

Banner laughed. "I needed something for effect, so I made it up. I thought it was weak, but it must've worked."

"Yeah." Hoff echoed the laugh. "And I gave that fat fucker a few other things to think about. There's something I want you to do. See if you can track down this Rodrigo Como character in Florida."

"And when I find him?"

"Buy him off for insurance purposes. Impress on him that if he plays with us, he plays with a winner. If he plays with Woods, different story."

"Meaning?"

Hoff paused. "Meaning he loses. Losses come in an assortment of forms. You can tell Como in good faith he won't like any of them. Can you jump on it right now?"

"Would you settle for a fast glide? Jumping and squirts don't mix too well."

To Forgive a Flibbertigibbet

Emotionally spent after the intense confrontation with Dr. Woods, Hoff tossed his keys onto the sofa room table of his condo. With tired indifference, he leafed through the mail, left by the concierge. Hoff's indifference evaporated when he saw the envelope scripted neatly in Leeandra's handwriting. He dropped the rest of the mail onto the table, went out on the balcony and sat on the chaise lounge to read her letter.

Monday, Nov. 6
Wichita Falls

Dearest Hoff:

It's almost midnight. Here in my room, all alone, I just treated myself to a wonderful bowl of imaginary chili from James Coney Island. I also imagined a tall, good-looking guy with me. He's the guy who's so nice even when I act like a ninny. When I got through imagining, I realized just how much I miss the real guy and how much I've tested your patience. Especially the way I acted in Dallas. Telling you that I love you, then pushing you away. That was two weeks ago, but it seems so much longer.

When we were in Dallas, I was being torn in two by Leeandra and Sister Cathedra. You could have called me Sister Confusion and I would have answered. I'm writing to ask you to forgive me for being such a flibbertigibbet. (Mother called me that when I was a little girl and did dumb things. The way she said flibbertigibbet reminded me of the jerky way a butterfly flies.)

I'm writing for another reason, too. If you don't already have plans, would you have Thanksgiving dinner with us in Amarillo? Casper, Ken and his family will be there, but mostly I'm asking you to come be with me. Perhaps you can stay for a few days.

I'm taking the coward's way out by writing. I'm afraid of hearing you say no over the phone. If your answer is no, you don't have to write or call. I hope you will come. I'm lonesome for you.

It's odd how you can be around so many people and still be lonely because the one person you want to be with isn't there. That's how it's been with me. I know this situation is of my own doing. At least, I think it is. I hope I'm not kidding myself. I'm good at that. And ducking what I feel and fear and don't want to face up to.

But I am facing up to one thing. I miss you.

I wish I could tell you Sister Confusion has gone for good. I don't think she has. But this me — Leeandra — needs you. I need you to love me and be patient with me. Above all, keep caring for me the way your eyes have told me you do. Will you?

I love you,
Leeandra

Hoff glanced from the letter toward the downtown office buildings three miles away. In seconds, he saw Leeandra's face framed in her long, straight blonde hair. The Leeandra he was seeing, who wrote the letter, seemed much younger than the one he remembered from Dallas. The letter's child-like simplicity showed in the face of this younger Leeandra. But it wasn't altogether her face. There was a part of Margo in this face, a blend of Margo and Leeandra. When a soft smile crinkled at the corners of her mouth, the face was all Leeandra. She brushed strands of hair away from her face and tilted her head a fraction, her Caribbean blue eyes soft and warm. A baptism by caring look that asked, "Will you?"

Chapter 18

Calm Before a Rage

Despite the piercing north wind, gray skies and a forecast of sleet, a standing room only crowd of ten thousand people filled the Lubbock Municipal Coliseum for the Sister Cathedra-Stevens Crusade on Thursday, November 16th, a week before Thanksgiving.

Danny Don Rhodes limped into the coliseum twelve minutes before the service started, angry about running behind schedule because Aunt Gertrude's ten-year-old Chevy sedan stalled. After ten minutes of trying, the car started. That vexation came on top of the irritation of having to convince her to let him borrow the car. Each time he used the spanking clean, dentless auto, the last thing he heard was her high-pitched, strident command, "Make sure you bring it back full of gas, you hear?"

During the one hundred-sixty-five mile drive from Channing, before the car stalled at the first light on Lubbock's north side, he thought about the threat against Sister Cathedra's life. He thought about the shooting deaths of the four evangelists and wondered why the killer hadn't been caught. He presumed there would be an army of extra security guards at the coliseum. But thoughts of threats and security were swept away when the engine stalled.

Because of his late arrival, he sat eight rows from the roof, far from the stage at the opposite end of the elliptical coliseum.

He was surprised at how few uniformed officers he saw in the big arena. An assailant could shoot her easily, he thought. He had no way of recognizing the three dozen plain-clothes officers assigned because of the murder of Reverend Harley Mann.

Despite the distance from where he sat, Danny Don was confident he could shoot Sister Cathedra easily. If he had brought the gun, getting into the coliseum with the 30-06 rifle his father gave him years ago—back when his father was around and they hunted together—would have been simple. Because of the cold weather, most people wore or carried long coats. Concealing the rifle under a top coat would be easy.

With a scope, he could shoot Sister Cathedra precisely between her big, beautiful eyes from twice this distance. He wondered how a marksman would go about making his escape, providing he wanted to escape. Getting caught could have advantages, assuming the shooter wanted to make a statement.

Were he ever to do anything like that, he would want to be heard. If he decided to shoot Sister Cathedra, it would be to make a point. In news conferences and television interviews, he could tell the world of the injustices inflicted on him. He could announce he'd evened the score and made someone pay, even though the someone was not guilty of transgressions against him.

Sister Cathedra must be guilty of something or there would not have been a death threat. He could mete out justice for the victim making the threat, and get his own point across. People must learn not to turn their backs on victims. It's unfair. The word ricocheted through a buzz of confusion. Un-un-fair-fair.

The service began, interrupting his sinister thoughts of getting even. He enjoyed Leeandra's a cappella singing. Her voice calmed him. When she sang, he thought of her as Leeandra, never as Sister Cathedra. His calm continued throughout her sermon. Her lilting words sounded almost like singing, and they suppressed his confusion and neutralized his anger. He continued to think of her as Leeandra as she preached. His thoughts of getting even went away.

He found peace and hope in what she said and was surprised at how fast the time passed. Her sermon was over, and she was inviting people to make decisions for Christ. Not until midway through the first verse of the invitational hymn did he remember an earlier thought. For the next verse and a half, he felt indecisive about whether to make his way to the floor of the coliseum to determine how close to her he could get—in case he should decide to make Sister Cathedra pay. Now, he wanted to get close to Leeandra to see if she was as pretty in person as on television.

He decided to go. After reaching the coliseum's floor, he edged through the crowd until he was less than twenty feet from where she stood on stage. She was a smiling, beautiful goddess with golden hair cascading down the back of her dark blue dress.

Danny Don felt a quiet awe, a peaceful shadow of reverence as he looked up. For the first time, when she held out her arms, exhorting people to respond to the call of Christ, he saw her as Leeandra and Sister Cathedra, one in the same. Could she care as much about people as her words from the pulpit evidenced? Could she care as much as the singing Leeandra?

As he stood with his scarred face tilted up, she glanced down at him and smiled. She didn't stare or grimace. Nor did her eyes dart away from his stringy, waxy burn scars. He saw compassion in her eyes before she looked back out across the crowd. He sensed a beauty inside her, a powerful, rejuvenating presence. Perhaps he could talk to her and find out if she really cared. If she did, it would make a huge difference. Having someone as lovely and as important as Leeandra care about him would give new meaning to his life. She would only care about someone who counted. He wanted to be among those who did.

He wanted to stand there and bask in her presence, but he made himself turn and edge toward one of the people helping register respondents. He got a man's attention, a smiling, elderly, white-faced man whose head shook in bobbing, clockwise little circles.

"Excuse me," Danny Don said, "could you help me?"

"Of course, how may I help?" The old man's shaking face smiled. He, too, seemed unfazed by Danny Don's scars.

"I need to talk to Leeandra...to Sister Cathedra. Can I talk to her?"

The man continued to shake and smile. "There are thousands of people who would like to speak to her, but I'm here to help. Tell me what's troubling you."

Tell you? Danny Don's head instantly filled with a gush of rage. You? Who the hell are you? He looked up at Leeandra, then back to the man with the shaking, smiling face. How can I tell anyone but her? What difference will it make if I tell anyone but her? None.

He mumbled something unintelligible even to himself, turned and pushed his way through the crowd and out into the early winter storm that fulfilled the weather forecaster's prophecy of sleet. Neither the gusting, cold north wind nor the whipping pellets of ice cooled the rage that boiled inside of Danny Don Rhodes as he thought, Leeandra doesn't care. Sister Cathedra doesn't care. She wouldn't talk to me. What a fool to think she'd care for someone like me.

Muddled Resolve

James Bresnahan frowned as he held the cinnamon disc on his tongue, watching the hubbub on the floor of the Lubbock Municipal Coliseum. He twisted the candy's cellophane wrapper into a tight strand and tucked it into the side pocket of his blazer. Fingering the cleft in his chin, he watched Sister Cathedra stand on stage, her arms lifted as the invitational portion of the service continued. Hundreds of people surged forward to make decisions for Christ.

When she entered at the start of the service, long blonde hair swinging rhythmically, he felt a clear resolve to exterminate her. Now, that resolve was muddled. He was favorably impressed by the crowd's response to her fervent appeal for people to accept Jesus Christ as their savior. A cappella, she sang two hymns in her clear soprano voice. Hers was a peaceful, soothing, angelic voice, much like the singing he remembered hearing in several of his boyhood visions. Sister Cathedra's singing was exponentially more powerful in person than on television. She adhered to the conventional arrangements. She didn't embellish with unneeded choreography as did the obnoxious Harmonia Tracker.

When she preached, she spoke of God's love. With brilliant simplicity, he thought, she recounted how God sent His only begotten Son, to atone for the sins of mankind. She did not ask for money.

Bresnahan chewed the thin remains of the candy. Perhaps Sister Cathedra was not one of the vermin. Or, perhaps she was just on her best behavior tonight. He would have to find out more, would have to decide. Vermin are resourceful in finding their escapes.

Zero Problems

In the lobby of the hotel where he was staying in Lima, Peru, Hoff thanked the concierge's runner with a generous tip. He unfolded the fax and read: "Lubbock Crusade an unqualified success. Zero problems. Collected more than fifty thousand dollars. Banner says no progress on preacher killings. See you Monday. Gracie." He wadded the message and deposited it in a large ashtray.

Never Another Chocolate Chip Cookie

As he exited the plane on Thanksgiving Day, Hoff grinned when he saw Leeandra standing at the end of the jetway in the Amarillo airport. Her head tilted a fraction, and a smile brightened her face.

When Hoff reached her, he put his garment bag down, clasped her shoulders and they looked at each other for a moment before he enveloped her with a hug.

"I'm glad to see you," she said, barely above a whisper.

He hugged her tighter and stroked her hair before he held her by the shoulders at arm's length, then kissed her briefly on the lips. "And I'm glad to see your smiling self. Where've you been for the last light year and a half?"

"How are you?" she asked.

"On top of the world! Why don't I get back on the plane and get off again? This is fun."

She laughed. "Why don't we head for home and have Thanksgiving dinner?"

"Second choice, but it'll do." Hoff picked up his bag, and they held hands as they strolled across the lobby. They got into the Stevens Crusade's twelve-passenger van in a no parking zone at the front door. She drove.

"The only good thing about driving this boxcar is I get by with murder in no parking zones." She looked at Hoff and laughed. "There's nothing in the Ten Commandments about parking."

"Whatever works. I'm glad to see you relaxed. I know you're ready for this break."

"And how. Except for going to Florida to see Aunt Emma and conducting the New Orleans service, I plan to catch up on doing nothing during the holidays. Next year should be calmer with fewer tent services. You were right about needing to let up on those."

"Especially now that you've become a television star."

Leeandra made a scrunched face. "Oh, hush!"

"It's happening. You were a big hit on *60 Minutes*, you know. Now you're scheduled for *The Today Show*."

"*The Today Show* appearance has been postponed, I guess you've heard."

"Yes. Disappointed?"

"No. Now that it's scheduled two days before the New Orleans service, we'll do it from the NBC station down there."

"I hoped you'd go to New York. I wanted to show you the sights. We could see *Cats*. You'd love that show. After the play, we could go to the Algonquin Hotel for dessert and coffee."

Leeandra smiled. "No shopping?"

"Only if you're in a good mood."

"I was in a good mood while we were shopping."

"But I'll never buy you another chocolate chip cookie. They give you the miseries."

"That was a rough day."

They were silent for several minutes as she drove.

"Are we having turkey and the trimmings?" Hoff asked.

"Yes. Ken Walker's wife and Casper are cooking. Casper inherited Daddy's interest in the kitchen."

"How is Casper?"

Leeandra tapped her knuckles against her forehead. "Fine, knock on wood. He's back to his normal, happy self."

"How has he reacted to the Antichrist ads and the death threat?"

"He seems totally unconcerned, as if none of it happened."

Hoff frowned. "I was surprised there was no ad when the crusade was held in Lubbock."

"Maybe the person is tired of going to the trouble." Leeandra glanced at him. "I missed having you in Lubbock."

"I got held up in Lima." The gold mine labor dispute proved surprisingly simple to settle after Hoff offered a union representative five thousand dollars. Meetings on expediting rail shipments of the ore delayed his getting home. "They're slow as the itch down there."

Hoff recognized the street Leeandra turned on to.

"Here we are," she said as she turned into the driveway.

After the introductions to Ken's family, Hoff took his bag to the garage apartment, hung up his clothes and returned to the house, which was filled with the appealing smells of dinner.

He spent several minutes looking at momentos, knickknacks and pictures scattered about the cluttered den. He dawdled in front of a framed picture of Leeandra when she was, he guessed, ten years old. She peeped out from behind Joe Ted, who stood with his arm around his wife's shoulder. Leeandra got her looks and blonde hair from her mother. Hoff wondered why Leeandra stood behind her father when the picture was taken.

Shortly before two o'clock, they gathered in the dining room. The table was crowded with turkey, ham, cornbread dressing, giblet gravy, vegetables, salads and relishes. Laughter punctuated the festive mood as they ate. When the meal was finished, Hoff and Ken helped Leeandra with clean-up duties.

Not until after the ten o'clock news were Leeandra and Hoff alone. They played "Scrabble" until midnight, laughing and arguing about the correct spelling of words.

The game was nip and tuck until Leeandra spelled "zincoid", earning fifty bonus points for using all seven tiles plus crossing a triple word score space.

"A hundred and seven!" Leeandra pronounced triumphantly when she finished adding up her score for the play.

"Are you sure that's a real word?"

"Positive."

He squinted at her. "This looks like divine intervention. I object."

The next morning, Casper prepared waffles and bacon. His demeanor seemed no different than any other time Hoff had been around him.

After breakfast, Hoff and Leeandra ran several errands. A blustery cold front hit shortly before noon, sending the mercury spiraling. By two o'clock, Hoff had a blaze going in the fireplace. Casper left to help a church group with its Christmas music program.

Hoff and Leeandra ate an early dinner of soup and turkey sandwiches on the sofa in front of the fireplace. They savored the fire as the cold north wind battered temperatures down under gray clouds that spat occasional granules of snow.

Leeandra held a cup of hot chocolate in both hands. "This is the life, isn't it? At home in front of the fireplace on a wintry afternoon." She smiled at Hoff. "With my fella."

He slid his hand through her hair and rubbed the back of her neck. "Agreed."

She sipped the hot chocolate and stared at the fire. "My life has really changed in the past year. Who would've ever thought I'd be on national television, flying first class, staying in suites at hotels? Preaching to crowds like we had in Houston and Lubbock. That's quite a difference from when you saw us in Sweetwater."

"It's called success."

"I wish Daddy could be here to enjoy it with us. He laid the foundation for so much of it. To think it started sixty-five years ago with Grandpa Preacher Bob's wagon. And his mules, Nutty and Putty." She lapsed into silence.

"Are you feeling more comfortable with everything, with Sister Cathedra?"

Leeandra didn't respond right away, then she answered quietly, "Sometimes....I'd just as soon not talk about Sister Cathedra."

"Suits me." He let several seconds pass, then asked, "When do you go to Florida?"

"Not until after Christmas. I'm looking forward to seeing Aunt Emma. She's actually my great-aunt by marriage, but we were close when she lived in Lubbock. She's been wanting me to visit. It'll be my first trip to see her since she moved to Innisbrook."

"That's a nice place."

"You've been there?"

"I've attended a couple of business meetings there."

Leeandra laughed. "I think you've been everywhere."

"Not by a long shot."

"I haven't traveled much. I don't count the tent crusade as traveling." She looked at the fire for several seconds. "If you could go anywhere in the world right now, where would it be?"

"Would you go with me?"

She looked at him for a moment, a happy sparkle in her blue eyes. "Yes."

"Anywhere."

"No fair! You've got to pick a place. You're on the phone with a travel agent and you have to make plans."

Hoff thought for a moment, then pretended to talk into a telephone. "I'd like to make reservations for two weeks at Nisbet Plantation Inn on Nevis. Ask them to confirm one of the bungalows on the first row facing the beach. Reserve a rental car—a Moke will be fine—from Mr. Howell in Georgetown. Ask him to meet our flight. We'll fly first class, by the way." He covered the pretend mouthpiece and said, "They're checking to see if there's a vacancy."

Leeandra laughed. "I love your 'by the way' on flying first class. That's big spender's nonchalance if ever I saw it."

Hoff moved his hand. "All set? Good." He pretended to hang up the phone. Once again, he slid his hand through her hair to her neck. "We'll have a picnic on Pinney Beach. Go snorkeling. Pig out on coconut tarts at the little native eatery in Georgetown. Take the ferry to St. Kitts. Have conch fritters for lunch at the hotel's beach cabana. I guarantee it will be your best vacation ever."

"Sounds perfect." The smile dissolved from her face as she looked at Hoff, her eyes almost purple in the dim light. Slowly, she turned to look at the fire. In seconds, she was deep in thought.

Hoff listened to the ticking Seth Thomas clock on the fireplace mantel for a long while before he said, "You're not going to leave me here all by myself, are you?"

She turned back to him and the smile returned. "Oh, no. It's a quiet, contented day, much too good to leave." With a sudden move, she sat forward on the edge of the couch and pivoted toward him. "I've done a lot of thinking since we were in Dallas. Remember what I said about the deaths of Daddy, Bur and the children directing me toward the ministry?"

He nodded.

"Something else dawned on me the other night. Their deaths were also among the many circumstances that brought you and me together."

He was about to respond when Leeandra scooted closer to him and leaned her head against his shoulder. "My happiest times," she said softly, "come when I let myself be myself....And when I'm with you."

Hoff kissed her on her forehead, and she said, "During the past month or so, part of me has always been with you."

He wrapped his arm around her and hugged her closer. "Thanks for inviting me for the holiday."

"I wanted to be with you."

They sat in silence, both looking into the fire, enjoying the warmth of the blaze and their feelings.

He kissed her forehead again. "I love you, Leeandra Kay Stevens."

She nestled against him. "I love you, too."

Hoff kissed her again, this time on the lips, a long kiss that became passionate and didn't end until their tongues explored each other's mouths.

Chapter 19

Awakening in Grand Style

Dr. Henry Woods rubbed his protruding, hairy belly as he stood naked at the sliding glass door in his third floor hotel room, overlooking the beach and the Gulf of Mexico two miles south of Port Aransas, Texas. He drank coffee and looked out at the clear blue morning, feeling lucky to find such nice accommodations at the last minute on Thanksgiving weekend.

He turned for a quick look at Cuddles, still asleep, lying on her left side, her wonderfully ample right breast exposed. He felt more relaxed than he had in months. The chief complainant against him in the investigation over misuse of church funds accepted his offer of twenty-five thousand in cash and left Austin. Without that witness's testimony, according to his attorney, the authorities would not get an indictment.

He had abandoned his effort to merge with the Stevens Crusade. The confrontation at Love Field left him angry, determined to lash out with his Rodrigo Como-supplied information. But the confrontation also made him afraid. In the days following the meeting, his resolve to retaliate faded much faster than the fear bred by the smoldering intensity of Jerome Hoffstedtler's eyes. His decision to abandon the merger effort was made all the more comforting by his success in buying off the crucial witness.

The payoff completed, he decided to reward himself with a quick trip to the Gulf Coast with Cuddles. He rented a Dodge van. As specified to the rental agent, only the two captain's chairs in front were in the van. He put a large air mattress in the back. During the drive from Austin, they stopped and fornicated on the mattress at a roadside rest area.

This afternoon, he intended to find an isolated stretch of beach where he and Cuddles could have sex. If the weather was warm, they could stroll naked on the beach, then fornicate in the surf.

After a last look at the brown pelicans flying along the wave tops, he shuffled to the bed. He would wake Cuddles in grand style. Sir Henry the Hard was at her service.

Money for Bus Fare

Danny Don Rhodes was leaving an antique store in Amarillo the day after Thanksgiving. He had sold the two gold pocket watches that had belonged to his paternal grandfather. The store's proprietress was sympathetic when Danny Don explained he needed money to pay for more corrective surgery on his scars. He was pleased with the two hundred and seventy dollars she paid, almost double the highest offer at the other two places, both pawn shops. While in the pawn shops, he priced used

VCR's. He continued to look forward to the time when he had one to play pornographic tapes. For now, he wanted money for another purpose, one so important he decided to sell the only two valuable family keepsakes he owned.

He buttoned his fleece-lined denim jacket before he stepped out into the windy, cold afternoon. He had enough money to cover bus fare and other costs of his trip to New Orleans on December 7th, the day before Sister Cathedra's crusade in the Superdome. Following the service in Lubbock, as he was driving home to Channing, he decided that only Sister Cathedra could atone for the sins of the world against him.

None Is Perfect. No, Not One

On Wednesday, December 5th, James Bresnahan watched Sister Cathedra on *The Today Show* on the small kitchen TV while he peeled and sectioned a grapefruit to go with his English muffin. He clicked off the set when he sat down to eat. A cold rain fell, turning pines into a soft, grayish green. He chewed a bite of muffin, which he ate without butter or preserves. In his head, he replayed Sister Cathedra's television appearance.

She says all the right things, he thought. So well trained, so perfectly programmed. The television appearance just prior to the New Orleans crusade, her well-coached demeanor and her impeccable grooming were too perfect. He recalled a quotation, but couldn't remember from whom. "None is perfect. No, not one."

At the service in Lubbock, her presence had been commanding. For two days, the sound of her hauntingly beautiful singing had filled his head. Her voice dictated that she be heard. Coming to grips with why he felt uncertain about Sister Cathedra was difficult. Now he was sure, committed to the fifth sweep of the silver broom.

After he tidied up the kitchen, Bresnahan glanced at his watch. He faced an hour-long drive to Fayetteville, and he must allow time to stop at the bank for cash for the trip. He did most of his banking in Fayetteville. Bentonville was too small a town, too prone to idle talk that could acquaint people with his personal business. In Fayetteville, he would catch his flight to Little Rock and the connecting flight to New Orleans.

He had an appointment with the Document Doctor for four this afternoon. In addition to another set of fake IDs, he wanted credentials that would admit him to the Superdome and allow him freedom to move about the day before Sister Cathedra's service. Doc Doc was confident he could provide the credentials and fill another of Bresnahan's requests: a seven millimeter Super "14" Contender. Technically, the weapon was a pistol with a long barrel, but at the range from which he anticipated shooting Sister Cathedra, it was a perfect choice. He popped a cinnamon disc into his mouth. He was eager to do more of God's work.

Another Important Success

Hoff propped his carry-on bag against the end of the sofa in his condo living room and hurried into the kitchen to refill his coffee cup. Leeandra's segment on *The Today Show* was next.

He returned to the living room sofa and nursed his coffee as co-host Karen Kennedy began. "She is widely regarded as a powerful, emerging force in television evangelism. Her name is Leeandra Stevens, although she is usually referred to as Sister Cathedra in her ministry." Leeandra's face appeared on the screen as Kennedy continued. "She is standing by live in the studios of NBC affiliate WDSU in New Orleans where she will conduct a service in the Louisiana Superdome Friday night." The screen was split, showing the faces of both women. "Welcome to *Today*."

"Thank you," Leeandra responded. She wore a red dress. With her blonde hair, she presented a regal crimson and gold visage.

"Is Sister Cathedra a stage name?" Kennedy asked.

"Sister Cathedra gets more attention than my own name and thus attracts more people to our services." Leeandra smiled confidently. "That's why we use it."

"Good answer," Hoff said aloud.

"Miss Stevens, what is the relevancy of your work?"

She was instantly somber. "The gospel of Jesus Christ is relevant because He offers salvation and eternal life. The response of so many people is powerful evidence of its relevancy." Her singsong lilt was pronounced. "This is not my work. It is God's. I happen to be one of the instruments through which His word is delivered."

"Don't you compete unfairly with local congregations? Siphon off money that might be used to meet local needs?"

"We work closely with congregations. Here in New Orleans, volunteers from twelve churches will help in Friday's crusade. Each church will benefit financially. We enjoy close relationships in all cities where we take our crusade. We contribute tens of thousands of dollars a year to congregations that assist us as well as smaller, new congregations. Our work provides names of many prospective new members for local churches. Our ministry extends beyond the usual Sunday morning boundaries. I would say that we augment the work of local churches."

Kennedy nodded. "We will show video from your service in Houston's Astrodome. Then I'll ask you a question." In the twenty-second clip, people filed toward the stage as Leeandra sang her solo. "Aren't you actually in show business?"

A smile softened her face. "We are an evangelical organization that spreads the gospel. Because we utilize television, you may consider it show business. I consider it worshipping our Savior, Jesus Christ."

"Are you an ordained minister?"

"I am ordained by God, not by a single denomination. I'm blessed with the opportunity to sing and preach the gospel thanks to the years spent building this ministry by my late father, Joe Ted Stevens, and his father before him. My sense of mission is reinforced each time another person accepts Jesus Christ."

Both women appeared on the split screen. Kennedy smiled. "Thank you, Miss Stevens. The best to you in your New Orleans crusade."

"Thank you." Leeandra smiled calmly into the camera.

"Terrific!" Hoff shouted and switched off his set with the remote.

He slipped on his suit jacket, picked up his bag and headed for his car. As he drove toward Hobby Airport to catch his flight to Miami, he thought about how well things were going. Leeandra's spot on *The Today Show* was another important media success.

Of more importance was the fact that he and Leeandra were closer than ever. Since Thanksgiving, they had talked every day, sometimes twice. Their time together in Amarillo had been relaxed and comfortable. For the first time, there hadn't been a backward step. He smiled, recalling how they kissed in front of the fire.

They didn't make love. During the long kiss that became passionate and writhing, he fondled her breasts through her blouse. When the kiss ended, leaving them breathless, he found himself strangely unsure what to do next, despite the dictates of his rigid penis. Leeandra made the decisive move. She walked to the fireplace and stood looking at the blaze.

In one of their subsequent telephone conversations, Leeandra admitted she had wanted to make love. "Maybe wanting is as big a sin, but I feel better that we didn't."

He also wanted to, but when the opportunity presented itself, he hesitated. Most of his inaction was caused by not wanting to risk making her angry. He couldn't figure out what the other part could be. Never before in his adult life had he felt such hesitancy. He grinned as he thought about how much he enjoyed being with Leeandra in Amarillo. At times, they acted like a couple of teenagers. They popped corn. She laughed and scolded him when he offered to do the popping. "I may not be much of a cook, but I can at least pop popcorn."

Hoff hoped his meeting in Miami to secure financing for a shopping center would end soon enough to get to New Orleans tomorrow. With luck, he would.

Chapter 20

To Assure No Interference

"Yes, sir, only the best will do on a big deal like this," James Bresnahan said and laughed politely. He wore freshly-pressed khakis with U.S. Audio Services Corp. embroidered above the left pocket on his long-sleeve shirt. The uniform and worker floor pass, bearing the name Ben Extett, came from the Document Doctor. Doc Doc also furnished the seven millimeter Super "14" Contender, pleased with his ability to fill such a challenging, last-minute order.

Bresnahan talked with a Superdome maintenance employee, one of many people scurrying to finish setting up for the Sister Cathedra-Stevens Crusade service in New Orleans tomorrow night.

"I'm here to test telephone and electrical circuits to assure there's no connectivity between the two that could cause inter-circuit harmonics. That kind of interference messes up sound recording, live audio feeds and such," Bresnahan explained. Although he knew nothing about the subject, he spoke with confident ease. "The sound system has to be up to network standards. I need someone familiar with this place to show me around. I've been to Tiger Stadium over in Baton Rouge and lots of other places, but never here. Mostly, I work the West Coast and Rocky Mountains." As he talked, Bresnahan extracted his billfold and pulled out a fifty dollar bill. "Would this make it worth your time?"

The worker, whose badge identified him as Jack Canada, grinned and reached for the money. "Just tell me what you want to see," he answered in a Cajun-flavored drawl.

An hour later, Bresnahan found what he wanted. The small, electrical panel room under the mezzanine-level seats provided a line of sight to the stage on the Superdome's floor. He would remove a small ventilation grate and shoot through the opening.

When promised another fifty dollars, Canada agreed to carry Bresnahan's equipment trunk to the electrical panel room.

"No need for you to report this to the Internal Revenue Service. I've got all kinds of fake receipts. These big-time religious moguls can afford it," Bresnahan said and laughed, handing the maintenance man the second fifty dollar bill after he set the trunk on the floor.

Jack Canada also laughed as he looked down at the money. The laugh turned into a tortured wheeze when Bresnahan drove the stiffened fingers of his right hand into the workman's Adam's apple. The wheezing stopped when Bresnahan delivered the chopping blow across the bridge of Canada's nose. Bresnahan had learned the moves when he took lessons in self-defense after being beaten up by a drunk outside his New Orleans mission five years ago. Within ten minutes, the workman's body, lifeless from strangulation, thudded to the bottom of a return air shaft.

Bresnahan loosened the screws on the grate to be removed, then retightened them so they wouldn't be noticed. He checked the contents of his trunk, adorned with a newly-painted U.S. Audio Services Corp. inscription, and locked it. Before leaving the room, he made sure the master key, also obtained from Doc Doc, worked. It did. He locked the room, strolled out of the stadium and headed for his corner suite at the Windsor Court Hotel. He was pleased at the smooth start of his mission and glad he had time for a strenuous, mind-clearing run before dark.

Findings about Casper

"Dadgummit!" Upset by the delay and pressured by last-minute preparations for tomorrow's service, Ken Walker spat out the expletive, the strongest in his vocabulary. The Stevens Crusade business manager looked at the activity going on around him.

Eighty volunteer choir members milled about the stage or sat on risers in the yawning, afternoon emptiness of the dimly lit Louisiana Superdome in New Orleans. They waited for Casper Stevens, more than twenty minutes late for the final rehearsal.

Ken turned to a band member. "Any idea where Casper is?"

"I saw him about an hour ago, back by the dressing rooms."

Ken skipped down the stage steps and hurried across the stadium floor into a corridor leading to the dressing rooms. They were empty. Casper is hardly ever late, Ken thought. Where could he be?

Ken stuck his head into a large lounge room where several volunteers sat, drinking coffee and talking. "Anybody seen Casper?" His question was answered with a "no" and a "sure haven't."

Ken began to check other rooms that lined the hallway. Frustrated by their emptiness and Casper's tardiness, Ken stood in the quiet corridor, struggling to control his vexation.

An unusual sound captured his attention. He listened intently for ten seconds before he walked slowly toward the source. As he got closer to a small room, dark with its door ajar, he was sure someone was crying and talking. After he listened for another moment, Ken was also sure it was Casper.

Ken frowned as he tiptoed to the door. He was about to knock when a surge of anguished, crying words stopped him.

"Oh, dear God, please forgive me." Words gave way to sobs that yielded to more words. "How could I have done these awful things to her, Your servant, my own sister?"

Shocked, Ken held his breath as he waited for another wave of sobs to subside.

"Forgive me, Heavenly Father, for the thoughts I've had about her, for thinking she's evil." A new spasm of tormented crying erupted, then waned quickly. "Oh, God, forgive me for thinking thoughts about her death, for making that call in my time of weakness, for placing those ads. Oh, God...." Casper's voice again succumbed to racking sobs.

Ken listened to the tortured confession in stunned silence, alone in the sterile hallway. Casper did those things! How could he?

Ken resisted the urge to charge into the room and confront him. After a moment of indecision, Ken took a single backward step, turned and ran onto the busy stadium floor. He scurried onto the stage and toward the lead musician.

"You've rehearsed the music with Casper, haven't you?" Despite his efforts to remain calm, Ken's question came as an urgent near-whisper.

"Yes," the musician answered.

"You'll have to rehearse the choir."

"Me?" the musician shot back. Surprise broke across his face. "Where's Casper? What's wrong?"

Supercharged barbs of impatience and apprehension raced through Ken. "Take over until he gets here! Understand?" Ken fled down the stage steps. He half-walked, half-ran toward the lounge. He charged into the lounge room, occupied by the same volunteers who were there earlier.

"Listen, everybody! I need your help. Casper is out of pocket. We have to find him. Go down every hall, yell his name until you locate him." Ken made himself smile. "He's probably catching a nap. The choir is waiting to rehearse." He clapped his hands. "Come on! Hurry! Gotta find him quick! We're wasting time!"

He bounded back into the hallway. "Casper!" he called loudly. "You," he shouted to the first man who emerged from the lounge. "Go that way." Ken pointed in the direction where he had heard Casper. "Casper!" he called out again.

"Relax, Mr. Walker," a man said. "We'll find him."

Ken forced another smile. "You don't know him like I do. He can sleep through an earthquake. Whoop it up, guys! Raise the roof. When you find him, get him out to the stage. We need him for choir rehearsal."

"Don't worry," another man said. "We'll find him.... Casper!"

Ken watched for a moment, then ran toward an office where he knew he could find privacy and a telephone. When he got there, he pulled the wallet out of his hip pocket. With his phone credit card on the desk, he punched out the number of Hoff's Houston office. As the phone rang,

Ken glanced at his watch. 2:31. His hands trembled.

"Mr. Hoffstedtler's office," Gracie said.

"Gracie, this is Ken Walker in New Orleans. I've got to talk to Hoff."

She recognized the urgency in Ken's voice. "What's the matter?"

"It's an emergency! I must speak to Hoff!"

"He's in Miami, in a meeting in his hotel suite right now." Gracie gave him the hotel's number, then asked, "What's wrong?"

"Tell you later." Ken hung up and tapped out the number..

Hoff was laughing when he answered. In seconds, he was grim as Ken's exigent, machine gun delivery sprayed him with the news.

"I don't know what to do next. I need your help." When there was no response, Ken asked, "Hoff?"

"I'm thinking." Hoff spoke slowly. "You're the only one who knows about this?"

"Yes."

"Is Casper calm? Can you handle him physically?"

"I'm sure I can."

Hoff was silent for a moment. "I'll get to New Orleans as soon as possible, come directly to your room at the Hyatt. Sit on things until I arrive. Don't tell anyone unless he comes unglued. If worse comes to worse, ask the house physician to give him a sedative."

"I'll do my best."

Listening to a Nose

New Orleans Police Lieutenant Dugas LeBlanc motioned for Banner Tatum to have a seat. LeBlanc sat behind his desk and watched Banner study the nameplate.

"My first name is pronounced Doo-gah. Equal emphasis on the two syllables," LeBlanc said. "I've spent my whole life spelling it and pronouncing it. I named my son William." When Banner finished his quick, polite laugh, the lieutenant continued. "What brings you to New Orleans?"

"My nose," Banner began. "You know how cops' noses can be sometimes." He briefed the lieutenant on the four evangelist murders.

LeBlanc scooted forward in his chair and leaned both elbows on his desk. "Are you working any fresh information?"

"No. I've been in touch with detectives working on all four cases. I'm convinced one perp is involved, but he's crafty. He's given us little to go on." Banner smiled. "If nothing else, coming to New Orleans is a good excuse to do some prime eating and enjoy some Dixieland. Is Preservation Hall still operating?"

"Oh, indeed it is."

"Are you taking any special security precautions for the service tomorrow night?" Banner asked.

"We'll deploy more men than we would normally and the organizers have private security personnel. Do you think we should do anything special?"

"This damned nose of mine tells me you should, but if our roles were reversed and you told me what I'm telling you, I'd probably classify you as a sob sister and offer you a Kleenex."

LeBlanc laughed. "Are you going to hear Sister Cathedra?"

"I'm going just to be there. I have no particular interest in hearing her. How about you?"

"I'll be there," LeBlanc answered. "My wife and I are big fans. Miss Stevens is a messenger of God's word. We love her singing."

Banner stood. "I wanted to check in with your department. Maybe I'll see you there tomorrow night."

"I'll look for you," LeBlanc said, shaking Banner's outstretched hand. "Give me a call if I can help while you're in town."

Tangled in Withered Vines

Seven hours after the telephone conversation with Ken Walker, Hoff strode into the lobby of the Hyatt Hotel adjacent to the Superdome in New Orleans. He called Ken from a house phone and went directly to his room on the eighth floor.

Ken poured Hoff coffee from a carafe and told him what had transpired since their conversation. The shouting orchestrated by Ken interrupted Casper before anyone else heard him. Ken surmised that Casper stayed in the small room while he composed himself.

"Not long after I talked to you," Ken said, "Casper rehearsed the choir. He acted as if nothing unusual happened. Right now, he's asleep in his room."

"Acted as if nothing unusual happened," Hoff repeated softly as he brushed his fingers back and forth across the hair on the back of his left hand. "Casper doesn't know you heard him?"

Ken shook his head.

Hoff said, "For the time being, I think we should hold off telling Leeandra, the police or anyone else. That could mess up tomorrow's service. I do think we should talk to Casper."

"Why? He may go to pieces."

"That's a risk, but he needs to know that we know. Knowing will be a relief, maybe keep him from doing something else stupid. Casper must be feeling a lot of guilt and pressure. That's why he got on the crying jag you overheard. This way, he'll know we're watching him." Hoff picked up his cup but didn't drink. "But, you know him best. I'm open to suggestions if you have a better idea."

"I don't."

"Where's his room?"

"Next door. Our rooms connect. The door's unlocked."

Hoff set his coffee cup on a table. "Let's go." He pushed open the door into Casper's room and heard him stir. By the light from Ken's room, Hoff made his way to the bed and said quietly, "Casper?"

"Huh?" Casper answered.

"Casper, wake up," Ken said. "It's Hoff and me. We need to talk."

"What?" Casper slurred the word and turned over, fogged with sleep.

"We know about the ads and the death threat." Hoff's voice was even, authoritative. "Wake up. We've got to talk." He clicked on the bedside lamp.

"What's going on?" Casper was up on one elbow, squinting at Hoff. "What're you talking about?"

Ken said quietly, "I heard you this afternoon when you said you placed the Antichrist ads and phoned in the death threat."

Casper sat up in bed, holding the sheet up to his chin to cover his bare chest. "Heard me?"

"Why don't you get up, wash your face and put on some clothes?" Hoff suggested. "Get your thoughts together."

Without a word, Casper complied, then sat contritely on the edge of the bed, facing Hoff and Ken, who occupied two side chairs.

Hoff waited for Casper to speak. Sitting there so quiet and erect, so subservient, Casper reminded him of a kid in trouble with his teacher.

"Why'd you do it?" Hoff asked.

"Do what?" Casper's glancing looks darted back and forth between Hoff's and Ken's steady gazes.

"Put the ads in the newspapers. Phone in the death threat against your sister," Hoff answered.

"Why would I do that?" Casper asked, his voice tense and squeaky.

"Casper," Ken said, his voice warm with compassion. "We're here to help. We're your friends. I heard you confess when you were praying this afternoon. You put those ads in the paper. You phoned in the death threat against Leeandra."

Casper held his fidgeting hands in his lap. "Leeandra," he said flatly, looking down at his hands. He repeated, "Leeandra."

Hoff and Ken glanced at each other.

"Go easy," Ken mouthed.

Hoff nodded and spoke quietly. "You called Leeandra the Antichrist. You made the death threat."

"Sister Cathedra," Casper said hoarsely, looking down at his fidgeting hands. He cleared his throat.

"Leeandra is Sister Cathedra," Hoff said calmly. "Your sister."

Casper sat in silence, kneading his finger tips as if searching for a touch of reality. "Sister Leeandra," he said, barely above a whisper. He continued to look down at his fingers.

"Casper?" Ken said. He got no response. "Casper!"

Very slowly, Casper looked up at Ken with a glazed, distant expression in his eyes.

"You don't like Sister Cathedra, do you?" Ken asked.

In the same ultra slow movement, Casper shook his head.

"Why?" Ken asked.

Casper looked down at his hands and remained silent.

"Casper!" Hoff said firmly, then lowered his voice when Casper looked up. "Tell us why you don't like Sister Cathedra."

"Because...." Casper began and paused as he looked back and forth between Hoff and Ken. "Because she takes my sister's place. She comes and Leeandra goes away."

Ken frowned. "Goes away?"

"Yes." Casper nodded very slowly. "Mother and Daddy went away. Now, Leeandra goes away, too. I don't like it."

Ken glanced at Hoff, then looked at Casper. "You're afraid when Leeandra goes away?"

Casper's nod was barely perceptible as the wail began.

Ken and Hoff watched with widening eyes as Casper vented his anguish with a wailing, O-sounding cry that grew louder and higher pitched. Casper's own eyes widened as he screamed, "Ohhhhh, God!" He fell over, face down on the double bed. He sobbed and beat his fists on the back of his own head.

Ken jumped to the bed and grabbed Casper's hands to stop the self-pummeling. Then he sat on the edge of the bed and tugged at Casper, guiding him onto his back.

"Oh, God, forgive me!" Casper sobbed wildly as his face came free from the pillow. "Oh, God...such torment. Save me, dear Jesus!"

As Casper cried with heaving sobs and clutched Ken's hand, Ken spoke in a soothing monotone. "It's okay, Casper. You're just tired...just a little mixed up, maybe. Don't worry. God loves you. We all love you. We're here to help. Leeandra will help, too."

Casper cried uncontrollably, taking in long, raspy gasps of air and wretching them out. Ken continued to speak in a quiet, reassuring croon until Casper's sobs ebbed.

"Get a cold wet cloth," Ken said to Hoff. When Hoff brought the wet washcloth from the bathroom, Ken swabbed Casper's face as he lay spent and quiet on his back, hands folded across his chest.

"I see the change every time she preaches," Casper said in a quiet, remote voice. He stared at the ceiling with its circle of light from the open top of the bedside lamp's shade. "I see Leeandra turn into Sister Cathedra. And then Leeandra's not real. She's not what God intends her to be. She's a false prophet, who says and does all the right things."

Casper's voice grew steadily quieter as he spoke. "There's false teaching. There's darkness around Sister Cathedra when Leeandra goes away. Errancy. I see errancy and danger." He paused. "I see...I see sin." He paused again. "I see...the Antichrist." Casper closed his eyes. "There's danger. She becomes what she is not. Sin. Darkness. There's darkness and danger." Another pause. "Leeandra isn't the Antichrist. She's not Sister Cathedra." He breathed evenly, deeply, his eyes closed.

Ken thought Casper had dropped off to sleep, but he spoke again in a slow, soft voice. "The Antichrist spreads confusion. Danger. Errancy. I'm tangled up...all tangled up in black, withered vines." He fell silent.

"Casper?" Ken asked and waited. "Casper?" Ken looked at Hoff. "I think he's asleep." Ken put the wet cloth on the bedside table.

"Maybe we should call a doctor," Hoff said.

"No, not just now." Ken moved from the bed to the closest chair. "Let's leave him be, let him sleep. That's best for now. I'll stay here with him tonight. If he's still like this in the morning or has another episode tonight, we'll call a doctor."

"I'll stay, too. I'll go get more coffee."

"Thanks, but there's no need for you to stay. He'll sleep." Ken looked at Casper. "He's a good kid, but he's not as strong as Leeandra." Ken was silent for a few seconds, then looked at Hoff. "Like a sheep, Casper needs a shepherd. His folks are dead. He sees Leeandra changing...going away, as he puts it. I can be his shepherd. I'd like to do that for him. He's like family to me."

Hoff took a deep breath, exhaling slowly. "You're good people."

"I think the hotel is full, so use my room tonight. My key is on the desk in case you want to go get something to eat."

"Can I bring you anything?"

Ken shook his head and glanced at Casper. "He's sleeping like a baby. Maybe he's gotten a big monkey off his back. This kid has been carrying a heavy load."

"Are you sure you don't want anything to eat? Coffee?"

"I'll pass. Thanks for your help. I didn't know how to handle it."

Ken smiled. "There are times when I also need a shepherd."

"That goes for all of us, but it seems to me you handled this whole thing admirably. And, I appreciate it. I'll be back within the hour." Hoff patted Ken on the shoulder, picked up the key in the adjacent room and headed for the lobby bar.

As Hoff waited for and then rode the elevator, he castigated himself for not following through on his earlier hunch that Casper was responsible for the Antichrist ads. Casper's jealousy and his lack of concern over the ads and death threat had triggered Hoff's suspicion. Even now, he could hardly believe Casper would do those things to his own sister. He didn't do them to Leeandra, Hoff thought. He did them to Sister Cathedra.

The lobby bar stocked Martin's twenty-year-old Scotch and Hoff ordered a double. He resisted the urge to call Leeandra. It was already 11:40. Hoff needed conversation to help dispel the tense twanging in his head. I guess I could use a shepherd, too, he thought. He finished his drink hurriedly, found a phone booth and called Andy Boxx.

"Andy! Hope I didn't wake you. It's Hoff."

"Evening, Hoff. You didn't wake me. I was half watching some shit-for-brains thing on the tube. Are you in jail?"

"No, I'm in New Orleans."

"It's kind of late for recreational talk. Got your tit in a wringer?"

"I just might." Hoff told Andy about Casper.

"Christ almighty. Sounds like you may have both tits in the wringer. What're you going to do?"

"Nothing for the time being. Calling a doctor or the cops would blow things for the crusade tomorrow."

"Yeah, but from what you told me, that little nipplehead is wound tighter than a dime store clock. He could come uncorked and do God knows what. Sounds to me like he needs a shrink."

"He may. It's a matter of holding off for a day or two." Hoff paused. "I wish you could've seen how Ken read that situation, how carefully he handled Casper."

"Well, you're there and I'm not." Andy laughed sourly. "The mind can be a screwball contraption, can't it?"

"It sure can."

"Speaking of screwballs, how're you doing?"

Hoff laughed. "I'm fine, thank you."

"How's it going between you and Sister Cawonderful?"

Hoff laughed again, thankful for Andy's humor. "Pure and simple, we've got a textbook courtship going. I'm enjoying the hell out of it."

"You? The consummate female bones jumper?" Andy laughed. "Damned if it doesn't sound like she has you where she wants you. You've got a screaming case of the sweet ass."

"I think you're right."

"Yessir," Andy said, "you've got it bad."

"Did you see Leeandra on television?"

"Yeah. She did good. Did she know in advance what questions were going to be asked?"

"No, but George Lee briefed her on possible questions and they rehearsed answers."

"It turned out well. Want me to hotfoot it over to New Orleans? I can guard Bourbon Street while you people are churching it up."

Hoff said, "You're all heart. Thanks, but Bourbon Street appears to be in good hands."

"Are you sure? We don't want anything to happen to a prime breeding ground for sinners."

"No shortage of sinners, I don't think. Sure you don't want to come over for the service?"

"Damned sure," Andy shot back. "That thing in the Astrodome will do me for a whole decade."

"Okay. Thanks for letting me bend your ear."

"Shit fire, that's what friends are for. You don't have to thank me."

"I know. I just wanted to say it."

"Have another Scotch. Tell the barkeep Doctor Boxx prescribed it. Call me if you need me." Andy hung up.

Hoff went back to the bar and ordered another drink. He wondered what Margo was doing tonight. Remembering the gin-sodden trip to New Orleans with her and their fornicating on Rampart Street made him smile. Margo the Magnificent. On an impulse, while in Miami, he called her in St. Thomas. She was now Mrs. Gordon Mayfield Butler. She sounded happy.

During that conversation, Margo asked, "Have you poked the preacherette?"

Hoff laughed. "You know it's a sin to tell where I've had my thing."

His humor faded as thoughts of Casper's antics pushed everything else aside. Hoff sipped his drink. He'd be glad when tomorrow night's service was over.

Chapter 21

Help from Children of God

Danny Don Rhodes lay fully clothed in the sagging double bed in his dank-smelling hotel room in New Orleans, exhausted by the twenty-two hour bus trip from Amarillo. The dirty, dull white neon sign outside said simply, "Hotel."

He was still angry at the ancient, stooped desk clerk who said he didn't know the hotel's name. The clerk had stared at Danny Don's facial scars and asked, "What the hell happened to you? Looks like you picked a fight with a blow torch and it won." Throughout the trip, people had stared. Children and old people were the worst.

On the bus, one little boy with chapped cheeks, green eyes and twin strands of snot down to his mouth affixed an expressionless stare on Danny Don. The little boy continued his blank look even when Danny Don stuck out his tongue and made faces. The boy's mother finally put the youngster down in her lap for a nap.

While waiting for his connection in the Dallas bus station, Danny Don's anger flared when he learned he could have flown to New Orleans for less money than it cost to ride the bus, had he made flight arrangements twenty-one days in advance.

He was pleased with the hotel room, better than he thought he could afford. Because he didn't own a credit card, the clerk made him pay twenty-three dollars cash in advance for the first night. After that, the grizzled old man explained, he could pay every other day. The room was warm, comfortable and contained a television with reasonably good color.

Outside, a cold front drove a biting wind through the streets of New Orleans. Tomorrow's weather forecast called for temperatures in the forties. His fleece-lined denim jacket with its special pocket sewn inside to hold the pistol would not be out of place.

Thoughts about the pistol, still in his suitcase, set off the vortex of apprehension in his stomach. He had taken a long time to decide on the .357 revolver rather than the rifle.

He was a crack shot with both, skills sharpened with recent practice sessions along Rita Blanca Creek in the open, sparsely-populated cattle country west of Channing. Nobody minded if he shot targets in the dry creek bed. Use of the pistol dictated a close range when he shot Sister Cathedra and eliminated the chance of escape. He decided that was okay. He wanted the opportunity to explain his act.

He convinced himself that people aware of his plight would help him, including those associated with the Sister Cathedra-Stevens Crusade.

They were children of God, merciful and forgiving people. He envisioned a special fund to pay for corrective surgery on his disfiguring scars. These children of God would understand his desperation. The idea of merciful, helpful people blotted up the swarming apprehension. They must help me. They are my only hope.

Time to be Leeandra

Hoff broke into a smile as Leeandra walked swiftly across the Hyatt Hotel lobby toward him, her long blonde hair swaying to her step.

"Hoff." A lilt enlivened her voice.

He kissed her briefly on the lips before he held her by the shoulders at arm's length. "Where've you been taking the beauty treatments?"

Her laugh contracted into a quiet, loving expression. "I'm so glad to see you."

He guided her toward the lobby restaurant, his arm around her waist. He enjoyed feeling the slow undulation of her walk. As they were shown to a table, he noted that several people recognized her.

"When did you get in?" she asked.

"Late, very late last night."

"Why didn't you call me?"

"I didn't want to disturb your beauty sleep, which obviously works very well."

"You're awfully good for a girl's morale. I'm glad we get to have both breakfast and lunch together today."

"Me, too." He looked at her for a moment. "Several people recognized you when we walked in. You were dynamite on *The Today Show* in your red dress. Very memorable." He paused. "Why did you wear red?"

"Because you said I look good in it."

"You do."

She smiled. "You are decidedly prejudiced."

"I willingly plead guilty to that." After they ordered breakfast, he said, "You might as well face it. You're a celebrity. You may have to start wearing disguises. Think you'd make a good Harpo Marx?"

Leeandra cradled her cup of coffee in both hands. "If you knew how little being a celebrity appeals to me, you wouldn't joke about it. I was happy as an anonymous tent singer. I don't want to be a celebrity. I want time to be Leeandra." The caring, quiet expression settled onto her face. "I want time to be with you."

"I take that to be good news."

She held the cup an inch from her lips, her Caribbean blue eyes focused on Hoff. "I love you," she said softly.

"And I love you," he answered. The waitress smiled at their exchange as she served breakfast.

Talk about Redemption

Hoff returned to Ken Walker's room as the business manager was hanging up the phone. Ken had been asleep on the floor in Casper's room when Hoff left to have breakfast with Leeandra.

"How's Casper?" Hoff asked.

"Calm. He talked in his sleep quite a bit during the night. From what little I could understand, he was having a conversation with Leeandra when they were children. They were playing. Casper told Leeandra he loved her and wouldn't let the tigers get her."

"Has he said much this morning?"

"Not a whole lot. He's ashamed of himself." Ken poured a cup of coffee from a carafe. "I gave him a pep talk. It seemed to help. Poor kid. He told me he couldn't save Joe Ted from dying, but he could save Leeandra from danger."

"What kind of danger?"

"That mumbo-jumbo he talked about last night. I don't know where he got that errancy garbage." Ken glanced at his watch. "I woke him up a few minutes ago. He'll be in here shortly."

"Should I talk to him?"

"Yes, but be positive. He needs all the support and acceptance he can get. Are you angry with him?"

"I feel sorry for him. I got my mad out of the way on the plane. If I'd gotten my hands on him then, I'd have wrung his neck."

"That's understandable," Ken said. "You love Leeandra, don't you?"

Surprised, Hoff hesitated. "Yes."

Ken smiled. "I think she loves you, too."

"Has she talked to you?"

"No, but neither of you is working overtime to camouflage your feelings. I was sure after seeing you together at Thanksgiving."

"What do you think?"

"I care a lot for Leeandra, a family kind of caring. I want what's good for her. I've developed a healthy respect for you. I think you'd be good to her, good for her. I hope you'd be loyal to her. Obviously, I wonder what'll happen to the ministry if you and Leeandra marry."

A timid knock at the door between Ken's and Casper's rooms stopped the conversation. At Ken's invitation, Casper stepped in. Apprehension flared in his eyes when he saw Hoff.

"Good morning, Casper." Hoff made himself sound friendly.

Casper nodded at Ken's offer of coffee and looked at Hoff warily. "I'm sorry for what I've done." Casper sat on the edge of the bed.

"I know you are," Hoff answered. "Ken and I realize you've been through a tough time. We're here to help you."

Casper glanced from Ken to Hoff. "You're not mad at me?"

"No. The real Casper wouldn't do that sort of thing, right?"

Casper nodded, visibly relieved.

"That's breakfast," Ken said in response to a loud knock. He tipped and dismissed the room service waiter, then wheeled the cart to where Casper sat. "Got to get you fed. Billy Dean is due in a few minutes to take you to the stadium for the walk-through."

"Are you feeling up to tonight's service?" Hoff asked.

Casper nodded as he chewed a bite of bacon. "I want to redeem myself. Should I confess?"

"During tonight's service?" Ken asked, frowning. Casper nodded.

"I don't think so," Ken said matter-of-factly. "Leeandra doesn't know. We want to wait a day or two before you tell her."

Casper looked frightened again. "She doesn't know?"

"No need for it now. She has plenty on her mind. Let's wait."

"Yes," Casper said quietly. "Let's wait."

"I like what you said about redeeming yourself," Hoff said. "That shows the kind of spunk we've always seen in you. I'm proud of you. Ken is, too."

"You are?" Casper asked quickly. He smiled weakly.

"You're important to the service. I'm confident we'll see the real Casper up there on stage tonight." Hoff grinned. "Am I right?"

Casper's smile was stronger. "Yes. I won't let us down."

Chapter 22

Mission Revisited

"Sorry you had to wait," the antiques shop clerk said. "Lots of people are in town for the big religious service tonight."

"No bother." James Bresnahan had waited patiently, puttering around the shop that occupied the space he rented for two years for his New Orleans mission. He stooped to examine a piece of scrimshaw in a display case. "I'd like to see the larger piece on the top shelf."

"Wonderful choice." The clerk continued her sales presentation as she retrieved the scrimshaw and laid it on a square of maroon velvet. "A very old and significant piece."

The clerk accepted an offer of ten per cent less than the marked price of four hundred dollars. Bresnahan paid in cash, including the two fifty dollar bills reclaimed from Jack Canada's body.

"I recall there was another type of place in this location the last time I was here," he said. "That was several years ago. Am I right?"

"Indeed you are," the clerk answered. "There was a church here, but it closed. I've heard it provided fake papers to illegal aliens." She smiled and shrugged. "No matter. We're here now."

"So we are." Bresnahan unwrapped a cinnamon disc. Before slipping the candy into his mouth, he repeated, "So we are."

Taunts in Dark Dreams

A strident disquiet buzzed inside of Danny Don Rhodes as he marked time in his dank-smelling hotel room before leaving to walk to the French Quarter.

Last night's dreams caromed through his head. He slept soundly for part of the night until his first dream. In that one, Joyce, his ex-wife, stared at him from the edge of the service garage at Hooper's Fina Station in Channing. Each time he looked up from patching the truck inner tube at his workbench in the back of the garage, the top half of Joyce's face peeked past the roll-up door's metal track. The rest of her was hidden behind the white concrete block wall.

Their eyes—his sandy brown, hers gray-green—met for no more than a second before she disappeared, vanished instantaneously as opposed to pulling her head back from his line of sight.

He wanted to sprint the twenty-five feet to the door to see where she went, but he was locked in place. The scar tissue from his burns kept him from moving. In the dream, he could work on the inner tube, scratch his crotch and do anything except pursue Joyce. He woke up after the third replay of the dream.

Danny Don remained awake for over an hour in the mildewy darkness of his room, eight hundred and forty-five miles from home. He lay on his back, covers clutched to his chin as he looked up into the dark. He awakened gradually, afraid, but not knowing why.

He hadn't dreamed about Joyce in six months. They had been high school sweethearts in Dalhart. She was a cheerleader. He played football. She beamed with pride when he trotted to the sidelines after scoring a touchdown on a long, fleet run.

She had left him three years ago, freed by the divorce he had no money to contest. Why had she returned to torment him in his dreams?

Using the tautly drawn covers as shelter, he chinked the hole in his mind's levee that held back his feelings for Joyce. He struggled to stop the trickle of realization that mixed with his hatred for her was a residual vein of love. No, not love, he thought with a rebutting rush. Not from me. Not for Joyce. Not for anyone. Never again.

He turned on the light to look at his watch. 1:50. He clicked off the pale, forty-watt bulb in the bedside lamp with its stained, ripped shade. He rubbed his scratchy eyes, stared into the dark of his windowless room.

Finally, he went back to sleep. He didn't know how long he slept before the next dream began.

Sister Cathedra appeared out of a mist at the foot of his bed, an immaculate vision of beauty and peace. He glanced away, but when he looked again, she was different. She had Joyce's face! No! He tried to shout, but he couldn't. The covers were too heavy, pulled too tight against his chin, trapping his voice inside his body. Sister Cathedra, as beautiful with Joyce's face as with her own, tried to sing, but she mouthed a wailing, discordant stream of sadness.

I'll fix you! In slow, laborious dream motion, he freed his right hand to reach for the blued .357 revolver with the polished black walnut grips. The pistol was stashed in an indistinct, nearby place. He felt its welcome heft as he grabbed the pistol and snapped off three quick shots at Joyce's face. He gawked in disbelief as squirts of motor oil popped out of the end of the barrel.

He stared in bubbling anger as Sister Cathedra with Joyce's face beckoned people out of the mist to stand at the foot of his bed.

Go away! he tried to yell, but the silent people kept coming. They were of all ages, sizes and colors—green, purple and yellow like the colors in Aunt Gertrude's patchwork quilts. Hundreds of faceless people emerged from the mist to stand in orderly rows around his bed. Sister

Cathedra with Joyce's face lifted her arms as the real Sister Cathedra did during invitations at the end of her sermons.

As her hands rose even with her shoulders, Danny Don shrank back into the lumpy bed, trying to flee from the silently crying, faceless horde. Even though they had no faces and no eyes, he felt their stares at his scarred ugliness. From behind them came a hoarsely whispered incantation from hundreds of voices, "Scar boy, scar boy, scar boy." Suddenly, they all had faces. He tried to cry out in fear and surprise. The first face he saw was Skeeter's, mottled with clots of ejaculate, her mouth twisted ominously as she said in a strangely metallic monotone, "Be quiet and stay in your box or I'll tie your little weenie in knots." Except for Skeeter and Sister Cathedra with Joyce's face, all of the people were disfigured with stringy, waxy burn scars. The faces also had rivulets of snot down to their mouths like the little boy on the bus.

With a bolting start, Danny Don woke and sat upright, his heart pounding. He felt feverish with alarm and sat for a full minute as he realized it was only a dream. With that realization came anger and he fell backward, enraged.

You taunt me, Sister Cathedra, he thought. You and the others. You stare. He felt like shouting out loud in his seething, white hot rage. He didn't, fearful because he was alone and far from home. His fear added to the rage, now a roaring storm inside his head.

His thoughts raced. You taunt me now, Sister Cathedra, you and your followers, you and your assumed faces. You...you...you Sister Counterfeit and the fakers who follow you!

Danny Don slid his hand under the pillow, gripped the pistol and felt better.

"Taunt me while you can." He spoke softly into the dark mustiness. "Stare at me with your big blue eyes while they still see." His voice was ominous as he talked to himself. "After tonight, you will never stare at anyone. Not after you become the sacrificial lamb to atone for the sins of the world against Danny Don Rhodes."

He lapsed into thinking silence. During the last three days, he had practiced saying the words about sacrificial lamb. He practiced the pauses. When interviewed about why he shot her, he would say, "Sister Cathedra was chosen to be the sacrificial lamb...to atone for the sins of the world against Danny Don Rhodes."

He tried to imagine the looks of shock and horror that would contort the faces of her followers tonight at the Superdome. He would be getting even with her followers, also. They, too, were guilty. They, too, would pay. Not next week. Not next month. Tonight.

Slowly, he rolled over, clicked on the bedside lamp and squinted at his watch. 4:33. He felt exhausted, his eyes raspy with the need for sleep. But the strident, disquieting drone in his head and the fear of more dreams kept him awake. He sat up, flipped back the covers and swung his legs off the edge of the bed. He pulled the revolver with its polished black walnut grips from under the pillow, limped across the hard worn carpet, opened the wobbly bottom drawer of the chest and slipped the pistol in between folds of the spare blanket.

He dressed and went out for breakfast. He got angry when the insolent, hawk-faced counter man wearing an "I Stop for Snort" tee shirt told him he didn't warm sweet rolls on the griddle. Danny Don settled for one heated in the microwave.

He spent two quarters for a *Times-Picayune* out of a vending machine before he realized it was yesterday's newspaper. His anger surged again and he wished for the pistol as he thought, I'd ventilate that quarter-eating mother fucker!

Back in his hotel room by a few minutes after six, he read the day-old newspaper, watched television and munched pork rinds. By ten o'clock, he was full of a scratchy need to be on the move.

Before he left the hotel, he checked to make sure the pistol was still between the folds of the spare blanket in the dresser. It was.

He limped toward the French Quarter. He had wanted to go last night, but his fatigue and the cold wind had kept him at the hotel. This morning's sun was bright, the wind calm. He paused in the median of Canal Street to enjoy the sun's warmth, to watch a passing streetcar and observe this Friday's mid-morning activity. He checked face after face. Nobody stared. His mood improved.

Danny Don moved on to Bourbon Street and walked along slowly, amazed that bars were already open. He passed a pornographic peep show, stopped to peer into the gloomy, dark interior and ambled on.

At St. Ann Street, he turned right and walked until he got to Jackson Square. He stopped for a cup of coffee and two cinnamon rolls from the sweet-smelling bakery with the French name he could not pronounce. He found a bench outside where he ate and watched the world go by. The rolls were warm, spongy fresh and full of raisins. His seat was in the plume of the ovens' sugary fragrance, adding to his enjoyment.

A pigeon walked up and cocked its head, assessing the prospect of a handout. Danny Don popped the last morsel of cinnamon roll into his mouth. The pigeon moved on. Danny Don stood and unsnapped his fleece-lined jacket as the bright sun warmed the day.

He moseyed across Decatur Street to the overlook next to the Mississippi River. He watched an empty ship glide by, riding high in the water, its propeller blades thrashing a mixture of air and river.

He walked through the French Market, then headed back toward Bourbon Street. He had decided to go back to the pornographic peep show and walked faster, his limp more pronounced at this pace. At the arcade, he cashed two one dollar bills into quarters and was pleased the clerk did not stare at him.

He selected a booth, fed in three quarters and watched the film of a couple copulating. He imagined the woman was Sister Cathedra and he was the man. He was punishing her, forcing her into this vividly documented subjugation. Instead of shooting her, he thought, I should fuck her to death, stroke by penetrating, punishing stroke.

He blinked himself back to the reality of the vile-smelling, dark closet with its lewdness lighting up the tiny screen, streaked with ejaculate. He was angry. Of course that's not Sister Cathedra, he thought. Of course it's not me. I'm too ugly, too scarred, unworthy of her prim, sanctified beauty.

Whirling anger ruined his mood. He banged the door open and fled from the darkened nest of cubicles. The remaining quarters clutched in his fist, he emerged squinting into the morning light.

The film was sick, he thought, the same sickness that pushes aside a scarred cripple. But I'll get even this very night.

He limped hurriedly along the street, oblivious to everything except his thoughts about shooting Sister Cathedra. Concentration is the key, he reminded himself. Concentrate on her, only her.

In the dry bed of Rita Blanca Creek, he had practiced focusing on the target. He practiced lifting the pistol out of the specially-sewn pocket inside his jacket without thinking. He practiced aiming without thinking. He imagined concentrating on the smiling face of Sister Cathedra as she stood on stage.

He limped toward his hotel. He would watch television and leave early enough to get a floor level seat near the stage. Only one thing occupied his mind—the spot in her forehead just above the bridge of Sister Cathedra's nose, slightly above her big, blue eyes. After tonight, those eyes would be closed forever.

#

As Danny Don stood in the median of Canal Street, waiting for a walk light, he was unaware that standing in the huddle of people waiting to cross the street from the opposite direction was Dr. Henry Woods. He had been drawn to the New Orleans crusade like the moths to the naked, one hundred and fifty watt light bulbs under the Stevens tent where he first saw Leeandra in Austin.

Hanging on his arm was a brightly-dressed, short-skirted prostitute named Candy. Last night, in his hotel room with its tenth floor view of the Mississippi River, Dr. Woods nicknamed her Divinity. He liked divinity candy. Divinity was an appropriate name for this tastily edible Candy with her trim, busty figure. At his suggestion, they played a game he called carnival. She sat on his face and he guessed her weight.

Magic Fettuccine

Leeandra and Hoff held hands as they sauntered toward St. Charles Street to catch the streetcar. As usual, Leeandra didn't carry a handbag.

"You won't preach too long tonight, will you?" Hoff asked.

The question stopped Leeandra. She laughed. "That reminds me of something." They resumed walking. "When I was a kid, my folks invited a preacher over for lunch almost every Sunday when Daddy was home. There were two preachers Casper and I dreaded because their blessings were so long. One was Brother Jenkins. He blessed everything on the table and everyone around it by name. He blessed pickles, relish, bread, butter, salt, pepper, every last thing. His blessings lasted forever."

Hoff laughed with her. "I guess that's another advantage of growing up as a heathen. Short blessings or none at all."

"I bet you don't even know a blessing."

"Sure I do."

"Recite it for me."

"You don't want to hear it."

"Is it profane?"

He assured her it wasn't, and she insisted he tell her.

"As a matter of fact, I know two. Do you want to hear the long one or the short one?"

"Both."

"Okay. Long one first. Thanks for the bread, thanks for the meat, excuse us, God, it's time to eat." As she laughed, he said, "I didn't say it was a theological masterpiece. Ready for the short one? Rub-a-dub-dub, thanks for the grub."

She laughed again. "I'm not sure that qualifies."

"Unorthodox, maybe, but the spirit in which it's said is worth something." Hoff paused as they got to a corner. "This is St. Charles. We can catch the streetcar by that sign."

"I've never ridden a streetcar before. Where are we going?"

"Copeland's Restaurant. The food is terrific. Here comes our ride."

They watched the streetcar brake to a grating, steel-on-steel stop and hopped aboard.

Leeandra sat next to the window and Hoff slipped his arm around her. As they rode, he tinkered with her ear lobe and told her about a newspaper article he read on the sixty craftsmen who keep the streetcars running. Some of the cars were eighty years old and were completely rebuilt. "The Transit Authority hired a consultant to talk to the guys who work on them and create a set of blueprints. That way, when the old guys die, the younger ones will know how to keep the cars running."

She looked at him. "You remember the darnedest things."

Hoff patted her on the shoulder. "I pride myself in a little bit of knowledge about a whole lot of things. When I get to be king, I can be my own minister of minutiae."

They continued the small talk until Hoff spotted Copeland's Restaurant ahead on the left. He pulled the stop cord. As they got off at the Napoleon Street stop, he said, "They have a dish you'll flip over. Cajun pasta. They add spicy Cajun ham to Fettuccine Alfredo. They call it Fettuccine Lamborghini." He sang to the tune of the *Hallelujah Chorus*. "Feh-too-chee-nee, lam-bor-ghee-nee."

"You're pulling my leg again," Leeandra said over her shoulder as they entered the restaurant.

"A quick question before you seat us," Hoff said to the hostess. "Do you have Fettuccine Lamborghini?"

"Oh, yes, sir. That's one of our specialties."

"See," Hoff said. They followed the hostess and were seated. "It's only fair to warn you I can't eat Cajun food without a beer."

"That list gets longer all the time."

"It's my only vice. Want to mix and share? The fried crawfish tails they call Cajun popcorn are delicious. And we must have blackened redfish and the Fettuccine Lamborghini."

Leeandra snapped the menu shut. "I'm sold."

When he placed the order, the waitress peered at him quizzically. "Are you aware all of those are entree-sized portions?"

He answered with a serious expression. "Yes, m'am, but you see, my tall, blonde lady friend is a professional weight lifter. She has a humongous appetite."

"Hoff!" Leeandra protested as the young waitress stared at her for a second before retreating. "You're terrible!"

"Better than admitting I'm a glutton."

Her smile dissolved slowly into her misty look. "Could life with you be this much fun all the time?"

"We'd have more than our fair share of good times. You and I both know life can't be all fun. It hasn't been for either of us." He smiled. "I would love you all the time, though. I'm off to a running start on that."

She nodded. With flicking visual forays, she absorbed every feature on his face.

"Cable cars in San Francisco. Grouper for breakfast on Virgin Gorda. Finding sand dollars on Padre Island." Hoff paused. "Popcorn in front of the fireplace. A bowl of James Coney Island chili." He paused again. "Just being together. We could start today, you know."

"Today?" Leeandra furrowed her brow. "How?"

"In lots of ways. We could simply declare that our life together has started. We could hop on a plane for Las Vegas, get married and decide where to go on our honeymoon." He smiled at the surprise on her face. "Better yet, we could go to the Caribbean."

"Just like that? Just leave?"

"If we want. There's nobody to stop us. You talk about feeling trapped. This is a good way to escape."

A thoughtful expression covered her face. "Leave before the service?"

"If you want."

Barely audible, she said, "That's not an altogether unattractive idea at the moment." She brushed strands of hair away from her face. "Not very realistic, though."

"I'll leave this afternoon if you go with me."

Leeandra shook her head in tiny, quick movements. "No," she said quietly. "For some reason, the idea of running away appeals to me. But I can't. Running away has never worked."

"You can't blame me for trying."

"I'm glad you care enough to try," she said as the waitress arrived with their food.

She tasted the fettuccine. "Oh, my! This is to die for!"

After lunch, Hoff leaned back and said, "Boy, I'm stuffed."

"Me, too." Leeandra smiled. "And content. Add fettuccine to our list of magic foods." She paused. "I've had the best feelings lately, feelings that everything is about to come together."

"In what way?"

"I'm not sure. But for the past few days, I've had a calm, relaxed, happy feeling."

Hoff turned his beer glass slowly on the cardboard coaster. "I'm ready for us to get together."

"Getting impatient?"

"Eager."

She leaned forward. "I believe forces are at work to...." She hesitated. "I don't know how else to say it...to bring things together." Her eyes were misty and soft. "I can't imagine that not including you and me." In a quiet, songful voice she added, "I love you."

Hoff squeezed her hand. "And I love you, Leeandra Kay Stevens."

Chapter 23

Disguise by Deformity

Danny Don Rhodes tore out the Sister Cathedra-Stevens Crusade ad from the day-old *New Orleans Times-Picayune* and kept it on top of the hotel room's television set. Doors open at six p.m., the ad said. At four o'clock, in the middle of the *Goldfinger* movie, Danny Don left his room. The revolver was tucked into the specially-sewn pocket inside his jacket. He fashioned the pocket himself, having learned to do simple sewing tasks after Joyce left.

As he left the run-down hotel, he gave no thought to what he was about to do. He had rehearsed his actions many times—lift the pistol from the pocket, concentrate on Sister Cathedra's forehead, take a breath, let half of it out, squeeze the trigger ever so slowly. There was no need to think. Doing it was all that remained. He did not pack his suitcase.

Only the top snap of his jacket was undone as he stepped out into the late afternoon's chill breeze on Friday, December 8th. His fleece-lined jacket felt good. He bent over slightly as he walked and exaggerated his limp. If anyone noticed the bulge in the left front of his jacket, they would think it was part of his deformity. Danny Don watched the faces that passed. No one stared.

Henry Waits Among the Masses

Hoff decided to join Ken Walker in the reserved seats near the stage on the floor of the Superdome. Most people using reserved seats would help greet, register and direct respondents during Leeandra's solo and the post-sermon invitation. He arrived at the stadium a few minutes after five and showed his staff pass to get in before the doors opened to the public. He wished that Larry Best, detained by meetings in New York, could be here.

Earlier in the day, Banner Tatum told Hoff security arrangements in the Superdome seemed okay, and he would attend the service "to keep an eye on things." Worried by the murder of Harley Mann last month in Tempe, Hoff had asked Banner to come to New Orleans.

Hoff got a cup of coffee in the reception room, then strolled to the media center to see George Lee. The PR man's assistant beeped for him.

A minute later, George came pounding into the room. His face brightened when he saw Hoff. "Hey, stranger, where've you been? I tried to find you for lunch." They shook hands.

"Busy day," Hoff answered. "Leeandra's bit on *The Today Show* was a winner."

"Yes. We're two for two with TV's big kids."

"I hear the New Orleans media gave us a good reception."

"Terrific. The CBS and NBC exposure helped a bunch. Leeandra turned thumbs down on a radio talk show appearance this afternoon. She wouldn't tell me why."

Hoff stifled a smile. "She likes to have time to herself before a service."

George steered them toward the coffee urn, refilled Hoff's cup and got one for himself. "Nothing other than local media due here tonight. I don't expect national coverage unless something out of the ordinary happens."

"Like what?"

George shrugged. "Who knows? Maybe the Jolly Green Giant will show up and be converted." They both laughed. "Or, it could be a slow day for the networks. Our filler is as good as anybody's. What's the latest on the death threat and those goofy ads?"

"Nothing much." Hoff hoped his quick response was casual enough. "At least the ads have stopped."

"Do you think that bad apple preacher in Austin is part of it? Ken told me about that, the scandal about him bribing a witness and his resignation from Centrum Church. What a screwed up mess."

"I don't think he's involved." Hoff had heard nothing from Dr. Henry Woods since their meeting at Love Field more than a month ago. Banner Tatum had located and talked to Rodrigo Como, who said, "Woods is an ass. He paid. I worked. I could care less what the preacher lady has or has not done. You go your way. I'll go mine." This week, Dr. Woods had resigned to avoid prosecution for bribing the witness.

"Have you looked outside?" George asked. "There must be five thousand people waiting to get in. Long wait to hear a preacher."

"Can you imagine standing around waiting so you can sit on your duff and wait another hour-and-a-half to sit through a sermon?"

"Not unless I'm getting paid," George said, "which I am. What's your excuse?"

"Lunacy, I guess. That and checking on my investment."

A press room phone rang and George was called away to talk.

Hoff walked back to the reception room, saw Ken and steered him to a corner. "Is Casper still doing okay?"

"Yes. In fact, he's excited about tonight, acting like his old self. I think he's okay. He's definitely relieved to have all that off his chest." Ken paused. "Looks like we'll have a big turnout. There were so many people waiting outside that we decided to open the doors early. Several thousand people are already seated."

"I think I'll go have a look and stretch my legs, unless there's something I can do to help you."

Ken shook his head. "Why don't we meet at the reserved seats about seven-twenty?"

"I'll be there." Hoff refilled his coffee cup and walked to the floor of the Superdome. People continued to file in at a steady pace. Those already in their seats talked and laughed.

#

In the milling mass of humanity, Hoff failed to see Dr. Woods, seated alone eight rows from center stage. He wore a lime green sport jacket and a new hair piece. As he waited, he read the New Testament.

Be Still and Know

James Bresnahan located two folding chairs and moved them to the small equipment room. He sat in one with his feet up in the other, reading a magazine. Gingerly, he rubbed the cleft in his chin, glancing at his fingers occasionally to see if there was blood. There was none. He had cut himself this morning while shaving.

The time had come to be patient. Patience, he had learned, was a vital part of his missions. He recalled the scripture, "Be still and know that I am God." Patience was also vital in knowing himself, in studying his visions, in learning to listen to the voice of God's ordaining direction.

Before settling down to read, he removed all but two screws in the grate. He would remove the grate after the service started, the least likely time for anyone to notice its absence.

Bresnahan sucked on a cinnamon candy and read an article about the future of American space exploration. Clad in his khaki uniform personalized with the name of Ben Extett, he felt no nervousness about what lay ahead. No one had paid attention to him today when he entered the Superdome. No one asked why he wanted two folding chairs. He double-checked the seven millimeter Super "14" Contender and returned it to the small trunk. Nothing else to do but read and wait. He licked his finger and turned a page.

No Pay, No Play

New Orleans Police Lieutenant Dugas LeBlanc excused himself from his wife and the couple who accompanied them to the Sister Cathedra service. He walked across the floor of the arena to where four uniformed officers stood talking. A twenty-one-year veteran of the force, LeBlanc knew three of the men.

"Were you briefed on the missing maintenance man?" one of the uniformed officers asked LeBlanc, who shook his head.

"A maintenance supervisor named Jack Canada," the officer said. "He didn't check out yesterday afternoon and didn't show up at home last night. Nor did he come to work this morning. We've been told to look for anybody that might be using his security badge."

"I'll keep my eyes peeled," LeBlanc said, "but I'm not on duty."

"I damned sure am," another of the uniformed officers said. "I badge my way into a Saints game on occasion, but this kind of deal is definitely no pay, no play for me."

LeBlanc smiled. "Keep your ears open. You might hear something you like." He walked around the floor of the Superdome, looking for Banner Tatum. When he didn't find him, LeBlanc returned to his wife and friends.

Travel by Weather Map

Danny Don Rhodes found a discarded *USA Today* on top of a box of trash a block from the hotel and brought it with him to pass the time. He read the weather page in detail, wondering if he would ever visit New York, San Francisco and other places on the map. Not once did he think about the travel eventuality in the context of what might happen to him after tonight.

He was civil when the smiling woman asked about the seats next to him. He moved into the aisle to let her and four friends pass by. He was pleased when the last woman to scoot past thanked him. She did not so much as glance at his waxy, stringy burn scars. He was calmer, more at peace than at any time he could remember since the explosion. He felt a sense of mission — his own rescue, even though it would come at Sister Counterfeit's expense.

False Alarm in an Overcoat

Banner Tatum stood near one of the Superdome's entries and glanced at his watch. The service was due to begin in nine minutes. People continued to flood into the stadium.

For the past hour, he had walked a random pattern, watching people. He stopped to watch when he spotted a tough-looking young woman carrying her overcoat in an unusual way. He relaxed when she dropped it and the coat collapsed in a heap. He thought, no rifle in there.

Front Row Seat

Hoff's watch read twenty-two minutes after seven when he unhooked the velvet barrier rope, stepped into the reserved seating area, hooked the rope in place behind him and walked to the front row. Ken sat talking to someone across a vacant folding chair.

"Hi," Ken said. He patted the chair. "Saved this for you."

Hoff sat. He was a hundred feet from the left front corner of the stage. He wasn't sure he liked the angle or being so close.

Ken twisted around in his seat to look at the crowd. "We should hit fifty thousand, maybe more."

From the moment Leeandra appeared on stage and they exchanged a nodding smile, Hoff sensed Sister Cathedra was not as dominant as she was at the Astrodome in Houston. Sister Cathedra had been totally absent today at lunch.

The hymns, prayers, standing, sitting and special music came and went amidst Hoff's thoughts about his love for Leeandra and the prospect of spending the rest of his life with her. He planned to propose on New Year's Day. He was sure she would accept, the perfect beginning for a new year.

Hoff watched Casper's happy enthusiasm and wondered how he could conduct himself this way in light of what he had done. Perhaps, he thought, Casper has a tough streak in him. Hoff preferred tough over psychotic.

When Leeandra sang her solo, "Ivory Palaces", Hoff watched with rapt attention. He feasted his eyes on her beauty and let his ears absorb her song — not the words, but the beautiful sound that was her. Her voice filled him with warmth. He smiled as he thought, love is its own strange, elusive elixir.

A Cold Muffaletta

Despite what he was about to do, James Bresnahan enjoyed Sister Cathedra's singing. He stopped reading his magazine to listen. Just as no one is perfect, he thought, neither is one totally imperfect. Her voice was a gift. Too bad she did not use it as she should.

He paid no attention to the sermon but waited for the invitational portion of the service. He brought a muffaletta sandwich and ate part of it, wishing he could reheat it. He decided to shoot her during the invitation, when hundreds of people would converge on the large vacant area in front of the stage. Others would leave early to avoid the post-service traffic jam. The milling thousands would be part of the cover for his getaway. Mostly, the element of surprise would be his cover. He was surprised that despite the assassinations of four evangelists, there was no evidence of enhanced security for Sister Cathedra here at the Superdome. Lack of security was a sin of omission on someone's part.

Flowing River of People

Danny Don Rhodes stiffened in his seat at Sister Cathedra's first mention of the invitation.

When hundreds of people responded during her solo, he briefly considered going to the stage, but decided to stick with his plan to shoot her at the end of the service. He steadfastly avoided listening, so as not to feel the impact of her beautiful voice. His decision was made. Reconsidering now would provoke an onslaught of confusion.

During her sermon, Danny Don concentrated on the spot in the middle of her forehead, just above the bridge of her nose. That spot where the .357 slug would impact. Where the bullet would begin its powerful, deadly penetrating mission of ushering him from his desperate, damning anonymity. Sister Cathedra's death would be the call to order for his story.

He stood when Casper took over the podium to lead the invitational hymn. Sister Cathedra, dressed in the simple, long-sleeve, dark blue dress, stepped toward the left corner of the stage.

He smiled. He was rankled when the big shots took their seats inside the purple funeral home ropes close to the stage. They would get a good look at what was about to happen. The choice of funeral home ropes was more appropriate than any of them could know.

He undid one of the middle snaps of his jacket, reached in with his right hand and touched the pistol, secure in its hidden pocket. The varnished, smooth black walnut of the revolver's grips felt like an old friend. A friend of mine, Danny Don thought, but definitely not a friend of Sister Counterfeit.

He resnapped the jacket. The time had come to take the first sideways step into the aisle. Not until he took the step did he realize the aisle was crowded with people. A river of humanity flowed slowly in response to Sister Cathedra's call for decisions for Christ. He was content to flow with them. No need to hurry. Time's infinity would wait patiently for Sister Cathedra. He felt unusually calm, quietly detached from the movement and noise around him. He looked up at the spot on her forehead as the shuffling pace slowed.

"Come home. Come home. Ye who are weary come home." The crowd's singing of the invitational hymn filled the Superdome, but to Danny Don the music seemed far away.

A logjam at the end of the aisle caused a short delay as volunteers directed people on toward the stage, some straight, some to the right, some to the left. When he moved again, he looked up at Sister Cathedra on stage. He was passively aware of the singing, of the babble of voices close around him, of the slow shuffling forward. He veered to the left edge of the aisle. As he got even with the first row of chairs, he angled toward the end of the stage where she stood. Dimly, he heard a man's voice say, "God bless you, brother."

Midway between the front row of chairs and the stage, as he shuffled along with his eyes fixed on the target spot between Sister Cathedra's eyes, a man appeared in front of him. The man thrust something forward. Startled, Danny Don looked wide-eyed at the man, who smiled and said, "Would you take a card to fill out? May I help you with your decision?"

"I want to pray," Danny Don mumbled as he took the registration card and stubby yellow pencil. He stuffed both into his pants pocket. The interruption angered him. I don't need help with my decision, he thought.

Again he moved toward the stage, now only twenty feet away. With his right hand, he began to unsnap his jacket. He looked up, concentrating on the target spot, oblivious to the other components of her face. Hitting the spot from this short distance would be easy.

A loud "praise the Lord" from behind disrupted his concentration momentarily, but he quickly closed his focus on the spot.

All of Danny Don Rhodes' being was concentrated on that one point where a projectile made by a being of God's handiwork would rip into another of God's handiworks. During target practice at Rita Blanca Creek, he had speculated about how much of Sister Cathedra's head and face would be blown away when the soft lead slug began its explosive expansion upon impact with her skull. Enough that the casket would be kept closed at her funeral.

Every snap on his jacket was undone. His right hand rested on the smooth, black walnut pistol grips. He slid his finger into the trigger guard, between the trigger and the back of the guard. He stopped shuffling long enough to look down at the edge of the stage, ten feet away, twenty feet from where she stood.

When he looked back up, he saw all of her face. She was singing, her face alive with happiness. Her blue eyes—those beautiful blue eyes—dazzled. Her long, meticulously-groomed blonde hair shone golden under the lights. He could not hear her because of the crowd's singing and a fast-growing burble of voices immediately behind him. There was no one between him and the stage.

His field of vision tunneled on the target spot as he lifted the pistol from the pocket inside his jacket. As the pistol came free, he was aware of only one thing—the white spot. The target.

There was no Sister Cathedra as he raised the gun. No Superdome as he brought it higher. No cause or thoughts of justice as his arm extended until his right elbow locked. There was nothing but the white target spot as he extended his left hand to grasp his right wrist. Nothing except the erupting, strange, unintelligible sounds—a barking, wailing voice very close behind him. Still there was the white spot—the target—as Danny Don cocked the revolver and his index finger began its squeezing pull on the trigger. He took in a breath and let half of it out.

He was aware of nothing in that slow-moving fraction of a second except the sudden, violent thrust in the middle of his back. The impact shoved him forward, bowed his back, levered his right arm and gun-holding hand up — up too far above the target spot between Sister Cathedra's eyes as the muzzle blast from the powerful .357 kicked the pistol still higher. What the hell? Danny Don thought.

He struggled to maintain his concentration, tried to regain the tight focus on the target spot. He saw all of her, saw her eyes become darkened pits of fear. He watched Sister Cathedra's outstretched arms fold like bird wings to bring her hands toward her face. She looked straight at him, her mouth drawing into an O. The wailing torrent of words behind him was louder, now mixed with an assortment of shouts. Danny Don brought the pistol back down toward Sister Cathedra's forehead.

Interruption by Confusion

James Bresnahan had begun to tighten his finger on the trigger when, though the scope, he saw the abrupt change of expression on Sister Cathedra's face. He recognized her fear. Something unusual was happening. He lifted his eye from the scope, but he was too far away to make out anything other than a knot of confused motion in front of the left side of the stage. Bresnahan put his eye back to the scope and crooked his right index finger around the trigger. He took a breath, exhaled slowly and began the gentle pulling motion with his trigger finger.

Slow-Moving Tide

Standing at the opposite end of the stage from where Danny Don fired his first shot, Banner Tatum whirled toward the source of the explosive sound. He fought his way through the crush of people responding to Sister Cathedra's plea to accept Jesus Christ.

Standing, craning to see from where he now stood on tiptoes twenty-two rows from the stage in the center, floor-level section, Lieutenant

Dugas LeBlanc jumped toward the nearest aisle when he heard the shot. He battled his way through the slow-moving tide of people who, unaware of what was taking place, continued to make their way to the area in front of the stage.

Ye Who Are Weary

Hoff jumped over the velvet barrier rope and sprinted toward Leeandra. He was looking away from the stage, up into the crowd when the gunshot ignited him into action.

He was conscious of the growing tumult to his right and of Leeandra's agonizingly slow, sagging retreat from the front of the stage as she pressed her hands to her cheeks. Hoff's screams of "Get down! Get down!" were lost in the crescendoing pandemonium that began to overpower voices that still sang, "Ye who are weary come home." People unaware or as yet unable to comprehend what was happening continued to sing. Hoff vaulted onto the stage.

"Get down! Get down!" He screamed as he ran. He watched her inch backward, half-bending, half-stooping in horrified, slow-motion recoil from the madness on the floor in front of her.

Known, Disrupting Babble

The unknown tongue! Danny Don Rhodes recognized the disrupting babble behind him as he steadied the pistol.

His vision tunnel closed back down on the target spot. Sister Cathedra moved ever so slowly away, but in a straight line. He began his slow squeeze on the trigger as the dark blur shot into the tunnel from the left. The wrenching hammer blow struck him in the back, spinning him clockwise as his index finger contracted on the trigger. Even above the rising tintinnabulation of screams and shouts, even with the loud crunch of a fist smashing into the side of his head, the .357's second shot was explosively clear.

Reaching for Leeandra

Hoff reached out to grab Leeandra, to get her off the stage. She took another backward step just as he reached her, causing him to surge past. He spun, lunged for her and heard the distant crack. In that same instant, he saw Leeandra's grimace and felt the smashing blow and burn in his neck. The bullet's impact kicked Hoff into Leeandra, and they tumbled toward the back of the stage, coming to rest six feet from the edge. He was on his back and realized she was crawling on top of him. In his mind's scrambled confusion, the odd thought materialized: Not here, Leeandra. Not in front of all these people.

He heard her scream, "Oh, Hoff, you're shot. Dear God, help us!" He saw her straighten up, and he heard the crowd's crescendo of screams and cries replace the invitational hymn.

"Shot? Me?" He couldn't tell if he was thinking or talking. He felt nothing except sticky wetness on his neck and the awful burning. He squinted up and wondered why Leeandra was so out of focus.

"Help!" she screamed. "Somebody help us!"

Warmth by Accomplishment

Thinking he had killed Leeandra, James Daniel Bresnahan calmly laid his rifle down on one of the metal folding chairs and picked up his magazine, still open to mark the article he was reading. He left the small equipment room, careful to lock the door. A scurrying panic was evident in the Superdome as he strode purposefully toward the nearest exit, the folded magazine tucked into the right back pocket of his khaki pants. He felt a warmth of accomplishment at once again performing God's will, using the silver broom to sweep away another verminous apostate. He unwrapped a cinnamon candy.

Before slipping it into his mouth, he said to himself, "Good-bye, farewell, Sister Cathedra. The broom and I came here and killed ya." He smiled as he continued his private conversation, "A bit jocular, I suppose, but I like it."

An Urge to Smile

On her knees, rocking back and forth as she cried, Leeandra yielded her hold on Hoff when two uniformed paramedics and another man sprinted to Hoff's side.

"Neck wound," the Hispanic paramedic pronounced crisply. "Compression bandage. Quick. We've got a bleeder."

"Tube him?" the other paramedic asked.

"Yes." The Hispanic barked into the microphone on his shoulder, "Life Flight on standby for the Superdome."

"Ten-four," came the brittle reply.

The man in a blazer and black turtleneck scooted to Leeandra's side and put his arm around her. "I'm Banner Tatum, a friend of Hoff's. We'll take good care of him."

"Is he dead?" Leeandra asked between sobs.

"No," a paramedic answered, then instructed Banner to press the large bandage against Hoff's neck wound. "Press firmly."

With quick, experienced motions, one paramedic held Hoff's head still while the other inserted the plastic tube into his windpipe.

"Losing consciousness," the Hispanic said, then spoke into his shoulder microphone, "Dispatch Life Flight to the Superdome pad."

"Ten-four. Dispatching Life Flight, Superdome pad."

"Please, God, save him," Leeandra wailed and looked up as more people rushed to help.

New Orleans Police Lieutenant Dugas LeBlanc stooped and asked Banner. "How does it look?"

Banner shook his head. "Don't know. They've called a copter."

The police lieutenant stood and yelled to three uniformed officers, "Clear a path to the landing pad. Move!"

Hoff was aware of the strangling pressure on his neck and tried to open his eyes. He recognized Banner's voice over the barrage of noise in the stadium. He heard someone ask, "Miss Stevens, are you hurt?"

"No," she answered. "Save him. Dear God, save him."

She's okay. He felt the urge to smile into the inky quiet that had begun to envelope him, penetrated only by bursts of raucous noise surrounded by ricocheting, fuzzy balls of intense white light.

Pieces of the Puzzle

Backstage, in what was to have been a reception hall, Banner Tatum sat in stunned, unmoving silence, his hands and the sleeves of his blazer stained with Hoff's dried, caked blood. George Armstrong Lee sat beside Banner as the sequence of horrifying events began to assemble itself in tiny, interlocking pieces.

Casper suffered a flesh wound in the thigh from Danny Don Rhodes' second shot. Ken Walker was with Casper at the hospital.

Danny Don sustained cuts and bruises as he was subdued, was treated at a hospital and moved to the police station. He kept shouting his demand to have a news conference to explain why he wanted to kill Sister Cathedra. Lieutenant LeBlanc was at the station, grilling Danny Don.

The police believed Hoff was shot by a single bullet fired from a weapon different than Danny Don's. The slug struck Hoff in the neck, just under his chin, but missed vital arteries and his spinal column. He was listed in stable but critical condition due to blood loss and threat of infection.

Backstage, Banner and George watched local news coverage. WDSU-TV crews were filming the flow of people toward the stage when the shooting erupted. A cameraman had zoomed in on Danny Don.

A heavyset woman, speaking the unknown tongue and dancing in religious ecstasy, jostled Danny Don an instant before he fired the first shot. She bumped him accidentally again, apparently unaware of the shot. A man, also thought to be a respondent to the invitation, rammed into Danny Don from behind and hit him an instant before the second shot was fired.

Banner's eyes rounded in surprise as he watched a slow-motion rerun. Except for having too much hair, the man who rammed into Danny Don was a dead ringer for Dr. Henry Jackson Woods.

"Son of a bitch," Banner said and nudged George Lee. "That's the bad ass preacher from Austin. If it weren't for him, that lunatic with the pistol would've killed Leeandra sure as shit."

#

Shortly before midnight, Banner and George Lee joined Leeandra, Ken Walker and others in the intensive care unit's waiting room.

Leeandra, pale and trembling, drank coffee from a white foam cup held in both hands. Blood stains blotched her dark blue dress.

Banner whispered to Ken, "What's the latest on Hoff?"

"The doctors say he'll live," Ken said. "He's lost a lot of blood, but he's stabilized. He's still listed as critical, but he's breathing on his own. I think Hoff had a special guardian angel looking after him tonight."

"It should've been me," Leeandra said softly, wiping away tears.

Ken moved to sit next to Leeandra and put his arm around her. "No, Leeandra. He saved you. It's God's will."

Banner drew two cups of coffee from the urn and handed one to George Lee before turning to Ken Walker. "Has anybody seen Hoff?"

"No," Ken answered. "The doctors say it'll be tomorrow before anybody can see him."

"Why don't y'all go to the hotel and get some rest," Banner said. "I'll hold down the fort here."

"I'll stay, too," George Lee added.

"I'm not going anywhere," Leeandra said quickly.

At 2:25 a.m., Lieutenant LeBlanc arrived at the waiting room. He told Banner and George Lee that police officers searching the Superdome discovered the missing grate in the equipment room. They found the trunk and gun left behind on a folding chair. They bagged two small cellophane candy wrappers found on the equipment room floor along with remains of a partially-eaten muffaletta sandwich. "We think that's where Hoff's shooter was holed up."

Banner shoved his hands in his pockets, and muttered, "Looks like he got away."

Chapter 24

Things that Make No Sense

At 8:30 on the morning after the shooting, Banner Tatum and George Lee took a taxi to WDSU-TV's studio to view more of the videotape recorded at the Superdome service.

Banner stared intently at an out-take of a standing Henry Jackson Woods, his face glistening with sweat and wracked by exaggerated, wincing blinks. He held a hair piece in his hand after Danny Don Rhodes lay subdued, face down on the floor. Dr. Woods sagged to his knees and began to sob.

From the television station, Banner and George called hotels until they located Dr. Woods, who was awakened by the phone.

"I called to thank you for what you did last night," Banner said. "You saved Leeandra's life. When Hoff gets better, I'll make sure he knows about it."

"How is Hoff?" the Austin preacher asked.

"Lost a lot of blood, but he'll live."

"That's good. He's the one who saved Leeandra's life, though." Dr. Woods paused. "How'd you know I'm in New Orleans?"

"I recognized you on one of the newscasts. Why did you come?"

"You may find this hard to believe, but I came for what I knew would be a wonderful worship service. It was. I went to the stage area to rededicate my life to Christ."

Banner hesitated. "No hard feelings, I hope."

"No."

"You're a hard one to figure. Your actions have never made sense."

"Weakness seldom makes sense," Dr. Woods answered. "But, it's part of life. It's but one of the things in life that makes no sense. Leeandra's death would've been a grievous addition to that list."

Hoff's First Visitor

At noon, a nurse came to intensive care waiting area and said one person could see Hoff for no more than ten minutes. Leeandra jumped to her feet and followed the nurse. Banner Tatum stood until she left the room.

Leeandra stood quietly at Hoff's bedside and trembled at the sight of the tubes in his nose and the IV dripping into his arm. His neck was heavily bandaged, the left side of his face bruised and swollen. His bed was surrounded by machines looking stark and menacing under the intensive care unit's glaring lights.

Not until she rested her hand on his was Hoff aware of her presence. "Hi," he whispered before opening his eyes.

She stooped and kissed his forehead. "Thank God you're okay."

Hoff studied her for several seconds. "You've been crying."

"Yes." Tears filled her eyes. "I thought you were gone." She tried to laugh. "I love you, Hoff."

"That's the best medicine a man can get." His voice was raspy, weak. He squeezed her hand. "Are you all right?"

"I've stopped shaking. Yes, I'm okay. How are you feeling?"

He smiled weakly. "Much better now that you're in here with me." He stared at her for a moment. "They tried to kill you, Leeandra. How could I have been so stupid as to let you get on that stage?"

"You couldn't have stopped me," she answered.

Hoff said, "I told you we should've run away."

"I wish we had."

He closed his eyes and she asked, "Are you in pain?"

He formed a "no" with his lips, but didn't speak.

"I talked to Andy Boxx," Leeandra said. "He said to tell you that he'll come take you home in his plane when you're ready."

"Good ol' Andy. I can always count on him."

"Banner has been so helpful, and Gracie sends her love. Hoff?" When she didn't continue, he opened his eyes. "You saved my life," she said, barely above a whisper.

He smiled. "Want to know why?"

Leeandra wiped tears from her eyes as she nodded.

"On New Year's Day, I was going to fly to Amarillo and propose to you. I've already bought the ring, but it's back in Houston."

"Are you serious?"

"Just in case some other lunatic gets after me, maybe I'd better ask now. I love you, Leeandra Kay Stevens. Will you marry me?"

She clasped his hand tighter. "Yes, Jerome King Hoffstedtler. I will marry you."

Another Visitor

On the fourth day after he was shot, Hoff was moved to a private room for another day of observation before he would be flown to Houston. He was dozing when the door opened. He smelled her before he opened his eyes and saw Margo approaching slowly. "Hello, magnificent one."

"I had to come see you," Margo said. She kissed him lightly on the lips. "Gordon was very understanding."

"Things okay with you?" Hoff asked.

"Yes." A smile flashed across her face. "I'm so glad you're okay."

"Me, too. If the shooter had hit me in the ass, I'd've been a goner for sure."

Margo squeezed his hand. "I met Leeandra. She's lovely. Banner told me you've proposed. Lucky girl. I hope she makes you happy."

Hoff said, "At times I'm sorry things didn't work out for us."

"Me, too." She shrugged. "We had some really good times. I'll never forget them."

"Me, neither."

Margo blinked back tears. "I had to come say hello. I'm so happy it wasn't worse. Lots of people feel that way." She kissed him again, a short, light brush of her lips on his. "I'm going to leave before I cry." She turned toward the door.

"Stay for a few minutes?" he said.

Margo stopped, facing the door. "I don't dare." She waved without looking back and left.

To the Edge of the Earth?

After getting dressed for the trip home, Hoff was tired and stretched out on the hospital bed.

"Jesus H. Christ! Sleeping in the middle of the goddam day," Andy Boxx said boisterously.

Hoff smiled, but kept his eyes closed. "Trying to, but I keep having nightmares. If somebody's not shooting me, they're waking me up." He opened his eyes when he felt Andy's hand on his.

Andy looked at Hoff for a moment, assessing the bandage and bruises. "Thought I taught you better than to go standing up in the line of fire."

"I forgot."

Andy patted Hoff's arm. "You done good. From what I hear, if it weren't for you and that preacher prick from Austin, Sister Cawonderful would've bought it."

Hoff nodded. "That's what they tell me."

"I saw on the passenger list that Casper isn't flying with us. What's with that little nipplehead?"

"He's got his nose out of joint because we're getting married."

"What a shithead." Andy looked around. "You opening up a florist shop here?" Without giving Hoff time to answer, he said, "I see you're packed. Prince and The Bomber are in their usual three-point stance."

"As long as nobody fires a starter pistol," Hoff said.

Andy laughed. "Glad to see the shooter didn't blast away your good humor glands. Come on, let's go."

Hoff sat and swung his legs off the edge of the bed. "Maybe Prince could find a quiet, cozy little place near the edge of the earth and get us away from all this insanity."

"Fat chance." Andy whuffed a laugh. "You know damned good and well that fraidy-cat Cuban won't go near the edge of the earth."

Hoff grinned, but the smile evaporated quickly. "You know, don't you, that I'm gonna find that shooter son-of-a-bitch if it's the last thing I ever do?"

"I figured as much. If you need any help, let me know."

"Can I interrupt?" Leeandra peered through the partially-open door.

"Sure," Andy said. "I'm tryin' to get old lazy bones out of bed."

Leeandra held the door for an attendant pushing a wheelchair.

"I can walk," Hoff said.

"Hospital rules," the attendant said and held Hoff's arm until he was seated, both feet on the fold-down rests.

Andy picked up Hoff's leather carry-on bag. "Liability issue. They're afraid you'll fall flat and sue 'em. Let's go home."

On the way to the car, Andy told them that Larry Best would have a catered early supper ready when they arrived at Hoff's condo.

"A bowl of magic chili?" Leeandra asked.

"Inside joke," Hoff said to Andy.

Andy grumped, "I hate inside jokes when I'm not inside 'em."

#

When the Boxx Oil and Minerals Westwind jet leveled off at twenty-two thousand feet, Andy retrieved a bottle of Dom Perignon and three crystal flutes from the galley. He set the glasses on a snack table and opened the champagne. "I've saved my congratulations for you two 'til now." Andy looked at Leeandra. "I have some non-alcoholic bubbly if you'd prefer."

Leeandra laughed and brushed strands of hair from her face. "I'm feeling worldly today."

"Great!" Andy poured the champagne and picked up his glass. When Hoff and Leeandra held theirs, Andy continued. "A toast. Usually, I'm full of nonsense, but I'm gonna be serious. May the two of you always love each other and find many years of happiness together. Drink up."

"Thank you, Andy," Hoff said. "You're a good friend."

"Yes," Leeandra added. "Thank you so much for everything."

Andy blushed, laughed and said to Leeandra. "You don't know how glad I am your name doesn't begin with 'M'."

Leeandra furrowed her brow. "What?"

"I'll explain later," Hoff said quickly. "Maybe over lunch on the beach in Barbados."